Surgical

Risk

A Kurtz and Barent Mystery

Surgical Risk: A Kurtz and Barent Mystery

Copyright © 2002 by Robert I. Katz

Cover design by Steven A. Katz

Surgical Risk

A Kurtz and Barent Mystery

by

Robert I. Katz

Other Books by Robert I. Katz

EDWARD MARET: A Novel of the Future

THE CANNIBAL'S FEAST

THE KURTZ AND BARENT MYSTERY SERIES:
SURGICAL RISK
THE ANATOMY LESSON
SEIZURE
THE CHAIRMEN
BRIGHTON BEACH

THE CHRONICLES OF THE SECOND INTERSTELLAR EMPIRE OF MANKIND:
THE GAME PLAYERS OF MERIDIEN
THE CITY OF ASHES
THE EMPIRE OF DUST
THE EMPIRE OF RUIN

To Bob

Chapter 1

"So this character comes into the Emergency Room," Nolan said. "He's well dressed. He looks normal. He smiles politely, apologizes for bothering us, and says he has six acupuncture needles up his penis." Crane, Liebert and Kurtz silently ate their pizza while they considered Nolan's statement. Six acupuncture needles up the penis, all of them felt, deserved at least a moment of silence.

Crane wiped olive oil from his fingers, opened the box and picked out the last slice of pepperoni. "Didn't that hurt?" he asked.

"It didn't seem to bother him," Nolan said.

"But why did he do it?"

Nolan grinned. "Probably because he's a pervert."

"He didn't say that, did he? 'I like to shove things up my penis because I'm a pervert.'"

"I guess not," Nolan said.

"Well, what did he say?"

"He said that he had an itch."

"Hell of an itch," Crane said, and took a bite out of his pizza.

Crane was stout, with broad shoulders and thick, muscular arms. Nolan was tall, stooped and lean. Both men were pale, pasty faced and sunken eyed. It was a body habitus endemic to surgery residents, a breed that rarely saw the sun and subsisted for the most part on pizza, take out Chinese and junk food.

"So what did you do?" Kurtz asked. Richard Kurtz had been an attending surgeon for nearly three years. He was almost as pale as the residents but somewhat better rested and much better fed. The others stared at him. Nolan gave a quick, cautious smile. Three nights before, a skinny kid with a pierced tongue, a pierced nose and probably a pierced brain, tripping out of his mind on amphetamines, with tattoos covering most of his torso, had tried to strangle one of the orderlies; but beyond the simple application of brute force the kid had no technique whatsoever. Kurtz had knocked him down and sat on him, an act which considerably reinforced Kurtz' already macho reputation. Privately, Kurtz thought the reputation absurd, but he wasn't going to fight it.

"We took him to the O.R., did a cysto and managed to grab them with a biopsy forceps. Turned out there weren't six of them. There were eight."

"Jesus," Crane said with a shudder.

Kurtz raised a brow, shook his head and took a sip of his coke. "That's even weirder than a gerbil up the ass," Liebert said.

They all nodded in unison but the gerbil story was old hat, and probably untrue. Kurtz had heard it from several different sources over the years. Supposedly one of Hollywood's top action heroes, a guy married to a gorgeous model whose face had appeared on every magazine cover in America, had come into the E.R. at New York Hospital with a gerbil up his ass. It made a great story—but no such case report had ever appeared in the medical literature.

"Does anybody know which particular foreign body in the rectum is responsible for the greatest number of E.R. visits?" Kurtz asked.

"Dildos," Nolan said immediately. "And vibrators."

"Very good," Kurtz said. "What's number two?"

"Cucumbers?" Crane said.

"Nope. They've been reported, but they're not in the top two or three. Anybody?"

Nolan shrugged. Crane ate his pizza. Liebert smiled like the good little medical student that he was, waiting to be enlightened.

"Depends on the study, actually," Kurtz said. "One says rubber balls, one says glass bottles, another one says wooden dowels." He shrugged.

Crane visibly winced. "I've seen a couple of vibrators. I haven't seen any wooden dowels."

"Trust me," Kurtz said. "You will."

"I read a letter in the *New England Journal of Medicine* a couple of years ago," Nolan said. "It was written by a British urologist visiting America. He was invited to look in on a cysto and he sees a sign in the patient's bladder saying, 'Drink at Joe's Bar.' At first, he thought it was the American penchant for advertising carried to an extreme, before he realized that the guy had shoved a swizzle stick up his urethra."

"That's bullshit," Kurtz said. "There are just as many nut cases in England as there are over here."

"Hey, I'm just telling you what it said."

Crane leaned back in his seat and covered a yawn with his fist. "I read a letter in *The New England Journal* from a physician who was out jogging in the middle of winter. It was really cold out and his running suit wasn't warm enough. By the time he got home, he could barely feel his penis. Nobody was home, so he dropped his pants and began to warm it up with his hand. At the same time, while he's standing there in the foyer, he begins to flip through the latest issue of the *New England Journal*, which is sitting there with the mail. Just then, the front door opens and in walks his wife. The letter said that she wasn't amused."

"I don't get it," Liebert said. "What do you mean?"

8

Crane rolled his eyes. Nolan grinned. "The wife thought he was jerking off while reading the *New England Journal*."

"And the *New England Journal* printed this?" Leibert said.

"I guess they figured it was sort of a human interest story."

Kurtz put his feet up on the edge of the desk, took a slow deep breath and willed his tight muscles to relax. The hall outside his office was dimly lit and silent. It was one A.M. Only an hour before, they had finished sewing up a young woman who had been stabbed in the chest by a jealous boyfriend. But at the moment things were quiet: no cases in the E.R., all the patients tucked in and sleeping, no vomiting or sudden fever or cardiac arrest. Nothing to do but sit tight and wait for the shift to end. They should go get some sleep themselves, Kurtz thought. You never knew.

"But wasn't he embarrassed?" Liebert asked.

"Who?" said Nolan.

"The guy with the acupuncture needles: wasn't he embarrassed?"

"Oh, him." Nolan yawned, seemingly bored with the subject. "Not in the slightest. The attending urologist told me afterward that the guy would probably get a stricture. He'll have trouble peeing for the rest of his life." He shook his head again. "Crazy."

"Crazy," Kurtz murmured. He put his feet down from the desk, opened a drawer and began to rummage through it. "You want to see crazy?" He found what he was looking for buried under a pile of old papers. "This is really crazy." He held it up.

Crane scratched his head. Nolan slowly nodded. Liebert blinked, wrinkled his nose and stared.

It was a chest x-ray. Three flat razor blades nestled between the lungs, obscuring the shadow of the heart. "A psych patient," Kurtz said. "His name is Bill Mose; he's a schizophrenic. He sits around, watches T.V. and smokes cigarettes." Kurtz shrugged. "You talk to him, he makes no sense whatsoever but he occasionally expresses the opinion that he's being persecuted. He considers himself to be misunderstood and perfectly well adjusted. He likes to eat things."

"Jeez," said Crane, "like Hannibal the Cannibal."

"He doesn't eat people," Kurtz said, "just things."

"I thought they didn't allow smoking in the hospital," Liebert said.

"They do for the long-term inpatients. Some idiot decided to make a civil rights case out of it and threatened to sue."

"What happened to him?" Liebert asked.

"We got the razor blades out with an endoscope. Within a week, he had swallowed a pencil eraser and a couple of pens, so we took him to the O.R. and did it again."

"Is he still alive?" asked Crane.

9

"So far as I know, he's upstairs," Kurtz said. "On the locked ward. He's been there for years."

Three nights later, a pharmacist's aide came to the door of the locked ward, peered in through the glass and waited until every patient within sight had moved away to a healthy distance. At this hour of the night, there were only a handful: Bill Mose and a few others whose inner clocks ticked to their own distinctive beat. The aide looked to be a new one. Mose didn't recognize him, but he obviously knew the routine, quietly waiting by the doorway while the patients shuffled off. As always, Mose was the last, but finally he too reluctantly moved down the hall, and the aide turned the key in the lock and entered, closing the door behind.

The patients ignored him, all except Mose, who pretended to as much apathy as the rest but whose attention focused like radar on the jangling keys that represented freedom.

The pharmacist's aide handed over his shipment of pills while the head nurse signed for them and a little redhead with a sour face named Weems began to put the pills into each patient's medicine drawer.

The pharmacist's aide walked back down the hall, scanned the immediate area to make certain that none of the patients were near enough to slip out and inserted his key. The door opened. The door closed. Sadly, Mose shook his head and shuffled up to the solid steel barrier, staring down the hall outside the unit to the elevators. As he always did, Mose grasped the doorknob and tried to turn it, expecting the usual solid resistance, but this time something was different. It took him a moment to realize what it was: the doorknob turned smoothly in his fist. The door swung open.

Confused, Mose peered out into the hallway, then back into the ward. He frowned, uncertain, then he slowly smiled. His heart pounding, fully expecting to hear the nurses' excited voices yelling behind him, he stepped out into the corridor, closed the door silently and padded down the hall, whistling between his teeth.

Dr. Sharon Lee let the hot water run over her face and stood under the shower for a long, luxurious moment, forcing herself to relax. It was three A.M.

Sharon Lee hated stat C-sections. Everybody did. A fifteen year old girl, with no history of pre-natal care, had come into the E.R. in labor and been rushed up to obstetrics with a frank breech. Sharon shuddered and breathed a long sigh and felt her heart finally begin to slow down. The residents had started without her and a good thing, too. Mother and baby were both doing fine but they had been very, very lucky.

Sharon had a clinic in the morning but it would take a half hour to get home and the same amount of time to get back. The call room beds were lumpy but the rooms were quiet and it wasn't worth the bother to leave and then return.

She finished her shower, got into clean surgical scrubs and crawled under the covers. Then she turned out the light and rolled over, snuggling into the pillow. Her eyes closed and within minutes she was asleep.

The sound of a door creaking open awakened her and she wondered for a hazy moment where she was before a pair of hands gripped her throat. She tried to struggle, to cry out, but the hands were too strong and soon a red haze settled over her eyes and her struggles grew weaker and then she shuddered one final time and was dead.

At nine A.M., as he did every weekday morning, Oscar Hernandez knocked on the call room door and waited. After a moment, he slid his key into the lock and pushed the door open. He stopped suddenly, gulped and stared. "Oh, my God," he whispered. Carefully, he closed the door and re-locked it, then he hurried down the hallway to the nearest phone.

Chapter 2

Kurtz' first patient in the morning was a burly construction worker who clung to a conviction that nothing was really wrong with him, despite the pain that made him wince whenever he moved his right side. The anesthesiologist, Vinnie Steinberg, had given the patient a sedative as soon as they entered the room and now his eyelids fluttered and he smiled sleepily while they put on the EKG and the blood pressure cuff. Steinberg took a quick look at the monitors, made a notation on the anesthesia record, winked at Kurtz and pushed the plunger on a syringe of propofol. The patient mumbled once more that he only had a "stomach ache," then his eyes glazed over and Kurtz went outside to scrub.

When he got back ten minutes later, Nolan and Crane had already put the drapes up and Nolan was standing by the patient's side, holding a knife and looking at Kurtz expectantly. "Go ahead," Kurtz said.

Nolan's knife slid in, split skin, fat, fascia and muscle. Crane helped him while Kurtz silently watched. Nolan reached the bowel, followed it along to the cecum and pulled it up onto the skin. The appendix sat there on the end, long, red and swollen, oozing a bit of serous fluid from the tip. "Just in time," Nolan said. Kurtz nodded. The appendix would have ruptured soon; the patient was lucky.

The operation went smoothly. Nolan circled the appendix with sutures, tied off the blood supply, put two clamps around the base, cut between the clamps and handed the specimen off to the nurse. Then he cauterized the stump, inverted it into the serosa, tugged the sutures tight, tied them and began to close.

"Okay," Kurtz said, and removed his gown. He ignored the whispering at the head of the table. The anesthesiologists were always talking about something and unless there was a problem with the patient, it didn't concern him.

"Hey, Richard."

Kurtz looked up. Steinberg peered at him over the drapes. "Did you hear the news?"

"News?" Kurtz frowned. "What news?"

Steinberg shook his head dolefully. "Sharon Lee," he said. "She's been murdered."

Scene of the crime: a bedroom. A single bed, a nightstand, a desk with a lamp, a bathroom with a toilet and a shower that connected with another bedroom on the other side, a green linoleum floor. All hospitals had such rooms, Barent had been told: a call room for the staff to sleep in at night when they had to be there but didn't have to actually work. There were two wings of such rooms, one for the residents and another for the attendings. The residents were required to spend their nights on call in house and so their rooms saw a lot of use. The attendings' rooms were usually empty. Barent wondered about this fact but doubted that it would be much help in narrowing things down. Most likely, everybody who had ever worked here knew it.

The Medical Examiner had already come and gone, having solemnly declared the cause of death to be strangulation. No surprises there, considering the deep bruises on both sides of the neck. The body was still lying on the floor where it had fallen, evidently after a struggle, since the bedclothes were tangled together and thrown about the room. The victim was wearing green surgical scrubs. The shirt was torn and pulled up over her face. She was a good-looking woman, if a corpse could ever be described as good-looking—slim, firm, nice breasts. Sharon Lee: Doctor of Obstetrics and Gynecology, thirty one years old, never married, no children, father dead, mother still living, one sister. Successful. Barent sighed and shook his head. Not any more.

Barent walked over to the window, parted the drapes and allowed the bright winter sunlight to shine in. They were on the Seventeenth Floor of a twenty story building on the West Side of Manhattan. Below, cars drove silently along the pavement. A row of apartment buildings, most of them less than five stories high, rose on the opposite side of the street. Beyond the apartments, the grass and trees of Riverside Park sloped down to the Hudson River, covered now with gleaming chunks of ice.

Easton had started out in 1912 as the Riverhead Psychiatric Institute, a rest home and rehabilitation center for wealthy alcoholics and neurotics. Then, in 1930, a grateful patient named Ernest Easton had died and left the place his entire fortune, on condition that the institution expand into surgery and general medicine. The Board at the time had eagerly accepted the proposed changes, but even today, more than seventy years later, nearly a quarter of Easton's patients were psychiatric, a situation that the present Board had no desire to change. Psychiatric patients rarely needed CAT scans, respirators or Intensive Care Units. Psych patients were, more often than not, low tech and cut rate.

The central courtyard of the building contained a playground, scattered trees and half a dozen picnic tables where residents of the locked wards were often brought for exercise, recreation and fresh air. In the late 1950's,

13

the hospital had constructed an office tower for its physicians called the Hampshire Building. The Hampshire Building was made out of glass and red brick. It connected to Easton by a Third Story walkway built over the street.

"He didn't escape through the window," Moran said.

"No." It was two hundred feet to the ground. Barent turned away from the window and blinked, his eyes adjusting slowly to the relative darkness of the room. "Why do you say 'he?'"

Moran puffed up his cheeks and surveyed the dimensions of the room. "Pretty young woman. It seems likely."

Privately, Barent agreed. Statistically, most murderers were male, and women, when they did commit murder, were rarely strong enough to do so with their bare hands. "We don't know that yet," Barent said. He said it as much to himself as to Moran, who looked down at the body and ignored Barent's comment.

Barent flipped through his notebook and opened it to a clean page. The notebook served to keep his thoughts in order but its primary function was to act as a prop, something to impress the witnesses, maybe intimidate them a little. People tended to think very carefully about what they were saying, watching their words get written down as soon as they left their mouths.

"What have we got?" he asked Moran.

Moran glanced at the lab techs methodically quartering the room, taking measurements, dusting for fingerprints, preserving it all on film. They went about their business as if Barent and Moran were not there. "Presumably she locked the door but forgot about the bathroom. The doors to the bathroom and the bedroom on the other side were both unlocked."

"I see," Barent said. "Unless she did check the locks and somebody else had a key."

Moran gave a little shrug of his shoulders and glumly nodded. Beyond the barricade at the end of the hall, a small crowd of people were clustered, doctors and nurses and other hospital employees curious about what was going on.

Barent looked once more at the still body, shook his head and walked out. He followed Moran down the hall and sat behind a desk in one of the small call rooms. "Bring in the janitor."

Moran gave him a reproving look. "I believe that the preferred term is 'environmental service technician.'"

Barent barely cracked a smile. "Of course."

The 'environmental service technician' was plump, about fifty, with faded gray eyes and a bewildered, frightened expression. He sat in the chair and hunched his head down onto his shoulders.

"Can you tell me what happened, Mr. Hernandez?" Barent asked.

Hernandez blinked at him. "I opened the door," he said. "She was lying there, not moving. I went and reported it. That's all I know."

"The door was closed?"

"Yes."

"Was it locked?"

"I put the key in and turned it. If it wasn't locked, I didn't notice."

"But it might not have been locked?"

Hernandez spread his hands to the side and shrugged.

"Have there been any robberies reported from any of the call rooms? Any fights?"

"I don't know about any of that stuff," Hernandez said. "You should talk to Security."

"Security..." Barent tapped his pen against the notebook. Hernandez eyes stayed glued to his own hands, folded in his lap.

"Did you notice anything different in the hallway outside or in any of the other call rooms? Any signs of a struggle? Dirt on the carpet? Blood? Overturned furniture?"

"No." Hernandez peered glumly up at Barent. "Nothing like that."

"Did you know Dr. Lee?"

"I seen her around. I never talked to her."

Doctors, reflected Barent, probably didn't have much to say to 'environmental service technicians.' "Alright, Mr. Hernandez. Thank you. That's all I have to ask you for now."

Hernandez looked at him uncertainly. "I can go?"

"Yes." Barent scribbled in his notebook. "We'll get in touch if we need to talk to you again." Hernandez quickly nodded, got up and lumbered out. Moran shook his head. "Too bad nobody else was up here," Barent said. "They might have noticed something."

"Yeah, and we might have had a few more bodies."

A point. A definite point. "Not much in the way of witnesses, though," Barent said.

"There is one guy outside who wants to talk."

"Who?"

"Guy named Richard Kurtz: a surgeon, former boyfriend."

"Really?" Barent was frankly surprised. Former boyfriends of murdered young women usually walked quickly and quietly in the opposite direction. "Show him in," he said.

Kurtz came in and sat down. He stared at Moran, who shrugged and left the room. Kurtz was tall and lanky, with a pale complexion, dark eyes and dark curly hair. He looked at Barent impassively.

"Why did you want to talk to me, Doctor?" Barent asked.

Kurtz barely smiled, a thin humorless line in his white face. "I figured that sooner or later you would want to talk to me. Better to get it over with."

"I see," Barent said. What Kurtz said was most likely true, but still, Barent didn't like being anticipated. He frowned, picked up a pencil and made a notation in his book.

Kurtz peered at the notebook and suddenly grinned. "When I was in the Army, I spent about a year as a clerk for C.I.D. One of the investigators used to carry around a tape recorder. It made the suspects real nervous. You could see their eyes watching the spools go around, getting down everything they would say. Then he'd smile at them and switch it off. 'This is just between you and me, now. O.K?' Real confidential." Kurtz shrugged. "Sometimes it worked."

C.I.D. Barent hadn't known that, but then of course he knew nothing at all yet about Richard Kurtz or any of the other people who worked here. Kurtz had just a hint of a drawl in his speech, not quite Mid-West but not pronounced enough to be Southern.

"You were a cop?"

"No. The cops were mostly career types. I was just a kid. I enlisted right out of high school. My family had no money and I figured it was a good way to get out of West Virginia."

That accounted for the drawl. "Where were you stationed?"

"Munich. Nineteen-Eighty-One to Nineteen-Eighty-Four."

"Munich." Barent puffed up his cheeks and gave a sour little laugh. "Munich...I passed through there once. Real nice city. I was in the Army a little earlier. Da Nang and Kwang Tri.

"How did you get to be a doctor?" Barent asked.

Kurtz gave Barent a long, brooding look, his head cocked to the side. "One of my classmates used to be a traveling groupie with the Allman Brothers' Band, though I don't suppose she put that particular qualification down on her application. She went into pediatrics. Another guy who was a pretty good friend of mine used to run with a street gang. He got kicked out of high school when he was sixteen. He told me about some fights he got involved in. It seems he didn't enjoy that part of it very much, so he would just hang out near the edges of the crowd and kick the ones who were down. He's a gastroenterologist in South Carolina now. We had a former Broadway producer, a professional trombonist, at least three lawyers, four with M.B.A.'s and probably ten or more who had been in the military." Kurtz shrugged. "The science nerd stereotype is not entirely accurate."

"The Allman Brothers..."

"So she said. I didn't check her references."

Barent took a moment to try the idea on for size. Kurtz was right. People—which certainly included Barent—were not likely to imagine their doctors "traveling" with a rock band or getting kicked out of school for juvenile manslaughter.

He shrugged. "What can you tell me about Sharon Lee?"

"I met her here in the hospital. We went out for about three months."

"Was your relationship sexual?"

Kurtz barely blinked. "Now and then."

"Why did you break up?"

"I guess you could say we got on each other's nerves."

"How so?"

"Sharon's father was a partner at one of the big law firms in the city: Cravath, Swaine...Milbank, Tweed... I forget which one. Her mother has lunch with the girls and goes to garden shows. Sharon was rich, smart, good looking and used to getting her own way." Kurtz smiled wryly. "She liked men she could order around."

"And were you a man that she could order around?"

"Well..." Kurtz drawled. "I wasn't Sharon's usual sort. When she met me, Sharon had just broken up with a guy named Barry Kantor who ran a car dealership in Rahway, New Jersey. Barry was a nice fellow but not very exciting and Sharon was in the mood for something different. It turned out that she didn't like different. Sharon thought I was some sort of natural man or something, just because I didn't hold a teacup the way her JAP friends did. She thought that was great, at first, but it wore thin pretty fast. I wasn't *sensitive* enough for her."

Barent could understand that. Kurtz didn't exactly look sensitive. He had a square jaw and massive shoulders and looked like he was carved from a piece of granite.

"She was Jewish?"

"The family was non-religious but the name used to be Levine."

"Who broke up with who?"

"It was mutual." Kurtz shrugged. "We both made a mistake."

Barent nodded, wrote a few words in his little book. He looked up. "You have any idea who might have wanted her dead?"

Kurtz stared at him, his eyes unblinking. Barent met the stare with perfect equanimity. After a moment, Kurtz let his breath rumble out and grimaced down at the desk. "No," he said.

"How about Barry Kantor?"

"He got married a few months later. Last I heard he had two kids. I doubt it."

"After you, who was she involved with?"

"I haven't the faintest idea."

"I see." Barent stared at the walls, then he shook his head. "Thanks for your time. I'll give you a call if I have any further questions."

Kurtz made no move to get up from his chair. "Can I see the body?" he asked.

Barent frowned. Kurtz looked like he meant it but it wasn't exactly the usual procedure. "You're sure?"

"Yeah," Kurtz said shortly.

"C.I.D., huh?" Barent closed his notebook. "I really shouldn't." Kurtz waited, hunched forward a little, sitting very still. "Okay," Barent finally said. "Come on." He rose to his feet.

The lab techs were almost done. There was only one left in the room, down on his hands and knees, gathering samples of dust from under the window. "Don't touch anything," Barent warned.

Kurtz nodded but didn't look at his face. He stared down at Sharon Lee's body, saying nothing, while Barent stared at him. Barent wasn't sure about Kurtz. Usually he was pretty good at reading people, but not Kurtz. Finally, Kurtz breathed a long, slow sigh and glanced back at Barent with tired eyes. "Thank you," he said.

Barent nodded. "Don't mention it."

Chapter 3

Except for those infrequent occasions when a delusional patient grew violent, there was rarely any excitement on the locked ward. Breakfast tended to be the high point of the morning and none of the patients missed it. There were three fold out tables in the Unit cafeteria, seating six patients each. Bill Mose always sat in the chair nearest the door. Only when he did not show up for breakfast did anyone become suspicious. The Head Nurse, a woman named Reilly, ordered, "Search the Unit." Within minutes it had been established that Bill Mose was no longer on the ward and Miss Reilly alerted Security.

Security already knew.

The voices were particularly loud this morning, so loud that Mose could barely make out what they were saying to him, but the message they carried was a familiar one nonetheless. He looked down at the knife in his hand and almost snarled in frustration. He had already tried more than once to get it down but the knife was just too big to navigate the back of his throat. There was a lot of noise here. Confused, he shook his head.

"Don't let him get us!" a little girl cried. She clutched a raggedy teddy bear to her chest and began to cry even louder.

A nurse—Mose knew she was a nurse from the white uniform—grabbed the little girl, dragged her into a room and slammed the door. Suddenly, the hallway was nearly silent. The knife in his fist swayed slowly back and forth, leaving trails of colored light in the air.

Mose giggled. He hadn't had such fun in ages. The nursing station was nearby, filled with interesting things. Mose shuffled up to it. A container of paper clips sat near the phone. Mose smiled, and his mouth began to water. Perfect, he thought.

Just then, a pinging sound from the end of the hallway distracted him. He looked up. A squad of five men dressed in uniforms emerged from an elevator and raced toward him. They stopped abruptly, a few feet away. One of them, a large, black man said, "Put down the knife."

The knife? Mose stared at the knife. A beam of light flew at him and Mose flicked at the air. The men backed slowly away. "Spread out," one of them whispered.

The big, black one looked at him. "We can't spread out," he said. We're in a hallway."

"Oh." The first man blinked at the walls. "That's right."

The big one reached down to his belt, removed a billy club attached to a loop and hefted it in his fist. "Let's get him," he said.

They stared at each other, then inched forward, the big one up front.

Flickering beams of sunlight shone in through a latticed window at the end of the corridor. The beans of light hurt his eyes and Mose stabbed at them. "Get away!" he shrieked. His hands trembled. Random twitches danced along his skin. He howled, stabbing randomly at the light that clawed at his eyes. While the men stared, he stumbled against the wall, shrieking, and the knife clattered out of his hand.

"Alright, men," the big man yelled. "Get him!"

It took all five guards to subdue him. Mose struggled wildly, squirming and twisting. He called constantly upon the name of Christ as he fought. "*Jesus!*" he screamed. "*Jesus*, help me! Help me! Ahhh!" He fought and shrieked and struggled and finally they had him face down on the hallway with his hands behind his backs. The big one pulled out a pair of handcuffs and snapped them on Mose's wrists and then he slumped down in relief, wheezing.

"Oh, man," he said. "I'm too old for this." He shook his head and hauled himself to his feet. "Okay, let's get him down to the E.R. They can call Psych." He looked at the knife lying on the floor and pointed. "And bring that. It's evidence."

Barent scratched his head and watched Bill Mose struggle. Two large orderlies had arrived from the Psych Unit upstairs a few hours before and methodically put Mose in a straight jacket. They had wanted to bring him back to the Unit but the E.R. docs had vetoed this idea, feeling obligated to work Mose up for any physical injury before releasing him. Mose seemed hardly aware of what they were doing. He panted and moaned and cried out to his own private demons while dribbling bloody saliva.

"What makes him any more of a suspect than anybody else in this place?" Barent asked.

The Chief of Hospital Security was a retired cop named Wellesley. Wellesley had a red face, a bull neck and enormous, rolling shoulders. His thighs were so large that they rubbed together when he walked, making him waddle. The buttoned down collar, maroon jacket and restrained black tie seemed absurdly out of place on Wellesley's squat, massive body. He seemed bewildered by Barent's question. "He's a known lunatic and he's been rampaging around the hospital with a knife."

This was true, Barent reflected, but it had no obvious connection to the death of Sharon Lee. "Dr. Lee wasn't killed with a knife," he said. "She was strangled."

"Then whose blood is on it? Nobody else has reported an injury." Barent looked at him and shrugged. "Probably his own. His mouth is bleeding. Is there anybody around here who knows this character?"

"I do." A tall young man with frizzy black hair, horn rimmed glasses and a pale face stepped out of the crowd gathered in front of the Emergency Room desk.

"Who are you?" Barent asked.

"William Werth. I'm his psychiatrist."

William Werth looked like an eager puppy. Barent peered at him doubtfully. "Is there any place around here we can sit down and talk?"

"Sure. Come this way."

Werth led him down the hall to an empty examining room and closed the door. The room had a treatment table covered with a roll of white paper, a metal cabinet filled with tape, gauze, sutures and other medical instruments, a round, vinyl chair on rollers, and a tiny fold down desk.

"I'll take the table," Barent said. He hoisted himself up and let his legs dangle over the edge. Werth sat in the chair.

"Okay," Barent said. He fixed his own glasses more firmly on his nose and glanced down at Werth. "That guy is your patient?"

"Ever since I've been here."

"How long is that?"

"Four years."

Four years...Barent shuddered. Not a place he would want to spend four years. "He's been here all that time?"

"He's been here for seven."

"Jesus," Barent muttered.

"We let him out sometimes, always with a group. You had to keep an eye on him. He tended to bolt."

"Does he have any family?"

"He had an older sister. She died a few years ago."

"Inpatient psychiatric care doesn't come cheap. Who pays his bills?"

"Actually, Mose is pretty well off. The sister left him everything."

"Really?" Barent's ears pricked up. "And if he dies, who gets it?"

"I'm not sure."

"Who would know?"

"Mr. Robinson might know. If he doesn't know, he ought to know who would know."

"Robinson?"

"The Hospital Director."

"Seven years..." Barent carefully removed a sharp pencil from his inner jacket pocket. He wrote *Robinson* and *seven years* down in his notebook. While he was writing, he looked at Werth out of the corner of his eye. "Any women up there?" he asked.

"On the Psych Floor?"

Barent nodded. "Yes."

"Sure, there are," Werth said. "But they're in a different Unit. We keep the men and women separate."

"Why is that?"

Werth folded his hands on top of the fold out desk and looked up at Barent with earnest surprise. "To put it in layman's terms, these patients are completely out of their minds. Reality is a concept that they cannot deal with, or even recognize—but the sex drive stays with you until you're pretty much dead."

"So what? I thought sex between consenting adults was legal in this state."

Werth swiped a hand through his hair and suddenly looked like a puppy that had just been spanked. "They're not consenting adults. In order to give consent you have to be mentally competent. If one of these women got pregnant, we'd get our asses sued."

Barent blinked at him. "That ever happen?"

"Not here." The look on Werth's face said that it had happened somewhere.

"So far as you know, did Mose ever have a relationship of any sort with another patient?"

"No," said Werth. "Never. Mose is a schizophrenic. They can't relate to other people. They have no capacity for any but the most superficial emotions." Werth shook his head. "He was one of the easier patients to handle, actually. He's totally dissociated from reality but except for his obsessions, he was almost always docile."

"Obsessions? What obsessions?"

"He eats things. Any small, inanimate object he can get his hands on."

Barent's brows rose. "Sounds like quite an obsession." He scribbled in his notebook. "And so far as you know, is there any relationship between these sorts of obsessions and a tendency to murderous behavior?"

"None at all." Werth shook his head again. "The two things have nothing to do with each other."

Barent tapped the tip of his pencil against the notebook while he considered. Certainly, Mose was now a suspect in the murder of Sharon Lee, if for no other reason than his obvious capacity for violence—despite what Werth said about it—and his lack of an alibi. Where had Mose been all night? Nobody seemed to know how long ago he might have vanished from the locked ward upstairs or where he might have been hiding. But Barent distrusted the whole situation. Murderers were rarely so obliging as to drop into his lap like a plum. Still...

"I'm going to have to take Mr. Mose into custody," he said. "His medical problems won't be neglected. He'll be brought to a Psychiatric Hospital." A quick grin flit across Barent's face. "One a little more secure than Easton. If it turns out that he had nothing to do with the murder, then he'll be returned here in a few days. Is that alright with you?"

"Do I have a choice?" Werth's pale, freckled face turned abruptly red.

"No," Barent said. "You don't."

Chapter 4

"Mose?" Kurtz whistled softly through his teeth. "I don't believe it. I simply do not believe it." He drained his beer and signaled to the waitress for another.

Bill Werth nursed a Rusty Nail, stirring it with a plastic straw every minute or so. "Running around the hospital with a knife didn't exactly help his cause."

"He's psychotic, for Christ's sake!"

"So?"

"What do you mean, *so*? Who knows why schizophrenics act the way they do?"

Werth shook his head. "Certainly not me."

Kurtz gave him a disgusted look. "I'm sure your patients would love to hear that."

"Let me amend my statement," Werth said. "We do know that schizophrenia is a disturbance of dopamine transmission in the brain, leading to delusions, hallucinations and an inability to accurately perceive reality. We have a pretty good idea of the pathophysiology involved in the condition, and we have had some minimal success in treating it. What we have been totally unsuccessful in doing is figuring out why a particular patient suffers from a particular delusion." Werth shrugged. "So sue me for malpractice." He sipped his drink and crushed a piece of ice between his teeth.

Shrinks. Nothing amazed them, nothing surprised them. And they were so used to dealing with failure that failure quickly ceased to bother them. Kurtz had the surgical outlook; you fixed what was wrong with them and they got better. Kurtz expected his patients to walk out of the hospital on their own two feet and not come back. "Do you believe he did it?" he asked.

"It doesn't matter what I believe," Werth said.

Kurtz heard him with only a part of his mind. He kept seeing Sharon Lee lying on the floor, naked and dead. Sharon and he had had a rocky relationship from the beginning and they had broken up more than two years before but that vision still bothered him. It bothered him a lot. "Where is he now?"

"I don't know. They took him away. Barent said he would be returned in a few days if the evidence cleared him."

"Bill Mose weighs about a hundred twenty, hundred thirty at the most. He couldn't have done it even if he wanted to."

"Sure he could." Werth held his drink up his mouth and took a long sip, then patted his lips with a napkin. "He could have if he stumbled across her when she was sleeping. And anyway, psychotics tend to be a lot stronger than they look. They don't have normal inhibitions. If they want something, they go all out."

"Bizarre behavior does not constitute evidence."

Werth sipped his drink again and frowned down at the melting ice. "Barent seemed pretty sharp. If there is any physical evidence, I'm sure they'll find it."

Kurtz barely heard him. He stared into his beer and felt like grinding his teeth.

"You want something to eat?" Werth asked.

Kurtz shook his head. "No." He glanced at his watch. "I've got to get going. I have a date."

"Kathy?" Werth asked. Kurtz nodded.

"Lucky girl," Werth said.

Bill Mose spent the first few hours exploring. Mose was confused. The place seemed like the locked ward he was used to but somehow, it wasn't. The people had different faces. The rooms had different layouts and were spaced differently around the floor. There were bars on the windows. The nurses were all male, large and well built. He didn't spend too much time thinking about it, though. Mose had always been intimate with the inexplicable. He accepted it. He had no choice.

He wondered a little about the events of last night but they were already hazy in his memory. The policeman had asked him a lot of questions and Mose had tried to answer them but the policeman had not seemed happy. Then there was another man; Mose was uncertain of his name but he had seemed to be his friend. A lawyer, the man had said, appointed to represent him. Mose recognized that word...*lawyer*. He had seen a lot of lawyers on T.V.

The food here was no different than it had been in the other place. The pills were the same. One of the large nurses handed him his thorazine with a cup of water and waited until he had swallowed it. Then they showed him his new room and his new bed and locked the door.

That was just fine with Mose. Mose tended not to worry too much about the future. The future was a concept that he had heard of but did not really understand or believe in. The bed was soft and Mose was tired and he lay down and prepared to sleep.

Tomorrow could take care of itself.

Kathy Roselli was a Teaching Assistant, working toward her Ph.D. in the English Department at N.Y.U., where Dina Werth had recently been promoted to Associate Professor. The two women were good friends. Dina and Bill Werth had introduced Kathy and Richard Kurtz at what they had described as a "dinner party." It had been an obvious fix up since Kurtz and Kathy were the only guests, a state of affairs that had annoyed Kurtz at first and seemed to please Kathy no better.

Kurtz quickly decided, however, that annoyance in this case would be counterproductive. Kathy had very pale, clear skin, straight, jet-black hair, enormous brown eyes and a lithe, willowy body that set Kurtz' imagination to happily dancing.

Kathy's annoyance lasted a little longer. "A surgeon?" she whispered, and glanced at Dina with a frown on her face.

"He's very nice," Dina said firmly. "Aren't you, Richard?"

Kurtz, who had found himself so hypnotized by watching Kathy's lips that the words coming out of them were just a blur, barely noticed the interchange. He had been trying to discuss the Knicks' chances of going all the way with Werth and he had completely lost the thread of both conversations. Kathy had white, even teeth and very full lips, moist and (he thought) succulent. He found his mouth watering as he watched her. "What was that?" he asked.

"Nothing," Dina replied. "Nothing at all. Would you like a drink?"

"I'll have some white wine," he said, his eyes fixed on those plump, succulent lips.

"I knew a lot of pre-meds when I was an undergraduate," Kathy ventured.

"Oh?" Kurtz replied.

"They studied quite a bit." That was kind of her, Kurtz thought, very kind. He really admired how delicately she put that.

"It's unfortunate," Kurtz agreed. He was determined to be agreeable. "Pre-meds aren't exactly popular, even among themselves."

"Well, they did seem rather narrow minded."

Kurtz nodded. "In general, an unsavory bunch," he said. "But some of us do manage to resist the stereotype. I try to keep an open mind, myself."

"Really?" She smiled at him. "Do you like opera?"

"Can't stand it," Kurtz said agreeably. "How about you?"

Her smile grew wider. "I prefer ballet."

"Ballet," Kurtz said. "I like ballet. I understand Alvin Ailey is in town. Would you like to go?"

She looked at him and said, "Maybe."

He called her a few days later and renewed the invitation. She accepted. That had been four months ago.

He met her tonight at a little place downtown called the Rathskellar. It had wooden tables and dim lighting and served beer, schnitzel and bratwurst. Kurtz ate there often. It reminded him of his days in the Army. Tonight, however, the menu sat listlessly in his fingers and Kurtz noticed neither Kathy nor his surroundings.

Kathy looked at him doubtfully. She had never before heard the name Sharon Lee, but he had blurted out the whole sorry story as soon as she arrived and now he sat silently, staring into his opened menu, unable to concentrate.

"You're sure you want to do this?" Kathy asked.

Kurtz blinked. "Excuse me," he said. "What was that?"

"The whole thing is terrible. Wouldn't you rather just go home and forget about dinner?"

"No," Kurtz said. "No. That's alright."

"What were you thinking about?"

He had been thinking of Sharon Lee's dead body and Barent and the investigation, and how the guys he had known in Germany would have handled the case. Kurtz had turned down the opportunity for full C.I.D. training because it would have meant at least one more tour of duty and he had already decided what he wanted to do with his life, but he did wonder sometimes how things would have turned out if he had decided differently.

"I was thinking of the Army," he said. "And Munich. Have you ever been to Munich?"

Kathy shook her head. "I was in Europe the summer of my sophomore year but I never got to Germany."

"My favorite place was the Hofbrauhaus, the largest beer hall in the world. It dates back to the fourteenth century. The waitresses look like linebackers in dirndl skirts. They carry four steins of beer in each fist. I remember one time, I was sitting outside on the balcony. It was sunset. It must have been July, maybe August. Two guys came in with a young woman and sat down not too far from where I was. She was the most German looking girl I've ever seen in my life, about six feet, blonde, broad shoulders, gorgeous. She could have been an advertisement for Lufthansa or the Hitler Youth. The guy I was with—his name was Jimmy Schwartz, from Brooklyn— he looked at this girl and he shook his head and he said to me, 'My God, it's Brunnhilde.' They must have seen us talking but I don't suppose they heard what he said because all of a sudden the girl turns to me, leans over and says, 'I know what you're thinking: typical American tourist. Right?' Turned out she was a kindergarten teacher from Wisconsin." Kurtz shook his head. "Things aren't always what they seem. You know?"

Kathy smiled doubtfully. "I'm afraid I don't see the connection."

"I just can't believe he did it," Kurtz said.

Kathy peered down at her menu and studied it for a long moment. "Did you know," she finally said, "that the state of Wisconsin was largely settled by German immigrants? So maybe things are exactly what they seem to be, after all."

Kurtz stared at her. "Really?"

"Really," she said.

"I didn't know that."

Kathy gave a small, apologetic smile. "Do you still want to stay?"

"Sure," Kurtz said. "We're here. We might as well eat."

"Okay...then I guess I'll have the sauerbraten, with red cabbage."

"A wise choice," Kurtz said. He looked at her, then looked down at his menu. "But I still don't believe he did it."

"You'll have to talk to Mr. Wellesley. He's our Chief of Security." The Hospital Director's name was Edwin Robinson, a tall, thin man with a bald head, prominent jowls and a red face. He wore a blue, three-piece suit with a watch chain stretched across the vest. Barent couldn't remember ever seeing one of those outside of an old movie. "I already have," he said. "But I was wondering if you could give me your impressions as well."

"Impressions? I have no impressions. I believe in facts, and if I don't know the facts then I keep my mouth shut."

Not a bad philosophy, Barent thought. "Did you know Sharon Lee?" he asked.

"We have over five hundred physicians on our staff. I believe I've met her. I don't really remember."

"How about Bill Mose?"

"The psych patient?" Robinson laughed softly. "I do remember him. He's been here for years. On Christmas and Easter, the hospital holds a special dinner for all the inpatients. The Administrative Staff helps to serve it. We feel that it's good for morale."

"Dr. Werth told me that you might know the disposition of Mr. Mose's money. It seems that he has some."

Robinson frowned. "He has a lawyer..." Robinson scratched his head. "What was his name?" Then he snapped his fingers. "Pike," he said. "Jeremy Pike. He's the one who pays all the bills."

Barent wrote Jeremy Pike down in his notebook.

"How about Richard Kurtz?" he asked. "Do you know him?"

"A surgeon. He finished his residency and went into partnership with Edward Ornella, one of our senior staff, about three years ago. People here seem to think highly of him. That's all I know."

Barent nodded, made a few more scribbles in his notebook, then closed it. "Thank you," he said. "We'll keep in touch."

28

The staff on the Obstetrical Unit seemed subdued, almost shell shocked. Barent hardly blamed them. Complications and crises were supposed to happen to the patients, not the doctors. Two of the nurses and one of the secretaries were quietly crying. Barent noticed one of them in particular, an attractive young woman with long brown hair and soft, green eyes. Her nametag said Peggy Ryan.

He spent an hour on the Unit, talking with most of the staff. The ones who had worked the late shift had been asked to stay until he finished with them. One or two seemed annoyed at this but none had actively protested.

"Did Dr. Lee receive any phone calls last night?"

"You mean at home?" The ward clerk at the main desk was named Rita Mendez. She was about forty, a thin, homely woman who seemed quietly competent.

"No. I know that she had an emergency case last night, and I know that somebody must have called her in. I mean while she was here, on the Obstetrical Unit."

Rita Mendez shook her head. "I don't think so, but I really couldn't say."

"Did she have any particular friends on the Unit, anybody that she socialized with, or even talked to very much while at work?"

"Nobody that I know of."

Sharon Lee, it seemed, was not the most sociable person in the world. She took care of business and kept her personal life private.

"How about the ones with the sniffles?" Barent asked.

"Were they friends of hers?"

Rita Mendez shrugged. "You'd have to ask them."

He did. Peggy Ryan was still tearful. Her voice tended to crack unexpectedly. "I hardly knew her," she said. "But she was so young and so attractive. She had everything to live for. It's terrible."

The other nurse, a woman named Alice McMahon who appeared to be in her late thirties, said pretty much the same thing. "Dr. Lee was the quiet sort. I don't think any of us knew her personally." She shook her head. "I hate it when someone I know dies, particularly someone with their whole life ahead of them. It makes no sense."

The secretary, a girl barely out of high school named Carol Jennings, could hardly speak. "How could this happen?" she sobbed. "How?"

Barent tapped his notebook and wondered the same thing.

Sharon Lee's office staff had consisted of a secretary named Barbara James and a nurse named Audrey Parker. Barbara James was a thin, middle-aged lady with prominent white teeth and dyed blonde hair. Audrey Parker was an overweight young woman with a plain, round face and acne. Both of them seemed to have the I.Q. of a flea.

"Arguments?" Barbara James looked at him stolidly. "No. I never heard any arguments."

"Had she received any threatening phone calls? Any patients upset about anything? Any of the staff who didn't get along with her, for any reason?"

"Upset? Phone calls?"

Barent wondered if maybe there was an echo in the room. "Yes," he said.

She shook her head. "No."

Audrey Parker was just as bad. She stared at his face with round, colorless eyes, her jaws working steadily on a piece of gum. "I don't know anything," she said. "Don't even ask."

Barent could believe it. Where had Sharon Lee gotten these two? And why? Maybe she had wanted to be the only attractive woman in the office. "I'm afraid that I have to ask," he said.

Audrey Parker shrugged, a ripple going down her shoulders, spreading across her chest and down to the tops of her fleshy thighs. Barent waited for an instant but she didn't say a thing.

Ten minutes later, he closed his notebook. Audrey Parker was right. She knew nothing and she couldn't have cared less.

Wellesley also had been cooperative but unhelpful.

"I miss it sometimes, the action; you know what I mean?" Wellesley had a wistful look on his face.

"How long were you in?" Barent asked.

"Twenty-three years." Wellesley sighed. "I know it's dumb. I go home at five every night. I drink a martini and watch T.V. and shoot a round of golf with the Missus. I get to watch the grandchildren grow. I'm not sorry to be out of it, but sometimes..." He shrugged. "Ah, well, you know how it is."

Actually, Barent didn't, and he sincerely hoped that he never did. Barent planned on leaving when he hit sixty and never looking back. Wellesley, he suspected, was merely indulging in a little nostalgia, brought on by shooting the breeze with another old pro.

"You like it here?" Barent asked.

"It's okay." Wellesley said it without enthusiasm. "The only problem is these people don't take it seriously. They hire me to do the job but they don't understand that ninety per-cent of security is the people who work here having the right attitude. After the World Trade Center went down, it worked a little better for a few months, but then it slacked off. I don't have enough men to make this place secure. I never will. They want it secure, they've got to take the initiative, ask people who don't belong what they're doing here, assume some responsibility." Wellesley shook his head sadly. "We have guards posted by the front doors, by the E.R. entrance and by the elevators. Anyone going up to the floors is supposed to show either a hospital I.D. card or a pass, which they get at the information desk in the lobby. After eleven at night, they're supposed to sign a book by the elevator. But the fact is that during the day the place is so crowded that anyone can just walk up. Late at night the system works a little better."

"I understand," Barent said, and nodded. About what he had expected. The evening and night shift guards had noticed nothing suspicious. The day shift people had been uncommunicative. They seemed embarrassed, probably unwilling to admit that a murderer had walked in and waltzed right out and they had never noticed the difference. "Can you give me copies of the sign in book for the past forty-eight hours?"

"Sure," Wellesley said.

They were unlikely to be much use but you never knew.

The nurses on the Psych floor had been equally unhelpful. Nobody had any idea how Mose had gotten out. "Probably somebody left the door open." The Head Nurse, a tall, red headed woman named Burke, who had a round face and nice green eyes, said it with gloomy satisfaction. "Maybe the orderly who delivered the pharmacy cart."

The orderly swore it wasn't him, but you couldn't expect him to admit it, and it didn't matter anyway.

Jeremy Pike was equally unhelpful. "The will was quite specific," Pike said. "A trust fund was established, sufficient to pay Mr. Mose's medical care for the remainder of his life. After that, any equity left over is to be donated to the American Cancer Society. Miss Mose died of cancer, you know."

Barent didn't, but he made appropriate, regretful noises and hung up. Scratch that idea, he thought. Nobody seemed to have a motive to frame old Mose.

The preliminary lab results and the initial autopsy findings on Dr. Sharon Lee were ready by the afternoon of the next day. The tox screening would take a little longer but Barent would be very surprised indeed if it showed anything. This was not a case where the subtleties of poison or drug overdose seemed likely.

He closed the door to his office, sat down behind his desk and read the report slowly and carefully. Cause of death: asphyxia. She had been strangled, which they already knew. Deep bruises on both sides of the neck. Microvascular hemorrhages in the lungs and in the brain. There were small bite marks on her breasts and some tiny lacerations in the vagina. But no semen. Too bad. If Mose had raped her, he hadn't ejaculated. There had been a Bic pen lying next to the body. They had examined it for blood or vaginal

31

secretions but it was clean. Barent grimaced. There were a number of foreign hairs on her scrub suit, but they could have come from anyone. The call room was not cleaned as often or as well as it should have been. A lot of hair and skin fibers were mixed in with the dust gathered from the room, and a few of these seemed to match the ones found on the scrubs. Similar fibers had been found on Dr. Lee's clothes, hanging in the call room's tiny closet. Some other, thicker strands seemed to be horse hair, in varying colors. Barent made a note to find out if Sharon Lee had been into horses.

Plenty of fingerprints—only to be expected in a room shared by many people—but none that the Police or FBI files had flagged.

Barent's eyes narrowed at the next section. He read it through carefully, then read it again. There were traces of blood under the victim's fingernails—A negative—which was Bill Mose's blood type. DNA analysis was not yet completed. Barent made a soft, clucking noise and smiled to himself. He picked up another folder, the one on Mose. They were still trying to figure out where Mose had been all night long but so far, no luck. That bothered Barent but it was a big building and much of it was largely deserted at night. Even during the day, it was rare that anyone would find a need to go into the basement storage rooms or the boiler plant. Mose's clothing was dirty, but no dirtier than the corners of Sharon Lee's call room. The knife was a typical dinner knife. Trays with dishes and dirty utensils had been found in five out of the twenty-one attendings' call rooms, some of them obviously there for a day or more. It seemed to have been customary for the doctors to bring food up from the cafeteria. There was no such tray in the room where Sharon Lee had been killed, but Mose could easily have picked the knife up in one of the adjacent call rooms.

Strip search of the suspect had revealed four small lacerations on his left upper arm. The blood stains on the knife were not from Sharon Lee. As Barent had suggested to Wellesley, they appeared to be from Mose himself. There were cuts on his tongue and the inside of his lips. Barent remembered what Werth had said about Mose's propensity for swallowing small objects and shuddered. Evidently the knife had been too big for him to get down. Luckily for Mose, the knife was rather dull. Otherwise he could easily have bled to death.

So that was it. If the DNA typing matched, the case was pretty much wrapped up. They would have enough to go to trial and Bill Mose would spend the rest of his life locked up in the custody of the State. Barent thought about that for a moment and found that he regretted it. It seemed so completely inadequate. Mose was going to spend his life locked up in any case, and Barent doubted that Mose would ever notice the difference between his old Unit and an institution for the criminally insane. People who commit murder ought to be punished. They should have to live in a cramped, crowded cell and sleep on a narrow cot and eat lousy food and dream of a world that they would never see again. Their lives should change, and not for the better.

Barent shrugged and closed the folder.

Chapter 5

"So who do you think is the most obnoxious surgeon in the hospital?" Steinberg asked. "It doesn't really matter, just give me a name."

"Farkas?" the resident said. "He's pretty obnoxious."

"Okay, Farkas. Now suppose Farkas turns to you in the middle of a case and says, 'Doctor, I need a laser beam. I want you to turn that overhead light into a laser beam.' What would you say to that?"

Like all anesthesiologists, Steinberg thought of himself as a philosopher and a diplomat but was really a repressed personality, hostile, passive aggressive and full of resentments over petty, imagined slights. Kurtz bent over his patient's abdomen, sewed over an ulcer and listened with half an ear as Steinberg talked to his resident, a kid named Chao.

"I'd tell him he was out of his mind," Chao said.

Steinberg shook his head. "Big mistake. Of course, he probably is out of his mind but telling him so is not going to help matters. Look at it this way—your job is to make the case go smoothly, right?"

The resident nodded, looking doubtful.

"Now telling him he's out of his mind is treating him like he's *not* out of his mind. It's pretending that he's really a normal human being, even though he's acting like a jackass. But you got it right the first time. He *is* out of his mind. You don't tell a lunatic that he's out of his mind. What's the point?

"So if Farkas asks you to do something asinine, the proper response is to give him a big smile and say, 'Gee, Dr. Farkas, I don't know if that's going to work. But I'll try!' Then after you've tried, you turn back to him and you say, 'Gee, Dr. Farkas, I couldn't do it. I'm sorry, but I tried!' And he'll probably think you're not the best anesthesiologist in the world but, oh, well, you tried. And that'll be the end of it.

"Now think what would happen if you did what you suggested. You tell him he's out of his mind, you'd get into an argument and then you'd both end up pissed off. How does that help the situation? Believe me, it doesn't. It's completely counterproductive. What you have to do is think of yourself as a psychiatrist of the operating room. You have to always keep in mind that the guy with the knife in his hand as almost as much your patient as the patient. Try to maintain what the psychiatrists call a 'therapeutic relationship.' Believe me, things will go smoother."

"Steinberg," Kurtz said amiably, "you are such an asshole."

"Whoops," Steinberg said, "the walls have ears. Now remember, be therapeutic."

Kurtz sniffed but otherwise maintained a dignified silence.

Chao smiled behind his mask as Steinberg beamed over the drapes at Kurtz.

"Okay, Steve," Kurtz said to Nolan. "Why don't you close?" Steinberg continued to beam. Kurtz gave him a disdainful glance and walked off, his head held high. Behind him, Steinberg chuckled.

Older hospitals, Kurtz reflected, did have a certain elitist charm. Most of the newer places had one large cafeteria, where patients and staff mingled indiscriminately, but Easton still preserved the tradition of a separate dining room for the doctors. The food came from the same kitchen that supplied the patients and the rest of the workers, but they dressed it up with a sprig of parsley or a carved carrot. The tables in the Doctor's Dining Room were made out of old oak and the chairs had armrests and cushioned seats. The walls were covered with faded oil paintings of distinguished physicians from the hospital's past and they charged about thirty per-cent more for the privilege of eating there.

Kurtz resented getting ripped off but he ate there whenever he wasn't tied up in surgery; it was expected.

He took a tray through the cafeteria line, shook his head sadly at the day's choices and settled for beef stew, with a side order of French fries and a slice of cheesecake. While he was paying, he surveyed the tables. It was a little past noon and the place was crowded. One table near the window had a few empty seats and he walked over and sat down.

Jim Farkas was holding court. "The Dow can't keep going up this way. I've been raising cash for the past two weeks. We're overdue for a correction; then I'll buy back in." Farkas was a plastic surgeon, and therefore rich. He was also middle aged and stout, with a bald head and a smooth, unlined face that popular rumor attributed to an advertisement for his own wares.

Phil Longo was an orthopedist, a frequent fishing buddy of Kurtz and Bill Werth. Dick Weber was a pediatrician. Pediatricians made a lot less money than surgeons, a fact that the pediatricians, along with all the other practitioners of the self-styled 'cognitive specialties' such as family practice and internal medicine, complained about constantly. In Kurtz' jaded view, a view shared by all members of the 'technical specialties,' the internists and pediatricians deserved to make less because when you came right down to it, they really didn't do much of anything, spending the majority of their working hours either dealing with chronic illness that couldn't be cured or prescribing pills for minor ailments that would go away in a few days no matter what you did for them.

Weber looked both bored and vaguely pissed off, which Farkas seemed not to notice. Longo flashed Kurtz a grin and squinted down at his tray. "I pity your coronary arteries," he said.

Kurtz nodded thoughtfully while he chewed a French fry. "My cholesterol is one-sixty. I've got good genes."

"Lucky you."

"I saw a cartoon once," Farkas said, "I think it was *The New Yorker*, a little guy is sitting in a chair surrounded by elephant tusks, African spears, carved wooden statues, paintings—all sorts of stuff. He's looking at his wife and saying, 'I've decided to put my money into things.'" Farkas nodded decisively. "That cartoon was supposed to be funny but it had a good point. Rare coins have been doing great and now is the time to buy them, just coming out of a pullback. Also art. I've picked up a collection of Miro lithographs for a great price. They should double in three years, maybe triple."

"You do any interesting cases lately?" Longo asked Kurtz.

"Yeah," Kurtz said. "Two weeks ago I had a guy with a hepatic cyst. Echinococcus."

Longo wrinkled his brow. "That's a tapeworm, isn't it?"

Kurtz nodded. "He's from New Zealand. It's common around sheep. People eat the eggs, the larvae migrate to the liver, or sometimes the lungs, and form cysts. If a cyst ruptures, it can be fatal."

"I've never seen a case."

"Hey, Kurtz," Farkas said. "You ever been to Sanibel Island?"

"Sanibel Island?" Kurtz said. "No."

"It's down in Florida, off the Gulf Coast. I've got a little condo there, place on the beach. Perfect for getting away from it all and forgetting the cares of the world."

Kurtz grunted and Farkas peered at him. "Weird, this thing about Sharon Lee. I'm glad they got the guy who did it. You used to go out with her, didn't you?"

"Yes," Kurtz said carefully, "I did."

Farkas nodded, and then, amazingly, he said. "Sorry to hear about it. She was okay." This display of compassion seemed to exhaust Farkas' store of sensitivity. He immediately took off on a tangent into the realm of Commodities Futures and how Fed policy on interest rates would affect the course of the market.

Kurtz frowned down at his stew, suddenly no longer hungry.

Longo gave a tight little grin and said to Kurtz, "I hear Sanibel Island is pretty nice. We should all go down there and borrow his place for a few weeks. You think he'd mind?"

Kurtz' secretary had gray hair and narrow shoulders and sat very straight in her chair behind the front desk. Her name was Rose Schapiro. The patients liked her. So did Kurtz. She was always cheerful, she never called in sick, she typed eighty words a minute and she had never lost an insurance form.

He arrived back at his office at one o'clock. Mrs. Schapiro looked up from her computer screen and said, "Have a nice lunch?"

"Not bad. Has Ed shown up yet?"

"He's in Room Three," Mrs. Schapiro said, "removing a mole."

"Good," Kurtz said. Edward Ornella was one of the Grand Old Men of the surgical staff but he was overdue for retirement and for most of the past year had been easing himself out. He had recently stopped operating and now confined his practice to consults and office work.

Just then, Ornella came out of the back treatment room, drying his hands with a paper towel and smiling. "Richard," he said. "Nice to see you."

"Hello, Ed."

"Well, I've made my contribution to the ledger for today." He threw the paper towel in a wastebasket and waggled a finger at Kurtz. "Now remember," he said, "time is money." Still smiling, he put on his coat and walked out of the office.

Mrs. Schapiro watched him go and shook her head sadly. "Ten years ago, he was a great surgeon."

"He's still a great surgeon, when he wants to be."

"I guess that's what I mean, then. It's sad."

"I don't believe he sees it that way. He's really looking forward to shucking the rat race."

"Do you think so?" Mrs. Schapiro laughed softly. "I don't think anybody looks forward to being old and useless."

Maybe not, Kurtz thought, maybe not. Not having to work for a living was hard for Kurtz to imagine, much less not wanting to. "Is Mr. Gallinas in yet?" he asked. Gallinas had a lump in his thigh that was probably a benign sebaceous cyst but every once in a while the most innocent appearing lump surprised you. It made sense to take it out.

"He arrived a few minutes ago. He's in the back."

"Okay," Kurtz said. He took off his jacket, hung it in the closet and put on a white doctor's coat. "Room Two?"

Mrs. Schapiro nodded.

Kurtz smiled and rubbed his hands together. "Lead me to him," he said. "And don't ever forget, time is money."

At four A.M., Herman Delgado climbed up the fire escape in back of a brownstone on the lower West Side of Manhattan. The stars shone overhead but there was no moon out and the night was very dark and very cold. Herman's breath steamed in front of him.

All good citizens, even the citizens of the city that never sleeps, were dormant at this hour of the morning. Herman Delgado had little fear of being seen as he lay on his stomach on the cold steel grating of the fire escape and cut a triangular patch out of the window with a glasscutter. He had fixed a piece of duct tape to the middle of the patch, and when he gave it a quick tap with his gloved fist, it came loose but did not fall. Gently, Herman Delgado lowered the piece of glass into the apartment inside, reached his hand in and released a clasp on the window. He slid the window up and clambered inside.

The apartment was dark. Delgado carefully closed the blinds and pulled a flash light from his pocket. A cone of light played over a stove, dishwasher and refrigerator. Confidently, as if he knew that nobody would be home, he walked down a narrow corridor and into the living room. The main light switch had a dimmer on it. He set it to low and turned it on. Herman Delgado smiled and rubbed his hands together.

The apartment was decorated with low, white leather couches, white shag rug, solid oak coffee table with a glass top, abstract paintings on the wall whose muted purples and pinks blended unobtrusively into the room's decor. Delgado moved into the empty bedroom and began to rummage through the dresser drawers. He took his time and did it right, searching thoroughly and carefully and not bothering to put things back where they belonged. In the middle left hand drawer, he found the jewel box. Opening it, he held up a white gold ring set with a single emerald cut diamond, nodded and stuffed it into the inner pocket of the denim jacket that he wore beneath his coat. He shuffled through the rest of the pieces in the box, selecting most of them and discarding only the few that he knew were not worth trying to fence.

When he was done, he walked back into the kitchen, peered out the window, just to make certain that nobody was lurking down below, then clambered back onto the fire escape and vanished into the night.

Chapter 6

"It still bothers you, doesn't it? Sharon Lee, I mean."

"What was that?" Kurtz asked.

Kathy smiled at him. "See? You're so pre-occupied, you hardly hear a word that people say to you."

Kurtz shifted uncomfortably in his seat and cracked a weak grin. "Did Nolan ask you to talk to me?" "Liebert," she said.

"Liebert?" Kurtz blinked. "I'll have to have a little talk with Liebert."

"Better not. He might complain to the Dean."

Kurtz nodded but he barely heard her. "Okay, I won't have a little talk with Liebert."

Kathy had a two-bedroom place on Bank Street that she shared with a post doc in history named Jennifer Levy. Jennifer was away for the weekend. Kurtz sat on Kathy's couch and sipped Scotch and soda and tried to act like what Steinberg might have called a "normal human being."

Kathy sat next to him and held her own glass of white wine with both hands and took a small sip.

"I'm sorry," Kurtz said. "I really am. I can't figure out why I feel this way. Sharon and I broke up almost two years ago. I hardly ever thought about her." He shrugged. "I'll get over it. I just don't know when."

Kathy nodded. "She was important to you at one time. You can't forget that."

"No." He gave a shaky laugh. In reality, while the murder of Sharon Lee was the focus for his current sour mood, Kurtz knew that he had been vaguely unhappy for quite some time. He had a sort of desperate longing for...something. Something he had trouble defining. Certainty, perhaps. Or maybe just significance...Kurtz had been on the staff at Easton for nearly three years. Long enough to get comfortable. Long enough to get bored. A lot of physicians felt this way. The process took these very smart, very hard driving, very competitive people and it tortured them: all the endless, obsessive work to master the enormous reams of material, the agonizing fear that a moment's ignorance or lack of attention could result in a mistake and the knowledge that even a small mistake could wind up killing someone. The stark reality was that you had to be perfect because nothing less than perfection was allowed—and nobody was perfect.

All that pressure...for years, always climbing the ladder toward the ultimate, elusive goal: four years of college, four years of medical school, five years of surgical training. Two years at least to build a practice. And then you were there: physician and surgeon, respected practitioner of the art. Real life. No more steps on the ladder, no more goals to strive for, nothing to do but do the same things you were doing day after day— operate in the morning, see patients in the afternoon, never let the battery on the beeper run down because a disaster could strike at any instant—always pretending that you were in control, that you were good enough to do the job when only God Himself was good enough to do the job because sooner or later everybody died.

Doctors were freaks about control. You had to know everything. You had to be on top of everything. Nothing happened by chance. And if anything—anything at all—went wrong, you could be absolutely certain that the god damned lawyers would look at the situation just exactly in that light. It was your fault—even if it wasn't. No excuses allowed.

And then Sharon Lee had been murdered and it seemed like the last straw, because nothing was more out of control than cold-blooded murder.

"I'm sorry," he said. "It's just the way I feel."

Kathy sipped her wine and looked at him over the rim of the glass and said, "Nobody can argue with the way that you feel."

"Yeah." He gave his head a little shake. "Like I said, I'll get over it." He stared into his drink and hoped it would be soon.

"Barent?"

Barent sighed. He knew this voice and he rarely enjoyed hearing it. "Yes?"

"It's John Costas. At The News."

"I know," Barent said.

"Hey, what's the matter? You don't sound glad to hear from me."

"Well, John, you don't usually make my job any easier. You understand what I'm saying?"

"Come on, Barent. I gave you great press on the Carmody murder."

"You gave us credit for catching the perpetrator. That was after calling us idiots for three weeks because we didn't."

"I was just doing my civic duty, Barent."

"And selling newspapers. Don't forget selling newspapers."

"Well, selling newspapers is my job."

"Really? Gee, I didn't realize that. And here I thought your job was journalism. You know: informing the public, telling the truth, exposing corruption—that sort of stuff."

"Ouch," the voice said amiably.

"What can I do for you, John?"

"I hear you have positive evidence regarding the suspect in custody, the wacko. I'm talking about the murder at Easton."

"Where did you hear that?"

The voice was cagey. "I have my sources."

Barent grunted.

"Well, do you?"

Briefly, Barent considered denying it but decided against it. Costas had no monopoly on inside sources. If Costas had heard it, then every other reporter in Town would be trumpeting the story and he might as well keep the son-of-a-bitch at least minimally friendly. "Yes. But that's off the record. Anyway, the Commissioner's called a Press Conference for tomorrow. He'll announce it officially then."

"Hey, no problem. Off the record's my middle name. I prefer it that way. If they can't check your sources, then they can't check your quotes. Know what I mean?"

"Yes, John," Barent said. "I'm afraid that I do."

Bill Mose was not bored. He woke up in the morning when the nurses told him to and he brushed his teeth and washed his face and then shuffled out to eat breakfast. After breakfast, he wandered into the social room and smoked cigarettes and watched T.V. Tom and Jerry were followed by Porky Pig and Porky Pig was followed by Chip and Dale. Mose lacked the ability to follow the plots but the colors and the action held his rapt attention.

Vaguely, as he watched, Mose became aware of an uncomfortable sensation somewhere in his abdomen. He ignored it. He had had such sensations in the past and they had always gone away.

He smoked his cigarettes, taking deep sucking drags. Ten other men sat on the couches, all of them smoking and staring at the T.V. When one cigarette burned down to the filter Mose would light another. Once, when he had finished a cigarette, he glanced around the little room. The patients stared blankly at the television screen. Two beefy aides sat in the corners. Nobody was looking at him. He smiled to himself and swallowed the filter, then puffed contentedly away.

Herman Delgado sat on the roof of his building and snorted a couple of lines in the frigid cold. Herman didn't mind the cold. The air was clear and still and the sky was very blue. From up here, the dirty snow down on the street looked clean, white and pure. Sitting out on the roof, he felt like he had the city all to himself. He liked that feeling.

Across the roof, a single pigeon had set up housekeeping in the old pigeon cote that Herman had placed there. When he was sixteen, Herman had seen *On the Waterfront*, with Marlon Brando. He had loved the scenes with the pigeons on the roof and he had gone out and bought himself a pigeon cote. What he hadn't figured on was the fact that birds made a lot of birdshit and cleaning up birdshit was not Herman's idea of a good time. So after a couple of days he had decided to ignore the pigeon cote. He left it where it was, though, and the stupid birds still used it.

His nose and the tips of his ears grew numb, partly from the cold but mostly from cocaine. Herman laughed softly to himself and watched his breath steam away in the frigid air. After a little while, he felt the need to move and he went back inside and climbed down the stairs.

Ten minutes later he was out on the street, feeling good. The money he had gotten for the stolen jewelry would keep him in crack and eager women for a month. He wriggled his toes in his new Bass shoes as he walked down the icy sidewalk.

A black Lincoln Town Car slowed as it passed by him and a window lowered. From the back seat, a grating voice issued. "Herman," the voice said. "I want to talk to you."

Herman hesitated, the hair on the back of his neck prickling. He forced himself to smile. "Boss?"

"Get in, Herman."

Herman shrugged and opened the door and slid into the back seat. The door closed and the limousine pulled away from the curb. Inside the car sat the man Herman had referred to as "Boss." Next to him sat the driver, a big guy named Tony, plus another man who did not turn around or even move but who Herman recognized with a jolt of sudden fear. In the back seat, smiling at some secret joke, moving his head to music that only he could hear, staring straight ahead, sat a man whose real name was unknown but who was called "Bose", because his deep voice had reminded the Boss once of the sounds issuing from a stereo speaker.

They traveled for about a mile with the Boss frowning out the window, then he turned to Herman with sad, hooded eyes and shook his head sorrowfully, saying nothing.

Herman stared at him. "Boss?" he said uncertainly.

The Boss drew a deep, resigned sigh. "Herman. Why do you have to be so stupid?"

Herman drew himself up, offended.

"You've been warned, Herman. You're not operating alone any more. You're part of an organization. You show initiative, that's fine. But initiative is supposed to contribute to the good of the organization. Simply put, Herman, you do a job and the organization doesn't get its cut, you become a liability that the organization can no longer afford."

Herman looked at him, at his set expression and empty eyes, and knew sudden fear. He turned to the man sitting next to the driver. "What's he mean?" he whispered.

The man said nothing. He gave a tiny, disgusted snort and shook his head. "No! You gotta help me!"

Bose turned toward Herman, holding a gun. The black opening at the end of the silencer on the barrel seemed to stare at Herman like an accusing eye. The gun went off with a soft pop. A tiny gout of flame came from the muzzle, and Herman felt something cold spread out from the center of his chest. He looked once at the little dribble of red leaking down the front of his jacket, then his eyes glazed over and the world faded. The last thing he heard before death took him was Bose' deep, beautiful voice saying, "Goodbye, Herman.

Chapter 7

It snowed again on the night before Christmas, covering the potholes and piles of garbage with a soft, white blanket. The sounds of bells ringing and people singing Christmas carols drifted through the air, and the city— or at least the section of it that was Lew Barent's main concern—seemed to have grown curiously and unusually calm.

Barent spent most of the week following Sharon Lee's murder on routine matters. In the mornings he sat behind his old wooden desk and did paperwork. On Tuesday afternoon and again on Thursday he went to court to testify in a case involving a prostitute who had stabbed her pimp. The case was unusual in that the girl was an undergraduate at N.Y.U. with no prior record who claimed to be putting herself through college on the proceeds.

"Men?" she sniffed at one point. "I don't have a very high opinion of men, thank you, but I didn't stab him because I hate men. I stabbed him because he beat me. He deserved it and I don't regret it one single bit."

She was blonde, freckled, pretty and demure and the jury seemed inclined to believe her. So did Barent.

On Wednesday morning Barent reviewed a report on the current activities of Bill Mose, who had done nothing at all out of the ordinary for a schizophrenic—which is to say, he had done nothing at all except eat, sleep, smoke cigarettes, stare at the T.V., go to 'occupational therapy' (which meant pasting paper and sticks of wood together with glue in a futile attempt to make 'art') and wander around the Unit.

On Friday morning he received a call from Harry Moran. "Lew?"

Barent breathed a sigh. It had been, he thought fleetingly, much too good to last. "What's up, Harry?"

"I'm down by the Hudson, opposite 23rd Street." Moran's voice stopped.

"Yes?" Barent prompted. "You were saying?"

"Oh, sorry. One of the blues was telling me something. It's a body in a trash bin. Hard to say how long he's been in there but long enough to be frozen stiff. Shot once in the chest."

Barent looked at the diminished pile of papers on his desk and sadly shook his head. "I'll be right there," he said.

Bill Mose was off his feed. Usually a careful and meticulous eater, he seemed to have lost his appetite. The uncomfortable feeling in his abdomen had grown over the days to a constant, throbbing pain. He looked at his food and felt nauseous. A sheen of sweat covered his forehead. When he sat up suddenly, a wave of dizziness washed over him.

On the morning of his fifth day in the new place, he found himself unable to get out of bed. When the aide came in to usher him up, he ignored the insistent voice and simply lay there, huddled in misery around the pain in his gut.

"Come on," the aide said. "None of that." He reached out a hand, shook Mose by the shoulder. Mose ignored him.

The aide shook his head. "It's time to get up. You know you're not allowed to just lie there." He gave Mose another shake, then grabbed him under the arms and attempted to haul him out of bed.

It was too much. With a convulsive heave, Mose's stomach spasmed. He groaned in misery and collapsed back onto the bed as a torrent of green bile spewed out of his mouth and covered the legs of the astonished aide.

"Shit!" the aide shrieked. "Look what you've done to me!"

Mose ignored him. He was too busy retching.

"Goddammit..." The aide stuck his head out into the hall and called out to the nursing station. "Get somebody in here with a mop and a bucket!" He wrinkled his nose. "And get a doctor!" He muttered, "They better pay me for these pants. God damn nut case..."

Three hours later, Mose was in an ambulance back to Easton. The staff psychiatrist had had enough presence of mind to evaluate his distended abdomen and high pitched bowel sounds, make a tentative diagnosis of bowel obstruction and put down a nasogastric tube. Mose pulled it out through his nose as soon as the ambulance got under way.

After that, they tied his hands together, which served little purpose since the damage had already been done but which made the aides feel better. The two policemen assigned to guard the prisoner *en route* watched impassively and said nothing.

When they arrived at the E.R., Mose was trundled in on a stretcher and deposited on a hard metal table while his entourage sat down in chairs to wait. After a half hour, Mose again began to vomit. The policemen looked at each other and decided to wait in the hall. One of the aides stuck his head out and said to a passing nurse, "This guy is throwing up. Can't you get a doctor in here?"

The nurse puffed up her cheeks and gave him an irritated look. "We're very busy," she said. "Someone will be with you shortly."

"But—" the aide began.

The nurse cut him off. "You'll just have to wait your turn." Defeated, the aide went back into the room and watched helplessly as Mose continued to retch, covering himself, the table and the floor around him with foul smelling, watery green fluid.

Finally, a harried looking intern came in, took as much of Bill Mose's history from the aides as they could recall, listened to the patient's heart, lungs and abdomen, called for x-ray, started an I.V. and phoned in a consult to surgery. Then he left.

Fifteen minutes later, a technician rolled in a portable x-ray machine. The technician glanced at the order sheet and said, "Chest and abdomen?"

The aides looked at him. One of them shrugged helplessly.

The technician grunted. "Help me up with him, would you?" he said. The aides lifted Mose while the technician slid an x-ray plate under his back. "Okay," he said, "step back." The aides left the room until the machine buzzed, then returned.

"Now the chest," the technician said. They repeated the process and the technician left to develop the films.

Mose, his stomach finally empty, closed his eyes and had almost dropped off to sleep when Nolan arrived, accompanied by Liebert. "Oh, boy..." Nolan muttered. "Kurtz isn't going to be too happy about this."

Liebert wrinkled his brow and gave Nolan a worried frown.

While they were examining Mose, the technician arrived with the films and Nolan snapped them into a view box on the wall. "What do you think, Doctor?" he asked Liebert.

"Dilated small intestine with air fluid levels. A bowel obstruction?"

Nolan gave him an approving look. "Very good," he said. "How about this?" He pointed to a hazy shadow surrounding a clear density in the middle of the abdomen.

Liebert wrinkled his brow. "I don't know," he said at last. "It looks like metal."

"Well, it's not soft tissue and it's not bone," Nolan said. He grinned. "He probably swallowed something." Nolan sat down, quickly wrote up an admission History and Physical and some orders while Liebert examined the somnolent Mose more thoroughly, daintily stepping around the puddles of vomit on the floor.

"Okay," Nolan said to Liebert. "Let's go tell the O.R."

A half hour later, Nolan and Liebert wheeled Mose into the operating room, his hands tied to the rails of the stretcher. Nolan had put down another N.G. tube but Mose had managed to twist himself around and once again pull it out. The two policemen, wearing surgical headcaps, shoe covers and white paper "bunny suits" over their uniforms followed along behind.

Liebert was still arguing. "The patient is incompetent. There's no consent. You can't operate without consent."

"It's an emergency," Nolan said. "You don't bother getting consent in an emergency."

"Kurtz shouldn't do it. He's too involved."

"Tell it to him."

Liebert frowned unhappily. "I already did. He told me he's on call, it's his patient and I should mind my own business."

"Good advice," Nolan said.

"Well, then we should get an ethics consult. There's always an ethics counselor on call. That's what they told us."

Nolan turned and gave Liebert an annoyed look as the stretcher skidded around a corner. "Look, kid, you want to call the chaplain or the hospital lawyer or whatever other bureaucrat they supposedly have available to help us poor nincompoops make difficult moral decisions? Jesus. These people get bothered so seldom with this sort of stuff it would take ten, maybe fifteen minutes for whoever it is to wake up and even understand what you want. Then he'd probably decide to consult the rest of the committee, because frankly, the people who are supposed to make difficult moral decisions are usually better at passing the buck than doing their jobs. All told, you're going to waste at least another hour, probably a lot more, and this guy needs to be operated on right now. So forget about it."

Liebert shook his head. "Hell," he said. "I'm only a medical student. I'm just trying to do the right thing."

"Well, the right thing to do right now is to shut up and let's start operating."

Kurtz met them in the O.R. Mose had already been placed on the table. The EKG showed a rapid but regular rhythm and his blood pressure was normal. Steinberg nodded to him when he walked in but was too absorbed in what he was doing to talk and Kurtz sat down in a corner of the room. Truthfully, Kurtz hardly knew how he felt about this case. Bill Mose was small, dirty, miserable and sick. He didn't look like Kurtz' conception of a murderer. Still, Kurtz knew that Liebert had a point. Maybe his personal involvement should have disqualified him from operating. Morosely, Kurtz shook his head. Mose was his patient and he wanted to do it, and he was going to do it. And if anybody had a problem with that, they could argue about it later—after it was too late.

With great concern, he watched what Steinberg was doing, ready to step in and lend a hand if he was asked. The induction of anesthesia was particularly dangerous in a bowel obstruction. The intestines were bloated and full and even if the stomach was de-pressurized with a nasogastric tube, there was no guarantee that the tube had gotten into every fold and corner. The patient had to be presumed to have a stomach full of vomitus, and if Mose happened to vomit after the anesthetic had deprived him of his normal reflexes but before the trachea was protected by an endotracheal tube, then the acidic bile would flow down into the lungs and the patient would most likely die from aspiration pneumonia—if he didn't drown outright.

"You ready?" Steinberg asked his resident. The resident nodded. "You checked your laryngoscope? The suction is on?"

The resident gave him a harried look and nodded again. "Okay," Steinberg said. He glanced once more at his monitors, then pushed a syringe of a short acting narcotic, waited thirty seconds and gave propofol, followed immediately by succinylcholine. He pushed down on the larynx with his left hand, compressing the trachea onto the esophagus, and waited.

The patient's eyes glazed over and he stopped breathing and thirty seconds later, he began to shake all over as the succinylcholine took effect and every neuromuscular junction in his body discharged at once. Then he stopped shaking. For three minutes at least, he would be completely paralyzed. "Go," Steinberg said.

The resident inserted the laryngoscope into Mose's mouth and lifted the jaw. "You see it?" Steinberg demanded.

"Good view." The resident kept his eye on the vocal cords and held up his hand. Steinberg, still keeping pressure on the larynx, handed him the endotracheal tube and the resident slipped the tube between the vocal cords and into the trachea.

Steinberg breathed an audible sigh of relief and turned to Kurtz. "He's all yours."

"Nice job," Kurtz said. He stepped outside to scrub and by the time he returned, Nolan had opened a huge incision from the sternum all the way down to the pelvis. The bowel lay inside the abdominal cavity, swollen and distended. Kurtz elbowed Nolan aside, reached into the pelvis and ran his fingers up the length of the descending colon, which felt entirely normal. The same for the transverse and the ascending colon. The ileum too was fine, undulating with peristalsis like a gigantic earthworm. Midway through the jejunem, he found it. "See here?" he said.

Nolan and Liebert peered in. Nolan nodded, reached in, felt the area that Kurtz had indicated and nodded again. "Something hard."

Kurtz lifted the bowel up onto the skin, made an incision and inserted a suction catheter. At least five hundred cc's of green fluid drained out. Then he put clamps on both sides of the obstruction, cut off the offending segment, plopped it into a basin and handed it to the scrub nurse. He stapled the ends together, told Nolan to close and went over to the scrub table. "Could I see that?" he said.

The scrub nurse handed him the basin. With the clamps on, the segment of bowel looked like a stuffed sausage. Kurtz picked up a knife and

48

cut into it. In the middle, blocking the passage, was a sodden mass of fibrous material. With a Kelly clamp and a pair of forceps, he delicately spread the fibers. In the center of the mass was...Kurtz frowned.

"What is it," Nolan asked.

Kurtz picked it out. It glinted in the light. "It looks like a gold ring," Kurtz said.

Chapter 8

Sharon Lee and Richard Kurtz had been a beautiful couple. Everybody said so. None of their friends could understand it when they broke up. "It's my fault," Kurtz would tell them. "She's too good for me." Since nobody felt it prudent to ask him exactly what he meant, the comment tended to forestall further questions.

What he meant, actually, was that Sharon Lee had been a lunatic. He never did completely figure her out, though when he met Sharon's mother he thought he understood her a little better. Children of alcoholic parents often grew up with a chip on their shoulder and a need for control, which made medicine an appropriate career choice because it was a field where Sharon's particular craziness was almost admired. Great doc, that Sharon Lee, really takes care of her patients. Except that she was nuts. Kurtz had given her a key to his apartment and once, when he called to tell her he had to break a date because he had an emergency case in the O.R., he arrived home later to find Sharon gone and the telephone ripped out of the wall. Kurtz shook his head in amazement, remembering. Nuts. If there was anything an obstetrician should have understood, it was the unpredictable nature of both their jobs. She was wild in bed, though. She had made love obsessively and passionately, groaning and crying out, almost screaming, which had embarrassed Kurtz at first but which he got a kick out of once he got used to it. But even in bed, she had to keep control. You get on top. Turn that way. Kiss my nipples. Rub there. *Harder*.

Kurtz figured that he was probably not the easiest person in the world to get along with but Sharon Lee had been something else entirely.

Kurtz sighed and looked out the window and sipped his brandy.

His apartment was on the Eighteenth Floor of a building across town from the Medical Center, overlooking the East River. One whole wall was covered with plate glass. Two nights after he had operated on Bill Mose, he lay on the couch in his living room with a snifter of Courvoisier X.O. and watched the water flowing by. The Gil Evans Orchestra with Miles Davis was playing softly in the background: "Summertime," from Porgy and Bess.

He and Sharon had been together in the summertime. For three whole months, they had spent all their nights together, sometimes at Kurtz' apartment, more often at Sharon's place on the lower East Side. There was a little park-like area out back, almost a courtyard, which had a winding stone path surrounded by a garden. They would lie in bed at night after making love and

50

hold hands and stare out at the stone path surrounded by yucca and Japanese maples and azaleas, the stars shining overhead and the moths flying through the beams of antique copper lamps that made their wings glow like they were on fire.

Real romantic. Except it had only lasted for three months, which was probably about a month and a half too long.

Sharon hadn't been a bad sort, he reflected. Be generous. Their personalities had simply been incompatible. Everybody has their little quirks. Their quirks just hadn't meshed.

After the breakup, they had hardly spoken for a year. After that...it no longer mattered. They were simply two people who knew each other. They said "hello" when they passed in the hallways and that was about it.

Kurtz had gone out with a lot of women. He had never felt like sticking with any of them...until Kathy. Kathy, he had to admit, was different. He thought about Kathy a lot lately. Kathy could let a man be. Kathy felt no obligation whatsoever to conform to anyone else's expectations and she didn't expect anyone else to conform to hers. Sharon, in addition to her need to keep the upper hand in a relationship, had always seemed to define herself in terms of other people: her snide, rich friends, her almost but not quite adequate boyfriend. Kurtz, frankly, had no desire at all to re-make himself into anybody's image of the ideal man.

Who might have wanted Sharon Lee dead?

That was the question, wasn't it? Barent thought Mose had done it... Even Bill Werth thought so, and truthfully, Kurtz had no good reason to think otherwise. Only a feeling.

Just then, the phone rang. Kurtz gave it a frown but it kept on ringing. Finally, he reached over and picked it up.

"Hello, Dr. Kurtz?"

"Yes?"

"This is Harry Moran. Sorry to bother you, but Detective Barent and I were wondering if you might be able to come downtown and talk with us."

"Now?" Kurtz glanced at the clock across the room. "It's eight o'clock. I have surgery in the morning."

"Something's come up. We think that you might be able to help."

"Is this about Sharon Lee?"

"We're not interested in your parking tickets, Doctor. You know what I mean?"

Kurtz hesitated. "Where are you?"

"We'll send a car."

"Coffee, Doctor?"

"No, thank you."

"You mind if I smoke?"

Kurtz grimaced at the air outside the glass separating Barent's office from the rest of the squadroom. The place was filled with desks, most of them empty at this hour. "If it's all the same to you, I'd rather you didn't. It gives me a headache."

Barent shrugged. "Sure."

The door opened. Moran came in, sat down in a corner and proceeded to look bored. Moran, Kurtz had already figured out, liked to look bored.

"We have a problem," Barent said. He stopped, frowned down at his desk and swirled his cup of coffee with one hand. "Harry and I are no longer as certain as we were that Bill Mose is the one who murdered Sharon Lee."

"Really..." Kurtz sat up straight in his chair. "That's a surprise."

Barent morosely nodded. "Two nights after she was killed, Sharon Lee's apartment was robbed. All of her jewelry was stolen."

Kurtz frowned, mulling this over. Barent gave him a moment to think about it, then said, "Yesterday afternoon, the body of a man named Herman Delgado was found in a dumpster near the Hudson River. He was murdered—shot in the chest." Barent held up a photograph of a white, circular smudge, perhaps six inches across. "You know what this is?" he asked.

Kurtz shook his head.

"It's a gloveprint. You wear them for awhile, leather gloves pick up oils from your hands and your fingers. The pattern of pores and ridges on a piece of leather can be just as distinctive as a fingerprint."

"Go on," Kurtz said.

"That's an enlargement of a print taken from Sharon Lee's apartment. It matches the forefinger of the right hand glove that Herman Delgado was wearing when he was killed." Barent reached into his desk and held up a small object. "And then there's this." He flipped it to Kurtz.

Kurtz caught it. It sat delicately in his large fingers, a man's gold ring, with a black onyx face. The letter "D" was inscribed on the face next to a single small diamond. The ring glittered in the bright light. "It looks like the ring I dug out of Mose," Kurtz said.

"It is the ring you dug out of Mose. The Pathology Department at Easton didn't want to give it to us, claimed it was confidential. We had to threaten them with a subpoena."

The ring had lodged in Bill Mose's small intestine and a mass of fibrous material, presumably a collection of cigarette butts, had adhered to it, making an obstruction that had blocked his small bowel. Kurtz turned it every which way, but it remained a simple gold ring.

"When he was a kid, Herman Delgado used to run with an uptown gang that called themselves the 'Blades.' He had a fairly extensive criminal record. Petty larceny, assault, car theft." Barent shrugged. "Of course none of this proves anything at all. D for Delgado? Who knows? There are twenty six letters in the alphabet and millions of rings around. No way to tell for certain where Mose ran across it. Still, psych patients don't move around much and there were never a lot of visitors up there on the Unit."

Barent leaned back in his chair, emptied his coffee cup and smiled. "No real evidence to tie Herman Delgado to the murder—though I think it's fairly safe to say he was the one who robbed Sharon Lee's apartment— just enough to make me look at the possibilities. For instance, it's possible that Herman Delgado knew something about Sharon Lee's murder. It's possible he was killed to keep him quiet. It's possible that he knew her apartment would be empty because he was the one who killed her—or he knew who killed her."

"Anything's possible," Kurtz said. "It's possible he knew she was killed because he read about it in the newspaper."

The corner of Barent's mouth twitched. "True," he said. "Sad but true."

"Why tell me?" Kurtz asked.

"Why, indeed?" Barent shrugged. "If Bill Mose didn't do it, then who did? You think maybe you could fit the bill?"

Kurtz pursed his lips and stared curiously at Barent's face. Barent was about fifty-five. He was short for a cop, barely five nine, but he had kept in shape. He had thinning black hair with a bald spot on top and gray eyes behind wire rim glasses. The eyes were looking at him keenly. "Gee, Detective," Kurtz said. "Why don't you go fuck yourself?"

Barent smiled thinly and almost laughed. "I could speculate about possible motives—Sharon Lee and you were romantically involved; perhaps there was jealousy, or resentment." Barent tipped his head to the side, peered into his empty coffee cup. "I have no real reason to think you did it. I have no reason to think you didn't."

"Well, I'm not going to give you one," Kurtz said.

"Could you re-fill this for me, Harry?" Barent handed Moran his cup. Moran poured it full from a pot in the corner of the room and brought it back. "Motive is the question," Barent said. "Was it just some punk looking for a cheap score?" Barent held a hand up and rocked it from side to side. "Unlikely. There are easier places to find someone to rob than a hospital in the middle of the night. And this business with Mose. Assuming of course that it wasn't Mose who killed her—about which I am still uncertain—the way he was set up shows a lot of cool nerve. It also implies an inside job, because the average crook on the street who's com- mitting murder would not have hesitated to kill a witness who stumbled on what he was doing. The murderer must have been able to recognize that this guy would never be able to identify him, was in fact a human being with about three functioning brain cells.

"And who killed Delgado? You might say that people in Herman's line of business get killed all the time, and you'd be right. But the timing is certainly curious."

Kurtz frowned at him, still angry but unable to think of anything constructive. "I think I'll take that cup of coffee you offered me," he said finally.

"How do you like it?" Moran asked.

"Cream. Two sugars."

Moran grunted, went over to the pot and poured Kurtz a cup. Kurtz sipped it. The coffee was good. No reason it wouldn't be good. Policemen, like physicians, spend a lot of time working at night. They probably consumed gallons of the stuff.

Kurtz felt off balance and vaguely unreal. He hated the feeling. Control, he thought. Kurtz had spent years dealing with an environment that defied absolute control, but one that he at least understood. He was no longer used to feeling so out of his depth and he resented it. Barent sat there while he drank, looking at him with a sad expression on his craggy face.

"So you think someone in the hospital did it," Kurtz finally said.

"I think someone in the hospital had something to do with it. I doubt they were working alone."

"Why not?"

Barent smiled his sad smile. "Who killed Herman Delgado?"

"Oh," said Kurtz. "Right."

Barent shrugged. "You're a smart guy, Doc. It takes a lot of brains to get through medical school, learn to do the things that you do. Most crooks are stupid, but in any line of work you'll find that some people are more successful than others and the really successful crooks are not stupid at all." He stared down into his coffee, shook his head sadly and sighed. "One more thing," Barent asked. "Did Sharon Lee ride horses?"

Kurtz looked at him sharply. "She rode all the time. They kept three horses on the estate. When she was a kid, she used to dream about going to the Olympics."

Barent wrote something down in his notebook, then looked up at Kurtz. "So much for dreams. I wish I could make something profound out of that but I can't. The only thing I can do is try to catch the people who killed her. Somebody had something to gain by Sharon Lee's death. Now who could that somebody be?"

Chapter 9

Kathy Roselli's father was a professor of Sociology at Stanford. Her mother taught Anthropology. Kathy had grown up in an environment where diversity of thought was supposed to be cherished (so long as it was politically correct thought) and where money was considered to be crass (though it was a constant source of irritation that the academic life paid so poorly). Other cultures—even the most brutally repressive—were accorded endless tolerance and respect but members of one's own culture who happened to think differently from themselves were assumed to be misguided.

Kathy, Kurtz knew, had enough insight into herself to realize that this outlook was, at heart, parochial and contradictory. "I think it was Woody Allen who said, 'Intellectuals are like the Mafia; they only kill their own.'" She had said this to him once while discussing her parents. Kathy liked to think that she had outgrown the dogmas of her youth. Kurtz sometimes had his doubts.

"How do I look?" she asked.

"You look beautiful," he said. "Stop worrying."

She sniffed. "These women spend half their time at the tanning salon and the other half getting their hair done."

"Very few of them start out with your natural advantages."

"Nice of you to say so." She examined her face in a hand mirror, searching for imperfections. There were none.

"I like your dress," he said. The dress was dark blue, slit up the side of one leg and cut low in front. Kathy's hair, usually hanging down her back in a dark cloud, was pinned up in a chignon. He held her coat for her and she slipped her arms in. While she was doing so, he kissed the back of her neck. Her breath caught and he felt her shoulders tremble.

"We could stay in tonight," he suggested.

"What would the doctors think?" she chided. "Not to mention their assorted wives and concubines."

"We could leave early."

"Why would we want to leave early? I'm sure the conversation will be fascinating: gall bladders and esophagogastrectomies, limited partnerships and closed end mutual funds. What could be better than that?" She gave her hair a last little pat, then turned around, gave Kurtz a grudging smile and reached up to straighten his tie, which he tolerated in silence.

"Come on," she said. "Let's not be late."

They said very little in the cab. A thin flurry of snowflakes drifted out of the sky and the wipers slapped at them lazily as they settled on the windshield. Kurtz stared without seeing at the lights and the snow and mulled over his conversation the other night with Barent. "Herman was twenty: the leading edge of the youthful underworld. These kids, they band together into gangs when they're twelve, thirteen, fourteen, sometimes even younger. By the time they're grown up, they've got ambitions. Herman served six months for armed robbery when he was seventeen. He was in and out a total of maybe a year after that on a variety of charges: assault, possession of marijuana, burglary. It's possible that this involves his old gang. It's equally possible that Herman was working alone or took up with another organization. We should know more in a few days. We'll keep you informed," he said.

"I'm not a cop," Kurtz said. "Why are you bothering?"

Barent smiled at him and blinked his eyes innocently. "It's possible that you may be able to help us."

Kurtz stared at him, the skin on the back of his neck suddenly prickling.

"It seems likely that the solution to the murder of Sharon Lee, and possibly Herman Delgado as well, can be found in Easton Medical Center. You already have some knowledge of police procedure. Believe me, we wouldn't ask you to do anything dangerous. Maybe gather a little information."

"Oh," Kurtz said. "Really."

Barent again gave him his humorless smile. Kurtz said nothing. "Like I said," Barent repeated, "we'll let you know."

Kurtz felt for a moment like an ice cold wire was penetrating his brain. He shivered. "Can I leave now?" he asked.

"Sure." Barent glanced at his watch. It was close to ten at night. "I'll have one of the boys drive you home."

That had been two nights ago.

The first drops of rain began to drizzle down and the cabbie turned up the speed on his wipers. Kathy sat next to Kurtz with a dreamy smile on her face.

Kathy's Ph.D. thesis was almost completed, something to do with the relationship between T.S. Eliot and J.R.R. Tolkien. The two men had been part of a literary group at Oxford that called themselves the "Inklings." When he was younger, Kurtz had not been much of a reader. He would much rather be on a trout stream or hiding in a duck blind with a thermos of hot coffee and a shotgun, but when he got to college, an inspired instructor in a required Philosophy course and another in Introductory Literature had grudgingly changed Kurtz' mind. Maybe his time in the Army had a little to do with it, seeing other people and other places, hearing other languages. Maybe it was simply growing up. Whatever it was, Kurtz had read both Eliot and Tolkien and he thought the association improbable, though he refrained from mentioning this opinion to Kathy.

The cab turned down Central Park South and stopped at a building near 56th Street. An elderly black man in a green uniform opened the door and they walked into a mirrored lobby with a red carpet leading across a marble floor to the elevators. The elevator let them out on the Fifteenth Floor.

The door opened to their knock and Phil Longo stood there wearing a tuxedo and holding a bottle of champagne. A pointed party hat with a crepe paper tassel dangling from the tip perched on top of his head. Longo had a big smile on his face. His eyes were bloodshot. "Happy New Year," he said. "Come on in."

Longo was tall, red haired and well built. Even drunk, he looked good. Longo always looked good. Kurtz wondered sometimes how he did it. His clothes were always straight, his expression attentive, even now through an alcohol haze. It was as if the liquor only affected the surface of his brain. The real Longo was immune to it, somewhere deep inside his head. Longo could spend ten hours in the O.R. on a miserable case and come out looking eager for a brisk round of golf.

"Kathy Roselli," Kurtz said. "Phil Longo."

"Pleased to meet you." Longo said. He blinked happily at Kathy's chest. Kathy gave him a smile and swept past him into the room.

The apartment was enormous, the furnishings varied and expensive. A Queen Anne desk sat in one corner of the foyer and a display case high- lighted a collection of American redware. Longo's wife, Kurtz remembered, collected antiques. Or was that his former wife?

"Nice place," Kathy remarked.

Kurtz nodded. "Phil is an orthopod. Orthopods do well."

"Better than general surgeons?"

Kurtz didn't even have to think about that one. "Absolutely," he said.

"You doctors have quite a hierarchy, don't you? Who's number one? The dermatologists?"

"If you're talking only about money, probably heart surgeons, or maybe plastic surgeons. Orthopedists, neurosurgeons and ophthalmologists are pretty close. Dermatologists do make a lot but not nearly as much as the surgical sub-specialists. On the other hand, you don't get called out in the middle of the night for acne or psoriasis, so if you're factoring in life style, dermatologists would have to be pretty close to the top."

Kathy frowned at the display case. "It's good to see that virtue is rewarded," she said. "Let's get a drink."

They sipped champagne and mingled. Most of the crowd were doctors, mostly male, along with their wives or girlfriends. And the conversation did tend to center around medicine and money. Also vacations. Everyone, it seemed, was just coming back from someplace or about to go someplace else.

"How well do you know Longo?" Kathy whispered to him.

"Pretty well. Bill Werth and I have gone fishing with him a few times and we've had some beers after work. I always thought he was a nice guy. He does a lot of charity work. He'll probably hit me up for a donation to Settlement House before the evening is over. His wife is on the Board. Why?"

"Just wondering. How about the rest of them? Do you know them all?"

"Most of them. Not all."

A tray of hors d'oeuvres swept past and Kurtz grabbed a mushroom stuffed with crabmeat and a shrimp coated with barbecue sauce and popped them in his mouth. Kathy chose an endive leaf with a slice of goat cheese in the middle and nibbled on it.

A woman who appeared to be in her early thirties came up to them. She had dark blonde hair piled high on the top of her head. Her nose was straight, her skin perfect. She was small, not more than five two, but her figure was softly rounded, with a tiny waist and swelling breasts. "Hello," she said, and held out a tiny hand. "I'm Sylvia Longo."

The hand was hot. What was that movie, the one with Kathleen Turner? Body Heat. The character's passionate nature was supposed to be reflected in her temperature. Sylvia Longo even looked like Kathleen Turner.

"This is Kathy Roselli," Kurtz said, "and I'm Richard Kurtz."

Sylvia Longo looked Kurtz up and down with a wide smile. She seemed to like what she was seeing. "Phil has told me all about you," she said. After the initial perfunctory handshake, she ignored Kathy.

"He has? Nothing truthful, I hope."

"He says that you're a wild man from the hills of West Virginia, rustic, true to life and unspoiled."

Kurtz nodded and sipped his champagne, wondering if he should be annoyed, also wondering if it was true. "And I thought the tuxedo hid the real me."

Sylvia Longo's eyes fixed on his face and Kurtz felt suddenly as if she could see right through his clothes. "It's amazing," she said. "We can talk about emancipation and equality all we want, but every woman I know dreams about being swept off her feet by some handsome, uncivilized savage."

"Really?" Kurtz blinked his eyes, and felt as if an electrical connection had suddenly been snapped. He turned to Kathy. "Is that why you like me?"

Kathy shook her head. "She said handsome."

Sylvia Longo's eyes flicked once to Kathy's face, then back to Kurtz. She grinned. "Well," she said, "enjoy yourself." And she walked off.

"Antiques?" Kathy said.

"Maybe it was the first wife."

They wandered through the crowd. A string quartet played quiet music in the corner of the room. A steady stream of waiters offered assorted hors d'oevres to the guests and a table near the kitchen was piled with opened bottles of Veuve Cliquot Grande Dame.

"Hi, Richard," Bill Werth said.

Standing next to Werth was a tall, fat man with a round, red face, who held out his hand. "How ya doing? I'm John Stills, O.B.- G.Y.N."

Kurtz shook his hand.

"You're Kurtz, aren't you?"

"I used to be," Kurtz said, "but now I'm Tarzan, Lord of the Jungle."

"Huh?"

"Never mind. Just a joke."

Stills wrinkled his brow and peered at Kurtz. "What do you think about this thing with Sharon Lee?" he said after a moment. "Pretty strange, huh?"

Kurtz examined Still's fat, innocently smiling face and reluctantly decided against strangling him. "Yup," he agreed. "Pretty strange."

"I did a lot of cases with her. Good surgeon, you know? Sort of a grouch but she knew her way around a uterus."

"So I've been told."

"Great party, isn't it?" said Stills.

"You bet."

Werth tried to suppress his grin and failed, and Kurtz gave him a sour look. "Where's Dina?" Kurtz asked him.

"She's around somewhere," Werth said. "I haven't seen her in a little while."

"She's in the bedroom with my wife," Stills said, "examining a Ming vase."

"We're going to have to leave soon," Werth said. "The babysitter has to be home by 11:30."

"Too bad." Stills smiled widely and blew an alcohol laden breath at Werth, who silently gagged. "We'll just be getting started by then."

"I," Kathy announced, "need more champagne."

"I'll join you," Kurtz said. Behind them, Werth made a helpless gesture in Still's direction and then rolled his eyes to the ceiling. Kurtz smiled at him blandly over his shoulder.

"A charming man," Kathy remarked, "rustic, true to life and unspoiled."

Kurtz gave her a wounded look and silently drank his champagne.

"You want to go to Vegas?" Jim Farkas peered blearily at Kurtz, glanced with drunken interest at Kathy.

"Las Vegas? When?" Kurtz asked.

"I'm getting together a little trip. Middle of March. We'll stay at the Mirage, maybe Bellagio. Longo's going, so is Stills."

"I'll think about it."

Farkas turned to Kathy. "I'm Jim Farkas," he said. "You like him?"

"Sometimes."

"He's a cheap bastard," Farkas said with a crooked smile. "You should drop him, get together with a guy who'll treat you right."

Kathy nodded. "I've been thinking the same thing. General surgeons don't make much money."

"You said it." Farkas felt through his pockets, came up with a card and handed it to Kathy. "Here's my number. You get tired of him, give me a call. I mean it. You're gorgeous."

"I'll keep it in mind."

"Okay." Farkas grinned at Kurtz, leered at Kathy and wandered off. Kathy fingered the card and smiled speculatively at Farkas' retreating back. She put the card in her handbag. "You never know," she said.

"Isn't money supposed to be beneath the notice of the true intellectual?"

"I'm beginning to acquire an appreciation for the finer things in life. Dr. Farkas is a very attractive man."

Farkas was short, stout and bald. Kurtz snorted. "Uh-huh."

Kathy laughed softly and hugged his arm. "I think you were right, after all," she said. "Why don't we leave early?"

Chapter 10

Barent spent New Year's Eve at home with the family. Betty made a turkey with stuffing and cranberry sauce and after dinner, they watched television in the living room. An old Western was on, *The Searchers*, with John Wayne and Montgomery Clift, one of Barent's favorites.

About ten o'clock, Michael, the Barents' oldest son, looked at his watch and said, "I've got to get going. I told Janet I would pick her up. We've been invited to a party at the LaRocca's."

Barent glanced at his wife, who gave an imperceptible nod. "Sure," Barent said. "Say hello for us."

Denise, their daughter, was already waiting for her date to arrive, a stockbroker named Paul Janus. Barent didn't like him.

The door bell rang and Denise glanced at Barent. "Don't be too late," he said.

Denise smiled, picked up her coat and kissed him in the middle of his bald spot. After she had gone, Barent felt his good mood beginning to desert him. A commercial came on the T.V. The house grew quiet. Betty watched his face with an expression that he found hard to interpret. Finally, he asked, "What's on your mind?"

"Oh, nothing." She shrugged and looked sad. "I was thinking that they grow up so fast." She smiled fleetingly. "I think Denise is going to marry Paul."

Barent shuddered. "God forbid," he said

"Why don't you like him?" Betty asked.

Barent sometimes wondered the same thing. "I'm not exactly sure," he admitted. "I suppose he's okay." He shrugged. "I guess he's just not my sort. He's sort of wishy-washy, you know?"

"You mean because he's polite?"

Barent grunted and gave her a sour look.

"I mean it," Betty persisted. "The way you talk to him, he ought to punch you in the nose."

"Hey," Barent protested, "if he wants Denise, he can put up with a little ribbing from her old man."

"Like the time you said to him that stockbrokers were parasites and why doesn't he get a job that might be of some use to society?"

"Did I say that?"

"Yes. You did. Believe me, I was just as embarrassed as Denise." Betty's knitting needles clicked furiously together.

"Come on," Barent said. "I didn't say anything like that."

"You did, too. You know you did. And I don't want you to say it again."

"Well, I don't believe it." Barent shifted his gaze to the T.V. but a few moments later looked back at Betty. "But if I said it," he added, "I must have meant it."

On the evening of January 2, Barent walked into a bar on East Houston Street. The bar had a sign in the window that said Exotic Dancers. It was the fifth such place Barent had visited since the early afternoon. He sat down at a corner table and waited to be served. The waiter, a fat white man with greasy black hair, a handlebar moustache and a dirty apron, came up to him. "What'll it be?" he asked.

"Heineken," Barent said, "and give me a burger, well done, with some fries."

The bartender grunted and Barent turned to see the show but there wasn't much to see. Maybe it was too early. On a small stage behind the bar, a solitary dancer swayed to the beat of some hard rock that, thankfully, was turned down low. The girl was blonde, of indeterminate age. She looked vaguely into it but moved without much enthusiasm. She had on a g-string and a bangle of fake pearls around her hips and nothing on top. Most of the patrons ignored her. Her nipples, Barent noted, seemed to be painted. That deep red color could not possibly have been natural.

The bartender re-appeared with a green bottle and a tall glass, poured out half the bottle, plunked it down in front of Barent and said, "Your burger will be out soon. Anything else I can get you?"

Barent nodded. "You see that guy?" He pointed to a thin black man wearing a tan fedora and a bright maroon jacket, sitting at the bar and watching the blonde dancer. "Could you ask him to step over here? Tell him Lew Barent would like to speak with him."

The bartender glanced at the black man, glanced back at Barent without changing the blank expression on his face, and walked away. A few minutes later, Barent saw him leaning over, talking to the black man. They both looked in his direction. Soon after, Barent's hamburger arrived. The bartender put it down and turned away without saying a word. A few minutes after that, the black man slid into the seat opposite Barent.

"Barent," he said. "Don't see you much these days."

"Hello, Croft," Barent said. "How's business?"

Croft's business was prostitution. Croft was a pimp, an unusual pimp in that he took a straight thirty per-cent cut, had his girls tested periodically for gonorrhea and AIDS and never abused them. They wanted to leave, set up on

62

their own, find someone else to peddle their wares, that was just fine with Croft. Plenty of others where they came from. Barent had a certain grudging respect for Croft, though he would never have let him know it. Barent, like most cops, had busted his share of prostitutes because that was part of the job but personally, Barent didn't believe in victimless crimes. Croft ran his business like it was a business. He was also a very sharp character.

Croft put a pained expression on his face. "Now what you wanting to ask me a question like that for?"

Barent cracked a smile. "Old times' sake, I suppose. It seemed so natural."

"Natural is over rated, you ask me. You got floods and earthquakes and cancer and everything else. What so great about natural?"

Barent couldn't argue. He shrugged and finished his beer. "I figured you might be here. You always were a creature of fixed habits."

"If you mean I'm a man who knows what I like, then you right."

"It occurred to me that you might be able to help me."

"Help you?" Croft smiled. He tilted his head back and peered out at Barent from beneath the brim of his hat. "Why should I do a thing like that?"

Barent let a hurt expression cross his face. "Didn't I put in a good word for you with the parole board?"

Croft looked doubtful. "You did? They never told me that."

"I need to know something." Barent went on as if Croft had not spoken. "You know a guy named Herman Delgado?"

Croft puffed his cheeks up, frowned. "Can't say as I do."

"Small time hood: robbery, assault. He used to run with a gang called themselves the Blades. He's dead—shot through the chest."

"Hard to establish a relationship with a man who's dead."

Barent shrugged. "Anything you can find out, I'd like to know. Who did he work for? Who didn't like him? Anything."

"Delgado..." Croft wrinkled his nose, nodded. "I remember the Blades real well: crazy little motherfuckers." Without another word, he got up and went back to his place at the bar and stared as if mesmerized at the jiggling breasts of the blonde dancer.

The burger was pretty good, Barent thought. He finished it slowly, left a nice tip and walked out. He had a few more people he wanted to see before heading home.

New York City was not where Richard Kurtz would have expected himself to wind up. Kurtz was an only child. His mother had died when he was three years old and he barely remembered her. His father was a quiet, hardworking man who never remarried. He had run the farm the way his father and his grandfather had before him and he seemed to assume that Kurtz would do the same.

Kurtz was a farm boy, small town all the way. He was a smart farm boy, though. He had graduated number three in his high school class, which surprised Kurtz almost as much as it would have surprised his friends, if they had only known it. They didn't know it because Kurtz never told them. He was embarrassed to admit it.

He knew he wanted out of there, though. His father might be disappointed in him but Kurtz was smart enough to know that scrabbling in the dirt for the rest of his life was not how he wanted to earn a living. Kurtz wanted out bad and the Army was the easiest, quickest way.

A lot of guys had hated the Army. Not Kurtz. Kurtz figured it was a good deal. You put in your time, did as you were told, they showed you a slice of the world and taught you some skills. Then they paid your way through college when you were done. For a poor kid, it was a very good deal indeed.

So here he was, thirty-six years old, with everything he had thought he wanted in life and somehow, it just wasn't enough. He looked out the window at the cold gray skies and felt a leaden weight on his soul.

I've been alone for a long time, Kurtz thought. A long time. Kurtz spoke to his father occasionally but they didn't have much to say to each other. Kurtz felt genuinely bad about that, but he didn't know what to do about it.

Kurtz had found himself waiting for Barent to call. He knew that he shouldn't. He told himself he was being an idiot, that Barent could only get him involved in something that he would regret, but he couldn't get the image of Sharon Lee, naked and dead, out of his mind. He wanted her killer found. His sense of the natural order demanded it. The thought that a murderer might be lurking in the hospital halls, walking to and fro, eating in the same cafeteria, perhaps working in the same operating room as Richard Kurtz, filled him with alternating horror and grinding rage. He found himself staring at the people he passed, wondering.

He had a week off starting Saturday. He performed no cases after Wednesday. He did not want to leave behind any patients who might go sour while he was gone. He saw a few people in the office, identified a hernia and a possible gall bladder and scheduled them for consultation by Medicine. By the time they were ready for surgery, he would be back.

As he walked into the office on Friday afternoon, he saw that Mrs. Nelson, Farkas' secretary, was sitting behind Rose Schapiro's desk. Farkas had surgery on Friday and the secretaries often covered for each other when their own doctors were scheduled to be out of the office. Mrs. Nelson was a plump, jolly woman with curly black hair. Kurtz liked her.

He saw his last patient, a lady who had had an axillary node biopsy for non-Hodgkin's lymphoma and who was now doing well after radiation therapy, and walked out of the office at four o'oclock, ready to party. Mrs. Nelson beamed at him. "Have a nice time, Doctor," she said. "We'll see you in a week."

Kurtz smiled at her. "Thanks. I'll do my best."

Freedom. He stopped on the hospital steps and breathed it in like a drug. It was January Fourth but the sun was shining, the day unseasonably warm. In a few hours he would be in an airplane, heading south. He could hardly wait.

"Jaime Ruiz," Moran said, "is a known psycopath."

"Yeah?" Barent squinted down the length of his cigar, puffed it alight and settled himself comfortably in his seat.

"Yeah," Moran said. "One time he sliced a kid's ear off in a bar because the kid didn't laugh when Jaime told a joke." Moran swerved the car to avoid a pothole and almost skidded on a piece of ice. "How come I always have to drive?" he complained.

"You like to drive," Barent pointed out. "I don't. I like to think."

Moran grunted.

"And do you know what I'm thinking at this particular instant?" Moran looked at him. Barent grinned. "You see that girl?" he asked. Walking along the street was a tall blonde with a red dress, a heart shaped face and a very hard body. "What about her?"

"Would it surprise you to know that I would very much like to walk up behind her, rip her clothes off and fuck her brains out, right there on the street?"

"Not at all," Moran said. "So would I."

"But you're not going to, are you?"

Moran pursed his lips and looked pained. "No?"

"I'm not going to, either," Barent said. "You know why?"

"Tell me," Moran said.

"Because my wife wouldn't like it."

"Yeah?" Moran said doubtfully.

"Yeah. There are rules, you see? Truth to tell, I've got just as many dirty little secrets running around my brain as anybody else. Even Jaime Ruiz. But I behave myself, because that's what all of us are supposed to do in a civilized society."

"Ah, of course," Moran said. "A civilized society."

"Yes, a civilized society. Did Jaime have an abused childhood?"

"I don't know. Why?"

"Because I don't care, that's why. I don't care why a psychopath does what he does. Lots of people have a tough life. Most of them get married, have kids, make money and follow the rules. They don't turn into psychopaths. So fuck him."

Moran looked at him. Barent gave a sour grin and blew a smoke ring into the air. "I'm looking forward to this," Barent said. "It's not every day I get to talk to a known psychopath."

The Vanity Social Club was on East 87th Street. It had opened only the week before and apparently was doing good business. Barent and Moran pulled the car into the parking lot on the side of the building and walked in. The front door opened onto a short corridor, which led up to a curled iron gate and a stand up desk where a tall Hispanic male in a tuxedo presided over those lucky enough to be allowed entrance. Beyond the gate, strobe lights flashed purple across the dance floor and a laser show went on over a stage where a redheaded singer was doing a passable imitation of Gloria Estefan. Her band would never be mistaken for Miami Sound Machine but they weren't bad, the sax especially.

Barent flashed his badge. "Detective Barent," he said. "Detective Moran. We're here to see Jaime Ruiz."

"You have an appointment?"

"An appointment?" Barent raised his eyebrows to Moran. "Do we have an appointment?"

"Why, I do believe so," Moran said. He screwed up his face in thought. "The precinct social director was supposed to call and make one. Why don't you check your book?"

The usher frowned down at his desk and said, "Just a minute." He walked off.

"An appointment," Barent said, and rolled his eyes. "Oh, man."

The usher came back and said, "Come with me." He led them around the dance floor to a set of stairs. Two more men with tuxedos stood at either side of the staircase. "Up there. Third door on your right."

"Thanks," Barent said.

He looked at Barent without expression, turned and walked away. "Well, what's the matter with him?" Moran asked.

The upstairs hallway was covered with a thick, burgundy carpet. Two crystal chandeliers hung from the ceiling. The third door on the right was open. The room inside looked more like a bedroom than an office, except for a dark, wooden desk sitting beneath the window. The window was covered with red velvet drapes. A wet bar sat in the corner. An enormous bed lay against one wall and a bleached oak wall unit covered the entire opposite wall. A thirty-five inch television screen was set in the wall unit. It was playing a movie: *Blade Runner*, by Ridley Scott. Three men sat in felt covered reclining chairs in the center of the room. Two of these were big and burly and looked Barent and Moran up and down with idle suspicion. The third man was dressed in tight black jeans and a red silk shirt open nearly to the waist. His neck was covered with an assortment of gold chains that hid the upper part of his chest. He had black, slicked back hair and a thin black moustache. A small diamond earring sparkled in the lobe of his left ear. He said, "You Barent?" He didn't look up.

"Yes," Barent said.

"I'm Ruiz." He glanced at Barent from the corner of his eye.

Barent looked around for a place to sit down but there were no more chairs and none of the three looked inclined to offer him one.

"You like this movie?" Ruiz asked.

"It's not bad," Barent said.

"This movie kills me. At the end, when the replicant hold the cop out over the edge of the building and think about letting him drop, that just tears me apart. But he knows he's dying so what would be the point? Let the poor bastard live. Why not?" Ruiz shrugged. "I would have taken him with me, but what the hell?"

"To each his own," said Barent.

Ruiz looked up at him. "What do you want?"

"I want to talk." Barent frowned. "I could talk better if I had a place to sit down."

Ruiz looked at him, looked at the two men setting on either side of him and gave his head a little jerk. One of the men rose to his feet and walked over to the bar. Barent sat. Ruiz turned back to the screen.

"You know a guy named Herman Delgado?" Barent asked.

"Herman Delgado?" Ruiz frowned. "That name's familiar. What did he do?"

"I don't know what he did. He's dead."

The expression on Ruiz' face did not change. After a moment, he yawned. "People die all the time. Why come to me?"

"Our records indicate that Herman used to run with the Blades. The Blades answered to you."

"Oh?" For the first time, Ruiz looked interested. "What happen to him?"

"Someone shot him in the chest and dumped him in a garbage can."

Ruiz puffed out his cheeks and nodded. "That's too bad," he said.

"You wouldn't happen to know why, or even who, would you, Jaime?"

Ruiz gave a small shake of his head. "My people, they come to me when they're in trouble, I try to help them. This Herman Delgado, he a short fellow, little beard?"

"Yes."

"I remember him. He mind his own business. He leave the old neighborhood maybe six months ago. I don't know where. I don't know why. I had no reason to ask. One of my people, he want to go into business for himself, I can't stop him. He ever need me, I'm here."

"Regular little Godfather, aren't you, Jaime?"

Ruiz looked hurt. "What for you want to insult me, Barent?"

"No reason, I guess. We cops tend to be like that."

Ruiz smiled slightly and spread his hands. "Anything else I can do for you, Barent?"

"If you hear anything, you'll let me know." It was a statement, not a question.

Ruiz' smile grew wider. "I always cooperate with the law. It's how I got to where I am today."

Barent reached into his wallet, pulled out a card. "It's got my number," he said, and handed the card to Ruiz.

Ruiz turned the card back and forth in his fingers, as if not quite certain what to do with it. Then he shrugged. "Sure, Barent. I hear anything, I'll give you a call."

Chapter 11

Cancun: sun, sand and fun.

Kurtz had asked Kathy to come along with him. She had seemed to think about it, searching his face with a crooked smile. Then she gave a tiny shrug and a shake of her head. "Thanks for asking," she said, "but I need to work on my thesis and I could use the time. Have fun." Kurtz couldn't argue, but it seemed pretty obvious that there was something else on her mind. He was moody the whole evening after that, which Kathy ignored—if she even noticed.

A blast of heat took him in the face as soon as he exited the plane and he shuddered luxuriously, filling his lungs with the heavy, perfumed air. He walked into the terminal, retrieved his suitcase from the baggage checkout and took a cab from the airport to the Hotel Meridian, a brand new tower of adobe, red stucco and glass rising twenty stories above the beach.

He spent the next two days taking long walks by the water, soaking up the sun on his bare chest, eating *ceviche* and snapper baked in a salt crust and *arroz con pollo* and loin of pork with *mole*, swimming in the sea and floating on his back in the enormous pool.

As evening of the second day approached, he lay on a lounge chair by the water, sipping a piña colada and listening with sleepy contentment to a mariachi band composed of five young boys in Mexican hats playing *Guantanamera* in the shade of a grove of palm trees. Three more hats lay on the grass and people passing by would stop and listen for a few moments and occasionally throw some loose change into the hats.

Threading their way through the crowded forest of lounge chairs, an elderly lady with curled gray hair and a bald fat man wearing a striped bathing suit and carrying a beach bag walked in his direction. They settled themselves on lounges. The man took a tube of Coppertone out of the beach bag and squirted some on his abdomen. Then he pulled a paperback book out of the bag and idly flipped through the pages while rubbing in the Coppertone with his other hand. Kurtz, lulled by the sun and the warmth of the breeze, his eyes half closed, could see the woman looking him up and down. She smiled, showing large, perfect teeth, and said, "What do you do, young man?"

Kurtz shook his head drowsily. "Excuse me?"

"I saw you with that drink and I wondered, is that a piña colada? I always wanted to try a piña colada. I always think about asking for one but then I always change my mind at the last instant and order rum and coke instead. Isn't that silly? So I thought I'd ask. Are you an American? You look like an American. What's your name? Where are you from?"

Kurtz stared at her and shook his head, still half asleep.

The fat man reclined the head of his lounge and lay back, his enormous abdomen rising up like a white dome through his unbuttoned Hawaiian shirt. He gave Kurtz a quick look, shrugged his shoulders and stared at the pool.

"I'm Esther Brinkman." She jabbed the fat man with her elbow. He ignored her. "This is Stanley, my husband. We're from the Bronx. Do you like Mexican food? We love it. We come here every year. We used to go to Acapulco and we tried Ixtapa once but Cancun is much nicer. They give you everything you ask for and they have their own water system, all along the beach, but don't try the restaurants in town, you might be sorry.

"I'm Richard Kurtz," Kurtz said. "I'm from New York."

"See?" Esther Brinkman jabbed her husband again, who grunted but didn't bother turning his head. "I can always tell, something about the eyes. Are you here all alone? A good looking young man like yourself?" Kurtz, beginning to get a hemmed in feeling but not knowing how to get away without seeming rude, said, "Yes, actually. I am."

"That's a shame. Stanley, isn't that a shame?"

Stanley nodded. "Uh-huh," he said. "A shame."

"So what do you do?" She held up a hand suddenly. "No! Don't tell me. Let me guess." She squinted at him, her little eyes almost closing, her mouth looking like a raisin. "You're in sales. You've got that look, something very persuasive." She nodded triumphantly. "I can always tell."

"I'm a surgeon," Kurtz said. It just slipped out, and immediately he thought, *You dope.*

"A surgeon?" Her eyes grew wide. "A real surgeon?"

"Yes," Kurtz said weakly.

She stared at him. "Stanley," she said, and clutched her husband by the hand. "He's a surgeon."

Stanley turned his head and gave Kurtz a blank look. He shook his head sadly and rolled his eyes.

"I have someone you just have to meet. Where is she?" Mrs. Brinkman half rose from her seat and urgently scanned the crowd.

Oh, no, Kurtz thought. "I have to be going," he said.

Esther Brinkman ignored him. Her eyes lit up and she frantically waved at someone behind Kurtz' chair, all five fingers wriggling in the breeze.

"Please," Kurtz said. "You'll have to excuse me." He stood, turned, stopped, stared.

Oval face, long lashes, wide green eyes. She was tall. From the tips of her toes to the top of her head must have been a solid, willowy six feet. She wore a white string bikini, which covered very little of her tanned, lush figure. Long blonde hair hung halfway down her back, tied in a ponytail. Her hands were on her hips, head cocked to the side at a wary angle.

"This is Lenore," Mrs. Brinkman said. "Our daughter."

Kurtz turned his head, stared at Mrs. Brinkman. She gave him a thin smile. He turned back to Lenore and cleared his throat. "Pleased to meet you," he said.

Lenore Brinkman said nothing and looked at her mother. She did not, Kurtz thought, look pleased. Mrs. Brinkman stared back at her, a triumphant little grin on her face.

"This is Richard Kurtz," Mrs. Brinkman said, "from New York. He's a surgeon."

"A surgeon," Lenore said. Her voice was smooth and deep, like molasses. Her eyes went back to Kurtz' face. She gave her head a tiny shake, pasted a look on her face that was less than enthralled, and breathed a resigned sigh.

Kurtz said, "Can I buy you a drink?"

"Sure," Lenore said. She glanced at her mother. "Not here."

Mrs. Brinkman smiled like a bright, predatory bird. "Have a good time," she said to Kurtz. "I knew you two would get along."

"I don't know what it is about the women in my family," Lenore Brinkman said. She had put on a white jumpsuit and they sat on the hotel balcony, sharing a plate of shrimp with hot sauce and two Dos Equis. The sun was setting over the ocean and the sky overhead was shot full of purple and orange streaks. Far across the sand, phosphorescent waves broke rhythmically on the beach. "They're all crazy. My uncles are such nice, sweet men but my mother and both her sisters are completely out of their minds."

"She seemed to know what she was doing," Kurtz said.

"She knows exactly what she's doing." Lenore peeled a shrimp, dipped it in sauce, and bit off half of it. "My mother is a very smart woman. She could have done something with her life, except that girls growing up back then weren't supposed to do something with their lives. Instead, she bossed around my father and drove me and my sister absolutely nuts."

Lenore Brinkman had a degree from Cooper Union in Graphic Art and worked in advertising. She was twenty-six years old. She was just getting over a relationship that had not worked out.

"Harrison's father is an S.O.B. and Harrison didn't have the backbone to stand up to him." She shook her head. "Things have been difficult for them lately. They're old money and money's been tight, to which I say *tough*. Let them learn how the rest of the world has to live. They deserve it. Harrison's father is president of a Savings and Loan." Lenore snickered and took a chug from her beer.

"I had my doubts about coming along but maybe my mother was right. Get away from it all." She shrugged and wrinkled her nose at the shrimp she was peeling. Then she said, "Look, I don't want to string you along. You seem like a nice guy but I don't know if I'm ready to get involved with anybody just yet."

Kurtz sipped his beer and stared at the thin crescent of sun still barely visible above the horizon. "I understand," he said. He thought about Kathy and wondered for an instant what she might be doing, back in New York. "Maybe I'm not ready either."

Lenore suddenly grinned. "Mom was all over you like a pekingese chewing a bone. You looked pretty funny."

"I was trying to escape without being rude."

"Sometimes you just have to be rude." Lenore put her feet up on the lower rail and leaned her head back. Her hair glinted in the fading light. "Doctors..." She glanced into her beer, then drained the glass. "Every Jewish mother's dream."

"Why is that?" Kurtz asked.

"Why?" Lenore shrugged. "I suppose it's cultural. Jews admire education and it takes a lot of education to be a doctor. And there's the old stereotype about Jews and money; it's at least partly true. Jews like money. Doctors make money."

"Everyone," Kurtz said, "likes money."

"With us it's different. For five thousand years, sooner or later a Roman or a Cossack or a Nazi or the Spanish Inquisition would take everything we had and either kill us or kick us out. But if you had money, maybe you could buy a ticket to somewhere else; maybe you could bribe the soldier who comes to arrest you; maybe you could get away. Money buys security and Jews are nuts about security, an attitude that I can understand completely. I mean, Jews know they're paranoid, but just because you're paranoid doesn't mean nobody is out to get you.

"Now me..." Lenore shook her golden hair out over her shoulders and ran her hands through it. "I liked art. Art is cultured. Jews are very into culture so my parents approved—they could tell their friends I was a genius. But culture is chancy. From a financial perspective, there is nothing in the slightest bit secure about culture. It is absolutely astounding the speed with which a genius can turn into a bum in the opinion of your family if you actually want to do something cultural for a living. You want to play the piano, learn to paint, study ballet: wonderful! You want to *be* a pianist, or an artist, or a dancer? Forget it; you'll never amount to anything. You're a bum. Of course, if you somehow manage to actually be successful, then you're a genius again." Lenore shrugged, and peeled another shrimp. "Oh, well."

Kurtz thought for a moment of his own boyhood, running barefoot through muddy fields in summer, trekking through snow that came up to his chest in winter. Nothing too cultural about that, and nobody he grew up with seemed to miss it.

"I'm twenty-six," Lenore said. "Mom's getting worried. A few years ago, if I wanted to go out with someone who wasn't Jewish, she'd threaten to disown me. I say 'she' because my father never had anything to say about it anyway. Now she's fixing me up with strange men." Lenore gave a little laugh. "I know my mother. She's willing to compromise. You're not a Jewish doctor, but you are a doctor."

The sun had set completely; only a faint orange glow still lingered over the horizon. A waiter walked around the terrace with a cart full of citronella lanterns, lit them and put them up on poles around the railing. Kurtz could hear the band beginning to play inside the Hotel. "Do you like to dance?" he asked.

"Yeah," she said.

"Let's dance," he said, and took her by the hand.

"Mrs. Delgado?"

She was short and fat, with round, plump arms and a round, moon face. She looked at him silently, with open suspicion.

"I'm Detective Barent." He showed her his badge. "This is Detective Moran. Could we come in?"

She stared at them, her large black eyes flitting back and forth between their faces. Finally, she stepped aside and they walked past her into the apartment. Paint was peeling from the walls. Tiny puddles of rust lay on the floor where radiator pipes had leaked. Cheap plyboard tables covered with vinyl, three rickety garden chairs and an old collapsed couch with springs showing through the fabric were the only furniture. The faucet over the kitchen sink steadily dripped.

Mrs. Delgado stood in the center of the room, looking at their faces silently and expectantly. Barent cleared his throat. "I'm sorry about your son," he finally said.

She shrugged. "Why do you care? He wasn't your son."

Barent frowned at this and felt the muscles across his shoulders tightening. "That's true," he said carefully. "But I have children of my own, and I sympathize with what you must be feeling." Barent meant it. His own youngest son, Benjamin, had died from leukemia three years ago, at the age of fourteen. Ever since then, Barent had had a lot of difficulty dealing with the bereaved parents of dead children, even if the dead children were career criminals like Herman Delgado.

73

Moran, who knew this, looked at him with moody surprise. "May we sit down, Mrs. Delgado?"

She glanced at the couch and shrugged. Barent sat. Mrs. Delgado lowered her weight into one of the chairs, which swayed beneath her. Moran continued to stand.

"Mrs. Delgado, it's my job to try to find the people who killed your son. Anything at all that you can tell me might be helpful."

"You a little late to be helpful. Herman, he run with a bad crowd but that the only crowd he ever know. It's hard for a boy to grow up right when he don't have no one to show him how." She sat up straight, her face closed in, her eyes fixed somewhere beyond Barent's shoulder, staring into nothing.

Barent nodded. He flicked a glance at Moran, who gave a minute shrug. He took a small cardboard box out of his pocket and removed the cover. Inside the box lay the ring that Kurtz had retrieved from Bill Mose's intestines. "Mrs. Delgado, could you tell us if your son had a ring like this?"

She looked at it without much interest. "I don't know," she said. "We don't see Herman too much. He spend most of the day sleeping. At night, he was mostly out." She shook her head sadly. "I don't know," she said again.

"Could you tell us who his friends were? Did he have a job? Who did he work with?"

The door opened. A girl no more than twelve stood there, dressed in a green blouse and jeans, frowning first at Barent, then at Moran. "Herman hang out with Jimmy Ramirez," the girl said. "Jimmy Ramirez his best friend. And Carlos Rivera—but Carlos move away and we don't see him no more."

"My little girl, Angela," Mrs. Delgado said. "She's right. You ask Jimmy Ramirez. I don't know nothing about Herman's business. He come in late. He say nothing. Sometimes he give me money." She shrugged. "That's all I know."

Angela sat down at the table, cradled her cupped hands beneath her chin and swung her legs back and forth under the chair. She watched Barent and Moran as if they were strange creatures in a zoo.

"Have you seen this ring before, Angela?" Barent asked.

Angela stared at the ring for a long moment, frowning, then gave a little shrug. Barent glanced at Moran, carefully closed the box and put it back in his pocket. "Thank you, Mrs. Delgado," he said. "Thank you, Angela."

Angela nodded her head. Mrs. Delgado said nothing. As the door closed behind them, Barent could see her staring at the cracked, faded wall. She looked as if she would stay there forever, Barent thought, staring, with no expression on her face.

74

Chapter 12

On the evening of January 6th, a street gang in the Bronx known as the "Black Dragons" invaded the territory of another gang that called itself the "King Cobras."

Two days before, a fourteen-year-old named Shawna, who had been sleeping with a Black Dragon named Jackson, had gone into a convenience store to pick up some lipstick. Shawna browsed the shelves, turned her head quickly around to see if anyone was watching, and pocketed the one she liked. She stopped at the counter, paid a quarter for a chocolate covered cherry and went out the door.

"Yo." A tall, well built young man smiled at her. He had a thin moustache and hair cut into a brush, with a gold skull set into the lobe of his left ear.

"What you want?" Shawna asked.

"What I want?" The young man looked her up and down and smacked his lips. "Why don't you come along with me and find out?"

"With you?" Shawna thought about it while she chewed her chocolate covered cherry. The young man's jacket was black and looked like real leather. He wore Adidas High Tops and his hair had twin lightning bolts cut down to the scalp on both sides. "You don't look like so much."

"No?" He smiled wider, reached into his pocket, pulled out a round tin container that said "Happy Days Chewing Tobacco" and pulled off the top. The tin was filled with soft white powder. He held it out to her. "I got what you want if you got what I want."

Shawna looked at the powder, looked up at the boy's grinning face and swallowed. Abruptly, she nodded.

The boy thrust the tin back into his pocket. "Come on," he said.

"What's your name?"

The boy looked at her. "Major."

Shawna followed Major down the street and up the steps of a dingy brownstone. He pulled open the door of an apartment and they both entered. Sitting around a table, passing a pipe, sat five more boys. They looked at her blearily and they all smiled. The door closed.

"Now wait a minute," Shawna said.

Major's eyes danced in the light. "You gone get all you can handle tonight, girl. Indeed you are."

Ten hours later, the boys allowed Shawna to leave. She was crying and she tottered down the street on unsteady legs.

Two nights later, fifteen young men, all of them armed with knives, three carrying pistols, walked into Cobra territory, seeking revenge. The Black Dragons moved in groups of three and converged on a small park where members of the rival gang were known to hang out. One bleary eyed boy sitting on a bench and smoking a joint by himself looked up and saw them. He shook his head, as understanding slowly penetrated. "Hey," he said.

One of the Black Dragons stuck a knife in him and he screamed. Boys came running from all over the small park, saw what was happening, pulled their own weapons and jumped into the fray.

Somebody on the street must have made a phone call because within fifteen minutes, the distant sound of sirens began to penetrate the screams. Slowly at first, then quickly, the gangs disentangled themselves and melted away. They left behind five dead bodies and seven who were too badly wounded to run. One of these was Jimmy Ramirez, who belonged to neither gang but who had had the bad luck to be conducting a cocaine purchase in the park at the time that the attack took place.

Five police cars, lights flashing and sirens screaming, came roaring up. The cops surveyed the scene, made their calls and within another few minutes, the ambulances arrived.

"Oh, man," Jimmy Ramirez said. He said it over and over. "Oh, man. Oh, man." He held a hand over the hole in his side but blood still leaked out. His eyes darted this way and that and he licked his lips with a tongue gone dry. "Oh, man." He mumbled something under his breath, coughed and then cried out at the sudden pain.

They carted him into an ambulance and sped off. At the E.R., the trauma team ripped off his clothes, put an I.V. into each arm and each leg and drew blood for routine labs and a Type and Cross. By this time, Jimmy Ramirez was almost unconscious, his blood pressure barely detectable. They rushed him out the E.R. doors and down the hall into an operating room where a surgical team stood waiting. Within minutes, Jimmy Ramirez was asleep and the surgeons began working.

The knife had carved a deep laceration in his liver. After six hours of surgery, his wounds had been repaired as well as could be. They still oozed but the liver was soft and held stitches poorly. Any attempt to place more of them was liable to make things worse. The surgeon put packs all around the abdomen, hoping that constant pressure would do the job, pulled the edges of the abdominal wall together and covered them with tape. He didn't suture. In a day or two, if Jimmy Ramirez lived, he would be brought back to the operating room for removal of the packs. They brought him to the I.C.U.

unconscious and left him there, oblivious to the soft sigh of the ventilator forcing oxygen into his lungs.

Two hours later, Jimmy Ramirez went into D.I.C.—disseminated intravascular coagulation—his clotting factors and platelets all used up in a futile effort to stem the flow of blood through his wounds. The I.C.U. staff poured in plasma and platelet transfusions as fast as they could, but there was too much organ damage. The platelets were chewed up as soon as they were transfused and Jimmy Ramirez began to ooze from every pore. The heart, deprived of its blood supply, slowed and then fibrillated. A surgical resident began to compress Jimmy's chest while the nurses desperately squeezed in more blood. After an hour, after twenty-seven units of packed cells, twenty units of platelets and ten units of fresh frozen plasma, Jimmy's heart had irrevocably stopped. The Chief Surgical Resident looked at the monitors, shook his head and announced, "Okay, that's it." Reluctantly, the team grew silent, stared at each other, drew long, weary breaths, shrugged and shuffled out. A respiratory therapist turned off the ventilator as she left. The nurses took a quick break for coffee, then wrapped the body in plastic and sent it down to the morgue.

The little man sitting in the chair across from Barent had coffee colored skin, black hair and a brush moustache. He wore a blue policeman's uniform. His name tag read *Arnaldo Figueroa.* "Call me Arnie," he said.

"Okay," Barent said. "Arnie." Barent had requested help, somebody who knew the neighborhood that Jaime Ruiz, Herman Delgado and Carlos Rivera had grown up in, and Arnie had been temporarily re-assigned from a precinct uptown. Barent liked him immediately. He was quiet but he paid attention. Arnie used to be a member of a gang that called itself the Latin Sharks but his mother had placed him in a Catholic middle school when he was thirteen and the nuns, Arnie was fond of saying, had "beat it out of him." He had been a policeman for two years.

"We're not getting anywhere," Barent complained. "First Delgado, now Ramirez. Every lead we have in this case turns up dead." Arnie nodded curtly. "I don't know how much I can do for you," he said. "I mean, I know a lot of those guys but they know me too. Ruiz' men wouldn't give me the time of day."

"I understand that," Barent said, "the problem at the moment isn't Ruiz. It's Carlos Rivera."

Moran, who was standing in the corner, glumly nodded. There were over fifty Carlos Riveras listed in the New York phone books. One of these was the former Fire Commissioner of New York. Seven were old men; two had left the city more than a year before; one was in jail; one was an Engineer who lived in Queens and worked for Computer Associates out on Long Island.

None of them could possibly have been the Carlos Ri- vera who used to be friends with dead, twenty year old Herman Delgado. "Right," Moran said. "We can't find him."

"Carlos Rivera..." Arnie said. "I barely remember him: a tall guy, good looking."

"I don't know," Barent said. The Carlos Rivera they were looking for had been busted at the age of twelve for dealing crack. He had been placed on probation as a youthful offender and then vanished from the criminal justice system. He had no other record. "We've got a picture but he was just a kid." Just a kid who peddled cocaine. The picture had showed a skinny boy with a sullen smile and brooding dark eyes.

"You say he's gone?"

"Angela Delgado says he hasn't been around for at least six months. The neighbors confirm it."

"I still have some contacts," Arnie said. "I'll keep my eyes open but don't hold your breath."

Barent sighed. "Anything you can do would be appreciated."

"Sure." Arnie nodded, got up and left, leaving a leaden silence in his wake. After awhile, Moran shook his head and scratched the side of his cheek. "Maybe it's time to pursue the other angle: Sharon Lee."

"I suppose we're going to have to." Barent moodily drained his coffee, walked over to the pot and poured himself another cup. "God damn it, we let on that the investigation is still open, the media will start asking questions and suddenly it's a circus. Right now it's a closed case. Nobody cares. We have room to move."

"Move where?" Moran asked.

"Yeah." Barent shook his head. "That's the question, isn't it? Jesus, you would think we could find out something as simple as who some two bit hood was working for."

"Maybe he wasn't. Maybe he was on his own. Maybe he had nothing to do with it."

"And maybe he just happened to fall into a dumpster after accidentally shooting himself in the chest." Barent cracked the wrapper off a Partagas cigar and puffed it furiously alight. "I admit the evidence tying him to Sharon Lee is hazy. But there's no doubt that Delgado was murdered and we are paid to find murderers. If it turns out that we're looking for two different murderers, then that's just fine with me."

The phone on the desk rang. Barent scowled at it for three rings and then picked it up. "Hello?" he said. "Barent."

Barent listened and said nothing for a long time; finally he said, "You're sure?" Then he nodded, drew a deep, slow breath and smiled.

"Okay," he said. "I understand. Thanks." He put down the phone and looked at Moran. "Tony Korda," he said.

Tony Korda was half German, half African-American. Tony's father, a soldier during the War, had met his mother in occupied Berlin and brought her back to the States. Tony, the youngest of five children, was born eight years later. Tony's father stayed in the military and rose to the rank of Master Sergeant. They moved frequently, spending time at half a dozen bases in half a dozen cities, finally settling in at Fort Monmouth, New Jersey.

Alone during the day while her husband was at work, and lacking any skills that would make her employable, Tony's mother drank. She took good care of the children when she was sober, but she was rarely sober. When Tony was six, at four o'clock in the afternoon, drunk, Tony's mother fell asleep while smoking a cigarette in bed and died in the ensuing fire. Tony was rescued by a fireman who arrived just before the building collapsed but he suffered third degree burns over forty per cent of his body and burns inside his lungs that left him with pulmonary fibrosis and asthma. He spent the next ten years in and out of hospitals.

Tony Korda always seemed to be in trouble after the fire that wrecked his childhood and took his mother's life. He never touched alcohol, and the smoke from marijuana made his lungs wheeze like burning coals in his chest but he seemed to consider any other psychoactive substance that he could eat or snort or shoot up to be in a different, more acceptable category. At the age of sixteen, he stole a car, took it for a ride with a girl named Lucy and, high on cocaine, wrapped the car around a tree. Lucy died and Tony Korda, still a juvenile, spent six months in detention. He behaved himself for a while after that, graduated high school and went to City College for a year. Tony did well in college but was expelled during his Sophomore year after rape charges were filed against him by a female student.

Twenty years later, Tony Korda controlled a small criminal empire. He was an intermediate link in a chain that began in the jungles of Colombia and ended with a street dealer handing a packet of white powder to a poor kid in a back alley somewhere in New York. He took a bite out of local extortion, ran prostitution in a small segment of the South Bronx, had at least three prominent labor leaders in his pocket, owned illegal betting parlors and had his finger in every scam that took place along the Upper West Side of Manhattan.

"Oh, I would love to nail Tony Korda," Barent said. Just the name was enough to start his blood humming. "I would really, really love to nail Tony Korda."

"What would Tony Korda be doing with a small time guy like Herman Delgado?" Moran asked.

"Anything." Barent shrugged. "They all start out small time. Run numbers, deal drugs...Croft wasn't sure. He said Ruiz and his organization have been doing some business with Korda recently." He stopped for a moment. The cigar smoldered in an ashtray, slow coils of smoke rising up to the ceiling while Barent leaned back in his chair, thinking. There was plenty of precedent for one gang joining up with another. Sometimes they did it willingly, sometimes not. And sometimes no accommodation was possible and one or both sides got wiped out. New York had seen plenty of gang wars. The Blades were no longer just a bunch of kids. Kids have dreams but grownups have ambitions and a guy like Tony Korda could help turn ambitions into reality.

Barent stretched himself in his chair and scowled down at the cigar, which had gone out. He picked it up, lit it again and stuck it in his mouth. "The word Croft got was that Herman tended to be a bit headstrong but Korda was generally satisfied with the quality of his work. That's exactly the way he put it: 'satisfied with the quality of his work.'" Barent loosened his tie, snorted into his coffee cup. "Jesus, a fucking connoisseur of criminal aptitude."

"What business would Tony Korda have with Sharon Lee?" "Well, that's what we have to find out, isn't it?" Barent said. He knocked the ash off his cigar into an overflowing ashtray.

"Ruiz claimed he hadn't seen Herman in six months," Moran said. "You don't think he could have been lying?" He cracked a smile.

"It's hard to believe," Barent said sadly. "He seemed like such a nice guy, for a psychopath."

Chapter 13

Wellesley had been right, Barent thought. Even at night, the place hummed with suppressed activity, dozing now and then but never quite sleeping. A crowd of people milled about the Emergency Room waiting area, reading newspapers, staring into space, wandering up and down the hall. The one security guard posted by the corridor that led into the rest of the hospital had left his position twice in the half hour that Barent had watched him, once to grab a cup of coffee and once to go to the bathroom. Anybody could have waited for the opportunity and walked right in.

Barent himself carried a pass issued by Robinson, the Hospital Director. So far, nobody had asked to see it.

He shook his head, pasted a preoccupied look on his face, stuck his hands in his pockets and walked briskly down the corridor. As he passed the guard station, the officer looked him over, evidently decided that Barent did not look sufficiently suspicious and looked away.

Oh, brother, Barent thought. He walked by without saying a word. He turned right at the end of the corridor and soon came to the elevator bank in the lobby. Another guard was posted here but he barely even glanced at Barent.

Barent pushed the button, waited, and when an elevator arrived, went up to the Sixteenth Floor. From the lobby upstairs, two sets of double doors led into patient units on either side. Barent chose the one to his right, pushed open the doors and walked down the hallway. The corridor was dimly lit. Most of the rooms contained two beds and most of these held sleeping patients. At the end of the hallway was a nursing station. One nurse sat at the desk, writing in a patient chart. She looked up when he walked past. "Visiting hours are over."

Barent flashed her a grin and showed her his pass. "I'm just looking around," he said.

She looked at the pass doubtfully. "Well, please don't disturb the patients," she said. "They're trying to sleep."

"You bet."

He came to a stairwell, pushed the door open and walked up one flight to the call rooms. In the residents' wing, a few tired looking young men and women dressed in scrubs wandered up and down the hallway. They looked at Barent curiously but none of them bothered him. The attendings' wing was silent. A row of blank, closed doors stretched down the hallway. Barent tried a doorknob. It was locked. He tried another. It turned and he entered. The room was empty, the bed neatly made. Idly, he pulled open the top drawer in the dresser. A dirty coffee cup, two old *Playboys* and a copy of *Road and Track* sat there. He closed the drawer and walked out. About half of all the doors he tried were unlocked. The floor seemed deserted.

He turned and headed back to the elevators and punched the button for the Obstetrics Suite.

O.B. was brightly lit. Most babies, he seemed to recall, were born in the middle of the night. A team of doctors and nurses dressed in scrubs was pushing a bed down the hall toward what appeared to be a delivery room. A woman, obviously very pregnant, lay on the bed, groaning, while a man who might have been her husband held her hand and walked along beside, looking helpless.

"I've got to push!" the woman moaned. "I've got to!"

One of the doctors grimaced as he guided the bed around a turn. "Not yet," he said. "Just pant. We'll be there in a second." They vanished into the delivery room.

A nurse in a white uniform came bustling up to Barent. "Can I help you?" she asked.

He showed her the pass. "I'm just observing," he said. "Ignore me."

The nurse puffed up her cheeks and frowned. "Well, fine," she said, "but don't get in the way. And stay away from the patients."

Barent had no intention of bothering the patients. Like most men, he was more than a little squeamish regarding the mysteries of birth. "You bet," he said.

The Obstetrics Floor was arranged in a circle, with labor and delivery rooms around the outside. The central core of the circle contained chairs, desks, carrels where doctors and nurses could work on charts or dictate records, a large pot of coffee sitting on a table and a bowl full of donuts. A secretary sat at one of the desks, entering data into a computer. Occasionally, a laser printer hummed and spat out sheets of paper. Barent sat down on one of the chairs and watched. Over the next half hour, he saw women being pushed in and out on beds and stretchers, doctors and nurses bustling about, prospective fathers pacing back and forth, wringing their hands. It all looked quite routine. "Aren't you the policeman?" a voice said.

He looked up. It was the nurse who had been crying the morning that Sharon Lee was killed, the one with the round, cheerful face, Alice something...McMahon? Yeah, that was right. McMahon. "Detective Barent," he said.

"Of course." She hesitated. "If you don't mind my asking, what are you doing here?"

"We'll be going to trial soon. The alleged killer of Dr. Lee went from the Psych Unit up to the Seventeenth Floor without being seen. I wanted to take another look at the layout of the elevators and stairs. The defense will try to claim that it couldn't have happened." As a story, it wasn't much, but it would do.

"Alleged killer?" she said doubtfully.

"It's always the 'alleged killer' until the jury finds them guilty, even if you catch them standing over the body with a smoking gun in their hand."

"If you say so."

"Are things always this busy at night?" he asked.

She grinned. "Usually."

Barent was curious. His real reason for being here was to see who came and went and what the staff up here did about it. Sharon Lee had performed a Caesarian section, gone upstairs and been murdered. Who would have known when the case was finished, or where she would have gone afterwards? Apparently, the immediate world.

"Alice?" A pretty woman with dark hair came up to them. Barent remembered her clearly: Peggy Ryan. "The lady in Room Two is nine centimeters. She'll be pushing soon." Peggy Ryan frowned at Barent.

"Hello, Ms. Ryan," he said.

"Hi," she said uncertainly. "Detective Barent?" Barent nodded.

"I've got to get going," Alice McMahon said, and she hurried off. "Can I help you with anything?" Peggy Ryan asked.

"You work here long, Ms. Ryan?" "About four years."

"You like it?"

"I love it," she said simply.

From one of the delivery rooms, a long, agonized shriek rang out. Peggy Ryan ignored it. So did everyone else. Barent shuddered. Peggy Ryan suppressed a chuckle and then smiled. "You get used to it," she said.

"Better you than me," Barent said.

Peggy Ryan smiled even wider. "It's in my blood. My father was a doctor here. I was planning on becoming a nurse ever since I was a little girl."

"Not a doctor?"

"I thought about it, but nurses are closer to the patients. Doctors rarely have time to get to know their patients and that bothered me. A nurse is all I ever wanted to be."

Barent could understand that. His own father had been a cop. Being a cop was all he had ever wanted to be. He inwardly shrugged. "Well," he said, and hauled himself to his feet. "I'm not learning anything here and I've disturbed you all long enough. Have a good night."

She nodded. "Thank you," she said. Another shriek came from one of the rooms. Barent winced. Peggy Ryan smiled again and hurried away.

83

Kurtz spent most of the next three days with Lenore Brinkman. They swam in the pool together, snorkeled off the beach and went jet skiing across the placid blue water of the bay. They hired a boat and went out to where the reef dropped off into deep water, and they pulled in kingfish and snook and near the end of the afternoon, Kurtz hooked a marlin. He fought the great fish for an hour while it sounded, the line humming off his reel, then he frantically took in slack when the fish charged for the surface and jumped, its body flashing blue in the sunlight, water spraying in all directions like foam. Then, abruptly, he lost it. The line went dead and he reeled slowly in, the hook at the end empty, a deep aching fatigue settling slowly into his arms and shoulders.

The mate shrugged. The Captain looked at him, an unlit pipe hanging from the corner of his mouth, and then squinted out again at the water, already searching for new prey.

"Oh, Richard," Lenore said, and put her hand on his arm. "I'm sorry."

He smiled wanly. "The one that gets away is supposed to be the biggest." He shook his head and sighed.

Always he thought about Kathy. Kathy sitting with her legs curled under her on the sofa, reading while flames crackled in the fireplace. Kathy looking at him across a table, the light from a candle throwing shadows into the hollow between her breasts. Kathy with her hair spread out over her pillow like a billowing, dark cloud, reaching up for him in the night.

The time he spent with Lenore seemed unreal, like time spent somehow in a dream, in a time outside of time. They had no work, no cares, nothing to do but swim and play and eat and dance and listen to music and make love. Except that they didn't make love. Not yet—but, he thought, soon. Kurtz didn't push it. He didn't want to. The thought of Kathy kept intruding and Lenore—he knew it though they never spoke of it—had memories of her own to contend with.

The three days that he spent with Lenore were perfect. He loved to look at her, the way her eyes flashed green, the way her teeth sparkled, the way her golden hair floated around her head. She was beautiful. She was perfectly conscious of the fact and perfectly, completely, un-self-conscious.

Lenore's mother kept out of their way, her smiling, satisfied face studying their progress from a distance, charting off the milestones. They both ignored her.

On the afternoon of the third day, they walked together along the beach, searching for seashells. The sun was large on the horizon. The water lapped at their bare feet in little waves, which made soft, sucking sounds as they died and drifted back toward the sea.

"Here's one," Lenore said, she stooped and picked up a shining, bright green shell with brown dots, half buried in the sand. She brushed off the clinging grains of sand and handed it to Kurtz.

"It looks like a cowrie," he said.

He put it in the canvas bag he carried at his side. A wave ran over their feet, and he felt himself sink in just a little as the water washed out the sand from under him.

Lenore wrinkled her nose. "That tickles."

She pulled one foot out of the sand and stumbled and Kurtz quickly took her arm to steady her. She gave him a strange look, then slowly, she pulled her arm back and they began to walk, looking for shells. After a few hundred yards, she looked up at him and gave him a crooked smile and took his arm again and leaned against him. Kurtz said nothing. He looked down at the top of her golden head and stopped. Slowly, he turned toward her and put his arms around her back, not exerting any pressure at all, letting her know she could step away if she wanted to. She fixed her eyes on the sand, her head buried against his neck. Slowly, hesitantly, her arms came up and across his shoulders. Then she raised her head, her eyes closed, and he kissed her.

The kiss lasted a long time, and when they broke it she sighed and leaned against him.

"Let's look for shells," she said.

Kurtz held her tighter for an instant before letting her go. "Alright," he said.

Three hours later, they met for dinner at *Le Palais*, a French restaurant on the top floor of the resort. It was night. Stars shone in through the windows and a full moon glowed down on the rippling water. Kurtz wore a dark blue suit with a tie and Lenore had on a green, silk dress. The restaurant was half full. The lights were kept low and the tables far apart. Candles flickered, and waiters and wine stewards dressed in tuxedos discreetly patrolled the floor.

"Madame, Monsieur, my name is Ramon. I will be your Captain for the evening."

Ramon was tall, slim, young, with curly black hair. He looked like a movie star. He handed them both menus, flashed them a white smile, and vanished.

"Mine doesn't have prices," Lenore whispered. "I hate it when they do that."

"Don't worry," Kurtz said. "Everything is expensive."

She smiled, and he felt his heart go thump. Christ, he thought, I feel like an adolescent idiot.

"Monsiuer, Madame, something to drink?" The wine steward was short, slim and balding, with a pencil thin moustache on his upper lip.

85

"Some wine, perhaps?" He offered Kurtz a wine list inside a red leather folder, then walked off while Kurtz studied it.

Kurtz ordered *Dom Perignon*, which the wine steward opened with a flourish and a pop of the cork.

"To good times," Kurtz said. Lenore smiled at him very slightly and they both drank. The waiter wheeled a cart over, removed the rounded lid from a tray and served the first course: lobster cocktail, with a sauce made from capers and mustard.

"This is wonderful," Lenore said.

Kurtz smiled in the flickering light and poured another glass full of champagne. "Are you trying to get me drunk?" she asked.

"Would you like me to get you drunk?"

She gave him a grin that vanished as soon as it appeared. "You don't have to get me drunk."

He nodded, and drew in his breath, the back of his neck prickling. She had a faint scattering of freckles across the bridge of her nose. Her green eyes looked black in the dim light. Her golden hair glowed. He stared at her and it seemed suddenly as if she moved in slow motion, as if the two of them existed in their own private world in their own private Universe.

She moved her fork. She raised her glass. She smiled. Kurtz blinked and the moment vanished.

Kurtz hardly remembered what he ate after that. He could look at nothing but Lenore's face, wondering. They had an orange soufflé for dessert, with coffee. The waiter spooned a creamy sauce on top and they ate it quickly, before it collapsed.

By the Captain's stand at the entrance to the restaurant, a man stood talking. Kurtz noticed him from the corner of his eye but paid him no attention. The man showed something to Ramon, who looked at it, looked back toward Kurtz, and nodded. The man stared at their table. He straightened up, squared his shoulders, and walked slowly toward them. He was tall, as tall as Kurtz, with curling, light brown hair and a straight nose. Lenore had her back to him. He stopped, looked down at them, seemed about to say something, then shook his head. He walked past the table and turned, facing Lenore.

She looked up and blinked. For a moment, she said nothing, then her face turned abruptly white and she raised a hand to her cheek. "What is this?" she said. "A joke?"

The man grinned sheepishly. His face was as white as Lenore's. His eyes flicked to Kurtz, then back to Lenore. "No, it's not a joke. Can I sit down?"

Kurtz looked up. The tall young man refused to meet his eyes. He stared at Lenore with parted lips and an almost desperate look on his face.

"What's going on?" Kurtz asked her.

"This," Lenore said disdainfully, "is Harrison Thomas, Office Manager of First Amsterdam Savings and Loan, whose ancestors landed on the Mayflower and whose family never, ever forgets it, or lets anyone else forget it either." She gave a little sniff. "My former fiancé."

"Oh," Kurtz said. "Oh." He grinned, then coughed, and suddenly he felt laughter beginning to bubble up. He couldn't help it.

"What," Lenore demanded, "is so funny?"

"Nothing." Kurtz looked back up at Harrison Thomas. "Sure," he said. "Sit down."

Lenore seemed about to say something, then stopped. Harrison Thomas flashed Kurtz a quick, grateful grin, then sat.

Thomas glanced warily at Kurtz once or twice, but aside from that his eyes stayed glued to Lenore's face. They sat for almost a minute. More than once, Harrison Thomas opened his mouth, but nothing came out. Lenore refused to look at him. He was a good-looking guy, Kurtz thought, a good-looking guy who knows he's fucked up. Again, Kurtz almost laughed—but this time he managed to stifle it. Placidly, he stirred cream and sugar into his coffee. He sipped it slowly, then sighed and shook his head.

Lenore's eyes snapped toward his face. "What's bothering you?"

"Nothing."

She frowned. Kurtz turned to Thomas. "Look, you wanted to sit down. Why don't you go ahead and say what you have to say?"

Thomas swallowed. "Alright." He turned to Lenore. "I was wrong," he said. "I'm sorry. I want you back. I love you."

Kurtz smiled at him, raised his glass of champagne and took a sip. *Bravo*, he thought. Short and sweet.

"You love me." Lenore said it clinically, in a level, detached voice. "Yes," Harrison Thomas said.

"But your father disapproves. You're supposed to marry a rich WASP bitch. Someone just like yourself."

"I don't want a rich WASP bitch. I want you."

"Finally figured that out, did you?"

"Yes."

"But what are you going to say to Daddy?"

"I already said it. He didn't like it."

For the first time, Lenore looked at him with interest. "No?"

Thomas shook his head. "No."

"Good," Lenore said.

Thomas looked at Kurtz longingly, silently begging him to leave. Kurtz cheerfully grinned back at him and sipped his champagne. Lenore smiled at Kurtz, then turned back to Harrison. "Go on," she said.

He glanced desperately at Kurtz, who blinked at him innocently. "Alright," Harrison said. "I love you. I want to marry you. I can't live without you."

"That's sweet," Lenore said. "Richard, isn't that sweet?"

"Sweet," Kurtz agreed. "Very sweet."

"I'll think about it," Lenore said. She rose to her feet and turned her head so that Kurtz could see her face but Thomas could not, and silently mouthed the words, *Thank you.* "I'm going to leave now," she said. "I can't take any more of this." She walked off, not looking back.

So much for the perfect evening, Kurtz thought. He raised his glass to Harrison Thomas and said, "Champagne?"

Thomas looked sick. His face was white; his hands trembled. "No," he said. "Thank you." Shakily, he rose to his feet. "I'm sorry. Really. I know how this must have looked to you, but there was nothing else that I could do. I meant everything I said. I was a fool."

"I understand," Kurtz said.

"Thanks." Thomas spread his hands to the side and helplessly let them fall, then turned and walked out, his feet dragging.

Kurtz looked at him go and breathed a long sigh. The table looked awfully empty. He turned to the wine steward and motioned him over. "I thought I noticed Hennessy X.O. on the menu."

"Of course, Monsieur."

"Good," Kurtz said. "I'll take a double." He smiled wanly. "And please ask Ramon to bring me my check."

Chapter 14

A light knock on the door woke him up. The sun shone in through the window shades, making slanting lines of light across the bed. Blearily, Kurtz looked at the clock. Eight A.M. "Just a minute," he called out. He put on a robe and opened the door. Lenore stood there.

"Can I come in?" she asked.

He grinned slightly. "Sure."

She sat in a chair by the table next to the window and stared down at the beach, already filling with sun worshippers. From this distance, they looked as tiny and silent as ants.

"Would you like some breakfast?" he asked. "I can call room service."

"No, thanks." She shook her head. "I can't stay long."

"Ah..."

She smiled at him briefly. "Yeah," she said. "I know." Her voice held genuine regret.

"He seemed," Kurtz said delicately, "to be an okay guy."

"He is an okay guy." She had on jeans and a white tee shirt with a *Big Apple* logo on it. Her hair was held back with a pink plastic hairband and she wore no makeup. But her cheeks glowed. "Look," she said. "I'm really, really sorry. I felt that I owed you an explanation."

"What's to explain? The situation is obvious."

She shrugged. "I guess it is, but I still wanted you to know: I liked you. I liked you a lot. If Harrison hadn't come back..."

Kurtz folded his hands together and nodded. Down below, a surfer had just caught a wave. He rode it toward shore and stepped off his board just as it slid up the beach.

"I loved Harrison. I guess I still do. And I'm proud of him, too. It couldn't have been easy telling his father to go to hell." Lenore grinned. "I'm going to take a lot of pleasure out of tweaking the old bastard's nose."

"It's okay." Kurtz shrugged. He added, "I liked you, too."

Lenore looked at him, nibbled the inside of her cheek thoughtfully. "I'm glad you understand. I would never have done anything to deliberately hurt you." She grinned. "What I regret more than anything else is the way last night turned out. I was...looking forward to it." She stared him in the eye and looked as if she were thinking it over. "I'm still tempted but I know I better not. I'm not sure how I would feel afterward."

Kurtz gave her a wan smile. "That's the nicest non-offer I ever received.

"What does your mother say?"

Lenore laughed softly. "She's not saying. She hasn't figured it out yet. She's not certain if a rich executive is as good as a rich doctor, but since you're both hunks and neither of you are Jewish, she's withholding judgment."

"Smart woman, your mother."

"Yeah." Lenore rose to her feet, leaned over and kissed him on the cheek, then shook her head with what seemed to be real regret. "I better not see you again," she said. "It wouldn't be smart."

Kurtz nodded. "Good luck," he said. He meant it.

"Thanks."

He let her out and thought for a moment about facing the day. Then he smiled to himself and yawned and climbed back into bed. Later, he thought. I'll think about it later. Right now, I'm too tired.

The rest of his vacation was restful and uneventful. He tried to enjoy himself. He swam and ate and worked on his tan, but something seemed to have gone out of it. He saw Lenore occasionally, across the pool or in the dining room. She would smile at him but that was all and Kurtz respected her wishes. He liked the way that Harrison Thomas hovered over her. Lenore was quite a girl, he thought with a pang. Quite a girl.

Two days later, he was on a plane back to New York, back to his patients and the mystery of Sharon Lee, and most of all, back to Kathy.

His plane got into Kennedy at eight P.M. on Saturday night. It was raining, a cold wet drizzle mixed with snow. He looked out at the rain through the window as they taxied up to the terminal and he shuddered. He hated New York winters, and the already fading memory of Cancun, of the endless sun and the glistening blue sea made the dreary weather even more repellant.

He caught a taxi cab and sat silently in the back, feeling the dark mood of the city settle into his soul as they drove into Manhattan.

"You got a nice tan," the cabby said to him once. "Been on vacation?"

"Mexico," Kurtz said.

"Yeah?" The cabby's ears seemed to perk up. "I was in Mexico once. Tijuana. Burritos and chili peppers. I got the runs. I thought the place was a hole."

Kurtz shrugged and said nothing. The cabby glanced back at him through the rearview mirror, saw Kurtz frowning at the rain, and grinned. After that they drove in silence.

His mood lifted a bit as he put his key in the lock and opened the door to his apartment. He put his suitcases down by the door, turned on the lights and hung his coat in the closet, then went into the kitchen. He made himself a Bloody Mary and sipped it while he inspected his answering machine. Four messages. The first two were advertisements, then one from Kathy confirming a date for the next afternoon. The last message was from Barent: "Dr. Kurtz, there have been some developments in the case that I would like to discuss with you. Please give me a call when you get in. Saturday until ten P.M. would be okay. Otherwise, please make it at the station during the week." The message ended with Barent's home phone number.

Okay, Kurtz thought, you asked for it. He dialed Barent's number and after a couple of rings, a woman's voice answered. "Is Detective Barent in?" he asked. "This is Dr. Kurtz."

The woman's voice seemed to hesitate. "We're kind of busy right now," she said. "Is it important?"

"I don't know. He asked me to call him."

"Just a second, then." He heard her yell out, "Lew, it's a Dr. Kurtz."

Barent's voice came on. "Good to hear from you. You have a nice vacation?"

"Passable," Kurtz answered.

"Hold on a second." Barent said something to somebody away from the phone, then came back. "Look, I know I said to call but things have gotten awful hectic at home." He added in a voice that sounded less than thrilled, "It's my daughter. She's just told us she's getting married. Could we talk during the week? Maybe Monday?"

Kurtz had patients scheduled for Monday afternoon but the morning was free. "Nine A.M.?"

"Perfect."

"I'll meet you at the station. Congratulations about your daughter."

Barent grunted. "Thanks," he said grudgingly. "I'll see you then."

They met for lunch at *Le Bibliotheque*, a little place on the Upper West Side. It was supposedly French, but the menu listed clam chowder and assorted varieties of cheeseburger as well as croissants and bouillabaisse, and none of the waiters spoke with an accent. Each wall held a narrow bookcase rising to the ceiling, stacked with dusty volumes by Ernest Gann and Thomas Costain and other authors popular in the Fifties and Sixties. The patrons were encouraged to browse while they waited for their food but few chose to do so. The choice of reading material was not encouraging.

Kathy, however, loved books of all sorts, even forty-year-old best sellers by authors who had long since died and faded into obscurity. "Look at this one." She held a fat volume out to Kurtz, who took it reluctantly and weighed it in his palm. *"Lord Vanity,"* Kathy said, "by Samuel Shellabarger. I read this when I was a kid."

"I've heard of him," Kurtz said.

"He was big: *Prince of Foxes, Captain from Castile.*"

"Before my time."

"I'm going to buy it if they'll let me." Kathy put the book on the table and placed her elbow on top of it, as if the book might get up and walk away if she didn't stake her claim to it.

"How's the thesis going?" Kurtz asked.

"Pretty good. I've established some interesting parallels between *The Wasteland* and Mordor, Sauron's ruined domain. My preceptor is pleased. So..." She looked at him brightly and smiled. "You have a nice time?"

"Not bad," he said.

"You meet anybody?"

He gave her a wary look. "Anybody?"

"Hmmm." She squinted at him out of one eye. "You know, vacations are different from real life. They're supposed to be. That's what getting away from it all is all about. No cares, no worries. Everybody has that exotic glow. You fall in love; you fall out of love. It's easy." She grinned. "I spent two weeks on Ibiza once. You know Ibiza?"

"An Island in the Mediterranean?"

She nodded. "A vacation paradise. Anything goes. I met a guy named Russell who played the guitar and wrote poetry. He was from New York. We had a great time. I even saw him a couple of times once we got home but he seemed different." Kathy examined a roll, broke it in half and nibbled on the crust. "Actually, he seemed like a jerk. Hard to believe it was the same person."

"I did meet somebody," Kurtz said.

She frowned at the roll, picked up her knife and buttered half of it. "Oh?"

"She had a boyfriend. It was nothing serious."

"I'm not sure I want to hear this," Kathy said.

Kurtz smiled. "Then why did you ask?"

"Idle curiosity," she said. "But maybe I should have kept my mouth shut."

Except for the fact that Kathy was a brunette and Lenore a blonde, they looked a lot alike. Kathy's hair was straight and black and hung halfway down her back. She wore a green blouse with a flowered pattern, slacks and comfortable shoes that were good for walking. A modern woman, Kathy. Smart, self-assured, no bullshit. "I missed you," Kurtz said.

"Good."

Kurtz smiled. "Barent left a message on my machine. He wants me to call him in the morning."

Kathy's fork stopped halfway to her mouth. She looked at him over a piece of lettuce and frowned. "Why?"

"I'm not sure. He thinks I can help."

"How? You're not a policeman."

"No, but I know the environment in which the victim lived and worked."

Kathy thought about that for a moment, then she said, "I imagine a case like this must become an obsession for a policeman. Good against bad. Innocence versus evil. There must be a lot of satisfaction in finding somebody who would commit murder. It must be terribly frustrating when you can't."

The waiter set a bacon blue cheese burger in front of Kurtz. He picked it up and took a big bite. "I can relate," he said. "I can definitely relate."

"See that you don't get hurt."

Good advice, Kurtz thought. He speared a French fry and silently nodded.

Chapter 15

Barent's office was coming to seem quite familiar. Kurtz sat in the chair across the desk, swirled his cup of coffee and listened silently while the detective talked.

"Tony Korda..." Kurtz said when Barent finished. He felt cold suddenly and rubbed a hand across the back of his neck. "I've heard of Tony Korda. I've seen his name in the papers."

The office seemed strangely quiet in the morning. Only a few patrolmen moved about in the squad room outside Barent's office and the haze of smoke was decidedly less than it had been the last time Kurtz sat in this chair. "So you have no more leads."

"Not exactly true. We have files on more than two hundred people who work, or used to work, for Tony Korda."

"But nothing to tie any of them to either Sharon Lee or Herman Delgado."

Barent barely hesitated, then said, "That's correct."

"Do you have any people in Korda's organization?"

Barent smiled faintly. "What are you, the Chief of Police? Even if we did, I wouldn't admit it to you." Barent shook his head in wonder. "Jesus."

Kurtz felt himself blushing. "Sorry," he said. "I guess you aren't interested in my advice. So what do you want from me?"

"Information." Barent nodded at Moran, who stood leaning against the door. "Harry thinks that it's time we went back to Sharon Lee. He's right. For the moment, Herman Delgado has proven to be a dead end."

"What do you want to know?"

"I want you to tell me who might have wanted Sharon Lee dead." Kurtz blinked. "I already told you I don't know that. How would I?"

"Hopefully, you know more than you think." Barent leaned back in his chair, stretched until his back audibly cracked, and cradled his hands behind his head. "There are only two types of violent crime," he said, "which of course includes murder; there are crimes of passion and crimes of pre-meditation. And there are only two reasons for crimes of pre-meditation: gain and revenge. Seen in this light, most murders are solved fairly easily. Most murders are crimes of passion, committed by a family member or another close associate of the victim. Crimes of pre-meditation are harder because the murderer will almost always plan on getting away with it and will do everything he can to cover his tracks. It's quite likely that the majority of such murders are never discovered to be murders at all. Some old guy dies of a heart attack or some other 'natural cause'"—Barent shrugged—"the body is cremated. Nobody's going to find out that the victim was poisoned, or maybe somebody held a pillow over his mouth. Nobody's even going to look."

"That's disgusting," Kurtz said. Barent shrugged again.

"It seems too simplistic. There are other reasons for murder. There are insane reasons."

"I would classify crimes motivated by reasons of insanity to be crimes of passion."

"There are also disinterested reasons—terrorism, for instance."

Barent frowned. Since the World Trade Center, terrorism was a subject that no New Yorker took lightly. Then he grudgingly smiled and glanced at Moran. "Smart. Didn't I tell you he was smart? A mind like a scalpel."

Moran dolefully nodded.

"It's true that in crimes of terror the victim may be merely incidental, in that the victim is killed not because of who he is, but because of what he represents, and as often as not any victim at all would do equally well for the purpose—but there is no doubt that crimes of terror are pre-meditated and cold blooded. And the motive is clearly and always gain, political if not personal."

"I suppose so," Kurtz said.

"Good." Barent nodded. "So who had reason to want Sharon Lee dead?"

"I still don't know."

"That's because you're not letting your imagination work. Alright, look at it this way—she had a sister, right?"

"Yes," Kurtz said.

"If Sharon Lee is dead, then the sister will inherit a larger share of her mother's estate."

Kurtz' brow wrinkled. "Are you seriously suggesting...?"

Barent held up a hand. "I'm not suggesting anything. I'm merely pointing out that from a monetary point of view, her sister would most likely benefit from Sharon Lee's death."

Kurtz drew a deep breath and allowed a slow smile to spread across his face. "Okay," he said. "I get it. It's a game: who can come up with the largest number of suspects."

"Exactly."

"Okay...you mentioned her sister. Her sister's name is Sheila. Sheila might well have been jealous of Sharon. Sharon was better looking and got top grades and became a doctor. Sheila married a Psychology Professor at Northwestern and had two kids. She's a housewife."

Barent turned to Moran. "Put another check by the sister." Moran grunted.

"And how about her mother?" Kurtz said. "Sharon's father left Sharon a lot of money. Now that she's dead, some of that money must go back to her mother."

"Good." Barent nodded approvingly. "Add the mother to the list."

"Then there are the other obstetricians. Sharon was in solo practice and she was a woman. An awful lot of women want to go to a woman gynecologist; they feel more comfortable. The men in the department might have felt threatened."

Barent looked thoughtful. "For that matter, every O.B.-G.Y.N. in the metropolitan area could have had reason to want her dead."

"True," Kurtz said, and shook his head. "I don't feel like we're exactly narrowing things down here."

"We can narrow them down later. For now, let's get every possible suspect on the list."

"Every possible suspect..." Kurtz ran his hand through his hair in disgust. "I assume she was involved with somebody. Sharon always was. So there might have been a boyfriend who was jealous. Or an aspiring boyfriend who might have been jealous. Or a boyfriend's girlfriend who might have been jealous."

"We'll check that out," Barent said. "Who would know?"

"Her sister might. Despite what I said about her, they were close. They talked on the phone at least once a week."

"Her sister's in Chicago?"

"She lives in Chicago. She's probably here, helping her mother. Sharon's mother is not the most competent human being."

"Anyone else?"

"She had some friends from college; I forget the names...Evelyn Something." He frowned into his coffee-cup. "I think it was Hobbs, Evelyn Hobbs. And Joyce Davenport."

"Good. Anyone else?"

"Jennifer Parks, her best friend from Medical School. I know Jennifer. She's a family practitioner."

"Did she have any business dealings? Any investments?"

"She had a broker at one of the big firms—I think it was Merrill Lynch. From what I remember, he was the staid, conservative sort, nothing too risky. He was an older man. Sharon inherited him, as it were, from her father."

"Did she get along with her patients?"

"She wasn't the warmest human being on Earth. I never did understand why she went into obstetrics. But she was dedicated to her work. She was a good doctor."

"That doesn't really answer my question."

Kurtz hesitated. "She tended to be impatient, and she didn't have the greatest bedside manner. You probably know that obstetricians get sued a lot. There are always things you can't control, complications that simply couldn't be avoided. Patients are generally not willing to accept that, and obstetricians don't like to admit it. Women come into the hospital to have a baby. Things are supposed to go right." Kurtz shrugged. "Studies have proven that you can fuck up every which way from Sunday and your patients won't sue you if they like you."

"What sort of complications are you talking about?"

Kurtz smiled wryly. "All sorts of things. When I was a third year student, I had a patient once with a two-headed baby."

Barent stared at him.

"It was really identical twins that didn't quite separate. There was one body with two legs, two heads, two arms and a third vestigial arm coming up out of the shoulder between the heads. The poor thing was a mess. It died after a few hours."

Barent grimaced at Kurtz' blandly smiling face. "Does stuff like that happen often?"

"Not often, but it happens."

Barent shuddered. "Do you know of any suits against Sharon Lee?"

"I think she had a few. I only know about one. It was absurd. A perfectly normal delivery but the kid came out floppy. A muscle biopsy showed viral inclusion bodies. The kid had a congenital viral myopathy, an infection picked up *in utero* from the mother. It was nobody's fault but the parents weren't willing to accept that. They sued."

"What happened to the baby?"

"I don't know. Sharon and I broke up around that time."

"Who carried her malpractice insurance?"

"Probably M.L.M.I.C. They're the largest carrier in the State."

Barent made a notation in his notebook. "We'll look into it. Did she get along with her colleagues?"

"Sure." Kurtz sipped his coffee, wrinkled his nose as he realized it had gone cold and went over to the pot in the corner to fix himself a fresh cup. "One thing you have to realize: doctors all have tremendous egos. They're all smart and hard working and successful. Every one of them thinks he's God's gift and most of them think all the other doctors are idiots, except, of course, for their own little group of colleagues and friends, who are idiots only part of the time.

"Sharon was no worse than most." Kurtz shrugged again. "She got along."

"She had no enemies that you know of?"

Kurtz shook his head. "No."

"Did anyone in particular—that you know of—dislike her?"

"Beats me."

Barent surveyed his notebook, frowning, and tapped the page with the tip of his pen. "You've given us a few leads. We'll work on them." He looked up suddenly and fixed Kurtz with a sharp glance. "Are you willing to do a little more to help us out?"

Here it comes, thought Kurtz. The catch. "Like what?"

"Doctors are touchy about their patients, confidentiality and all that. But confidentiality doesn't extend to other doctors. Do you think you could get us some information about Sharon Lee's patients?"

"What information?"

"Just their names." Barent thought about it, added, "Addresses and phone numbers if you can."

"You could subpoena them."

"We could." Barent nodded. "If we have to, we will. But that would certainly tip people off, now wouldn't it?"

"You have some hope of keeping this investigation a secret?"

"You never know. Right now, the murderer thinks he's gotten away with it. He might be more careful if he knew we were still looking. We're going to try to keep the lid on as long as possible."

"How long is possible? Sooner or later you're going to have to indict Bill Mose or admit that you don't have a case."

"Mr. Mose is recovering from his recent surgery. He won't be fit to appear in court for,"—Barent looked up at Kurtz with a bright smile on his face—"how long would you say? A month?"

Kurtz frowned at the haze of smoke outside the office and thought about it. "A month sounds about right." Then he shook his head. "There's no way that I can get any information about Sharon's patients. The hospital computer system doesn't code to doctors' names, only patients' names. If I have a patient's name, I can find out the doctor, but it doesn't work the other way around."

Barent shrugged his shoulders and frowned into his coffee. "Oh, well."

"Was there anything else?"

"Yeah." Barent opened his desk and pulled out a sheaf of paper. It appeared to be a long list of words that Kurtz could not make out. "The hospital computer: what type is it?" Barent asked.

"You mean what brand? I think they're Dells."

"VAX? UNIX? Java? Microsoft NT?"

"Microsoft something. I'm not sure about the rest."

"Are there terminals at all the working areas? The nursing stations? The secretaries' desks?"

"Absolutely."

"And how are appointments made? The old fashioned way, or by computer?"

Kurtz warily eyed the sheaf of paper in Barent's fist. "When a patient calls to make an appointment, the secretary or clerk who takes the call is supposed to punch the name and time into the system."

Barent looked happy. "Perfect. And how about afterward? You said that there's a central computerized listing of patients. Are all the patients' visits listed as well?"

"Of course."

Barent extended the sheaf of papers to Kurtz, who eyed it with suspicion and made no move to take it. Barent carefully placed it down on the desk in front of Kurtz. "That's a list of names," Barent said. "Every individual who was ever known to be associated with Tony Korda or Jaime Ruiz. I would like you to see if any of them are listed in your hospital's computer."

"That's all?"

"Names, dates and times."

"Diagnoses?"

"If you think it's relevant."

"If I think it's relevant," Kurtz said with disgust. His eyes flickered from the sheaf of paper up to Barent's face and back down to the paper. "I know I'm going to regret this." He picked up the paper and settled it in his lap.

"Thank you," Barent said simply.

"You know," said Kurtz, "there's one suspect neither of us has mentioned."

"Who's that?"

"The one we don't know about—and haven't thought of."

Barent nodded his head. "True." He pointed to the sheaf of paper sitting in Kurtz' lap. "But maybe his name is on that list. Let's hope."

Chapter 16

Barent had not lied to Kurtz, not exactly, but he had deliberately allowed him to labor under a misconception. The problem right now was not that they had no case, but rather that the case they had was too good.

"Baloney." Ted Weiss was the Assistant D.A. He was average height, thin, with straw colored hair and narrow blue eyes. "Mose has no alibi and Sharon Lee had his blood under her fingernails. You can't tell me that doesn't make a case."

Barent put a pained look on his face. "Come on, Ted, give me a break. What about the burglary? What about Herman Delgado?"

"What about them? So her apartment was robbed and Delgado most likely did it. Apartments get robbed all the time. You have nothing to tie Delgado to the murder. Sure, he turned up with a hole in his chest, but so what? People like Herman Delgado get murdered all the time. You have no evidence to point to Korda or anyone else. You've got nothing." Weiss stabbed his finger at the air to add emphasis. "Nothing except a lunatic whose blood is under the victim's fingernails."

Barent opened his mouth to protest but Weiss held up a hand. "You're going to mention the ring. Don't. A *ring,* for Christ's sake! A nut case swallows a gold ring and that's supposed to be evidence? It could have come from anywhere. Anywhere at all!"

Barent sighed and slumped down in his chair. Hard headed, by the book: that was Ted Weiss. "I know it's flimsy," Barent said. "I know it's circumstantial. But it makes sense. This thing with Mose..." He waved his arms in the air helplessly. "It's too easy. It's too pat."

"What is this?" Weiss asked. "Policeman's instinct?"

"Yeah, you could say that."

"Try taking 'instinct' to the jury."

"The investigation," said Barent, "isn't over. I hope to be able to confirm my suspicions."

"Okay." Weiss nodded. "I understand that. But you have to understand that I'm under a lot of pressure with this case. A doctor...a young, pretty, *female* doctor. Right now it's a scandal. The family is going to sue the hospital. They'll get a nice settlement and that'll be that. Everyone is embarrassed but the case is closed. It's a one in a million occurrence and everybody sleeps well at night. If we let on that we don't know who did it, the public will be upset, and when the public is upset, the mayor gets upset. When the mayor gets upset, my boss gets upset. Guess who gets upset then?"

Barent was already upset but he didn't say it. "Give me another few weeks."

Dolefully, Weiss shook his head. "I'll give you *two* weeks. You come up with something better than you've got in two weeks or I'm going to indict Mose. I've got no choice."

"Two weeks..." Barent slowly nodded, his mind already considering the possibilities. "Thanks," he said grudgingly.

"Don't mention it," Weiss said. "And by the way, just so we understand each other, you should realize that I'm doing this as a favor because I think you're going to come up with nothing. *I* think Mose did it. But I'm giving you the time because I want you to be satisfied. I hope you appreciate that."

"They used to pay people to draw blood from patients. Usually they were med students trying to earn some extra money; sometimes it was a nurse or a nurse's aide or a lab tech." Nolan shrugged. "Anybody with hospital experience could apply for the job; it didn't pay very much.

"There was this one guy—he was a pharmacy student—the guy was a whiz with a needle. I mean, he could get blood from a stone. He was always the first one finished with his rounds. Five hundred pounder with no veins? No problem. Just call Joe. But after a while people began to get a little curious. How could this character be so much better than anybody else? How did he do it? Joe would never tell. You'd ask him, he'd just smile and say, 'Trade secret, man, trade secret.' So one day one of the other phlebotomists decided to find out. He waited until Joe was in with a patient who was known to be a particularly difficult stick and he opened the door suddenly and looked in. There was the patient, lying back on the bed and there was Joe with an extra long needle stuck in her chest." Nolan looked at the nurse. "Scissors," he said.

The nurse gave him the scissors. "In her chest?" Liebert said.

Nolan tied off a stitch, then dabbed at the wound with a four-by-four and waited a moment. No bleeding. Satisfied, he nodded his head and said, "He was using cardiac needles and drawing the blood from their hearts."

Kurtz shuddered. Franklin hunched his head down onto his shoulders and gave Nolan a disapproving look. Franklin was the serious sort. Crane had rotated out at the end of the month and Franklin had replaced him on the Service. Franklin was short, thin and quiet, and seemed to have no sense of humor at all, but he had good hands.

"Tie here," Kurtz said.

Franklin didn't look up but he did as he was told—two sutures around the cystic duct and the gall bladder, bulging from a stone obstructing the outlet, was swinging in the breeze. Nolan cut between the sutures and the specimen was free. Franklin handed the gallbladder off to the scrub nurse and Kurtz inspected the wound carefully. There was minimal bleeding from the liver bed but nothing unusual. "Lap pad," he said.

The scrub nurse picked up a white square of cloth about the size of a kitchen towel, soaked it in a bucket of sterile saline and handed it to Kurtz. He packed it into the abdomen and they waited.

"What happened to him?" Liebert asked.

"Who? Joe?"

Liebert nodded. "They fired him."

"That's all?"

"What else were they supposed to do? Hey, his job was to get the blood. He was getting the blood. So his methods were unorthodox, nothing illegal in that."

"But what if somebody had died?"

Nolan gave him a pitying look. "They didn't."

"But what if they had? Isn't it assault? Or even murder?"

"More like malpractice, I think. But they *didn't*, so why make waves? Get rid of the asshole and forget about it, and hope the whole thing stays buried."

Liebert wrinkled his brow. "I see," he said doubtfully.

"You know kid, you tend to be a little naive, sometimes." Nolan looked at Franklin and said, "Doesn't he tend to be a little naive?"

Franklin grunted and Nolan rolled his eyes.

Kurtz removed the lap pad. The wound stayed dry. "Okay," he said. "Close it up." He glanced at the clock and thought about the sheaf of papers sitting on the top shelf of his locker. It was 10:15 A.M. He had no patients scheduled in the office until after lunch: time to do a little searching through the computer.

Nice, Barent thought. *Real nice.* The Lee's home was a Tudor mansion set on three acres of rolling ground outside Stamford, Connecticut. Large oak trees straddled the driveway. The grass, even in winter, looked green and neat. A hedge of rhododendrons sat under the box windows and ran the length of the house. A marble fountain filled with a ring of dark, frozen water sat next to an iron lamppost.

Moran parked the car in the circular driveway. Barent pressed the doorbell and a short, plump woman dressed in a maid's uniform answered the door. "Yes?" she said.

"I'm Detective Barent and this is my partner, Detective Moran. Mrs. Lee is expecting us."

"Come in." Barent and Moran entered. "Please wait here." The maid turned and walked away. Barent looked up. An enormous crystal chandelier hung in the foyer. White marble tiles separated by black inlays covered the floor. To their left, a white, carpeted stairway curved up and around, leading to a second floor balcony that looked down on the foyer. A painting hung on the wall above the balcony. The painting was at least six feet long and brightly colored, a large white ball fading into green shadow, surrounded by dancing triangles in magenta, blue and rose.

"You like the painting? It's a Vasarelli." A tall, thin woman stood in the hallway. Her skin was wrinkled and she had bags under her eyes. She wore a light gray business suit with a lavender blouse. Her mascara was smeared.

"I like it very much," Barent said. He squinted upward. "But the style is hardly characteristic of Vasarelli. It looks more like an Ernst Gottlieb."

The woman frowned and looked up at the painting. She cleared her throat. "Well," she said. "You are Detective Barent?"

"And Detective Moran."

"I'm Estelle Lee." She held out her hand and Barent gravely shook it.

"I'm sorry to bother you, Mrs. Lee, but it seemed necessary."

"That's quite alright, Detective. We all have our jobs. Please come with me."

Estelle Lee tottered as she walked. They followed her down a hallway and into a room that was completely lined with glass. The room looked out upon a red brick patio bordered by a dense line of mountain laurel. Beyond the mountain laurel stood a chain link fence surrounding a swimming pool covered with ice. A small, wrought iron table with a tea set on top stood in the middle of the room. "Please sit down," Mrs. Lee said. "Tea?"

"No, thank you," Barent said. Moran, as usual, said nothing.

A woman who looked like a younger version of Estelle Lee walked into the room. She had a look of what appeared to be perpetual disapproval pasted on her face. "I'm Sheila Hirschfeld." She said it without a smile. "Sharon's sister."

Barent shook her hand. Sheila Hirschfeld seated herself on a chair next to her mother. The two women stared at Barent, unblinking.

"As you know," Barent said, "we'll be going to trial very shortly, and there are certain things that we need to have clarified in order to tie up any possible loose ends in our case. First of all, can you tell me: who might have had anything to gain by your daughter's death?"

Estelle Lee's lips compressed into a rigid line. "How is that question relevant at this point?"

Barent looked at her sadly. "The defense will undoubtedly argue that people other than Bill Mose might have had reason to kill Sharon. We have to be prepared for that."

Sheila Hirschfeld leaned forward. "Nobody had anything to gain by Sharon's death. Nobody."

"I know this is difficult for you, Mrs. Hirschfeld, but please believe that I'm on your side. I want your sister's murderer to be brought to justice as much as you do."

"I doubt that, Detective. I seriously doubt that."

"My daughter is right," Mrs. Lee said. "Nobody could have had anything to gain by killing Sharon."

It must have been a nice view in the summer, Barent thought, with the trees all covered with leaves and the mountain laurel blooming. Not all cold and gray like now. He sighed to himself. Why did you have to hit people over the head? "Didn't Sharon have money?" he asked. "Her father was extremely wealthy."

The two women exchanged glances. Mrs. Lee cleared her throat and swayed a bit, then caught herself. Her hand, he noticed, trembled slightly and her eyes were puffy. Tea was certainly genteel, but without doubt Estelle Lee had been drinking something a bit stronger before their arrival. "Sharon had a trust fund," Mrs. Lee said precisely, "that was set up for her education. So did Sheila. Other than that, all of her father's money went to me."

"I see." Barent gravely made a notation in his notebook, then looked up. "Had she had any arguments with anyone lately?"

"Arguments?" Sheila Hirschfeld said.

"Disagreements. Fights. With anybody, anybody at all."

"Such as who?"

"You would know that better than I."

Sheila Hirschfeld shook her head. Estelle Lee stared out at the mountain laurel. If she heard them, she gave no sign.

"No," Sheila Hirschfeld said. "Not that I'm aware of."

"Do you know a man named Richard Kurtz?"

Again, Mrs. Lee and her daughter looked at each other. Mrs. Lee looked away without expression. Sheila shrugged. "He's a surgeon," Sheila said. "Sharon used to go out with him."

"What did you think of him?"

"I didn't like him," Sheila said. "He was overbearing and opinionated."

It occurred to Barent that Sheila Hirschfeld more than likely suffered from a touch of the same disease. "And you, Mrs. Lee?"

She shrugged. "I don't remember him particularly. He was a young man. Sharon went out with so many of them."

"Who was her latest?"

"Pardon me?"

"At the time of her death, was she involved with anybody?"

"I don't know," Mrs. Lee said in a faint voice.

"Mrs. Hirschfeld?"

Sheila blinked. "No," she said. "I don't think so."

Barent examined her face for a long, silent moment. "Are you sure?" he asked.

Sheila opened her mouth but no words at first came out. She swallowed, cleared her throat, and then said, "Yes."

He tapped his pen on his notebook and looked at her. She looked back at him without blinking. "Do either of you know a man named Jaime Ruiz?" he asked.

"No," Sheila said. Estelle Lee shook her head. "I never heard of him. What does this Jaime Ruiz have to do with Sharon?"

Barent sighed. "Probably nothing." He rose to his feet abruptly. "Thank you, Mrs. Hirschfeld, Mrs. Lee—you've been most helpful."

Sharon's mother barely nodded. Sheila frowned, then said slowly, "Call us if we can be of any further assistance."

"Of course." He turned on his heel and went out, Moran following.

They were back in the car and a mile down the road before Barent spoke. "What do you think?"

"She was lying," Moran said. "I wonder why."

Barent nodded. "Her sister is dead. Who does she think she's protecting?"

"Maybe her memory," Moran said. "Maybe someone else." Then he looked at Barent. "Ernst Gottlieb?"

"Ernie Gottlieb, friend of mine back in grade school; a regular genius with circles and triangles, if you know what I mean."

"Hmm," Moran said.

Barent chuckled. "Hey, she wants to talk art, we'll talk art." Barent looked out the window at the trees passing by and narrowed his eyes. "How much you think that stupid painting cost?" he asked. "A hundred-thousand? More?"

Moran shrugged.

"From what I remember, Ernie Gottlieb became a plumber. You think he makes as much money as Vasarelli?"

Moran grinned. "More than you and me, anyway."

"That is for sure," Barent said. He puffed on his cigar, watched the smoke curl up toward the ceiling. "That is for goddamn sure."

Chapter 17

There were over two hundred names on the list. After an hour and a half, Kurtz had gotten through barely fifty of them. Patient data was accessed under the patient's Medical Record Number. If all you had was a name, you could type that in and the computer would give you the number, which you could then use to get biopsy reports, lab results and dates of both inpatient admissions and office appointments—but it took longer.

None of the fifty had ever been treated at Easton Medical Center. Kurtz was not surprised. It had seemed worth following up but it was a long shot at best. He glanced at his watch—he barely had time for a quick lunch before afternoon office hours.

Kurtz grabbed a sandwich in the Doctor's Dining Room, sitting by himself in a corner, then hurried back to his office. Mrs. Schapiro sat at her computer. "Mr. Callahan is a little early," she said. "Ellen showed him into an examining room."

Callahan. Kurtz repressed a shudder.

He took off his jacket, slipped on a white coat, swiped a hand through his hair, straightened his tie and practiced a smile in the mirror.

Ellen Grunfeld gave a perfunctory knock on the door and entered. She was a plump young woman with light blue eyes, ash blonde hair and a plain face. She wore a nurse's uniform. "Mr. Callahan is feeling poorly today," she said, and handed him a manila folder.

Mr. Callahan, Kurtz thought, is a grade A pain in the ass. "Mr. Callahan is under a lot of stress," he said.

Miss Grunfeld smiled knowingly. Kurtz took the chart and entered the examining room. Callahan sat on the metal treatment table with his white, hairless legs dangling over the side. He wore boxer shorts with blue polka dots and a sleeveless tee shirt. His outer clothes lay folded on a chair. Kurtz glanced at his chart. Five foot eight, two twenty. "You've gained a little weight, Mr. Callahan."

Callahan nodded sadly. "I know you said to exercise, Doc, but I can't exercise. My varicose veins are killing me."

Kurtz had operated on Callahan for a lipoma—a benign fatty tumor—on his back over a year before and the man had nearly driven him crazy. "Have you been watching your diet?"

"Like a hawk. I've cut back on the red meat, no animal fats, no tropical oils, no salt, lots of roughage. None of it does any good. I'm like cast iron in there,

Doc—constipation like I wouldn't wish on my worst enemy. I got cramps almost all the time."

"Cramps," Kurtz said.

"Like I wouldn't wish on my worst enemy." Mr. Callahan repeated it with a brave smile. "And I think I got a hernia."

"Yes, you said so on the phone. Lie down and let me take a look at you."

Kurtz palpated Callahan's abdomen, feeling for any masses, then listened to the bowel sounds with his stethoscope. "Where is this hernia?"

Callahan pointed to the region below his umbilicus. "Give me a cough," Kurtz said.

Callahan coughed. Callahan's smooth, rotund abdomen quivered slightly, but that was all. Nothing bulged. Kurtz palpated the area carefully. "Cough again." Callahan coughed and Kurtz shook his head. "I don't think so, Mr. Callahan."

"No?" Callahan looked disappointed.

"Any blood in the stools?"

"Blood?" Callahan seemed momentarily bewildered. "No, I never noticed any blood."

Kurtz looked at the chart. The only trouble with Callahan was that he ate like a pig and sat around on his fat rear end dreaming up problems for himself. "You're fifty-six," Kurtz said.

"Fifty-seven in March."

"Have you ever had a sigmoidoscopy?"

Callahan's face brightened. "No," he said. "Should I?"

"Well, anybody your age should have screening for colon cancer. A sigmoidoscopy is routine; a colonoscopy would probably be better."

"Really? When can we do it?"

"They're usually done by the internists," Kurtz said.

"Oh." Callahan's face fell. "I don't trust the internists. You're the one who saved my life. Can't you do it?"

"I appreciate your confidence, Mr. Callahan, but I hardly saved your life. It was very minor surgery."

"But it could have been cancer. You don't know how relieved I was."

"I can imagine," Kurtz muttered.

"What?"

"Nothing, Mr. Callahan."

"Well, can't you do it?" Callahan repeated.

Kurtz stared at the chart, peered at Callahan's eager, beseeching expression, and mentally threw up his hands. "I suppose so, Mr. Callahan."

"Great," Callahan said. "When?"

"You need a bowel prep. That takes a little time. Set up an appointment with Mrs. Schapiro outside. The nurse will tell you exactly what to do."

"Thank you," Callahan breathed. He grabbed Kurtz' hand with both of his own and shook it. Kurtz extricated the hand with some difficulty.

"That's quite alright, Mr. Callahan. Quite alright. I'll see you in a few days."

By four thirty, the last patient had left, and by five o'clock, Kurtz had finished dictating his charts. Mrs. Schapiro and Miss Grunfeld had gone home a few minutes before. He locked the door, turned out the lights and walked down the stairs to Bill Werth's office. Werth already had his coat on. "You ready?" Kurtz asked.

"You bet," Werth said. "Let's go."

They caught a cab and drove across town to Werth's apartment, where Dina and Kathy were waiting for them. Dina came up and kissed Werth on the cheek. Kathy gave Kurtz' hand a squeeze and he glanced at Dina, who was looking at them both with a fond smile on her face. He felt himself blushing. Kathy snickered.

Dina Werth was a pretty woman, dark hair, dark eyes, thin nose and graceful neck. She was on extended leave of absence from N.Y.U. since the birth of her first child two months before. "Come on," she said, "let's get out of here before Junior realizes I'm gone."

"Who's with him?" Kurtz asked.

"My mother. She's in the kitchen, stuffing his little face."

Werth smiled and made a shooing motion toward the outside hall. They tiptoed out. When the door had closed behind them, Dina breathed a long sigh. "Freedom," she said, "Thank God."

Werth looked at her sorrowfully. "I tell you, she's an unnatural mother."

"Baloney. You try staying cooped up with a howling infant, you wouldn't last ten minutes."

"You're absolutely right," Werth said placidly. "But it isn't a fair comparison. Men aren't emotionally equipped to deal with babies. It's genetic."

Dina slapped him gently on the cheek. "Sexist pig."

"No, really. I'm a psychiatrist. I know these things."

Dina turned to Kathy. "Shall you kill him? Or shall I?"

"I wouldn't dirty my hands."

They caught another cab to the Garden, grabbed a quick bite to eat and settled into their seats.

The Knicks were playing the Bulls and the crowd roared from the opening tip off. The game should have been a slaughter. Jordan was long since gone, Pippen traded. The Bulls were a shell of their former championship team, but somehow, the Knicks were just not into it. They moved sluggishly. They shot poorly. By the end of the first quarter, they were down by ten.

"Looking bad," Werth said.

"They'll come back," Kurtz said. "I have confidence."

The second quarter went a little better than the first. Houston made a baseline jumper that hit nothing but net. Ward stole the ball, went to the basket, was fouled and made both free throws. The two teams traded baskets and then Camby muscled his way inside for a gutsy rebound and got hammered as he put the ball back up. He sank one free throw and suddenly the lead was only four.

"Look," Werth said, and grabbed Kurtz by the arm. "Isn't that Bill Cosby?"

"Where?" Kathy asked.

"Down there." Werth pointed to the expensive seats on the arena floor. Kurtz squinted, then stared. Huddled close together on the edge of the court in a private box large enough for eight, not far from a man who might indeed have been Bill Cosby, were two people that he thought he recognized. "Hey," he whispered to Werth, "what do you think of the blonde?"

Werth looked, and silently whistled. "She must be a movie star."

Kurtz gave a non-committal grunt and nodded thoughtfully.

At halftime the Knicks were down by only two. The buzzer sounded and the crowd rose to its feet. "Come on," Kathy said. "I need something to drink."

Dina sat up and stretched. "My back still hurts," she said. "And it's already been two full months. The little sucker better be worth it."

"See?" Werth said. "Unnatural."

They pushed their way through the crowd and up to a concession stand outside. The line moved quickly. They had just paid for four sodas when Kurtz heard a familiar, unmistakable voice say softly, "Hey."

He turned around, telling himself sternly to be casual. "Lenore," he said with a smile. "How are you?"

Harrison Thomas held out his hand. "Nice to see you."

Werth, who was standing on line with a wide grin on his face, gave Kurtz a pointed look. "Bill Werth," Kurtz quickly said. "This is Dina Werth and Kathy Roselli." He turned to Kathy. "Lenore Brinkman. Harrison Thomas. I met them down in Cancun."

"Ahh..." Kathy said, and smiled. "Cancun." She held out her hand and Lenore shook it.

"Where are you sitting?" Thomas asked.

"Pretty high up. You can barely recognize the players."

"The Company buys season tickets. We have the whole box. Would you like to come down with us?"

Kurtz hesitated. "We'd be glad to," Kathy said. She had been quite obviously examining Lenore, who had been doing the same to her. They both smiled, apparently liking what they saw, which made Kurtz, for some unaccountable reason, begin to feel an uncomfortable itching sensation between his shoulder blades.

They went back into the arena and made their way down to the floor just as the third quarter was about to begin. "It is Bill Cosby," Werth whispered.

Somehow, Kurtz found himself sitting next to Werth and Harrison Thomas, with Dina, Kathy and Lenore on the other side of the box. The three women kept their heads together and chatted continuously, occasionally looking over at Kurtz and giggling. Whatever they were talking about, they seemed far more interested in the conversation than the game. Kurtz watched them surreptitiously, but if they noticed him glancing over, they ignored it completely.

Camby made a spectacular dunk and followed up with a twisting, fall away jumper from the top of the key that bounced off the rim. Houston grabbed a missed shot on the other end and slammed it home. The game went back and forth for the rest of the quarter, neither team managing to gain a lead of more than two or three points. As the fourth quarter began, both teams seemed to dig in. The pace slowed, the defense tightened. The shots became harder and the passes crisp and pinpoint and the ball moved back and forth, neither team able to penetrate. With fifteen seconds left in the game, Chicago was up by one with possession of the ball. They inbounded. Sprewell jumped in and swatted it away. Both teams scrambled and the ball popped up, floating above a pile of jumbled bodies. Jackson leaped in and grabbed it. Under the basket, Camby waved his arms wildly and Jackson shot the ball down court. Camby jammed it in just as the buzzer sounded.

"Wow," Werth said, and grabbed his head with both hands. Kurtz let his breath out slowly and shook his head.

"Great game," Thomas said. "Absolutely a great game."

Kathy and Lenore looked at them with superior little smiles on their faces. "Men are so competitive," Lenore said.

Thomas, Werth and Kurtz exchanged perplexed glances. Kurtz scratched his head while Werth frowned up at the ceiling. Thomas shrugged. "We're going to get something to eat," he said. "Care to join us?"

"Sure," Kathy said. "Why not?"

Dina Werth frowned and glanced at her watch. "We better get home, before Junior drives my mother out of her mind."

"We'll catch a cab," Werth said. "Don't worry about us."

"I'll go get the car," Thomas said.

"I'll go with you," Kurtz said.

"Why don't you meet us on the corner," Thomas said to Kathy and Lenore. "Thirty-fourth and Broadway. I'll swing around and pick you up."

Kurtz and Thomas went down three flights of stairs to the garage. "Second aisle and around to the left," Thomas said. He wore a black trench coat and black leather shoes. His fine curly hair was neat on his head.

"Strange, running into the two of you this way," Kurtz said. "I never thought I'd see either of you again."

Thomas turned, flashed him a quick smile. "The company has season tickets for the Knicks, Nets, Rangers, Mets and Yankees. You never know when you might have to stroke a client."

"You and Lenore seem happy."

"Couldn't be happier. The wedding is set for June."

Kurtz nodded. "What does your father have to say?"

"He doesn't." Thomas smiled at him again. "This is it," he said, and stopped next to a dark blue Mercedes 560. "Hop in."

Thomas opened the door as Kurtz went around to the other side. The door opened. A gun pointed at Kurtz' face.

"You heard the man," a voice said. "Hop in."

Chapter 18

There were two of them. The one sitting up front with Harrison was tall and burly, with brown, slicked back hair under a black fedora. He wore a dark blue suit and a sedately striped red and gray tie. His gun pointed unerringly at Harrison's head. "Straight ahead and turn left when you get out of the parking lot," he said. The gun, Kurtz noted, was a Ruger .22 caliber; he hadn't seen one of those since he left the army. It barely fit inside the gunman's hand.

"What's this all about?" Harrison asked quietly.

"You'll find out."

The one sitting in back with Kurtz was smaller, very thin, with long, hairy fingers and a five o'clock shadow over sunken cheeks. He held his gun loosely in his fist but it never strayed far from the center of Kurtz' chest and his eyes never left Kurtz' face. The gun was a Colt .44 magnum. Small man, big gun, and vice versa.

"Who's he?" the one up front asked.

"His name's Kurtz. He's a surgeon."

The little one put a sour look on his face and rolled his eyes. "Where's your girlfriend?" the big one asked.

"Waiting for us on the corner."

The two gunmen exchanged quick glances. "Turn right," the one in front said.

Harrison turned and the headlights of a passing car shone in briefly through the windshield. The big car's engine hummed smoothly. Both hoods looked attentive but vaguely bored, as if they had done this sort of thing many times before. After his one question, Harrison drove without speaking, hunched silently over the steering wheel, staring straight ahead. Kurtz sat quietly in the back, studying the situation. The knowledge that he was a doctor seemed to have relaxed the little hoodlum, and why not? Surgeons liked to think of themselves as men of action but an M.D. and a loud voice wasn't much good against a bullet. Kurtz hoped he could take advantage of that. Meanwhile, the little gunman sat in back with a sleepy smile on his face. Once, he stifled a yawn behind his fist.

They went crosstown on Thirty Fourth Street until they had almost reached the Hudson River. "Turn left," the one in front said. Harrison turned the wheel and they drove downtown along the West Side Highway. To their left, expensive walk-ups gave way to small old buildings sub- divided into storage space and single room apartments. To the right, the Hudson River flowed to the sea, dotted with chunks of ice. Between the roadway and the River sat a row of pilings and empty, rotting wharves. "Pull in," the big one said. Harrison turned and went off the road, into what used to be a parking lot, the big Mercedes bouncing in and out of crumbling potholes.

"Drive down to the end."

Harrison grimaced. He blinked and seemed to have trouble pulling air into his chest, but he did as he was told. The car drove out to the end of the lot. Ahead of them, past the edge of a rusting metal bulkhead, the Hudson gleamed in the moonlight. To their right, an empty warehouse, its windows long since shattered, lay crumbling. "Stop the car. Get out. Slowly."

The big hoodlum kept his gun on Harrison's back as the door opened. They stepped out of the car.

"You too," the little one said.

The air was frigid but Kurtz barely felt it. A whisper of cold wind caressed his cheek as he straightened.

The big one motioned at Harrison with his gun, waving him forward, and Harrison took three steps. "Stop," the gunman said. "That's far enough."

Kurtz stood with his back against the car, his breath coming faster, his heart racing. Things seemed unreal. It occurred to him vaguely that the crystalline blackness of the nighttime sky, the rippling moonlight on the ice of the river, the decaying old warehouse might be the last sights that he would ever see. His thoughts moved in slow motion and the stars seemed to twinkle overhead forever. The little hoodlum smiled at him, a strange, crooked grin, like he was smiling at something only he could see. For a moment, they stood there, and then the big gunman reached into a pocket and pulled out a set of steel rings and slipped them over the knuckles of his left hand. He wriggled his fingers, settling the rings more comfortably, and then he stepped forward and delivered a long left hook to Harrison's face. Harrison cried out and his legs crumpled. He fell, kneeling in the dirt. A black trickle of blood oozed from his mouth and dripped onto the frozen ground.

The gunman reached down, grabbed Harrison by the hair and tilted his face up. "Tell your father it will be him next. You understand?"

The gunman kicked him in the ribs, then kicked him twice more. Harrison rolled weakly onto his back, his eyes slits in his face, his breath wheezing.

A clatter of gravel came from the wharf. Kurtz saw a quick motion from the corner of his eye as a rat darted behind a moldering log. The little gunman's eyes flickered. *Move*, Kurtz thought. His left arm snapped up. His fingers clasped the gunman's wrist, wrenched the little man's arm down and to the side, and snapped his elbow over Kurtz' raised knee. The little man screamed shrilly.

113

The big gunman turned. His eyes flashed in the moonlight and his gun came up and spat flame. The little man gave a tiny cry, shuddered, moaned once and went limp. Kurtz grabbed the pistol from his slack fingers, raised it and fired. The big man groaned, clasped his hand to his side and fell heavily. Then he rolled, scrambled to his feet and, crouching low, ran a zigzag pattern over the rough ground and darted around the edge of the building. Silence.

Kurtz' breath whooshed out. He let the little gunman drop to the ground and examined him quickly. He was dead. Then he went over to Harrison, who was lying on his back with his head twisted to the side. A single lock of hair drifted over his forehead in the cold wind. Kurtz dropped to one knee and put a hand on Harrison's neck. The pulse was strong. His breathing was shallow but steady.

The big Mercedes stood black and silent in the frigid night. Kurtz went over to it and opened the door. He leaned across the front seat, picked up the cell phone and dialed 911.

The CAT scan was negative. Harrison had briefly awakened, smiled at Lenore and then drifted back to sleep. Kurtz and Kathy stood next to her while Lenore stared at Harrison's face and silently wrung her hands.

"Well," a familiar voice said, "isn't this a surprise?"

Barent stood there, a faint smile on his face. Moran was behind him.

Kurtz snorted softly and shook his head.

Lenore glanced at Barent once without interest before her eyes went back to Harrison. Kathy stared at Barent with obvious curiosity.

"Any place around here we can talk?" Barent asked.

"My office alright?"

"Fine."

"I'll be back," Kurtz said to Lenore. She nodded without looking up.

"I'm going along," Kathy said. "I want to hear this."

"That okay with you?" Kurtz asked Barent.

Barent shrugged. "Sure."

They trooped to the elevator, not saying anything, went down to the Third Floor and took the walkway over the street to the Hampshire Building. The hallways were brightly lit but the building was empty. Kurtz turned on the light in his office, sat behind the desk and said, "Sit down."

Barent took the visitor's chair while Moran crossed his arms and leaned against the wall. Kathy sat on the couch.

"I thought you only worked homicides," Kurtz said. "Why are you involved in this?"

Barent grinned faintly. "I'm interested in bodies." He shrugged. "There's a body."

"I see."

114

"The dead man was easy to identify. His name's Charlie Flanagan. He free lances, but he's done a lot of work in the past for Tony Korda, which I hope is a coincidence that can help us."

"How about the big one?"

"We're not sure. Probably Jimmy Raines. He fits the description you gave, and he's been associated with Flanagan."

"I was lucky," Kurtz said. "He took his eyes off me." Moran smiled ruefully and shook his head in wonder.

"What made you try it in the first place?" Barent asked.

"Are you kidding? I figured there was a real good chance that I would wind up dead if I didn't."

"Didn't they say to warn Thomas' father that he would be next? You can't give a warning if you're dead."

"The general situation did not inspire confidence."

Barent leaned forward. "These guys are pros. What made you think you could get away with it?"

"One would think that you resented my survival," Kurtz said.

Barent said nothing. Kurtz put his feet up on the edge of the desk and stretched, trying to work the kinks out of his tight muscles. The adrenaline had almost worn off and his nerves were frayed. "The only thing that bothers me is that I missed. I should have killed him. He was barely ten feet away, for Christ's sake." This was not exactly true. What really bothered him was that he had been less than perfect. Kurtz knew it was absurd but it was the way he had been taught to think. Excuses were not allowed.

"Have you ever killed anyone?" Barent asked.

"No," Kurtz grudgingly replied.

"You were rushed," Barent said.

"I suppose."

"These guys were not expecting you to be there. They were expecting Thomas and the girl. They would have beaten up Thomas and maybe the girl also, and then delivered their warning. And we would never have heard a word about it."

Kurtz looked at him doubtfully. "You don't know Lenore."

"Don't be a dope. I know these guys. If Thomas or his girlfriend had said anything to anybody but Thomas' old man, then either they or the old man would have wound up very dead. You can be certain that *that* message would have been delivered loud and clear.

"And also, we can assume that the old man wouldn't have let them talk because if Korda, or anybody like Korda, was putting pressure on him, it means that he's involved in some business that he needs to keep hushed up."

Kurtz nodded, thinking it over. It made sense. "I suppose so."

Barent stood up. "Tomorrow, Harry and I will have a talk with Mr. Oliver Thomas. I'd like you to come down to the station house. We'll have you look at some photos. Maybe you can identify the other one."

"It will have to be after four. I have surgery in the morning and then some patients to see in the afternoon."

"Fine." Barent's eyes flickered to Moran. "Harry will meet you."

Moran gave a soft snort and fixed his eyes on the far horizon. "How are you doing with that list of names?" Barent asked.

Kurtz shook his head. "Nothing yet."

"Keep on trying. Maybe something will turn up."

Chapter 19

"So tell me," asked Liebert, "what brings a man to colon and rectal surgery?"

Kurtz gave Liebert a long, brooding look and then grudgingly smiled. Liebert reminded Kurtz a little of himself at a much younger age. The kid's cheerful certainty seemed somehow to be a rebuke, but a rebuke for exactly what, Kurtz could not quite figure out. Maybe his lost enthusiasm. Usually Kurtz enjoyed morning rounds but lately things had been coming unglued. The events of last night seemed unreal next to the easy familiarity of the Surgical Floor, but they sat in the back of his mind like a lead weight. This whole thing with Barent and Moran, Bill Mose and Sharon Lee and Tony Korda was ridiculous. He was a surgeon, not a cop, not an undercover agent. What did he think he was doing? "General surgery is more than just colon and rectal," Kurtz said.

"But it's mostly colon and rectal," Liebert said. "So why would anybody want to spend their entire career poking around in somebody's rear end?"

Kurtz shrugged. "It's a living."

"I'm going into radiology," Liebert declared. "I've decided that people are gross."

"Wise choice," Franklin said, "lucrative, pleasant, good hours, no worries."

"Boring," Nolan put in. "Very boring."

"Not to me." Liebert shook his head. "I mean, *this* is boring. Think about it; we're spending an hour and a half looking at incisions, prescribing pain meds, changing dressings, listening to people moan about constipation, diarrhea and urinary retention. You really find that exciting?"

Nolan looked amused, Franklin annoyed. "You know, kid," Nolan said, "you've got the wrong attitude. You're a med student. You're supposed to look eager, even if you think it's all bullshit—wow, surgery sure is amazing! You guys sure are great! Don't you want to get a good grade for the rotation?"

"I am eager," Liebert said. He gave Nolan a smug smile. "I'm eager to finish up surgery and start radiology."

Liebert pushed the chart rack down the hallway. They stopped outside of each room and discussed the case for a few moments and then went inside to examine the patient.

Mr. Benson had bladder cancer. The urologists had done a radical cystectomy over a year before and Kurtz had been asked to assist with the

117

ileal conduit, isolating a piece of small intestine to which the ureters would be sewn and then inserting the conduit through the abdominal wall so that the urine could drain into a bag. Unfortunately, the cancer had recurred and despite radiation was spreading into the pelvis. Benson was on a morphine drip. He was somnolent but every once in a while he let out a faint moan in his sleep. His wife, a thin woman with a narrow, bony face, who seemed to be here twenty-four hours of every day, looked up as they came into the room. "How are you today, Mrs. Benson?" Kurtz asked. He deliberately did not ask how Mr. Benson was. They all knew how Mr. Benson was. Behind Kurtz, Liebert shuffled his feet and the residents assumed a solemn manner.

"I'm fine," she said. Her voice was so faint they had to strain to hear her. "Thank you."

Kurtz nodded. He glanced at Benson, then backed out into the hall. Liebert and the residents followed. "How much is he on?"

"Morphine?" Nolan asked.

"Yeah."

"Eight milligrams an hour."

"Up it to ten."

"Isn't that awfully high?" Liebert asked.

Kurtz shrugged. "Depends on what you mean by 'high.'"

"Enough to cause respiratory depression?"

"It might cause respiratory depression, but he's in pain," Kurtz said. "I won't allow that."

"But ten milligrams an hour could kill him!"

Kurtz gave him a level look. "We don't let our patients lie there and suffer." He turned to Nolan. "Give him whatever he needs."

"Right," Nolan said.

Liebert gulped. He seemed about to say something, then thought better of it. Something that might have been a smile pinched the corners of Kurtz' mouth. "Benson is going to die," he said, "and there's no power on Earth that can prevent that. But he doesn't have to die in pain. It's all we can do for him."

Liebert blinked his eyes rapidly and nodded his head. The next room was Stan Nugent's. Nugent's problem was similar to Benson's, but not so far along. Nugent was seventy years old, skinny, bald and pale. His wife, a short, stout woman with gray hair and red lipstick, stood at his bedside. Kurtz had operated on Nugent for colon cancer ten months before. Nine months later, Nugent had returned with a bowel obstruction. Kurtz had taken him to surgery and explored him but he had closed without doing anything except a colostomy. Nugent had metastases to the omentum and the liver. He had been on chemotherapy for a month now, which may or may not have been killing the cancer but was certainly killing Nugent.

They played a little game. Nugent didn't want to know he had cancer. They talked around his diagnosis, employing euphemisms like "abnormal cells" and "probable cure." Nugent would listen to Kurtz with an avid gleam in his eye, his attention fixed like a laser bolt on Kurtz' every word. Kurtz had seen many patients close to death, and he had always been amazed—even awed—at the quiet courage with which most of them faced it. But a few got like Nugent: cross and demanding. They pouted. They threw tantrums. Kurtz felt guilty about it but he had come to hate dealing with Nugent. The man clung to life like a miser, clawing with all ten fingers, blindly and with willful ignorance.

"You're doing better today, Mr. Nugent," he said. "Your white count has stabilized." Nugent's white count had 'stabilized' at less than a thousand. He was a setup for every infection in the book, but so far the germs had not found him worth bothering.

"That's good, Doc," he whispered. "That's good." He licked his lips with a dry tongue and gave Kurtz a knowing, sly smile. "So when can I get out of here?"

"Perhaps in a week or so, Mr. Nugent."

"Good." Nugent whispered, and nodded his bald head. "Good." Nugent was much too sick for his wife to take care of but he no longer needed to be in the hospital. The floor social worker was trying to arrange for nursing home placement. When that came through, Nugent would be gone.

Kurtz patted him on his stick thin shoulder, and they left. Mrs. Nugent stared after them as she did every morning, with wide, beseeching eyes, but she said nothing.

They pushed the chart rack back to the Nursing Station and Nolan, Franklin and Liebert sat down to write the daily orders. Kurtz glanced at his watch. He had time for a cup of coffee and a donut before going to surgery.

"This guy Kurtz is some piece of work," Moran said.

Barent stared out at the midtown traffic. A thin haze of foggy exhaust covered the street and Barent imagined his lungs crinkling inside his chest, silently screaming for mercy. "Nolan told me a little story about Kurtz: it seems that he was in the Emergency Room a few months ago, examining a patient with abdominal pain, when suddenly this character in the next room runs amok. Nolan said he was a biker, shaggy beard, black leather, tattoos running up both arms, smelled to high heaven and weighed close to three hundred pounds. His 'friends' had dropped him off, raving out of his mind on Angel Dust. The biker starts screaming, rips apart a row of cabinets, then grabs a nurse and begins to strangle her. Our boy Kurtz hears the ruckus, comes in and calmly knocks three of the biker's teeth out. After that the biker got more mellow." Barent took a cigar out of his inner pocket, frowned down at it and then squinted at the smog outside. He shook his head sadly and put the cigar back in his pocket. "There's a lot of competition among the residents to be on his Service. Kurtz is a pretty popular guy at Easton. Have you looked at his records?"

Moran nodded. He kept both hands on the wheel and maneuvered deftly through the traffic.

Barent said, "Regimental pistol champ, marksmanship medal, runner up in the Divisional boxing tournament, first degree black belt in Tae Kwan Do."

"He was a soldier," Moran said.

"Hey, most people like to sit around when they get the opportunity, maybe relax a little. Not our boy Kurtz."

"A black belt is not much use in his line of work," Moran commented.

"Yeah? Don't forget the biker. And then he takes a gun away from Charlie Flanagan and chases off Jimmie Raines in the middle of a job. Sounds pretty useful to me. You got a black belt in Tae Kwan Do?"

Moran took his eyes off the road, grinned at him briefly. "Shotokan," he said.

"What the hell is that?"

"Tae Kwan Do uses a lot of kicks. Shotokan is mostly hands and arms. Legs have more power but hands are quicker. We like to think that we can get inside their guard and knock them out while they're still thinking about it."

"No shit?" Barent said.

Lenore Brinkman was sitting at a table by herself, looking tired and pale. Kurtz hesitated, then walked over, his coffee and a bran muffin balanced on a tray. "How are you doing?" he asked.

Lenore smiled at him wanly. "Not bad," she said.

"Mind if I sit down?"

"Sure. I could use the company."

The doctor's cafeteria was closed for breakfast. Not enough business at this hour. Even the main cafeteria was almost empty. A cup of tea sat in front of her, along with a Danish pastry from which one bite had been taken. She had circles under her green eyes.

"You should go home and get some sleep," Kurtz said. "Don't worry about him. He'll be fine."

Lenore sighed. "I know that." She sipped her tea and shook her head slowly, a sad expression on her face.

Kurtz put sugar and cream in his coffee and buttered his muffin. "Then what's bothering you?"

She shrugged. "I like your girlfriend," she said.

"Kathy?"

Lenore grinned, a brief upturning of her lips. "How many girlfriends do you have?"

He grinned back. "I like her, too," he said.

Abruptly, Lenore's smile vanished. A tiny shiver seemed to pass through her. "What did Harrison say to you last night? I mean about us."

Kurtz looked at her, his muffin raised halfway to his mouth. "He said you couldn't be happier. He said you were going to be married in June."

"Well, he's wrong."

Kurtz blinked his eyes. He said nothing.

"We're not going to be married in June. He was lying to you." She smiled wryly. "It's not his father this time. At least part of it is my mother, the way Harrison winces whenever he's around her. He doesn't act that way when it's just me; I've got blonde hair; I dress nicely. He doesn't have to think about the fact that I'm not eligible for D.A.R. membership. My mother, on the other hand, cannot pass for anything other than what she is. And she wouldn't want to. Harrison doesn't have to like her. Half the time *I* don't like her. But he's not allowed to be ashamed of her." She shrugged and let her eyes wander out the window to the cold morning sky. "He's a nice guy but a tiger can't change its stripes and neither can a bigot." Lenore shook her hair out and gave a sigh. "Maybe that's a little too strong. I don't know—but I know I'm not going to be marrying Harrison Thomas." She shrugged. "So much for love. Mother doesn't know yet. She'll think I'm a fool."

"I see," Kurtz said. Lenore's eyes were fixed on his face. It was beginning to rain outside; he noticed it with a part of his mind. A distant roll of thunder made the windows vibrate. "I'm sorry to hear that," he said.

She smiled sadly. "Are you?"

He sipped his coffee and thought about it for a long moment. "I don't know," he said.

"We're here. First Amsterdam Savings and Loan." Moran flipped down the sun visor with the New York City Police logo on it and pulled the car into a parking spot next to a hydrant. They got out of the car and took an elevator up to the top floor. The elevator opened on an atrium lobby with a vaulted ceiling made out of glass. A receptionist sat behind a small black desk, which was bare except for a white push button telephone and a computer screen. "Detective Barent," Moran said, "and Detective Moran. We have an appointment to see Mr. Thomas."

The receptionist looked as if she doubted it. She scanned the computer, frowning prettily and nibbling on her lower lip, then her face cleared. "Yes, I see. You're right on time. Please wait just a second." She picked up the phone and spoke into it, "Your nine o'clock appointment is here, sir." She put down the phone, said to Barent, "Go right on in. First door on your left."

Barent pushed open the door and they entered a corner office, at least twenty feet by twenty, with views of the East River on one side and downtown on the other. Oliver Thomas sat behind an executive sized desk made of dark oak. "Gentlemen," he said. "Please sit down."

The desk was too big to reach across and Oliver Thomas didn't offer to shake hands. Oliver Thomas had gray, wavy hair and a smooth, pink face. His suit was gray with a thin blue pinstripe and his tie had a flowered pattern in pastel pink and green. He wore cufflinks in the sleeves of his white shirt, solid gold ovals with tiny diamonds in the center. "What can I do for you?" he asked.

"We're here to discuss the incident last night involving your son."

"Ah..." Oliver Thomas nodded politely. His eyes wandered around the corners of the room. He seemed bored. "What is there to discuss? Two thugs kidnapped him at gunpoint and then assaulted him. These things happen routinely in the City of New York. Luckily, his injuries are minor."

Barent smiled. Harrison had awakened this morning. He had a headache but was otherwise recovering without complication. His mother had swept in during the night, wearing diamonds and a floor length mink, barking demands and making herself generally difficult. Lenore had yawned in her face and then ignored her. Harrison had slept through her visit and Mrs. Thomas had gone home, angry and frustrated. Harrison's father could have had no way of knowing about the warning that his son had been instructed to give him, but if Barent's suspicions were correct, then Oliver Thomas must have known what the attack implied without having to be told. But there he sat, as cold as ice. "Perhaps nobody informed you of the details," Barent said.

Thomas glanced at his Rolex and frowned very slightly. "Do you have any questions for me, Detective? If you don't, then I'm really quite busy."

"How long have you known Tony Korda?" Barent asked.

Thomas stared at him, an uncomprehending look on his face. "Excuse me?"

"I said: How long have you known Tony Korda?"

Oliver Thomas blinked twice, then looked down at his desk. A tiny dark line appeared between his brows. "Who is Tony Korda?" he asked.

"Tony Korda is a well known criminal. If you don't know him personally, you should know of him. Most people in New York have at least heard the name. You don't know him?"

"No."

"Think about it for a few minutes. Search your memory. You're absolutely sure?"

Oliver Thomas frowned. "I'm afraid I don't like your tone, Detective."

"I'm really sorry about that, Mr. Thomas. I wouldn't want you to get upset." Barent smiled thinly. "You're absolutely certain that you never heard of Tony Korda?"

"I already said so."

Barent sighed. "That's sad." He looked over at Moran. "Isn't that sad?"

Moran nodded, his face expressionless.

"Here's the way I figure it," Barent said. "You run a bank, not one of the biggest banks in the country but how big a bank do you need?" Barent shrugged. "He can't be simply stealing your money or you—as the man in charge of the money—would be screaming to high heaven. Besides, you steal money from somebody, you only get a chance to steal it once. And why kill the goose that lays the golden eggs? No. Korda already has plenty of money but what he doesn't have is a way to turn his money into *legitimate* money. I figure that the cash comes in and the cash goes out, and the I.R.S. never knows the difference." Barent slid the palms of his hands past each other and whistled between his teeth. "Clean as a whistle."

Oliver Thomas' pink face had grown redder as Barent talked. "That's slander," he said.

"It's only slander if it isn't true."

Oliver Thomas smiled. The smile went no further than the sides of his mouth. "It's only true if you can prove it."

Barent nodded. "The guy who beat up your son works for Tony Korda." This might not be true, Barent reflected, but he wasn't going to let Oliver Thomas know that. If Korda wasn't pulling his strings, then somebody else was. "You know what he said to him?"

Oliver Thomas said nothing.

"He said, 'Tell your father it will be him next.' Not too subtle, was it? Now why would Korda want to do that to you? Could it be that your relationship is not as cozy as it once was? Could it be that the sums of money that he is attempting to deposit are getting perhaps just a trifle too large for you to handle? And could it be that you are expressing this opinion to Tony Korda just a bit more forcefully than he wants to hear?" Barent shook his head sadly. "That's the problem dealing with a guy like Korda: once you start, there's no way to stop. He owns you."

"Nobody owns me," Oliver Thomas said flatly.

"No? When you were an ordinary rich banker, way back when, and these guys first approached you, you could have gone to the police and maybe got protection, but now it's too late. Are you immune to a bullet in the back?"

Oliver Thomas breathed a long sigh. He put the fingers of both hands together in front of his face and nodded thoughtfully. "And why would I ever get involved in such a scheme in the first place? What could possibly be my motive?"

"That's the easiest question in the world. Rich people are rich because they have a fondness for money. You can't have too much money. Besides, Lenore tells me that business has been bad lately. Hey, no need to be ashamed. It's happening all over. Everybody made bad loans back in the roaring Nineties. Why should you be any different?"

Oliver Thomas stiffened. "I told my son not to get involved with that girl. She's not our kind. And she has no respect."

"Respect for what? The way she tells it, you're a simple anti-Semite."

Oliver Thomas shook his head in disgust. "I see no need to respond to that comment."

Barent grinned. He spread his hands in an open, expansive gesture. "Hey, look at it this way. You were right: I've got no proof. But I do have enough to interest the Feds. Could your books really stand up to an audit?" He shrugged. "Maybe they can, but could your business stand up to the publicity? People lose confidence in a bank that's under investigation. Your customers frankly don't give a shit about your problems. There are plenty of other banks out there. Cooperate and we can avoid all that."

Oliver Thomas grinned wryly and for the first time looked almost regretful. "As you've already pointed out, Detective, I'm not immune to a bullet in the back."

Barent nodded. "True." He waited but Oliver Thomas only smiled. After a minute the silence began to drag, and Barent shook his head. "I'm sorry we couldn't do business," he said. "Give me a call if you change your mind."

Chapter 20

Jogging wasn't a lot of fun at this time of year. After a mile or so, Kurtz' fingers and toes no longer felt the cold, but his chest burned and his ears felt numb, even under the hood of his sweatshirt. Still, he did it. If nothing else, it gave him time to think while he accomplished something useful.

He had finished with Moran nearly an hour before. It had been a quick interview. "This one," he had said. The fat face looked a little younger, a little thinner, staring sadly into the camera, but it was nevertheless unmistakable. The guy must have really liked that hat. The suit—even the tie— was the same.

"Jimmy Raines," Moran said. He reached inside his jacket, got out a pack of cigarettes, looked at Kurtz and then put them back. He reached into another pocket, took out a battered stick of gum, removed the wrapper and put the gum in his mouth. "Pure chewing satisfaction," he said.

Kurtz shrugged. "It's your office. I'm not stopping you."

"For a moment, you looked like my wife. The guilt was too much for me to bear." Moran looked down at the picture of Jimmy Raines and cracked a smile. "I'll have him picked up."

So now what?

Kurtz jogged along the sidewalk on Central Park South. You couldn't push the pace too much on hard pavement if you wanted to avoid shin splints, but it was a good street for jogging, long, wide and straight, but not too crowded. Not too empty either. In the spring and summer, Kurtz ran inside the Park, but in winter, particularly at this time of day, Central Park was almost deserted and you were just asking for trouble.

He had run three miles already, two more to go. He reached the eastern edge of the Park and headed uptown in the fading light to his apartment.

He passed no one that he recognized. He thought about that as he ran. Growing up in a small town, you knew everybody. The sense of community, of belonging, was inescapable. You didn't have to think about it. In New York City, there were a thousand times as many people, and none of them belonged to each other. The City was too big, too anonymous—eight million people all scurrying about like ants in a hill, immersed in their own concerns. You had to have friends to survive in a place like New York, people you cared about, or you'd go crazy. Kurtz had always thought of himself as a loner, but there were limits, and New York City was the loneliest place that he knew.

He had almost died last night. He had seen death many times during his career as a physician but it was always somebody else, usually a stranger, almost always sick and old—except, of course, for Sharon Lee. Let's not forget Sharon Lee. Last night was the closest he himself had ever come to it. When Jimmy Raines had pointed the gun at him, Kurtz had not seen his whole life flashing before his eyes. He had seen Kathy.

Barent and Moran had told him there would be no risk when they asked him to help them. And there shouldn't have been, not to Kurtz. He was a consultant, a very minor player in the game they were playing. Last night had been an aberration, a chance occurrence of the sort that could have happened to anybody, its relationship to the death of Sharon Lee hazy and fortuitous at best. How many random killings were there every year in New York. A thousand? More? He thought there were more. He didn't want to be one of them.

He was looking forward to getting home. He had nothing planned for tonight except dinner, a brandy, some nice music and a good book, try to relax and go to bed early. He needed it.

"Richard scares me sometimes," Kathy said, and felt a rush of relief at having finally admitted it. "I don't like that feeling."

Dina looked at her strangely. "What do you mean?"

"Last night is a perfect example. He almost killed a man. Afterward, he talked about it as calmly as you could please. His only regret about the whole thing was that he missed."

Dina curled her legs underneath her on the couch and nibbled on a piece of carrot dipped in Blue Cheese Dressing. "Richard could very easily have been killed himself. Harrison Thomas almost was. Would you rather he had been?"

"No, of course not."

"Well, then?"

Kathy shook her head helplessly. "I look at him sometimes and he looks like a stranger, like somebody I barely know and can't understand. He's unpredictable. He has a capacity for violence that frightens me."

"Has he ever been violent with you?"

"No, of course not."

"Has he ever harmed or threatened anyone you know?"

Kathy shook her head. "No. It's not that."

"Have you ever even seen this 'capacity for violence' that has you so upset?"

"Just once." Kathy drew a deep breath. "We were on the way to a show. Richard hailed a cab. The cab pulled up next to us and just as Richard went to open the door, a man ran up and slid into the back seat."

"Then what happened?"

"Richard got a strange look on his face, not quite a smile. He said to the man, 'Excuse me, I believe this is our cab.' The man looked at us and said, 'I got here first, buddy. Get yourself another.' Richard looked at the man. Then he looked at me. He seemed embarrassed. The cabbie said, 'Come on, close the door. I ain't got all day.' Richard shrugged, reached in, grabbed the man by the collar and dragged him out."

"Really?" Dina coughed on her carrot stick. "He did?"

"He held him up by the front of his jacket, gave him a shake that rattled his teeth and said, 'You must have been mistaken.' Then he put him down on the sidewalk, held the door open for me and got in."

"What did the guy do then?"

"Nothing. His face was white as a ghost."

"I'm not surprised."

"The cabbie drove off. He didn't say a word. Neither did Richard."

Dina reached down, hesitated between another piece of carrot and a stick of celery, finally picked up the carrot and crunched it between her teeth. "It seems to me," she said carefully, "that Richard is not the one who's breaking the rules. In both of the cases that you mention, Richard only responded to provocation. While most people would perhaps have let the whole thing go, I don't think Richard was inappropriate. I think the character got just what he deserved."

"Who appointed Richard to give people what they deserve?"

Dina frowned at her. "Nobody wants to get involved. Nothing is anybody's business. Isn't that why society is falling apart? Well, Richard doesn't mind getting involved."

"No," Kathy said. "He certainly doesn't."

"Richard Kurtz is not your average wimp, that's for sure. Think about it," Dina said. "Most women would like that."

Kathy sipped her drink, a Black Russian. "Richard told me that he met somebody when he was down in Mexico." She stared blankly at the tray full of vegetables. "He said it was nothing serious."

Dina rolled her eyes. "Famous last words. Why did he tell you?"

"I asked him."

Dina made a clucking noise with her tongue. "I always figured if you didn't want to know the answer, then you shouldn't ask the question." Dina gave her a look of indulgent disapproval. "I told you to go along with him."

"I had to work on my thesis."

"Oh, sure."

Dina was right, of course. She could have put the thesis off for a week. The real problem was that she wasn't sure where she and Richard were going and even worse, she wasn't at all sure where she wanted them to go. *God damn it*, she thought. Things were happening too fast. "It was Lenore," she said.

"Lenore?" Dina pretended to shudder, then whistled between her teeth. "Tough competition. Where did Harrison fit in?"

"Harrison was temporarily out of the picture."

"Don't tell me: he realized that he'd been an idiot and rushed down to Mexico to win her back."

A tiny smile crept across Kathy's face. "That's exactly what happened."

"Men," Dina declared, "are absolute fools."

We're all fools, Kathy thought bitterly. Why did I ever get involved with a man like Richard Kurtz, anyway? Richard was fun to be with. He took her to the best shows and restaurants in town. He was the soul of consideration. When she discussed her work and her classes and her friends with Richard, he listened. He seemed interested. He responded appropriately. But she always had the feeling that somewhere deep inside, he was remote from the concerns that were most important to Kathy Roselli. Richard Kurtz was like a juggernaut, going along on his merry way, oblivious to the rest of humanity.

"Yeah," Kathy said. "You said it."

"What is this, for crying out loud: *The Father of the Bride?*"

Tears glinted at the corners of Denise's eyes and she stamped her foot in helpless anger. "Daddy..."

"What? What did I say?" He threw his hands up and looked beseechingly at his wife. "Is it a mistake to think that thirty thousand bucks might be a little too much to spend on a party? Jesus Christ!"

Betty Barent looked back and forth between her husband and her daughter. "You go and get ready for Paul," she told Denise. Then she smiled narrowly at her husband. "You and I will discuss things after din- ner."

"But Mother—"

Betty held up a finger. "Don't worry about it. Go out and have a nice time. You hear what I'm saying?"

Denise looked at her father doubtfully, then shook her head and trudged upstairs.

"Don't tell me," Barent said. "You're taking her side, aren't you?"

Betty was ironing. She held up a shirt, an oxford with narrow blue and white stripes and a solid white collar. "You like this shirt?"

"It's fine. Don't change the subject."

"Subject? What subject?" She took a spray bottle and moistened a pair of pants. "If you mean our daughter's wedding, I already said we'll talk about

128

it after dinner, and that's the last word I'm going to say on *that* subject." She fixed him beneath an imperious gaze. "You understand?" Barent stared at her, his breath coming quicker, then he caught himself.

"Fine," he said gruffly. "Just fine."

"You always get like this when you've got a tough case. How many times do I have to tell you, don't bring your work home from the office? It's not good for the family. Frankly, I blame Harry Moran for all this. He's been working with you long enough, he should be able to catch one little murderer by himself. Goodness knows, he's had enough practice."

Barent's brow wrinkled. He stared at her. She ignored him. "I'm going to have a drink," he announced.

"Good," Betty said. "Make me one too. A scotch on the rocks." She finished with the oxford shirt, picked up another. "On second thought," she added. "Make mine a double."

"So then she says, 'This is Denise's wedding and she's going to have the sort of wedding that she wants. Just remember, after she's married, she's not going to be your little girl anymore. She's going to be Mrs. Paul Janus. Denise Barent was stuck with you. Denise Janus won't be. You're smart, you'll give her the sort of wedding she won't have to resent—that is, if you want her to ever come home for the holidays and maybe bring the grandchildren along too.'"

Moran rolled his eyes and shuddered. "Oh, man, I can see it now. My little girl's only seven but it's inevitable."

Barent rolled a cigar in the fingers of his right hand and stared down at it moodily while rubbing his temple with the left. "My God, what a headache I have. Mrs. Paul Janus..." He winced. Barent had suffered from headaches for as long as he could remember. He had asked a doctor about them once. The doctor had said they might be migraine but were more likely to be caused by tension. He had suggested aspirin and a different line of work.

"It's going to be a Church wedding..." Barent added.

Moran looked at him and nodded sympathetically. Barent had grown up in a non-religious household. He had converted to Catholicism when he married Betty because it was important to her. Barent himself could not have cared less. But ever since Benjamin's death, Barent had refused to step foot inside a Church. He had developed a conviction that God was not to be trusted.

Moran drove along silently while Barent stared out the window, shaking his head every once in a while, feeling sorry for himself.

Finally, Moran said, "This investigation has gotten all screwed up, you know?"

"Yeah," Barent shook his head one last time and dragged his mind back into the present. "It's definitely ass backwards. We should have made these calls the day after the murder. That's what happens when you jump to conclusions."

They pulled to a stop in front of a small enclave of four identical brownstones set in a cul-de-sac, each facing outward in a different direction. Presumably the houses had been constructed long ago with the intent that they would form their own little neighborhood; they had the same brick facing, the same verdigris on the roof, the same six stone steps leading up to the front porch. All four houses were surrounded by a red brick wall and arranged around a communal backyard. Old mercury vapor lamps on bronzed fixtures were attached to their sides, arching out over the street. It was only four P.M. but the sky was growing dark and the street lights were already on, throwing a faint blue light.

Sharon Lee had lived here for five years before her death. Moran pulled the car to a stop by a hydrant and they walked up the front steps. The lobby was tiny; there was a gray metal door, two mail slots in the wall and a staircase leading up to the second and third floors, both of which Sharon Lee had rented. The downstairs neighbor, according to the lease, was named Mario Gilbert. All the landlord had known about him was that he paid his rent on time.

Barent rang the doorbell. There was no answer. Moran looked at him and shrugged and Barent rang again.

"Just a moment," a muffled voice said.

The door opened. A young man, slim, with soft brown eyes and light brown hair cut short along the sides and long in the back stood blinking at them. "Yes?" he said.

"Are you Mario Gilbert?"

"No. Mario is at rehearsals. Can I help you?"

Barent and Moran exchanged glances. "Who are you?" Barent asked.

The young man's brows rose. "Well, I could ask you the same thing." Then he shrugged. "I'm Ronald Evans, Mario's roommate."

"The landlord didn't tell me about you," Barent said.

Ronald Evans grinned. "That's because I don't pay rent."

"Oh," Barent said.

Ronald Evans folded his arms across his chest and tapped his foot while he waited. He seemed content to tap and wait all day.

"Have you lived here long?" Barent asked.

"Why," asked Ronald Evans, "do you want to know?"

Barent pulled out his wallet and flashed his badge. "I'm Detective Barent. This is Detective Moran. We're interested in finding out anything we can about Dr. Sharon Lee."

"What took you so long? She's been dead for three weeks."

"We were working on the information that we already had," Barent said.

"Huh." Ronald Evans gave a little snort. "Sounds like a fuck up to me."

"Look, can we come in and talk?" Barent asked.

"Sure, sugar pie," Evans said. He stepped aside and swept his arm down from his shoulder, beckoning them inside. "Come right in."

The living room was furnished like a Nineteenth Century salon, with antique, cherry wood stands and plush couches with deep cushions, a style that had always reminded Barent of a Nineteenth Century whorehouse. "Sit down," Ronald Evans said. He looked at Moran and smiled like a bird that has its eye on a particularly luscious worm. He sat on a couch covered with a floral print and patted the seat. "Why don't you sit by me, Sugar?"

Moran sat in one of the chairs, his face expressionless. "Could you tell us about Sharon Lee?" Barent asked.

"Well, she wasn't the friendliest person on Earth, that's for sure," Ronald Evans said.

"How so?"

"She had the nerve to call *me* macho, just because I told her to keep her hands off my property. Can you believe that?" He blinked at them.

"Are you by any chance speaking of Mario Gilbert?"

"Yes." Ronald Evans' hands began to tremble. His lips drew down in a thin quivering line and he seemed for a moment to be on the verge of tears. Then a sardonic smile crept across his face and he said in a normal tone of voice, "Though why he would be interested in a smelly old thing like her, I'm sure I don't know."

Moran stared at the ceiling, then the walls. He stifled a yawn behind a closed fist.

Barent plowed ahead. "Are you saying that Sharon Lee and Mario Gilbert were sexually involved?"

"Well, *involved* is probably too strong a word. Mario did seem intrigued, but when I reminded him that AIDS is most commonly transmitted through heterosexual sex, he thought better of the notion."

"I see." Barent rubbed at the bridge of his nose. His headache, which had receded for a little while, was returning with a vengeance. "So far as you know, was Sharon Lee involved with anybody at the time of her death?"

"You do like that word, don't you? *Involved.*" He shrugged. "I couldn't tell you if she treated them all the same once the lights were out but I can tell you that she spent time with a lot of different men."

"Did you know any of these men?"

Evans shook his head. "No."

"Would you recognize any of them if you saw them again?"

"Maybe. A few days before she died, I saw her outside with somebody. He was big, with dark hair. I might recognize him."

"Did you ever hear fights or arguments coming from her apartment?"

"No." Ronald Evans shook his head decisively. "Never."

Barent looked once more around the apartment, then his eyes came back to Ronald Evans' face. "What is it that you do for a living?"

Ronald Evans' eyes fluttered. "I'm an actor."

Barent grunted. "I would never have guessed."

Chapter 21

"So where are you going after radiology?" Nolan asked.

"Obstetrics," Liebert said.

"Give me a clamp," Nolan said. The scrub nurse handed him a clamp and he closed the jaws on a small bleeder. Franklin touched the electro-cautery to the clamp and the bleeder sizzled.

"I liked O.B.," Nolan said. "I almost went into it."

The patient was a fifty-seven year old with diverticulosis. They were removing the sigmoid colon. Aside from a few adhesions, which tended to bleed when they were lysed, everything was going smoothly. Kurtz held a retractor and let Nolan do the case. One thing about Nolan, he loved to talk. Kurtz himself didn't say very much during a case. Talking broke his concentration, but Nolan's hands moved with smooth assurance at almost the same speed as his mouth.

"Only problem was, I could never tell where the baby's head was at. I'd stick my hand in there, call out 'plus one, plus two' as if I knew what I was talking about, but it was only a guess. Funny thing though, I was almost always right. Unless everybody was faking it, which I suppose is possible. Still, it didn't seem too smart to go into O.B. if I couldn't tell how far down the baby's head was at. You know what I mean?"

"I guess so," Liebert said.

"You guess so..." Nolan snorted. "You ever deliver a baby?"

"Not yet."

"You will. Your first time, they'll stick you in front of some nice lady who doesn't speak English and is having her seventh kid. You won't have to do anything but catch it when it pops out. Just make sure you don't drop it."

Liebert looked at him with wide eyes and gulped.

"Pretty nurses up there too. They like medical students. You don't have a girlfriend, do you?"

"Not now," Liebert said, his ears perking up.

"Tie," Nolan said. The scrub nurse handed him a piece of suture and he tied it twice around a small artery. Franklin cut between the ties.

"Ask out Alice McMahon," Franklin said. "Alice has made whole generations of medical students happy."

Nolan guffawed. "Alice McMahon? A little old, isn't she?"

"She's experienced," said Franklin. "Experience counts."

"A little plump, too."

Franklin gave him a hurt look.

"There's a real cute one up there," Nolan said, "I forget her name. Peggy something. Try her."

"Ryan," Franklin said. His voice was frigid. "Peggy Ryan. She's married."

"Yeah?" Nolan cut through a segment of omentum, picked up a scalpel and extended the incision further into the pelvis. "I heard she got divorced."

Kurtz cleared his throat. Nolan looked at him quickly and seemed to get the message. "Anyway," Nolan said. "You'll like O.B."

"I doubt it," Liebert said gloomily. "O.B. is even grosser than surgery."

The scrub nurse, Kurtz noted, seemed a little stiff. The last thing Nolan needed was to get himself reported for sexual harassment. Maybe after the case, he should have a little talk with Nolan. It probably wouldn't do any good, though. He glanced at the clock. They should be out of here in an hour. Then he could finish up that list of names on the computer.

"Why are we doing this?" Moran asked.

Barent looked at him, stuck an unlit cigar in his mouth and chewed on it. "Stir the pot. See what comes to the top."

"But what's the point?"

"I don't know," Barent said. He removed the cigar, frowned at it and dropped it in the wastebasket. "I just know we're not getting anywhere fast. Frankly, I don't understand this case. I don't understand how things tie together. Too many things have happened that don't seem to have anything to do with each other."

"Maybe because they don't," Moran said. Barent morosely nodded.

"Excuse me, Mr. Korda," Moran said in a mincing voice. "We're policemen and we're investigating a murder that we think you might have had something to do with and other than that we don't have a clue. You mind helping us out here, maybe give us a confession and save us the trouble?" Moran shook his head. "Take it from me. We're wasting our time."

"Maybe we are," Barent said. "And maybe we aren't. And maybe he'll let something slip."

Moran snorted through his teeth.

"Okay, so probably he won't. So look at it this way: maybe it'll be fun."

Moran shrugged.

Tony Korda ate lunch most days at a place on the East Side called the Bangkok House, one of the city's best Thai restaurants. Barent himself was not a great fan of chili peppers, regarding people who ate food that was designed to hurt them as being slightly crazy. Tony Korda was reputed to love the stuff.

Korda was spooning a bowl of soup into his mouth as Barent and Moran walked up. Five men sitting at adjacent tables looked at them with open suspicion as they approached. Barent had never met Tony Korda, but he was easy to recognize. One side of his face was covered in pink scar tissue. The fingers of the hand that held the soupspoon lacked fingernails and were shorter than they should have been.

Barent smiled politely. "Mr. Korda?"

Korda looked up. "Cops," he said with disgust. His voice was thick and grating, as if a membrane covered his vocal cords. Korda shook his head. "Always cops. I'm eating. This can't wait until I'm finished with my lunch?"

"Sorry," Barent said. "We're in a hurry."

"Always in a hurry." Korda put down his spoon and looked at them. "You think you're tough guys, don't you? You come in here, disturb my lunch, you're not in a hurry. You just want to show me that you're tough guys." Korda picked up a snowy white napkin and patted his lips. "There are laws against police harassment. I got enough lawyers on the payroll, they tell me these things. What do you want?"

"Herman Delgado," Barent said. "Jaime Ruiz and Sharon Lee."

"I don't know any Sharon Lee," Korda said.

"How about the other two?"

"I know Ruiz. Delgado?" Korda shrugged.

"How about Oliver Thomas," Barent said.

Korda blinked at him. A thin smile spread across his face. "Who?"

"Oliver Thomas runs a bank. His son was assaulted the night before last by two men named Jimmy Raines and Charlie Flanagan. They told the son to tell Oliver Thomas that 'he would be next.' Does this mean anything to you?"

Korda stared at them. A waiter in a white jacket put a plate holding four small pastries and a bottle of Singha beer down in front of him and walked off without uttering a word. Korda's eyes flicked to the pastries, back up to Barent's face. "You like Thai food?" he asked.

"Not really," Barent replied. Korda looked at Moran. "You?"

Moran shrugged.

"I was caught in a fire when I was just a kid," Korda said. "My lungs and the inside of my mouth got burned. These things are called curry puffs. They're supposed to be hot." Korda smiled. "I can barely taste them. They make my lips tingle, but that's about all."

"You want to try some?"

"No, thanks," Barent said.

Korda grunted and began to eat.

"So you don't know Oliver Thomas?" Barent asked.

"Never heard of him," Korda said. "If I ever do hear of him, I'll give you a call. Right?"

"Yeah," Barent said. "That's right."

"You got any more questions?"

"Not at this time."

"Then you mind letting me get back to my lunch?"

"Sure. Have a nice day." Korda grunted.

Barent rose to his feet and Moran followed him out the door. "You enjoy that?" Moran asked.

Barent looked at him. "Shut up," he said.

"That's what I thought."

The pick up order on Jimmy Raines had so far resulted in nothing. Raines' last listed address housed an insurance agent and his family.

"Raines?" The insurance agent scratched his head. "I don't know any Raines.

"Honey, come on out here?"

A plump woman wearing an apron and a harried expression came out of the kitchen. A four-year-old child was clinging to her leg and howling. "What was the name of the guy we rented the apartment from?"

"It was a year ago. Who remembers? It was some realtor." The woman reached down, picked up the four-year-old and held him against her ample breast. She trudged back into the kitchen.

"Yeah, she's right. Of course it was. Yeah, how could I be so stupid?" He hit himself in the forehead with the flat of his hand. "It wasn't even a guy. It was a woman. Raines?" He shook his head. "Never heard of him."

"Who was the realtor?" Moran asked.

"Let me see now..." The insurance agent walked over to a bureau in the living room and began to rummage through the drawers. "Here it is." He held up a card, then handed it to Barent.

" Highland Estates Realty," Barent read. "Joan Gray, Licensed Realtor."

"That's the one."

Barent handed him back the card. "Thanks."

Joan Gray wore a pink polyester pants suit over a white, frilly blouse. Her hair was short, blonde and curly. A sincere smile seemed pasted to her round, pink face. Her skin was flawlessly smooth. She reminded Barent of a younger Shelley Winters. "Why, yes," she said. "I remember him very well." She smiled down at the picture of Jimmy Raines. "I rented him the apartment." She opened a ledger book and flipped the pages. "Here. It was nearly three years ago. It was a two year lease. He didn't renew it."

"Do you have a forwarding address?"

"No, I'm afraid we don't."

"Is there anything you can tell us about him, anything that you remember?"

A quick frown briefly marred the smooth perfection of Joan Gray's skin. "He was rather loud, and he wore a black hat. I remember that particularly, because it was summer and the hat didn't fit the season."

"Nothing else?"

"Sorry." She shook her head. "No."

The drive back to the station was silent. Barent was in a bad mood. He hated this part of the job, driving all over town to talk to people who rarely had anything useful to say. For awhile, after he had been promoted to Detective First Grade, he had let the younger men go out into the field and interview witnesses. He had found, however, that he needed to see people's faces and listen to their voices to be effective. So much of the job was talking to people, trying to figure out when they were lying and when they were sincere. He couldn't picture them in his mind if all he had to go on was somebody else's dry summary.

"Put out an all points," Barent finally said. "We've had nothing but bad luck and dead ends with this investigation. I'm tired of it. I want Jimmy Raines."

Moran looked at him with his flat, gray eyes and nodded. "Raines is from Woodmere, on Long Island," Barent said.

"I'll give them a call," Moran said. He shrugged. "Maybe he went home to lie low."

Nice place, Barent thought. When he had been here the other night, he hadn't really looked at the decor. It was open and airy, dark blue carpet on the floor, soft, orange vinyl chairs lined up in neat rows, a pastel abstract painting that was probably supposed to look cheery hanging on the wall. Piles of magazines sat on low tables between the chairs. A fat little man was reading a newspaper—*The Times*. He held it open, struggling to keep the edges from folding down out of sight. A young woman was turning the pages of *Vogue*, barely glancing at them. She seemed to have difficulty concentrating. She kept looking at her watch. A white formica counter set up beneath a window took up one corner of the room. Behind the counter, a thin woman with iron gray hair and a straight back looked up. The nametag pinned to her blouse said, *Rose Schapiro*. "Can I help you?" she asked.

Barent leaned forward. "I'm Detective Barent," he said in a low voice. "I was wondering if Doctor Kurtz could spare me a few minutes of his time."

Mrs. Schapiro's brow creased. "We're very busy," she said. "Doctor Kurtz is already running late. Could Doctor Ornella help you?"

"I'm sorry, it's Doctor Kurtz that I need to speak with. If he could, it won't take long."

"Wait a moment." Mrs. Schapiro rose to her feet and vanished down the corridor. She came back in a few seconds and said, "Come with me." She conducted him into Kurtz' office. "He'll be with you in a few minutes. Please sit down."

"Thank you," Barent said.

Mrs. Schapiro vanished. Barent sat down in a chair opposite the desk and waited. It was more than a few minutes, but finally Kurtz came in.

"Barent," he said. "What can I do for you?"

Barent removed a manila folder from his briefcase. "This arrived yesterday afternoon from the insurance company. I can't make heads or tails out of it. It's the list of Sharon Lee's malpractice claims."

"What's the problem?"

"I don't understand it. What is 'failure to detect amniotic fluid embolus' supposed to mean? And here's another: 'failure to monitor for the presence of placenta accreta.' I figured you could help me with this. You got any thoughts regarding 'placenta accreta?'"

Kurtz grimaced. "Sure. Let me see."

Barent handed him the list. Kurtz scanned it rapidly, holding the sheaf of papers by the edge as if afraid he might soil his fingers, shaking his head and swearing to himself under his breath.

Barent ventured an opinion: "Doctor Lee seems to have gotten herself involved in a lot of difficult cases."

"Are you kidding?" Kurtz snorted in disgust. "Medicine has risks. So does surgery. Having a baby is supposed to be a happy occasion but a lot of things can go wrong. An obstetrician in New York City pays over a hundred thousand a year for malpractice insurance, and this crap is the reason why."

"A hundred thousand?" *That's a lot of babies*, Barent thought.

"This first one," Kurtz said, "amniotic fluid embolus. Sometimes during labor, some of the amniotic fluid—that's the liquid the infant swims in while still in the womb—gets squeezed into the mother's blood. It goes to her lungs. It can cause hypotension, difficulty breathing and even cardiac arrest. It can be fatal. But there's no way to prevent it and no way to detect it until it happens, and it's nobody's fault. The patient was successfully resuscitated and she did just fine.

"This other one: placenta accreta. That's when the placenta grows into the uterus. Sometimes they bleed during pregnancy, but just as often everything is completely normal until after the baby is out and then you have to do an emergency hysterectomy or they bleed to death. Again, there's no way to prevent it and usually no way to detect it beforehand. Now this patient, it was her first kid. She wanted more kids and she's pissed off but what she doesn't understand—or doesn't want to admit— is, first, Sharon Lee saved her life, and second, her beef is with God, not the medical profession." Kurtz shook his head. "Or what's just as likely is that everybody understands it just fine but her husband or her mother or her lawyer think they can gouge a few bucks out of the system. "The third one—that's the one I was telling you about: the viral syndrome? Again, no way to prevent it. No way to detect it. The family doesn't want to accept that, they sue."

Kurtz shrugged and handed the folder back across the desk to Barent. Barent took it grudgingly and said, "Alright, thanks." He had hoped there would be more in it. "We'll see what we can do. Have you had any luck with that list of names we gave you?"

"I've finished. No luck at all. None of them have ever been treated at Easton."

"Too bad," Barent said. He gazed off into space for a moment, thinking. "Thanks again for your time," he said. He tucked the file of malpractice claims back in his briefcase and rose to his feet. "We'll get right on it, such as it is."

The patient with the amniotic fluid embolus had survived without sequelae and made a complete recovery. She had had one other child a year later, and had moved to Texas when her husband's business relocated. A notice of intent to sue had been filed with the court but the actual suit had never been brought.

The lady with placenta accreta was named Lily Schultz. She had also made an uneventful recovery after the emergency hysterectomy that saved her life. She and her husband had adopted a second infant and moved to California. The lawsuit they had filed was still pending. Barent called the plaintiff's attorney, a man named Jonas Morley.

"Hey, I advised against it, but the family insisted. I had a choice of taking on the case or seeing it go elsewhere. I figure we'll settle for a nominal sum." Barent could almost hear Jonas Morley shake his head. "It's too bad about the murder. You lose a lot of sympathy for your client when something like that happens."

"Yeah," Barent said, "it must be tough to lose a case that way."

"You being funny?" Morley said.

"Not at all. What do the Schultzes do?"

"You mean their jobs?"

"Yes."

"They're both schoolteachers. She's First Grade. He does High School Chemistry."

"They're still in California?" Barent asked.

"Sure. Sun and fun. Why would they come back here?"

"No reason I know."

"You bet. Anything else I can do for you?"

"No," Barent said. "Thanks."

The third one looked more promising. The suit had been filed by a couple named Carmen and Emilio Gonzaga, who lived in a poor section of

Brooklyn. The suit had fought its way through the courts, neither side willing to settle, and the Gonzagas had lost.

The infant, a boy, though barely able to move his arms and legs, had survived until after his second birthday. He had been brought into the Emergency Room at Long Island Jewish with a fractured skull, and had died. Child abuse charges had been filed against Emilio Gonzaga but were dismissed for lack of evidence.

Transcripts of the trial were requested and arrived the next day. Barent reviewed them quickly, hesitated, blinked, and looked again. A slow smile spread across his face.

"Something?" Moran asked.

"Take a look. The wife's testimony, where she states her full name." He passed the sheet of paper to Moran.

Moran whistled. "Carmen Rivera Gonzaga..."

Emilio Gonzaga worked as a laborer at a warehouse. Barent and Moran went out to see him the next day. The warehouse floor was a huge, enclosed space, with row upon row of metal shelving piled all the way up to the ceiling. The walls were corrugated aluminum. Men in hardhats, bales and bundles in their arms, scurried in and out of the building, while cranes lifted packages back and forth from the shelves. A tall man with a barrel belly came up to them. He carried a clipboard and wore a yellow hardhat tilted back on his head. "Can I help you folks?"

"Are you the foreman?"

"That's me."

"We're looking for a guy named Emilio Gonzaga. We understand that he works here."

The foreman gave them a doubtful look. "You police?"

"Yeah."

The foreman nodded. "You look like police. Gonzaga in trouble?"

"We just want to talk to him."

The foreman glanced down at his clipboard. "Come with me." They followed him to a far corner of the warehouse where a group of men ferried bales of foam insulation onto a flat truck. "Wait a second. I'll get him."

The foreman walked over to a thin man wearing jeans and a tight green tee shirt. He had a lean face covered with old acne scars and a pack of cigarettes rolled up in one sleeve. As the foreman spoke to him, he looked over toward Barent and Moran and shrugged. Then he nodded and walked up to them and silently waited.

"Are you Emilio Gonzaga?" Barent asked.

"Si."

"You ever hear of a doctor named Sharon Lee?"

"Lee?" Gonzaga frowned and said softly. "What for you ask me that?"

"Please answer the question."

Gonzaga shrugged. "Sure I know her. I hate that bitch. She killed my son. You here because she's dead?"

Barent frowned at Moran. "How did you know she was dead?"

"You kidding? I read it in the newspapers. You think I can't read?"

"Did you happen to read how she died?"

"The papers say some nut job strangle her. That's good. She deserve it."

"Sharon Lee was strangled on the night of December Twenty-Second. Where were you that night?"

"December Twenty-Second? Who remembers?"

"Try," Barent said.

Gonzaga's face screwed up in thought. "I played cards with two friends. Then I go to bed."

"Until what time did you play cards?"

"I'm not sure. Maybe midnight. Maybe a little earlier."

"Who were the friends?"

"Roberto Santana. Tomas Vasquez."

"They work here?"

"Santana does. Tomas a friend from the neighborhood."

"Was your wife at home that night?"

Gonzaga looked annoyed. "Of course she at home. Where else my wife gonna be?"

"Do you know a man named Tony Korda?" Barent asked.

Gonzaga shook his head. "No."

"Jaime Ruiz?"

Gonzaga reached up slowly, unrolled the pack of cigarettes from his sleeve, tapped one out and lit it. Smoke dribbled out of his nose and spread around his face like fog. "No," he said. "I don't know no Jaime Ruiz."

"How about Herman Delgado?"

Gonzaga frowned. "No."

"Carlos Rivera?"

Gonzaga gave him a slow, suspicious look. "Carlos Rivera my wife's brother."

"Do you know where he is? We've been trying to find him."

"What for?"

"Please answer the question."

Gonzaga shook his head. "Carlos leave home maybe a year ago. He say he going to Florida. We not hear from him since."

"I see," Barent said. He nodded and scribbled something in his notebook. "Now," he said. "Where were you on the night of December Twenty-Eighth?"

Gonzaga stared at him. "I don't know," he said. "I don't remember."

"You remembered where you were on the Twenty-Second. Why can't you remember where you were on the Twenty-Eighth?"

Gonzaga shrugged. "Some things you remember. Some things you don't remember. It's not a crime to not remember."

Barent smiled at him gently. "That's certainly true. Thank you for your time." He turned to Moran. "Come on."

As they walked off, Barent could see Gonzaga smoking his cigarette, his hands in his pockets, staring after them. "What do you think?" Barent asked.

"I think you're both right," Moran said. "It's not a crime to not remember."

"Have someone talk with Santana and Vasquez," Barent said. "See if they confirm his story. Some things aren't crimes." He settled his glasses more firmly on the bridge of his nose and smiled thinly. "Some things are."

Chapter 22

"Harry, how you doing?"

"Fine, Lieutenant. Just fine." Moran shook hands and sat down. He grinned. "You look busy."

"Yeah." The other man glanced at the pile of paper sitting on his desk and gave Moran a crooked smile. "So what's up?"

Ed Lipsky worked out of a precinct on the Lower East Side. Moran had briefly worked under him after graduating from the Academy but had soon moved uptown, where he had remained ever since. Lipsky was burly, not quite fat since a lot of his bulk was muscle, with a broad red face and a crooked nose. His hair, salt and pepper when Moran had known him, had since turned entirely white. "The record says you were the last one to bust Jimmy Raines."

Lipsky nodded. "Sure. I remember Raines. A real dirt bag."

"I was wondering if you might tell me a little bit about him: friends, habits, anything that might prove useful."

Lipsky shrugged. "Raines..." He leaned back in his seat and folded his hands above his ample stomach. "He pays a lot of attention to his clothes, wears a suit and tie, thinks that makes him better than the other dirt bags."

Moran nodded. "Go on."

"He's a crazy fucker, likes to think of himself as a sophisticated hit man. He uses twenty-two caliber softpoints. The bullet mushrooms, stays inside the target and rattles around. Innocent bystanders don't get hurt."

"Makes a big hole in the victim," Moran observed.

"They're supposed to."

"I seem to recall a James Bond character like that."

"Scaramanga. *The Man with the Golden Gun.*"

"You think Raines has seen it?"

Lipsky shrugged.

"Anything else?"

"Jimmy had a girlfriend named Linda Angel, a stripper at the Flamingo Club in Queens. Her real name is Sophie Glass but Linda Angel sounds better, you know what I mean?"

"Sure. Go on."

Lipsky frowned, thinking about it. "His mother lives on the Island someplace."

"Woodmere."

"That's right."

"We're already looking into it. Anything else?"

"No." Lipsky shook his head. "That's about it."

"Alright, Lieutenant. Thanks."

"Lipsky chuckled. "You catch Raines, you tell him hello for me."

"We'll do that."

Jimmy Raines stood on the corner of Bank Street and Seventh Avenue and watched the traffic go by.

Jimmy Raines had been busy. Jimmy did indeed think of himself as better than the other dirt bags. Jimmy was a professional. He didn't do it for the money, though the money was just fine, thank you. He did it because he loved it. Jimmy had long ago figured something out about himself—he liked to hurt people. Even more, he liked to exert power over them, shock them out of their middle class complacency, show them the error of their ways. The real world, Jimmy figured, was composed of only two types of people: lambs and tigers. Jimmy was one of the tigers. The lambs, they got up in the morning, ate breakfast, went to work, got home in the evening, had dinner, maybe watched a little T.V. They thought they were safe. Oh, most of them had an intellectual knowledge that violent crime was a fact of everyday existence in New York City, but every one of them thought it couldn't happen to them, not if they stuck to well lit streets and avoided bad neighborhoods. They didn't realize that a jungle was lurking just outside their door. Jimmy got a real kick out of showing them they were wrong.

The other night, that guy Kurtz... Jimmy had been pretty shaken up by the way things had turned out. Kurtz was a lamb. The lambs were not supposed to grow teeth. Kurtz probably thought he was hot stuff, but he wasn't. Charlie had grown careless and Kurtz had gotten lucky. Professional pride—and a prudent reluctance to leave witnesses—impelled him to show Kurtz the nature of his mistake.

Jimmy had been following Kurtz for two full days, biding his time, planning his strategy. It wasn't enough to simply bump the guy off. You had to bump him off in a way that would make him realize just how stupid and insignificant and hopeless his position in life really was. He had to understand that he was a lamb and Jimmy Raines was a tiger.

Jennifer Levy came streaking out of her bedroom, pinning her hair back as she ran. "Gotta go," she said. "I'll be late." Kathy, who had never been a morning person, sat at the kitchen table with a cup of coffee and the paper and stared at her, bemused and vaguely revolted by such a display of energy before eight A.M. Jennifer was teaching a class on 'Woodrow Wilson and the

Origins of the Great War.' Jennifer was always in a hurry and always on the verge of being late. The door opened. The door slammed.

Kathy drew a slow, silent sigh. Blessed quiet. She finished her coffee and slowly ate a cheese omelet and some home fries and by the time she had finished, she felt more human. The amount of fat in a meal like this was ridiculous. Kathy knew it but every once in a while she indulged herself. Ever since the events of the other night, Kathy had felt skittish, sleeping poorly, waking up every couple of hours from bad dreams that she could not quite remember. She took the dishes over to the sink, rinsed them off and placed them in the dishwasher, then went into the bedroom to shower.

An hour later, dressed and alert, she opened the door.

A big man smiled at her. A gun pointed at her face. She stared at it, seeing nothing but the small black hole in the middle of the barrel. She started to say something—she hardly knew what.

"If you scream, I'll kill you," the man said. "Shut your mouth and go back inside."

She shut it.

"Very good," the man said. "We don't want any trouble, now do we?"

"Beautiful girl," Nolan said.

"Yeah." Kurtz nodded. Her name was Cary Schneider. She was twenty-seven, an aerobics instructor. She had first noticed the lump in her breast while examining herself in the shower. At first she had dismissed it. Twenty-seven was much too young. It couldn't be, not *her*, but the lump refused to go away and after a few months of feeling it, Cary Schneider made an appointment to see Kurtz and now here she was, about to undergo a mastectomy for breast cancer. Kurtz was glad she was finally asleep. She had seemed in a good mood, resigned to the surgery, already talking about the reconstruction that would follow. She had laughed and told a stupid joke in the holding area, something about a duck with one wing, while the anesthesia resident put the I.V. in and then, all of a sudden, she burst out crying. The men had looked at each other helplessly. Kurtz said, "I'm sorry, Miss Schneider." It was all he could think of to say. He thought about taking her hand or patting her on the shoulder but it seemed somehow inappropriate. Luckily, one of the nurses saw what was happening and bustled over. The nurse didn't say anything aside from the usual platitudes, but maybe the fact that it was coming from a woman helped. Cary Schneider's sobs turned to quiet sniffles and then they wheeled her inside and put her off to sleep.

Kurtz picked up the scalpel and made the incision and soon the beautiful, quivering breast was lying grotesquely alone in a bucket.

145

"The lesion here is small," Kurtz said. "If you can leave the underlying musculature and not take the lymph nodes then the later reconstruction looks pretty good."

Liebert nodded while he held the retractor.

The O.R. door opened. A nurse poked her head in. "Doctor Kurtz, there's a phone call for you."

"Could you please take a message?" Kurtz said. "I'm busy."

"She says it's important."

She? Kurtz looked at the nurse, then frowned at the wound. The edges were dry, the flaps already sewn. "Okay, Steve," he said to Nolan. "Let me go get it."

Nolan nodded. "No problem. I'll just finish closing."

Kurtz stripped off his gown and gloves and then went out to the Nursing Station. One phone was off the hook, waiting for him.

He grabbed a cab outside the hospital and gave the cabbie the address. "And hurry it up," he said.

The cabbie looked at him with bored eyes. "Sure, whatever you say." The cab went infinitesimally faster. Kurtz stared out the window, seething, ticking off the streets in his mind as they crawled by.

"He hurt me," she had whispered. "He *hurt* me." Her voice had been almost incoherent, on the verge of hysteria.

"Call the police," Kurtz said. "I'll be there as soon as I can."

Fifteen minutes later, the cab pulled up in front of Kathy's apartment. He paid the tab, ran up the stairs and knocked.

The door opened. A fat man stood on the other side, smiling, wearing a black suit and tie, holding a gun. "Come in," the man said. He backed away, keeping the gun pointed at Kurtz' face. "Come in slowly. Close the door."

Standing by the couch, Kathy was quietly sobbing. Her face was puffy, a purple bruise beginning to form under her eye.

"Jimmy Raines," Kurtz said.

The man frowned. "You know me," he said. "That's too bad."

"So do the police. I've already identified you."

Raines shrugged. "It means nothing if you're not there to say it in Court." Raines shook his head. "The other night," he said, "you shouldn't have done that. It wasn't smart. We would have beat up Thomas, delivered the message, you would never have seen either of us again. But no, you had to get cute. You had to think you were a tiger, when all you really were, was a lamb." Raines looked honestly regretful.

Kurtz backed away one step. "You always use that gun?" he asked. "Yeah. What of it?"

"Ruger twenty-two. I'm pretty good with a handgun." Kurtz smiled thinly. He felt his heart beating, felt the air moving slowly in and out of his lungs. "Anybody ever tell you that you look stupid in that hat?"

Raines frowned. He blinked his eyes and looked momentarily hurt.

"Twenty-two caliber long rifle shells will go through an inch and a half of pine," Kurtz said. "Softpoints, maybe an inch or a little less. Which do you use?"

Raines mouth twitched. "Softpoints. People aren't pine."

Kurtz shrugged. "Whatever, a moving target is hard to hit," he said. "And you've got to hit two of us. How good are you?"

Raines sighed, shrugged and raised the gun. Kurtz jumped.

Kathy screamed and the gun jerked, just for an instant. Kurtz had not jumped toward Raines. Curling himself into a tight ball, he rolled beneath the kitchen table. He came up carrying it in front of him like a shield and charged toward Raines.

Raines fired. The bullets hit the table and mushroomed. Lead fragments and chips of wood flew in all directions. Kurtz grunted in pain and kept coming.

Screaming, Kathy picked up a lamp and hurled it, then she threw herself to the floor and huddled behind the couch. The lamp hit Raines in the shoulder and his aim momentarily wavered.

Kurtz slammed the table into Raines' gut. Raines fell heavily onto his back and the gun went flying. Kurtz fell next to him, still clutching the table. Eyes glaring, lips pulled back in a snarl, Raines staggered up and jumped for the gun but Kurtz grabbed him by the ankle and Raines fell across his chest. Raines kicked out with both feet while Kurtz desperately held on to one leg. Kurtz groaned and felt his fingers begin to slip but managed to bring his other arm up, got hold of the bottom of Raines' pants and pulled him back. Raines turned toward him and they grappled, rolling over and over until they crashed into the wall. Kurtz struck out with the heel of his hand, snapping Raines' head to the side, but Kurtz' right shoulder was numb and the blow lacked force. Raines brought his knee up into Kurtz' abdomen and Kurtz felt his grip give way. Both men wobbled to their feet, Kurtz gasping, Raines' eyes fixed on the gun lying on the other side of the room.

"Come on," Kurtz said. "Try it." Oh, sure, try it. Kurtz' head spun. He put a cold smile on his face, raised his hands in a karate stance and willed them not to tremble. He tried to look mean. It must have worked. Raines stared, hesitated, said, "Shit" in a disgusted voice, then turned and ran out the door.

Kurtz breathed a long sigh in the sudden stillness. He blinked down at the front of his shirt. The bullets had shattered against the wooden table. The table was peppered with deep gouges and small holes where fragments of lead had gone through. One fragment had lodged in Kurtz' right arm, another in his shoulder. The right side of his shirt was turning red.

Kathy was still sobbing, her face in her hands. Kurtz walked over to her and reached down to help her to her feet. She shrugged his hand away with a violent motion and looked up at him, her face twisted through the tears. "Don't touch me." Her voice was a hiss. "Just don't touch me."

Kurtz drew a deep breath, staring down at her. "Alright," he said softly. "I'm sorry." He stood there for a long moment, swaying. Then he felt dizzy suddenly and sat down on the couch.

Kathy's sobs turned to strangled laughter and then back into sobs. Still crying, she picked up the phone.

Jim Farkas was the plastic surgeon on call that morning. He met them at the Emergency Room. "Jesus," he said. "What happened to you?"

"A mosquito bit me," Kurtz said. Farkas looked at him doubtfully. "It's the middle of winter."

"It must have been a roach."

Farkas grunted. He snapped an x-ray into a view box and peered at it. "Looks like bullet fragments to me. Two of them."

"Amazing," Kurtz said. "Absolutely amazing what you can tell with those things."

"Superficial," Farkas said. He shrugged. "You'll live."

He said to Kathy, "Lie back. Hold still." She did as he asked. His fingers moved gently over her face. "These are just bruises," he said. "There's nothing for me to sew up. They should be gone in a few days." He shook his head. "I told you to drop him. He's bad news." Shaking his head and chuckling, Farkas walked off.

"The man's real funny, you know?" Kurtz said.

Three hours later, he was out of surgery and discharged from the Recovery Room, the bullet fragments removed from his arm and shoulder and sent to Pathology.

Barent met him up on the floor. "How are you feeling?" he asked. "Not bad," Kurtz said. "Not bad." He smiled. The room was swirling around him and he felt like throwing up but he was telling the truth. He sighed and felt himself sink back into the pillows, content for the moment just to be alive. But then he fuzzily remembered Kathy and all of a sudden his euphoria melted away.

Barent looked uncomfortable. He seemed to have trouble looking Kurtz in the face. "I'm sorry about this," he said. "I never intended for you to put yourself at risk."

"It had nothing to do with Sharon Lee or your investigation. It was just bad luck."

Barent made a clucking sound through his teeth and then frowned. "Maybe, but for the moment at least, your involvement with this case is ended. You've done everything you can, anyway."

"Really?" Kurtz felt a sensation that he had trouble identifying. It might have been relief but it might have been regret. "Just like that?"

Barent gave him a curious look. "What do you mean? I asked you to help. You helped. I'm grateful. What else do you want?"

Kurtz drew a deep breath. His head was still spinning from the anesthetic and it was hard to concentrate. "I thought I was a part of the investigation," he said.

"You're not paid to get shot at," Barent said.

"I'm getting shot at anyway." Kurtz shrugged, then sucked in air at the sudden pain. "Harrison mentioned my name," he said. "But how did Raines know about Kathy?"

"He was probably following you."

"But why do it like that? Why not just ambush me at my place? Why involve her?"

"Who knows what he was planning? Probably he would have raped her, robbed the apartment, then killed you both—tried to make it look like a random event."

"Great. That's just great. Just another day's work in the City of New York."

Barent shrugged. "Sad but true. Keep your eyes open, if you want, but don't be obvious about it. Call me if you need me. I'll be in touch if we learn anything."

149

Chapter 23

Santana and Vasquez confirmed Gonzaga's story. They had been together playing poker until close to midnight. Carmen Gonzaga claimed to have been sleeping. She had no idea when her husband had come to bed.

"Sharon Lee was killed sometime between three o'clock and five o'clock in the morning," Barent said. "He has no alibi."

"Sure," Moran pointed out. "But we have no evidence."

Barent grunted. "Find Jimmy Raines. He's evidence."

Linda Angel—or Sophie Glass—was married to a construction worker named Archie Borden and lived in a working class neighborhood in Queens. She had a crying infant in a stroller and a harried expression on her face. She said she had not seen Jimmy Raines in more than three years. Barent believed her.

Raines' mother was a small, round woman with curly gray hair and wrinkles around the eyes. She looked at Barent sadly. "Is Jimmy in trouble again?" she asked. Barent had flashed his badge as soon as she opened the door but hadn't said a word.

"What makes you say that?" he asked.

"It's always the same thing. Jimmy's always in trouble."

"Have you seen Jimmy lately?"

"No."

"Has he called?"

"Officer, the last time I saw Jimmy was three years ago. He was being carted off to prison. I told him then that I didn't want anything to do with him, ever again."

She looked sincere. Sad, but sincere. "Does that sound heartless to you?" she asked. "Do I sound like an unnatural mother?" She shook her head. "I wonder about that sometimes. But all of us had had it up to here with Jimmy"—she made a throat slitting gesture with the forefinger of her right hand—"I did my best with him but nothing worked. He was always in trouble. Maybe it's my fault. Maybe I should have raised him different. I don't know." She raised her arms and let them fall helplessly to her side.

"You'll let us know if he contacts you?"

She shrugged. "He won't."

Apparently, he didn't. Barent heard nothing from Mrs. Raines and a surreptitious watch on the neighborhood turned out to be entirely fruitless.

But two days later, they got a break.

Vincent Graham was tall and thin, with graying hair and a lean face. He wore tailored blue suits that fit him with understated elegance and he carried a black leather briefcase. Nobody figured him for a drug dealer. The staff of the Ritz-Carlton in Chicago were properly appalled, therefore, when Vincent Graham was arrested in the lobby with a briefcase full of cocaine.

Graham smiled a gentle smile at the plainclothesmen and sadly shook his head. He held his hands out for the cuffs and went along quietly. His lawyer met him at the station house and they immediately proceeded to deal.

Vincent Graham named as many names as he could think of, dates, times, places. He had a remarkable memory. One of the names he dealt was Jimmy Raines, who turned out to be living in a neighborhood of quiet apartments near the Lake.

When the police turned up at his door, Jimmy Raines looked through the peephole, said, "Just a minute," in a bored voice, settled his black fedora on his head, grabbed his gun and a packed suitcase from the kitchen table as he walked by, opened the window of a side bedroom and calmly climbed down the fire escape. At the bottom, he looked around. Nobody. He smiled then, and walked away, brushing some dust from his jacket as he went. At the mouth of the alley, a low voice said, "Freeze," and the cold barrel of a pistol pressed suddenly against his head. He froze.

Two days later, Jimmy Raines was back in New York.

He looked, Barent thought, like a stocky undertaker: black pants, white dress shirt, round sloping shoulders. The police had done something with the jacket, fedora and tie. "Harrison Thomas?" Jimmy Raines said, and shook his head. "Richard Kurtz? Never heard of them. You've got the wrong guy."

"Really?" Barent pasted a doubtful expression on his face. "That's too bad. We wouldn't want to send an innocent man to jail."

"Jail?" Raines looked pained. "What are you talking about? I've been living in Chicago for the past year."

"Chicago and New York are about an hour and a half apart by plane. You can live anywhere you want, but we have reliable witnesses who say you were in New York on January 17th and 20th."

"It wasn't me," Raines said.

Barent ignored this. "And that scab on your side looks a lot like a bullet wound."

"No way," Raines said. "I fell down and scraped myself."

"On what?"

"On the edge of a table."

"Sure." Barent shook his head sadly. "And then of course there's the gun with your fingerprints on it, but maybe you lost the gun on the subway and somebody who looked just like you happened to find it. Like I said, we wouldn't want to send an innocent man to jail."

"Hey, man," Raines said. "Give me a break here, would you?"

"Sure we'll give you a break—if you give us a break."

"I want a lawyer," Raines stated.

"A lawyer?" Barent folded his hands across his chest and leaned back in his chair. "You can have a lawyer any time you want one. A lawyer's not going to keep you out of jail." That was not necessarily true, Barent reflected. In this city, at this time, nothing about the legal process was certain. Raines could look the jury in the eye and deny everything—he undoubtedly would deny everything—and they might even believe him. You never knew. But it didn't seem likely.

"Look man, I don't *know* anything." Raines swiped a hand through his hair and suddenly looked like he meant it.

"No?" Barent said. "Tell me all about it."

"Charlie took the job. Charlie Flanagan. All we were supposed to do was beat up the kid and his girl and tell them to warn the old man not to fuck around. That's all I know. I was just along for the ride. I don't know who hired us. There wasn't any need for me to know."

"You don't know?"

"No. I swear it."

"And how about Richard Kurtz and Kathy Roselli? Anybody hire you to kill them?"

"Kill?" Raines held his hands out to the side. "What do you mean, kill? I wasn't going to kill anybody. I just wanted to give them a little warning, maybe convince them to keep their mouths shut."

He looked sincere. No doubt he had had a lot of practice. "Well, Jimmy, that's too bad for you," Barent said. "Because your little warning didn't work. Now, let's be realistic here." Barent leaned back, stretched, put a thin smile on his face. "I want Tony Korda, and I want Jaime Ruiz, and if you can't give them to me, then I've got no reason at all to cut a murdering piece of shit like you any sort of a break whatsoever."

Raines hung his head. "I want a lawyer," he said again.

"Yeah, we'll get you a lawyer. And good luck to him. You're going back to the Pen, Jimmy. You're going back for a good long time." Saying it made Barent feel a little better. He stared at Jimmy Raines' hang dog face and realized morosely that Raines wasn't lying to him about Ruiz and Korda. "Shit," he muttered to himself. Another dead end.

"How's the shoulder?" Ornella asked.

"Better," Kurtz said. "I'll be back in the O.R. tomorrow."

"That's good," Ornella said, and frowned down at a copy of the *New England Journal of Medicine* from April of 1978. "How's Nugent?" he asked.

152

"About the same." About the same didn't mean exactly the same. If anything, Nugent was worse, a little weaker, a little thinner, blood counts dwindling lower. "We're still waiting for nursing home placement," Kurtz said.

"At this rate, he'll be dead before he can get there," Ornella said. Kurtz nodded. He might be; and it wouldn't be the first time that a patient had died in the hospital while waiting to leave it. "How's your young lady?" Ornella asked.

"Fine," Kurtz said.

There must have been something in his tone because Ornella grinned and said, "Trouble in Paradise? Don't worry, she'll get over it. And if she doesn't, there are plenty of fish in the sea."

Kurtz didn't feel like discussing it. He hadn't seen Kathy since the assault. He had called her twice. Her voice had been cold. She had been reluctant to talk, but he had persuaded her to get together tomorrow evening.

Ornella looked around the lobby of the office suite and sighed. Mrs. Schapiro had already gone home and the place was empty except for the two of them. Kurtz hadn't seen his partner much lately. Ornella was scheduled to officially retire on March 15th, but he had been coming into the office much less frequently in the past couple of months. "I like the changes you've made," he said. "The old place looks good." The old place looked like a new place, which was the way Kurtz wanted it. During the past year, he had replaced the fading carpet, painted the walls and purchased the art, the white formica desks and the brightly colored vinyl chairs.

"Can I help you with that?" Kurtz asked.

Ornella smiled wanly. "No, thanks." He had brought in a couple of big cardboard boxes and was cleaning out his desk. Apparently he had never done so in all the years he had worked here. He did it slowly, looking at each piece of paper as he went, weighing it in his fingers, trying to decide whether or not to discard this particular piece of his past or to save it. He had already gone through the Nineties, the Eighties and the Seventies. So far, more pages had gone into the boxes than into the garbage.

"Look at this," Ornella said, and held it under Kurtz' nose. It was a ticket stub for a Rangers game from 1963. "I remember that game. Bobby Hull and the Blackhawks." He shrugged. "The Rangers lost." He hesitated, then shrugged, and carefully deposited the ticket stub in the trash.

"You sure you don't want it?" Kurtz asked. "You might need it."

"Hmph." Ornella grunted and continued slowly to skim through the fossilized layers. "You got any interest in a *Life* from 1957?" He held it out to Kurtz. Frank Sinatra and Ava Gardner smiled at him from the cover.

"Not me." Kurtz shook his head. "Maybe you could donate it to a museum."

153

Ornella gave him a sour look and dropped the magazine in the garbage. He turned back to the desk, rummaged slowly through the papers. He was almost down to the bottom of the first drawer. He had been at it for nearly an hour already. "Wow," Ornella said. "Talk about memories."

He held a faded white piece of paper out to Kurtz. It had embossed lettering on it:

Benefit Dinner and Dance to Celebrate the Opening of the Hampshire Building
7:30 P.M., June 24, 1959
R.S.V.P.

"I went with Lily. It was quite a night." Lily, Kurtz remembered, was Ornella's wife. She had died of cancer nearly ten years before. Ornella's eyes grew misty as he stared at the invitation. He carefully placed it in one of the cardboard boxes.

"I met her when I was an intern. She was a nursing student." Ornella shook his head and wistfully smiled. "I used to sneak her into the dorm. All of used to sneak our girlfriends into the dorm."

"What dorm?" Kurtz asked.

"The old Intern's Dormitory. Back then, an intern was an *intern*. We all lived here. Spent the whole year hardly budging from the Medical Center. You'd finish a night on call, then work all the next day and drag yourself back to the old dorm, ready to collapse." Ornella breathed a sigh and shook his head. "Man."

Kurtz thought about his own internship and shuddered. "Where was this dorm?"

"Right here. They tore it down to put up the Hampshire Building. Jesus, we all hated the place. We used to sleep in scrubs in case we had to run in. The phone would go off, we'd jump out of bed, run down the stairs and into the tunnel and across the street to the hospital. Sometimes three, four times a night."

Kurtz blinked. "Tunnel?" he said.

"Yeah. It was nice of them. You shouldn't freeze your butt off if you got called in and it happened to be the middle of winter. Thanks a lot. They put the walkways up over the street when they built this place."

"Whatever happened to this tunnel?"

Ornella shrugged. "Beats me."

"Tunnel?" Wellesley said. "I never heard of it."

"It may not exist any longer. Supposedly it used to connect an Intern's Dormitory to the Medical Center. This was before the Hampshire Building."

"I never heard of it," Wellesley repeated.

Barent tapped his pen on his notebook. "Who might have the blueprints?"

Wellesley picked up his phone. "Maybe Engineering."

A half hour later, Barent and Wellesley were in the office of the Chief Engineer, a man named Suzuki, who looked Asian but spoke English without an accent. "There was a whole series of tunnels back then," Suzuki said. "The main hospital was much smaller than it is today. There were separate buildings for Orthopedics, Eye Surgery and Neurosurgery, and of course, the Intern's Dormitory. They were all connected underground. See here?" The blueprints spread out over the table were yellowed and crumbling around the edges, but they were still legible.

"What happened to these tunnels?" Barent asked.

"Some of them were incorporated into the basement of the present building. Others were boarded up. The last one still in use was the one leading to the dormitory, where the Hampshire Building is now."

"Any of them still accessible?" Barent asked.

Suzuki frowned. "Maybe," he said.

Barent smiled at Wellesley. "Let's go see."

It was easy to see why the police had missed the tunnel entrance when they searched the place after Sharon Lee's murder. It looked like a ventilation grate, tucked away in a far corner of the deepest layer of the sub-basement. A Yale lock held it tightly to the floor in the corner of a storage room filled with antique pieces of medical equipment. Barent recognized an iron lung and two bullet shaped devices that were probably obsolete EKG monitors. A ghoulish contraption that looked like an electric chair sat in a corner. "What's that thing for?" he asked.

Robinson frowned at it, his jowls quivering. "I think they used it for electroconvulsive therapy."

Barent shivered and Robinson gave him a peevish look. Robinson had insisted on coming along but was evidently hoping that the search proved a dead end. From Robinson's point of view, nothing to do with this case was going to help the bottom line and he just wanted it to all be over with and disappear.

Suzuki held the blueprint up to the dim light. "This is definitely it," he said. They stared at each other. Barent wordlessly gestured to Suzuki, who stepped forward with a set of keys. The second key seemed to fit the lock but would not turn the bolt. The fifth key, however, slid right in and the lock clicked open. Harry Moran and Arnie Figueroa put on gloves, grasped

155

the heavy steel frame and lifted. The grate resisted for a moment, then rose upward and slid to the side.

"Bingo," Barent said.

Chapter 24

"So okay," Barent said, "It was a dead end. So sue me."

Moran seemed to be having difficulty repressing a smile. The grating had concealed a set of concrete steps, which led down to a molding wooden door. The door swung open at a touch. On the other side of the door, a long, gloomy tunnel, walls and floor constructed of unpainted concrete, curved away to their left.

Suzuki held a lantern up and squinted at the blueprints. "This leads under the playground, toward the Administration Building," he said.

Barent looked at Moran, who shrugged.

Robinson glanced at his watch and frowned.

"Let's see," Barent said. The tunnel was large enough for two people to walk together. The air smelled moldy and damp. After a few hundred feet, the tunnel branched.

"Which way?" Barent asked.

Suzuki shook his head. "Beats me."

"Forget it," Barent said. "Let's get a team down here. They'll know what to look for."

Within an hour, the tunnels had been thoroughly searched. As Suzuki had told them, they crossed the entire grounds of the Medical Center in a connecting web. The branch that had once led across the street to the old Intern's Dorm had long since been filled in. In one isolated branch, huddled against the wall, they found a dusty old blanket, four empty bottles of Grolsch beer and an antique, desiccated condom (Later, when informed of the condom, Edward Ornella at first frowned, then shrugged and slowly smiled.). And that was all. Nothing to indicate that Bill Mose, Herman Delgado or anybody else had been down here in the past 30 years.

Barent believed in the virtues of serendipity, in luck both good and bad. Barent believed that if you scratched at a problem long enough, if you turned over enough rocks, then sooner or later the bugs would scurry out into the light and expose themselves. You had to be persistent. You had to keep digging.

When bewildered by a case, Barent always returned to the victim. The victim, after all, was the focus. The victim, whether she knew it or not, contained the key to every crime. Barent had interviewed many survivors of attempted murder. He had always been struck by the fact that the victims were almost never surprised by the attack; they understood it, and in a strange way, almost accepted it. You had to know the victim.

Barent did not understand Sharon Lee. She seemed to have lived her life almost without touching other people. Even her best friends hardly knew her. Evelyn Hobbs, Joyce Davenport, Jennifer Parks...he had called them as Kurtz had suggested. They had no clue. Evelyn Hobbs was a buyer for an importing firm and had spent most of the past six months in Paris and Hong Kong. Jennifer Parks claimed to have seen Sharon Lee no more than three times in the past year. Perhaps the fact that they were both doctors explained it. Jennifer Parks had a schedule that would have exhausted most men, with office hours for eight to ten hours each day, a husband and two children to take care of. Joyce Davenport had gotten married and moved to Seattle over a year ago. She had nothing to offer.

Alice McMahon, Peggy Ryan, Rita Mendez...forget it. Nolan, Stills, Franklin, Farkas, Werth...Barent had interviewed over fifty members of the hospital staff during the course of this investigation. Almost all of them seemed like perfectly nice people, which of course meant nothing in itself since murderers quite often appeared to be nice people except for the fact that now and then they killed somebody. If any one of them had possessed a motive to kill Sharon Lee, Barent had been unable to discover it.

Barent sat in the cool darkness of his office and thought about Sharon Lee.

Two weeks ago, shortly after the robbery that may or may not have been committed by Herman Delgado, Barent had gone to Sharon Lee's apartment.

He had of course been there shortly following the murder, but at that time the place had been mobbed with uniformed policemen and technicians from the crime lab. It had been hard to think. Now it was quiet. Now he could stand in the center of the apartment and try to get a feel for the essence of the dead woman.

A stack of cartons stood in the corner, half filled with clothing already removed by her sister from the dresser drawers. The artwork was "modern" but indistinct. It looked quite a bit like the stuff hanging in Kurtz' office, pastel, pretty and boring (not that Barent considered himself an expert on art, his old pal Ernie Gottlieb notwithstanding). The place was neat. A book of Erte prints and another book of photographs by Annie Liebovitz sat out on the coffee table. A baby grand piano stood in one corner. Barent hit middle C and winced. The piano needed to be tuned.

Sharon Lee had left no scrapbooks, no photo albums, no mementos hanging on the walls, no little trophies brought back from trips to Greece or Puerto Rico or Spain. A small stack of opened mail lay on the kitchen table, all advertisements and bills. Impersonal, that was the impression: neat, clean, sterile...except for one thing, one small touch of humanity: a framed photograph sat under a lamp on a table next to the couch: a picture of Sharon Lee and her sister, arms around each other by the sea, laughing.

Barent nodded to himself, rose to his feet and grabbed the keys to his car.

An hour later, he pulled the car into the driveway of the Lee household and parked. The same plump maid answered the door. "Is Mrs. Hirschfeld at home?" Barent asked. He held out his badge.

The maid's eyes flicked to the badge, then up to Barent's face. "Please come in," she said.

Barent waited in the foyer, peering up as he had before at the Vasarelli painting above the second story landing. He heard a clatter of heels on the tile floor and turned. Sheila Hirschfeld stood there. "Detective...?"

"Barent," he said.

"Yes, of course," she said quickly. "I hadn't expected to see you again." She bit her lip and flushed, evidently realizing how this sounded.

"I felt that we needed to talk."

She stared at him. "Oh? What about?"

"Can we sit down, Mrs. Hirschfeld?"

Barent looked at her with a grave expression on his face. After a moment, she looked away. "Yes, of course," she said again. "Come with me."

She led him back to the same garden room they had sat in before. This time, there was no tea. She sat on the edge of a cushioned hassock, clasped her knees tightly together and looked at him without speaking. Barent took the chair across from her.

"How is your mother?" he asked.

"She's fine."

"Is she at home?"

"Yes, but she's resting." Barent nodded.

"That's good," he said. "It's better if we speak alone."

She stared at him. "Why do you say that?" she asked. Her voice was little louder than a whisper.

"I felt that you would be more candid with me if we were alone." Barent looked at her and lifted one eyebrow.

She seemed about to say something but the words would not come out. She cleared her throat. Barent waited.

"What do you mean?" she finally asked. Amazing, Barent thought, how they always asked that.

"Detective Moran and I both had a strong feeling that you knew more than you were telling us."

Her lips thinned. She was offended. They always got offended, especially if they were lying. "I can't imagine what you're talking about."

159

Barent shook his head and allowed his lips to curl ever so slightly. "When Detective Moran and I were here last, you seemed reluctant to speak, particularly when the subject of your sister's romantic involvements came up."

She stared at him. Slowly, one hand rose, the fingers coming to rest ever so gently on her throat.

"The fact is," Barent said, "that we have acquired evidence strongly suggesting that someone other than Bill Mose may have murdered your sister."

She swallowed, her eyes still fixed on Barent's face.

"You said that you spoke to your sister often, I think you said at least once a week."

"That's right," Sheila said, and gave a tiny nod of her head.

"It's been stated by a number of witnesses that your sister was involved with someone at the time of her death. Yet no one has been able to tell us who that person might have been, and no one has stepped forward. Can you tell me, Mrs. Hirschfeld?"

"No." Barent could barely hear her.

"You can't tell? Or you won't tell?"

Sheila shook her head and gave a nervous little laugh. Her posture was hunched and defensive, the expression on her face, faintly disdainful. "When I thought that you had arrested the man who killed her, I saw no point in dragging Sharon's good name through the mud. This changes things." She frowned, staring out the window at the line of shrubs by the edge of the woods, and looked back at Barent. "I can't tell you. I don't know his name. All I know is that he's married."

"I see." Barent nodded slowly. "Can you tell me anything else about him. Did she describe him in any way?"

Sheila hesitated. "You had to know my sister, Lieutenant. She... had a thing about men. She collected them. My sister was very good looking, even beautiful. She was intelligent and dedicated to her work. But somehow, she had a lifelong struggle with her own self-esteem. She needed constant affirmation of her attractiveness and worth. I think the fact that this last one was married only added to the appeal for her. It takes a real woman, after all, to steal a man away from someone else."

"She never mentioned a name? She never described him?"

"No." Sheila shook her head. "Never." She added, "I disapproved. I told her so. After that, she was reluctant to talk and frankly, I didn't want to hear about it."

"Did she mention where she met him? Or what he did?"

"She did talk about meeting him secretly. I had the impression that the people she worked with knew him and would recognize them together. I assumed he was another doctor, but I don't know that for certain."

Her face was downcast, and Barent felt a pang of guilt. It wasn't pleasant having to drag people back through things that they would rather forget. "Thank you, Mrs. Hirschfeld," he said.

She nodded her head, staring out the window at the frozen ground. "If you think of anything else that might help us, please give me a call."

She shrugged. "Of course."

A bank of high, rolling clouds obscured the full moon outside. It looked like it might rain. They could dimly see a barge floating past on the East River. A searchlight funneled upward from somewhere on the Brooklyn shore.

Kathy sat slumped on the couch in Kurtz' living room. She seemed to have difficulty looking him in the eye. An open bottle of champagne sat on the coffee table. Kathy fingered her glass and every once in a while took a tiny sip. She touched the bruises on her face with the tip of a finger and grimaced. "Why aren't you angry with me?" she asked.

"Angry?" Kurtz blinked at her. "Why should I be angry?"

She gave him a dull, guarded look. "I betrayed you. I lured you into coming to my apartment and you were almost killed."

This, of course, was true; but Kurtz had long ago learned when to slug it out and when to roll with the punches. By now, considering that they were both alive and relatively unhurt, Jimmy Raines and everything to do with him was water under the bridge. At least, he hoped so. "What else could you do?" he said. "You had no choice."

She set her lips into a mulish line. "I could have refused."

"And what then? He had already hit you." Kurtz shook his head. "You had no choice," he repeated. "There is no way that you could have refused."

"I was so *scared!*" she said, and suddenly she was crying.

He took the glass from her and set it on the table. "Come on," he said. "Don't do that." Gently, he took her in his arms and she clung to him, sobbing. After a while, her sobs grew quiet and after a few final sniffles, they ceased.

Her face still buried against his chest, she said, "I can't see you anymore."

Just like that. *I can't see you anymore.* He opened his mouth and then closed it. "Oh," he finally said.

She pulled away from him and huddled in the corner of the couch, looking miserable. "Maybe it won't be forever," she said. "Maybe just for a while. We're very different sorts of people, you and I. You're so certain about things." She shook her head, looking forlorn. "I need some time to think."

"I'm certain about things..." Kurtz sighed. Absently, he noted that it had begun to rain. "I wish I were," he said, "but I'm not certain of anything. Anything at all."

She blinked at him, then looked away.

"You're blaming me for what happened. Aren't you? That's not fair."

"Maybe it's not," she said sadly. "But it's the way that I feel."

He stared at her, frustrated and helpless. She meant it. He could see that. It was *his* fault some cold-blooded bastard had paid to have Harrison Thomas assaulted. It was *his* fault that a lunatic assassin had decided to hunt them both down.

And was it also his fault that drug addiction and poverty and ignorance and hate led people to kill each other on the street? And Sharon Lee, was that his fault, too? Maybe it was, he thought. Maybe if he had never met Sharon, maybe if he had never broken up with her, her sad life would have turned out differently. Maybe if Sharon Lee had never been born, then she would never have been killed. Yeah, it was her mother's fault. Her mother's fault all the way.

"I don't accept that," Kurtz said.

"I know you don't. That's why I can't see you anymore."

Chapter 25

The next morning, a Ford minivan rolled up across the street from the Hampshire Building and parked in an empty space by a hydrant, where it stayed for the next twelve hours. At three o'clock, a foot patrolman walked by, wrote out a parking ticket and tucked it under the wiper on the front windshield. Then he walked off. At five o'clock, people began to stream out of the building. By seven, the place was deserted, with all the lights off and the front doors locked. At eight, the van's engine started up and it pulled away from the curb.

Easton, like most hospitals, published a staff directory, with colorful, brightly smiling pictures of every physician associated with the institution. Barent and Moran had taken the directory down to Bank Street, hoping that it might jog the memory of Mario Gilbert or Ronald Evans. "Why, gentlemen," Ronald Evans had said with a bright smile, "how nice to see you again."

"Can we come in?" Barent asked.

"But of course." Ronald Evans fluttered his lashes at Moran. "Will you sit next to me this time, Sugar?"

Moran gave Ronald Evans a brief, meaningless smile as they entered the apartment. A thin young man with deep set green eyes and black curling hair sat in a chair in the living room, listening to something classical on the stereo. He gave the detectives a questioning look and rose to his feet. "Mario," Ronald Evans said, "these are the policemen that I told you about. Detective Barent and Detective Moran."

Mario Gilbert glanced warily from one of them to another but held out a hand to shake. His grip was firm. "Nice to meet you," he said. "What's up?"

"Mr. Evans has told you about our previous visit?"

"Of course. You're investigating Sharon Lee's murder."

"Yes. We were particularly interested in knowing who her friends were."

"Friends?" Mario Gilbert narrowed his eyes. "I assume you mean boyfriends."

"Boyfriends, girlfriends." Barent shrugged. "Anyone she might have spent time with."

"Isn't the big one luscious?" Ronald Evans blinked at Moran and licked his lips. Moran ignored him. Mario Gilbert frowned.

"I mean, did you ever see such muscles in your life? Yum!"

Mario gave Ronald a sour look. "Ronald likes to talk dirty but he's really a housewife at heart. Pay him no mind."

"Oh, you," Ronald said with a sly grin.

"We really didn't have much to do with Sharon," Mario said doubtfully.

"Mr. Evans said that you and Sharon Lee were quite friendly. He said that she displayed a certain...interest in you."

Mario looked at Ronald and frowned. Ronald smiled up into space. "Sharon was an acquaintance," Mario said firmly. "Nothing more."

"I see," Barent said. Ronald continued to smile, looking quite satisfied with himself. Barent gave a little shrug. "It doesn't matter." He held the directory out to Mario. "Would you do us the favor of looking through this book? It's a hospital directory for Easton Medical Center. We would like to know if you recognize any of the people in it."

Mario kept his hands at his sides. "Do we need a lawyer?" he asked.

"You might be witnesses," Barent said. "I don't consider you to be suspects. Please; I'd appreciate your help."

Mario and Ronald looked at each other, exchanging glances that Barent could not interpret. Finally, Mario nodded. "Let me see it." He weighed the book in his hand, shrugged his shoulders minutely and sat down on the couch. Ronald sat next to him and they proceeded to flip through the pages. They paused a few times, once over a picture of Sharon Lee, smiling brightly for the camera. But that was all. When they reached the end, Mario closed the book on his lap and shook his head, looking up at Barent with what appeared to be genuine regret. "I'm sorry," he said. "A few of them look familiar. But I don't think so."

There were over a dozen who looked "familiar." None of these were people who Barent had previously interviewed. Barent sighed inwardly, thanked them both and left. He assigned a team to investigate all the men whose pictures had made Mario and Ronald hesitate. He didn't expect much to come of it, but it was worth a try and he would have been remiss in not following through.

Sharon Lee's mysterious lover had most likely been a doctor, according to her sister. Ronald Evans had already told them that he had been a big man with dark hair.

Robinson had been reluctant to authorize the surveillance, worrying about adverse publicity. "Something like this could do us tremendous harm. Patients don't like to think that one of their doctors might be a murderer. You'll do it quietly?"

"Surveillance isn't much use if people know you're doing it," Barent said. "Of course we'll do it quietly."

Robinson had morosely agreed.

Inside the van, a cop named Ferruci turned to his partner, whose name was King, and said, "I hate stakeouts. I always gotta pee."

"Me too," King said. "I wish they'd given us one of the new ones. They've got toilets."

They drove across town to the Precinct House, parked in the lot outside and brought their videotape in to be stored for the night. The next morning, a similar van rolled up to the front of the Hampshire Building and repeated the process.

Each morning, the crime lab reviewed yesterday's tape, cataloguing the face of each person who entered the Hampshire Building, looking for clues. It was a tedious procedure. In all, over 700 people had walked through the doors during the first day. The police fully expected most of these to be unrecognizable, people with no record of criminal activity. They hoped to spot at least a few that were known to the police, a few who might forge a link between Easton Medical Center and Jaime Ruiz or Tony Korda.

On the third morning, Barent was going over the negative report of the previous day's tapes, when a knock sounded on his office door. "Come in," he said. The door opened and Ted Weiss stepped inside.

"Morning, Ted."

"How's it going, Lew?" Weiss asked.

"Not bad."

"You satisfied yet?"

"No," Barent said.

Weiss took a cigar out of his jacket pocket. He scratched a kitchen match across Barent's desk, held it up to the tip of the cigar and puffed until the cigar glowed like a coal. "What have you got? Anything?"

"Take a look." Barent tossed a manila file folder across the desk to Weiss.

Weiss flipped through the file, stopping now and then to examine a piece of paper more closely, occasionally shaking his head. Finally, he looked up. "Not much," he said.

"No," Barent agreed.

"Mostly speculation and wishful thinking."

"I wouldn't go that far."

"I would." Weiss puffed thoughtfully on his cigar. Barent lit a cigarette of his own, blew smoke toward the ceiling and waited.

"The papers are starting to sniff," Weiss said. "I got a call from John Costas yesterday morning wanting to know what the delay was in indicting Mose."

"Is he the only one?"

"So far."

"I know Costas," Barent said. "Leave Costas to me."

Weiss continued to puff, slow coils of smoke issuing from his mouth and drifting to the corners of the room. "You haven't convinced me," he stated. "But you have raised a whisper of a doubt." He held up a hand in front of his face, the thumb and forefinger almost touching. "A whisper," he repeated. "The merest whisper."

Barent puffed on his cigarette. He tapped his pencil eraser on the desk. He leaned back and studied the cracks in the ceiling.

Weiss grinned. "How is Mr. Mose?"

"Kurtz tells me he's still recovering. He won't be able to appear in court for"—Barent looked at his watch and narrowed his eyes—"at least another two weeks."

"I don't think I can stall for another two weeks," Weiss said. "Not without coming clean. I think you better come up with more than you've got in one week or Mose is going to have to make a sudden, miraculous recovery.

"And talk to Costas."

"Hello, John?"

"Who is this?" The voice on the phone registered open suspicion. "Barent?"

"Yep."

"You don't call me, Barent," Costas stated. "I call you. I ferret out the news. You do your best not to tell me anything. A call like this is a perversion of the natural order of events. What is going on here?"

"I just had a little visit from Ted Weiss."

There was sudden silence on the other end of the line.

"Ted is worried," Barent said. "He thinks you're losing your touch."

"He thinks...?"

"Ted thinks you've lost your ability to figure out when you've got a good story."

Barent could almost hear Costas thinking over the phone. "Alright, what gives?" Costas asked, his voice suddenly serious.

"I've got a deal for you," Barent said. "You've been getting curious about the Sharon Lee story."

"True. Go on."

"Actually, I was pulling your leg. Ted doesn't really think you're losing your touch. Ted admires you. 'That Costas,' he said to me, 'a real nose for news.'"

"Don't make me gag."

"Alright, I'll give it to you simply. We have evidence suggesting that Bill Mose is not the murderer. We'd like to keep it quiet just a little bit longer."

"That's what you want, huh?" Costas said. "Well, what I want is the Pulitzer Prize for Journalism. Now that you've confirmed my suspicions, why shouldn't I report it?"

"So far, you're the only one who's asking questions. If you stop asking them for a few more days, I'll give you an exclusive when the story breaks."

"You mean it?"

"I mean it."

"Then I'll take it," Costas said immediately. "Eat your heart out, Connie Chung."

"Three more days," Liebert said. "Thank God!"

Nolan sadly shook his head. "It's a pity seeing a young man make such a mess out of his life. Isn't it, Jack?"

Franklin grunted.

"No," Nolan said. "I mean it. Radiology? How can you do it to yourself? After a few years radiologists start to glow in the dark and then they die from cancer. And their kids all have genetic mutations."

"At least they have kids," Liebert said. "Surgeons aren't home enough to get their wives pregnant."

"Touché," Nolan said. "Touché."

Liebert smiled smugly.

Kurtz took Stan Nugent's chart out of the rack and quickly reviewed it, wishing that Nolan and Liebert would shut up. After his talk with Kathy the other night, he had been in a totally foul mood, a mood that the intervening time had only made worse.

The chart was not good. Nugent's hematocrit had fallen to 17 as the chemotherapy wiped out his bone marrow. Yesterday, the nursing home placement had finally come through and Nugent was scheduled to leave tomorrow morning, but nursing homes did not accept unstable patients. "Do you know what the term 'hematocrit' means, Doctor?" he asked Liebert.

"The hematocrit is the percentage of the blood that's composed of red blood cells."

"That's correct; and what's a normal hematocrit?"

"40 to 45 in an adult male. 35 to 40 for women."

"Good," Kurtz said. "And what do you think we should do for Mr. Nugent?"

"He needs blood," Liebert said.

"So?"

"So we have to keep him. He's not stable enough to leave."

"We don't have to keep him." Kurtz turned to Nolan. "Give him three units of packed cells," he said. "Get his crit up to at least 35, then send him out."

Kathy was wrong. It wasn't that he was so certain about things, but life was full of decisions. You had to make them. There was no point in mooning over them from here to eternity and there was no point in regretting them, either. You made the best decisions you could with the information available and you tried to learn from your mistakes.

Liebert's face clouded over but he said nothing. Kurtz smiled at him. "You look doubtful," he said.

"That doesn't seem fair," Liebert complained.

"To who?"

"To the nursing home."

"The nursing home is not your patient. Nugent is your patient and Nugent wants more than anything else in the world to get out of here. Nugent is going to die. He knows that, whether he's willing to admit it or not. He would rather die somewhere other than the hospital and we're going to help him do it."

Lenore had bundled Harrison up and taken him home a few days before. Kurtz hadn't had a chance to speak to her again after that one morning in the cafeteria, and that was just as well. He thought too much of his relationship with Kathy to risk it.

What a jerk.

"But if he's going to die anyway," Liebert said, "then we're wasting the blood."

"You know what D.N.R. means?"

"Of course: Do Not Resuscitate."

"Is Nugent D.N.R.?"

"No, he's not; but he's terminal. He should be D.N.R."

"Maybe he should. But as long as he's conscious and in his right mind, the only one who can declare him D.N.R. is himself. And until he's D.N.R., we're obligated to do everything possible to treat his condition, whether it's a waste of medical resources or not.

"And don't worry about the nursing home. They'll follow his crit, and when it drops low enough, they'll send him back here. But if Nugent is lucky, he'll be dead before that happens."

He had thought about Lenore a lot lately but Lenore had her own problems and Kurtz didn't want to add to them. He had a feeling that her relationship with Harrison was not quite as dead as she thought it was. She and Harrison had been involved for a long time. She had hovered over his sickbed like a guardian angel, hardly ever leaving his side. Maybe in a few days he'd give Lenore a call, after he had calmed down. Maybe.

They followed Kurtz into the room. Nugent was lying curled on his side in the bed, his limbs shriveled, his skin waxen. His bald head gleamed in the light and he looked at the little group with a thin, feral smile. "Tomorrow, I'm getting out of here," he said in an eager whisper.

"Yes, Mr. Nugent," Kurtz said.

"It can't come too soon for me." Nugent's watery eyes wandered around the little room. "I can't stand this place," he said.

"Yes, Mr. Nugent. I understand your feelings."

"Good riddance," Nugent whispered.

"Congratulations, Mr. Nugent," Kurtz said. "And good luck."

Chapter 26

Barent wiped a scatter of ashes off the front of his shirt, sipped at his coffee and breathed a sigh. "Denise is busy picking out patterns," he said. "Silver patterns, china patterns, linen patterns. Everything's got a pattern. And all the bath towels and the napkins are supposed to be monogrammed. You have monogrammed bath towels and napkins?"

"We usually use paper napkins," Moran said.

"We've got linen napkins someplace. Betty brings them out maybe twice a year on the holidays. They're not monogrammed. Denise Janus will have monogrammed linen napkins."

"Is Betty happy?"

"Ecstatic," Barent said morosely.

"Well, then."

"Fathers are definitely superfluous in these things. Husbands too. Paul seems just as bewildered as me."

"That's probably the point. The women exclude the men from all these rituals and that's supposed to bring the Father-in-Law and the Son-in-Law— who probably up to now couldn't stand each other—closer together."

"I still can't stand him," Barent said.

"You'll get over it."

Barent frowned down at his cigarette. "I hate sitting around and waiting."

"Me too."

Barent had had a little conversation with the priest who would perform the ceremony, Father Michael Ianello. Father Michael was a mild mannered man with a weak chin and thinning hair. He looked like a pushover. He wasn't. Barent had let Father Michael know that he didn't like priests, he didn't like churches and he had no use for a God who allowed bad things to happen to good people. Father Michael had simply shrugged, "If you want to talk about it, we can talk," he said. "But if all you want to do is bitch, then I really couldn't care less."

For a moment, Barent was floored. "What do you mean, you couldn't care less? You're supposed to save souls, aren't you?"

"I mean I couldn't care less. One thing I realized a long time ago: you can't save souls who don't want to be saved. I've got no interest in butting my head against a brick wall. You want to go to Hell, that's your business."

Actually, Barent rather admired Father Michael.

He drew in another long sigh and tried to turn his mind to the job. "Anything turn up on Sharon Lee's credit card records?"

"She went to San Diego in October for a conference on fetal monitoring. She had a single room. Could she have met somebody?" Moran shrugged. "Sure. Plenty of doctors go to conferences. Plenty of people go to San Diego."

"Nothing local?"

"She ate out a lot, and from the prices it looks like she sometimes paid for somebody else, but it was never more than twice at the same restaurant. I went to the three most recent. Nobody remembered her."

"The surveillance better come up with something."

A knock sounded from the door. "Yes?" Barent called out loudly.

A uniformed policeman stuck his head in. "Phone call for you, Lew."

"Who is it?"

"Guy says his name is Oliver Thomas."

Kurtz smiled warily upward at the corner of the hallway where the wall met the ceiling. Even though he knew it was there, he couldn't see the miniature lens that the surveillance team had installed. There were similar lenses in all the corners of all the floors of the Building. Kurtz opened the door to his office suite, went inside and said to Rose Schapiro, "Who's first?"

Mrs. Schapiro looked at him with a cheery smile on her face. "Mr. Callahan," she said. "He's here for his sigmoidoscopy."

Kurtz audibly groaned. Mrs. Schapiro smiled at him brightly. "Miss Grunfeld brought him back to the endoscopy room."

"Thanks," he said, and walked in. Callahan was sitting on the table, dressed only in a thin cotton gown opened down the back. His hairy legs dangled over the edge of the table.

"How are you today, Mr. Callahan?"

"Not so good, Doc," Callahan said. "I still got that constipation." "Did you follow the instructions Miss Grunfeld gave you?"

Callahan nodded proudly. "Nothing to eat after noon yesterday except clear liquids. A Fleet's enema this morning." Callahan shook his head in amazement. "That Fleet's cleaned me out good. I feel like a new man."

"Well, turn over on your side and let's take a look."

The sigmoidoscopy appeared to be entirely normal; Callahan's rectum and lower colon were pink and shiny, but Callahan moaned and grunted pitifully throughout the procedure and refused to stay still, his toes curling and his heels kicking at the examining table every time Kurtz advanced the scope. "Almost done now, Mr. Callahan," Kurtz said. "Please try not to move."

"You're killing me, Doc," Callahan groaned. "Jesus, Doc, you're killing me."

171

"It's just cramps, Mr. Callahan. I have to pump air in to expand the bowel, otherwise I can't get a good view. Now try to keep still and it will be over soon."

"I never had cramps like this. This is like a weasel tearing at my insides."

"Uh-hmmm..." The fiberoptic scope worked its way up Callahan's bowels like a roto-rooter reaming out a pipe, while Kurtz squeezed the air bladder with one hand and peered through the lens, dreaming wistfully about weasels and gerbils. Finally, the scope was in all the way to the hub. "I'm coming out now, Mr. Callahan," Kurtz said. "Try to relax."

"Good," Callahan groaned. "Good."

A few minutes later, Callahan was sitting up on the table, wheezing, his face covered with a sheen of sweat. "Are you okay?" Kurtz asked.

Callahan looked at him doubtfully. "I think so. You sure you didn't rupture me?"

"I'm sure."

Callahan nodded grimly and compressed his lips. "Well, what's the word?" he asked. "You find anything?"

"No. It's a normal exam. Everything checks out fine."

Callahan heaved a deep breath. "Alright, then," he said. "What's the next step?"

"What next step?" Kurtz blinked at him. "There's nothing wrong with you."

"But Doc, what am I gonna do about this constipation?"

"See me next January," Kurtz said. "We'll do another sigmoidoscopy."

"It's been going on for a little over four years," Oliver Thomas said. "A man approached me. He was well dressed. His voice was cultured. He seemed to be a gentleman. His name was Gordon Stone. He knew all about my financial difficulties. He offered me a way out and I accepted. At first it was only Stone; after awhile it was another man also, a man named Roberto Alvarez. One of them would deliver a bag full of money. I deposited it into an account. A few weeks later, I transferred the money out to another account in the Cayman Islands. What happened to it after that, I have no idea." Oliver Thomas shrugged.

"Always these two men?" Barent asked.

"Yes."

"Never anybody else?"

"No."

"In whose names were the accounts?"

"Gordon Stone"—Thomas seemed to hesitate—"and Raymond Santiago."

"Not Roberto Alvarez?"

"No. All Alvarez did was deliver the money."

"How many accounts are we talking about?" Barent asked.

"Here or in the Caymans?"

"Both."

"Here, there were two; one for Stone and one for Santiago. There are five different accounts in the Cayman Islands, three in Stone's name, two for Santiago. I never made a deposit into the same account more than twice in a row."

"This Gordon Stone, was he white?"

Oliver Thomas frowned at him. "Of course."

"And what did you think when guys like Alvarez came into the picture?"

"I protested."

"Got you real far, didn't it?"

Oliver Thomas shrugged.

Barent nodded thoughtfully. "That's the trouble dealing with people of inferior ethnic backgrounds; they can get you mixed up in things that are downright sleazy."

"I'm afraid I don't like your tone, Barent." Thomas looked down at his desk in bleak disgust. "I know I made a mistake. I should never have gotten involved with these people, but I was on the verge of bankruptcy." He laughed softly. "I was born rich. I've always been rich. I don't know how to be poor and I didn't want to have to learn."

"Any of these people ever mention Tony Korda?" Barent asked.

"Korda?" Thomas blinked at him. "You brought him up before, didn't you?" Thomas shook his head. "No. Never."

"How about Jaime Ruiz?"

"No."

Barent frowned and looked at Moran, who shrugged silently. "So, why are you telling us?"

Oliver Thomas stared off into the far corners of his office. He took a long time before answering. Finally, he shook his head. "I'm in too deep. I don't know how to get out."

"Maybe you should have thought of that before you got involved."

"You're right." Oliver Thomas shrugged. "Can you help me?" he asked.

"I don't know. You've committed federal crimes, crimes over which I have no jurisdiction. I'm a cop, not an F.B.I. agent."

Thomas sadly nodded. He opened the middle drawer of his desk and pulled out a thin, black notebook. "Here is a listing of the people involved, the dates and the amounts of all the transfers." He tossed the book across the desk to Barent. "Take it. Do anything with it that you want."

Barent picked it up gingerly, weighing it in his palm. Then he tucked it under his arm. "Give me a few days," he said. "We'll see what I can do."

"Richard?"

The voice was familiar but for an instant he couldn't place it. Then he realized who it was and his heart gave a thump. "Lenore," he said.

"I would have called you sooner but I hadn't heard. I was in Boston, at an exhibition. Are you alright?"

"I'm fine," he said. "How did you find out?"

She laughed softly. "Doctors don't get shot at every day, even in this town. It was in the newspaper."

"Oh," he said. "I guess it was."

"And Kathy? How is she?"

For a moment, the words stuck in his throat, then he said, "She's fine."

"That's good. The paper said she was beaten."

"Some bruises. They'll heal in a few days." Lenore's voice was deep and smooth, like molasses. He noted it absently. "Kathy and I are not seeing each other at the moment," he said.

Lenore said nothing. He could imagine her on the other end of the phone line, frowning while she mulled this over.

"I'm glad you called," he said. "I've been thinking about you." He swallowed, the words suddenly sticking in his throat. "Would you like to have dinner with me tomorrow night?"

Her voice seemed to hesitate for a brief instant. "I can't," she said. "I'm having dinner with my parents."

"Then how about Friday?"

"Friday sounds good," she said.

Day after day, the Ford minivan pulled up across from the Hampshire Building in the morning and left in the evening after all the staff and patients had gone. Every morning, the lab developed the film gathered from the day before and sent it upstairs to be reviewed by their resident expert and his team. On the fifth morning, Arnie Figueroa suddenly stopped the tape he had been watching, re-wound it and watched it again. Then he picked up the phone. "Lew?" he said. "I think you'd better come down here."

Ten minutes later, Barent and Moran were sitting next to the monitor screen, watching the tape. Barent watched it through twice, then he rubbed his hands together and gleefully smiled. "That the one?" he said to Figueroa. He pointed to a face on the screen.

"That's the one."

Barent nodded, still smiling. He turned to Moran. "Remember him?"

"Sure," Moran said. "The maitre'd at the Vanity Club, Ruiz' receptionist."

Figueroa frowned. "He is?"

174

"Yeah," Barent said. "Isn't that why you called us?"

"No." Figueroa shook his head. "I called you because that's Carlos Rivera."

Barent stared at the screen. "Well, hallelujah," he finally said. "Which office has he gone into?"

"Number twenty-three." Barent looked at Moran, who was flipping the pages of the hospital directory. Moran found number twenty-three, nodded and looked up. "Longo," he said.

Chapter 27

Once a month, Jaime Ruiz came for dinner at Tony Korda's mansion in the Fieldston section of the Bronx, more often than that if circumstances seemed to warrant it. Tonight was routine.

Korda was a man who tried to have no illusions about other people or himself, particularly himself. He had been a wild kid, he knew that, with a real chip on his shoulder, but that was years in the past. Korda did not regard himself as a cruel man, not anymore. When he was very young, he had acted out of rage, then out of necessity. Now...now, he enjoyed himself.

Ruiz picked up his soup spoon, dipped the spoon in the bowl and raised it to his lips. Korda smiled. Six months ago, Ruiz had not known what a soup spoon was. Now, he wouldn't have dreamed of using anything else. It was amazing, Korda thought, how often those who lived by breaking the major rules of society insisted on aping the little ones.

To Korda, it was all a game. He had long since passed the point where he needed the money. Now, he did what he did to amuse Tony Korda.

Korda was an intelligent man. While his college career had long ago been aborted, he was nevertheless widely read. *In the long run, we are all dead.* Sartre got that one right.

"How has the take been going on the betting parlors?" Korda asked in his grating voice.

Ruiz quickly swallowed. "Good," he said. "Up fourteen percent."

"Any problems?"

Ruiz' lips thinned. His nostrils flared. "The connection to the Caymans is coming unglued."

"The banker still antsy?"

"Yes," Ruiz said shortly.

Korda sighed to himself. With Ruiz it was all personal. *Machismo*, that's what it was. Face. Ruiz believed in imposing his own brand of discipline on the world. Korda believed in doing as little as necessary to achieve his objectives. In the long run, extraneous moves had a tendency to weaken one's position. "Has he paid back your original investment?"

Ruiz hesitated. "Yes."

"Then let him go. We don't need him."

"He's been useful. He can be more useful," Ruiz said.

"I don't agree with you."

A butler brought in the next course, a salad. Both men picked up their salad forks. The butler left.

"He's an investment that has already paid off and now is going sour. Take your profit and put it somewhere else."

Ruiz stared at him, his breathing rapid. "It's a mistake," Korda said mildly, "to let other people know what you're thinking."

Ruiz hesitated. "Maybe you're right," he said. He grinned wryly then and took a deep breath. "Flanagan and Raines, they mess up pretty bad. The police know."

"Exactly," Korda said. "Forget about Oliver Thomas. There are plenty of other sharks in the sea."

Two days later, a member of the surveillance team named Cesar Herrera made positive identification of a man named Hector Cruz going into Doctor Philip Longo's office. The day after, there were two more, both young, male and Hispanic. All were known associates of Jaime Ruiz. None were listed as patients in the computer system of Easton Medical Center.

"Tell us about Longo," Barent said.

Kurtz rubbed a hand across his forehead and winced. "He's a nice guy," Kurtz said. Then he amended, "He *seems* like a nice guy. I know him pretty well. Bill Werth and I go fishing with him. We went out to Montauk last summer and chartered a bluefish boat. Then in the fall, we went up to the Beaverkill for trout."

"Go on."

"His practice is tremendous. He employs two physical therapists of his own. He works hard. He has a reputation for being better than most in the O.R. He doesn't yell at the nurses, which puts him one up on a lot of surgeons, believe me." Kurtz grinned weakly. "He's a normal human being."

"Strange way of putting it," Barent commented. He blew smoke at the ceiling, then said: "These therapists, you know them?"

Kurtz shook his head. "No. I've never met them."

"Isn't that strange?"

"Not at all. A lot of people work here. I don't know most of them."

"What are their names?"

"I couldn't tell you."

Barent blew smoke at Moran. "Find out from Wellesley." Moran nodded.

"How about his secretary?"

"He has two of them, both full time. Most of the surgeons' secretaries cover for each other when their own boss is in the O.R., but not his. With the therapists always there, they've got plenty of work to do, even when Longo isn't around."

"Do you know their names?"

Kurtz shook his head. "Sorry."

Barent glanced at Moran, who nodded again. "How is he with money?"

"What do you mean?"

"Bad investments? Any debts? Does he like to gamble?"

Kurtz frowned. "He goes to Atlantic City now and then, and he's going to Las Vegas next month with Farkas—he's a plastic surgeon—and some of the other guys. I never heard of him being a compulsive gambler, if that's what you mean."

"What else?" Barent asked.

Kurtz shrugged. "What else...?" He stared off into space, thinking about it. You thought you knew a guy, and then something like this happens. What was relevant? "He collects antiques, or his wife does. His wife is on the Board of Settlement House. Longo does a lot of charity work."

Barent glanced at Moran. "Sounds like a fine, up-standing citizen."

Kurtz spread his hands to the side. "I always thought so."

"Whatever is going on has got to involve money," Barent said, "and you can bet it's some sort of a scam."

"Blackmail?" Moran said. "Fraud?"

"Big time physician, runs his own physical therapy..." Barent smiled cynically. "My wife threw her back out a few years ago. Let me tell you, they bill plenty for physical therapy and insurance covers nearly all of it. I would bet on insurance." Barent turned to Kurtz. "You ever been in Longo's office?"

"Sure. It's like any other office." He thought about it. "A little bigger than most. He has a treatment room for the P.T."

Barent's pencil went tap-tap-tap on his notebook. "Tell me about his wife."

"She's his second wife. Her name is Sylvia. They've been married for about five years."

"What's she like?"

"I don't know her too well." He thought about the New Year's Eve party and gave a tiny shudder. "She's got a reputation for getting what she wants. Settlement House is the best funded charity around here."

"I don't know much about Settlement House," Barent said.

"They run a homeless shelter, collect food and second hand clothing for poor families, sometimes help people get jobs."

"What happened to the first wife?"

"Divorce." Kurtz grinned fleetingly. "Surgeons get divorced a lot. Women think it's glamorous, being married to a surgeon. They find out pretty quick that they spend most of their time by themselves."

"How long did the first marriage last?"

"I'm not sure. I think about ten years."

"Any kids?"

"Two."

"Alimony?"

"I have no idea." Kurtz shrugged. "Probably."

Barent leaned forward, the tips of his fingers pressed together under his chin. "Think about it," he said. "Maybe something else will occur to you. We'll talk again."

"Wait a minute," Kurtz said. "What does all this have to do with Sharon Lee?"

"Damned if I know," Barent said. "Maybe nothing."

"So what are you going to do about Oliver Thomas?" Moran asked.

"I'm going to alert the F.B.I.," Barent said. "What else would I do?"

"Why haven't you done it yet?"

Barent blew a smoke ring up to the ceiling and watched it spread out. "No hurry," he said. "No hurry at all."

"Sure," Moran said. Then he grinned. "Anything new on the wedding plans?"

Barent blew another smoke ring and gave Moran a woebegone look. "They've finally decided on a menu," he said. "First, the open bar and hors d'oeuvres while the stragglers wander in, then we all move to the buffet table. After the buffet, the sit down dinner will feature shrimp cocktails followed by a salad followed by a choice of London broil and baked potato or saffron rice and Hawaiian chicken. Filet of sole with asparagus will be offered for the diet conscious. Music and dancing between the courses, naturally. Dessert will be the usual Viennese table, with, of course, the cake."

Moran grunted in sympathy.

Truthfully, Barent hadn't fully decided yet what to do about Oliver Thomas. The list that Thomas had given them was intriguing. Gordon Stone, Roberto Alvarez and Raymond Santiago were presumably false names. Neither the police nor F.B.I. files had any record of them. Gordon Stone—whoever he was—made deposits in the three to four hundred thousand dollar range. Raymond Santiago put in more like fifty to a hundred thousand at a time. Big operator and small operator. Stone's deposits were regular, always on the third Monday of every month. Santiago put money in on no discernible schedule but rarely missed more than a few weeks at a time.

Barent had been operating all along on the supposition that Tony Korda was the elusive mastermind behind this whole affair, the spider at the center of the web. Unfortunately, he had been able to gather no evidence to prove it.

He had one person in custody at the moment who might—despite his earlier denials—be able to give him some answers. Jimmy Raines was awaiting trial for kidnapping, forcible restraint, felony manslaughter and attempted murder.

"Tell me about Tony Korda," Barent said.

Raines looked at him with his flat, dead eyes. "Go to Hell."

Barent smiled. "Jimmy, you're facing enough time to last you the rest of your life. You're sure you don't want to think about making a deal?"

"A deal?" Raines looked around the little room as if searching for a place to spit. "You're a cheapskate, Barent. I'm not interested."

Barent leaned back, allowed a smug, happy look to wander across his face. "Well, maybe you're right," he said. "A little word to the prosecutor about cooperation with the police—what's that worth? A lousy five years? Ten?"

Raines snorted through his teeth. "Not good enough."

"No?" Barent loved the look on Raines' face, desperate and desperately trying not to show it. Raines' face was thinner. His skin, once as smooth as a baby's, now hung off his cheeks in sagging jowls. "We could probably go a little higher. If you really know what you're talking about, make a significant contribution toward the elimination of organized crime in the City of New York, there could even be a place for Jimmy Raines in the Witness Protection Program."

"Witness Protection is federal," Raines said.

"I've got friends."

Raines gave a small, bitter laugh. "Sounds good," he said. "Only problem is, I've got nothing to sell. Was Korda involved? I've got no idea. I free lance. Sometimes people approached me. I never knew who they worked for; it was better that way. Sometimes Charlie Flanagan asked me to help him out on some of his action. Sometimes I say 'yes.' Sometimes I say 'no.' If I say yes, then an envelope full of cash appears under my door."

"And what if you get caught?"

Raines laughed again. "Then I'm on my own."

Barent was not surprised. Keeping your mouth shut was the number one rule in the criminal code of survival. You get caught, you're on your own. You talk, someone, somewhere, sticks a knife in you. It may be years down the road and a thousand miles away but it was as inevitable as the changing of the seasons. "I bet you really enjoy swinging in the breeze," Barent said.

Raines shrugged. "It was the best deal in town. Believe me, they all paid well."

Barent sighed and rose slowly to his feet. "Sorry we couldn't do business, Jimmy."

"Charlie told me this last job was sort of weird," Raines said. He said it in an even, offhand tone. "He got a call. He never saw the face. Whoever it was mentioned people Charlie knew, jobs he had done in the past, enough so it had to be on the level. Charlie said the guy had a strange voice," Raines said. "A real deep voice, like that guy in the movies, I forget his name, the one who played Darth Vader."

Barent's ears pricked up. "James Earl Jones?"

"Yeah." Raines nodded. "Him. Charlie said he would recognize that voice."

"Charlie's dead," Barent said. Raines shrugged. "Yeah."

A voice...Barent thought about that for a moment, then shook his head. A voice without a face to match it wouldn't get too far with the D.A. "I'll keep it in mind," he said. "Don't count on anything. A voice isn't much."

The next afternoon, the report arrived regarding the physical therapists and the secretaries. The therapists were named Donald Lake and Evelyn Morris. The secretaries were Janet Crowley and Kimberly Jones. There was no history of criminal activity listed for any of them in any police or government file.

"Look at this," Barent said.

Moran looked at the file. Prior to the current staff, Longo had employed a number of different nurses. "Jean Evans...Margaret Donaldson... Louise Klein. So?"

Barent shrugged. "These were all young women. Young women tend to be transient. They get married; they get pregnant; their husband moves; a better job comes along. A high turnover is pretty common. But about five years ago, suddenly Longo had no more turnover. That suggest anything to you?"

"The ones he's got now are in on the scam," Moran said.

Barent nodded. "I would bet on it."

"Think we've got enough for a warrant?"

Barent gave him a look that said Moran should have known better. "No way," he said. "So the Doctor sees patients—big deal. We have nothing to tie him to Sharon Lee. We have no evidence that any crime at all has been committed."

"Why do you need a warrant?" Kurtz asked. "Robinson gave you permission to go in."

Barent hissed disdainfully through his teeth. "Robinson gave me permission to enter the building but the offices are leased to the physicians. I can't go into the office without a warrant or Longo's specific permission. At this stage, I'm not about to ask. If Longo's got anything in there, all he has to do is say 'No.' He knows we're on to him; he destroys the evidence and we're left with nothing." He shook his head. "It's not enough. We need more."

"Where do we get it?" Kurtz asked.

Barent looked at him and scratched behind his ear. "I don't know."

Chapter 28

Kurtz had briefly considered *Lutece*, or maybe *La Caravelle*, but you couldn't get a reservation at any of the top French restaurants on such short notice, not for a Friday night. Anyway, the place down in Cancun had been French, which might actually have been a good association to make but which, he came to the reluctant conclusion, seemed just a little too contrived. Indian, he decided—foreign enough to be exotic but familiar enough to seem comfortable, at least to a New Yorker.

The place was called *Shangri La*. It occupied the penthouse of an older building off Fifty-Ninth Street. The floor was tiled in squares of pink and black marble and copies of temple sculptures adorned the walls. A man dressed in white robes sat in one corner on a raised dais and played the sitar. The waiters wore turbans and red jackets with gold epaulets on the shoulders.

Kurtz had requested a table by the window. There wasn't really that much of a view, but at night the dirt and the potholes became invisible, and any street corner of the city became something to see, full of flash- ing headlights, brightly lit windows and the constant, swirling motion of people wandering by below.

"Very nice," Lenore said.

"I think so."

A waiter brought over a basket of crispy *papadums*, spooned mint and tamarind chutneys onto two small plates and handed them both menus.

Kurtz watched her while she studied it. It was hard not to. She was wearing a light blue silk blouse that showed just enough décolletage to be enticing without being crass, a matching skirt and a string of pearls around her neck. Her golden hair was arranged in short bangs over her forehead and then fell loosely down her shoulders and back.

"Shall we each order what we want, or shall we share?" Lenore asked.

"Why don't we each order what we want and then share?"

She grinned. "Sounds good to me."

Kathy would have wanted to come to a consensus regarding each dish. The thought occurred to Kurtz fleetingly, then he dismissed it.

They gave their order. The waiter wrote it down impassively, gave a little bow and departed. A few seconds later, a girl who appeared to be no older than fifteen brought them two oversized bottles of Golden Eagle beer, popped them open and poured half of each bottle into two frozen steins.

"Cheers," Kurtz said, and took a sip. Tiny crystals of ice had already formed on top of the beer.

Lenore was looking intently into her glass. "I've never seen that before," she said. "Do they keep the glasses in the freezer?"

"I guess they do."

"I like it."

Lenore, Kurtz figured, was the sort who took things as they came. What she didn't like, she ignored. Maybe living with a mother who was just a tad unpredictable (to put it charitably), had something to do with it. Then again, intrusive, manipulating parents just as often produced children who were hostile, rigid and full of preconceived notions into which every new experience had to neatly fit. More often, in fact.

The waiter wheeled over a cart and placed a platter of golden fried vegetable *pakoras* and four meat *samosa*—triangular pastries filled with spiced ground lamb—down on the table. "One of the few advantages to living in a city like this is the fact that you can find any sort of food to eat any time you want it. I love this stuff," Lenore said.

"The food was pretty simple where I grew up. Mostly meat and potatoes."

"A deprived childhood, without a doubt."

"Oh, I don't know. People weren't shooting at me in West Virginia."

Lenore's face immediately fell. "Oh, Richard, I'm sorry. I forgot."

He grinned faintly. "It's alright. It only hurts when I move."

"I guess you better not move," she said, and grinned back.

They finished the appetizer and within a few moments the waiter wheeled over the main course: a platter of rice with peas and chopped onions, flavored with cardamom and fennel seeds, *chicken tandoor*, shrimp in a coconut curry and *saag paneer*, a dish of buttery creamed spinach with cubes of homemade cheese.

Lenore rubbed her hands together. "Oh, boy," she said.

A dozen different spices were blended into each dish and they were all tingling hot. They ate for a little while without speaking, putting out the fire with spoonfuls of *raita*, a yogurt sauce with cucumber and dill, and gulps of the ice cold beer. Finally, Kurtz sighed and pushed away his plate. "Great stuff," he said.

"Yes, it is," Lenore agreed. She stifled a lady-like burp behind a fist. "But it's not really Indian, though. Most Indians are Hindus and Hindus don't eat meat. They call it *Northern* Indian but it's Pakistani, mostly. Pakistan is a Muslim country and a lot of Americans, particularly New Yorkers, aren't too fond of Muslims these days, not after the Ayatollah, Saddam Hussein and September 11th."

183

"I didn't know that."

She shrugged, looked down at the cars passing by on the street and sighed. Then she said, "I understand that they caught the man who shot you. He's the same one who beat up Harrison."

"Yes. He was living in Chicago."

"I'm glad."

"So am I.

"So," she said delicately, "is Harrison. He told me."

She was still looking down at the street. The expression on her face was guarded. "You still see Harrison?" Kurtz asked.

"I still talk to Harrison. On the phone, mostly." She looked him in the eye and grinned wryly. "He says he would like to remain friends. I don't know how realistic that is but I feel obligated to give it a shot. I'm not too happy about the way things turned out."

"I see," Kurtz said, a non-committal comment, but one that seemed suddenly wiser to express than the sentiment (the very sincere sentiment) that things between Lenore and Harrison had most certainly happened for the best. It must have been fate.

Lenore grinned wider. "Yeah," she said.

For dessert, they had small ovals of sweetened cheese with slivers of pistachio, sprinkled with rose water, and tiny cups of thick coffee flavored with cinnamon and mace.

"Would you like a brandy?" Kurtz asked.

She shook her head. "I don't think so. Not after the beer."

Kurtz glanced at his watch and said, "It's a little early to call it an evening. How about a movie?"

"I don't think I'm in the mood for a movie," she said. She squinted one eye at him and looked for an instant like she was mulling something over. Then she grinned at him with one side of her face, gave a tiny shrug and said, "How about your place?"

The bar on East Houston was busier at night. There were three dancers now, two blondes and a brunette, and they swung their hips like they meant it. The stage behind the bar was lit with strobe lights that changed color every few seconds, red to magenta to blue and back again. Barent winced. The music was something by the Pointer Sisters, not exactly Barent's cup of tea. He had looked at the flickering lights for no more than a few seconds and already he could feel a headache coming on.

He wandered to the back of the bar where it was a little quieter and found Croft sitting in a booth with two women, drinking *Roederer Cristal*. Croft wore a brown leather jacket and a paisley tie. On the table sat a tan fedora with a leopard skin band around the rim. One of the women was black, with creamy smooth skin and long, curling black hair. The other was blonde, with blue eyes and full, red lips. They both wore tight, low cut dresses and they both sat very close to Croft.

"Barent," Croft said. "Didn't expect to see you here so late. Sit down. This is Heather"—he smiled at the top of the blonde's head—"and this is Chantal.

"Ladies, this is Officer Barent, of the New York City *Poli*ce Department."

Heather and Chantal both cast Barent doubtful glances. Neither of them said a word.

"Heather. Chantal." Barent tipped his hat and slid into the seat opposite Croft.

"Drink, Barent?" Croft asked.

Barent shook his head. "I'm on duty."

"Damn," Croft said. "I'll have to watch my mouth." Heather was looking at Barent warily. Chantal snuggled up to Croft's arm and smiled as if she hadn't a care.

"I need some information," Barent said.

Croft looked miffed. "What am I, a library? Can't a man enjoy a quiet evening after work with his lady friends?"

Barent smiled at Heather. He craned his head forward and said, "Boo." Heather blinked and looked startled.

"Now look what you done," Croft said. "You scared her." He patted Heather on top of her head. "Daddy won't let the big bad *poli*ceman hurt his little girl." Heather looked up at Barent uncertainly.

"Tony Korda and Jaime Ruiz," Barent said.

Croft winced. "Not in front of the children."

"Then take a hike, girls," Barent said pleasantly.

Both women looked at Croft. He nodded and they rose from the table without a word and walked over to the bar. Croft stared after them.

"New merchandise?" Barent asked.

Croft shrugged. "Korda and Ruiz not my business. I told you what you wanted to know. Why you bothering me now?"

"It wasn't enough."

"It was all I had," Croft said. He shook his head, chugged back his glass of champagne and poured another. "Look, Barent, there ain't nothing new in this. Kids, they play their little kid games, like cops and robbers. But in the ghetto, they be serious games. You know how many kids in the ghetto die before they grow up? One quarter get shot or stabbed or stomped on or O.D. And what you think happens to the rest? Not one in ten gets out of there unless he got people he can count on, someone to watch his back. So kids, they need protection, they form a gang, and after awhile they ain't kids no more and then what? Kid games not enough. They want to play grown up games. But they don't know how. So if they not too dumb, they look for a bigger gang to take them in, show them the ropes. That's the way it is with Ruiz and Korda, or so they say on the street. Me?" Croft shrugged. "I don't mess with things that don't concern me."

Barent shrugged. "I've heard the story before; this city is filled with rejects from the criminal major leagues."

Croft nodded sagely. "That exactly what it is. Ruiz, he a little rough around the edges, maybe not too smart but smart enough to know it. He need a little polish, a little shine. Korda, he give him some jobs, shine him up real good. Ruiz handle them, Korda give him some bigger ones. Pretty soon, Ruiz and his boys playing in the big leagues, they a part of the team."

"Unless they decide to form a team of their own."

"It happens." Croft poured another glass of champagne. "You sure you won't have some?"

"No, thanks." The thought, actually, made him feel ill. Even from across the room, the music made his skull vibrate and the flickering lights were inescapable. Barent's head was beginning to seriously pound.

Croft pursed his lips and swirled his champagne. "You know that fella wrote *The Godfather*? Mario Puzo? After he wrote *The Godfather*, he wrote another book called *Fools Die*. You think Ruiz know how to read?"

Barent peered at Croft doubtfully. "When did you get so literary?"

"Not much to do in prison. Place had a good library."

As soon as the door closed behind them, Lenore stepped toward him, still with that same faint grin on her face, put her arms up over his shoulders and kissed him. It was a very nice kiss, an expert kiss. She used her teeth delicately, nibbling on his lower lip. Lenore wasn't going anywhere, wasn't planning on doing anything else with the rest of the evening except stand there and let her lips rove over his, her tongue peeping out enticingly every once in a while to tease his. He put his arms around her back and she reached up to run her fingers through his hair, all the while keeping their lips glued together.

Kurtz felt dizzy. He felt like maybe neither of them were getting enough air. He remembered reading somewhere that hawks sometimes died while mating. They flew as high as they could, joined together, folded their wings and plunged toward the earth at two hundred miles an hour. Only when they were finished did they uncouple and fly off. If they didn't finish in time, they died. Kurtz felt like he might die right here from lack of oxygen. He felt like Cary Grant in that old Hitchcock movie, kissing Ingrid Bergman, the one where he was a secret agent and she was reluctantly infiltrating the gang of bad guys. The censors at the time didn't allow a kiss that lasted more than a few seconds, so they had to vary the kiss, mixing it up with little sighs and whispers of conversation, so that they could claim it wasn't really *one* kiss, it was a series of kisses that went on almost forever, and which wound up being far more erotic than one single kiss could possibly be—and that was a pretty good way to feel, even if (especially if) little red lights were dancing before your eyes and you seriously thought that you might blissfully slide into unconsciousness.

"I can't breathe," Kurtz whispered.

She went right on kissing him and he went right on kissing her back. It was amazing. Not since high school had a kiss (or rather a kissing *experience*) been so satisfying, and that was only because kissing was at that time as far as he had ever gotten and he could barely imagine anything better. The thought occurred to him that maybe he should start to vary the action, slide a hand up under her skirt, maybe let the tips of his fingers wander over her breast but nope, if this was as good as it seemed, and it seemed pretty amazingly good, then Richard Kurtz was going to let things happen as they happened and be blissfully content to go along for the ride.

As it happened, after what seemed to be about five hours but was actually somewhat less, Lenore broke off, leaned back, looked up into Kurtz' eyes and said, "Undress me."

Despite what trashy novels always said about it, Kurtz had never found undressing a woman to be the phenomenal experience it was cracked up to be, mostly because women's clothes were a lot more complicated than men's clothes, and unless you really knew what you were doing, you always wound up fumbling for zippers and buttons and clasps that you either couldn't quite reach or that wouldn't quite come undone. It probably would have been more romantic to simply rip the clothes off a woman, let her know you really wanted her and couldn't wait a single second longer, but most women, whatever they might say about the virtues of unrestrained passion and romance, tended to get a trifle upset when their no doubt expensive blouses and skirts and lingerie got ruined (Kurtz could remember one smart young lady in college who always wore a one piece jump suit with a single long zipper in the front when she was in the mood. A man could peel a woman out of a garment like that as easily and romantically as you please without having to fumble around like a jerk.).

But hey, what the hell? If Lenore wanted it, Lenore got it, especially here and especially tonight. She stood there with her eyes half closed while Kurtz gently, oh so slowly, opened the buttons on her blouse, pausing after each one to kiss the golden skin that the button had concealed, and by the time he had opened the last one and slid the blouse down over her shoulders, her breathing was rapid and she audibly sighed. She was wearing a low cut, lace edged bra, so sheer it was transparent. She kissed him again, hard, and he unclasped the bra, paused for a moment to look at her and then slid her skirt and bikini panties to the floor and then she was gloriously naked.

187

She smiled wickedly and looked suddenly thoughtful. "There's something very sensual and erotic about standing here undressed with a man who still has all his clothes on," she said.

"I never realized that. Should I keep them on?"

She frowned slightly. "I don't think so." She reached up and unbuttoned the top button of his shirt, then hesitated and stepped back with an impish grin. "No," she said. "You do it. I want to watch." His clothes were off in maybe a thousandth of a second, or maybe a millionth. She squinted at him as if assaying what she had found and then nodded in approval and stepped forward and then his arms were full of squirming, gasping Lenore.

Ten seconds later, they tumbled into bed, giggling.

Lenore wasn't loud enough to wake the neighbors but she made a gratifying amount of noise, which Kurtz thought was very considerate of a woman, letting a man know how much she was into it. It certainly puffed up the old ego. Once, when Kurtz slowed down, thinking he might be hurting her, she groaned out, "No. Keep going," which was just fine with Kurtz.

And then it was over, at least for the moment, and they lay there panting, arms and legs twined together and Kurtz thought with a sleepy glow that he had rarely been so content in his life. Somehow, Kurtz had slipped down on the bed and Lenore was clutching his head to her breasts. One perfect, pink nipple was bobbing next to his eye. He kissed it and she gave a tiny purr.

"I'm not usually this aggressive," Lenore said in a low voice. She yawned. "I want you to know that."

"No problem," Kurtz said, and kissed the nipple again. It was beginning to pucker. "Believe me."

"Kathy might come back to you. I wanted to stake my claim." She gave him a wicked, sleepy grin. "I like that," she said. "Don't stop. And try the other one."

Which also was just fine with Kurtz.

Chapter 29

Barent woke up with his headache intact. He briefly considered calling in sick but glumly rejected the idea, dragged himself out of bed and drove to the office, his temples throbbing. Once there, he poured himself a cup of coffee, swallowed two aspirin, picked up the phone and slowly dialed Kurtz' office. Mrs. Schapiro answered and asked him to hold. After a few moments, Kurtz picked up. "Barent," he said, "What's happening?"

Barent winced. The sound of Kurtz' voice was like a knife slicing through his brain. "I was wondering if anything else might have occurred to you," he said. "About Longo."

Kurtz hesitated. "No," he said. "Sorry."

"Too bad," Barent said morosely, "I was hoping it might have."

"Sorry," Kurtz said again, then, "Are you alright?" he asked.

"What do you mean?"

"You don't sound too good. Is anything wrong?"

"Just a headache," Barent said. "I get headaches. I asked a doctor about it once, he said maybe it was migraines. You know anything about migraines?"

"Not too much. Do you take ergotrate?"

"No. Should I?"

"I think you should see a neurologist. They know more about headaches than I do."

Barent grunted. "I was in a bar last night, talking to a guy who had given me some information. They had these colored strobe lights. I don't know why anybody thinks it's sexy, seeing women dancing around in strobe lights. They don't look sexy to me; they look like aliens from outer space."

"Colored lights?" Kurtz said.

"Strobe lights. Red, purple and blue. Jesus, my head is killing me."

"Lights..." Kurtz said. His voice was distant.

"Yeah," Barent said, "lights. What about them?"

"Son of a bitch," Kurtz whispered. "Lights..."

"Hello, again," Barent said.

"Just can't stay away, can you?" Ronald Evans simpered. "Did you bring that luscious hunk with you?"

"No," Barent said, "the hunk is back at the office."

"What a shame. Well, what can I do for you?"

"Is Mario home?"

"No. He's at work."

"Maybe you can help." Barent reached into his jacket pocket and pulled out a series of black and white photographs. "Do you recognize any of these men?"

Ronald looked at him doubtfully. "Again?" he said. He took the photos and shuffled through them. When he came to the fifth one he stared for a moment, his brow wrinkling, then nodded briefly. "For sure," Ronald said. He tapped the picture with a fingernail. "This one."

Barent realized he had been holding his breath. He let it out slowly. "Finally," he murmured, "we're in business."

"It was the lights," Barent said. "Mercury vapor bulbs cast a blue light. Red hair looks dark brown under mercury vapor lights. That was smart of you," Barent said to Kurtz. "Real smart." Barent's headache had disappeared. "You got any more of that brandy?" he asked.

They sat in Kurtz' apartment. Kurtz leaned forward and re-filled Barent's snifter. "I'm glad it worked out," he said shortly.

"We made some black and white prints from the pictures in the hospital directory. Without the red hair confusing the issue, they recognized him right away."

"Great," Kurtz said morosely. Longo. Kurtz still had trouble with the idea. Longo? "I don't get it," he said, and shook his head. "He's a successful surgeon. He doesn't need the money."

"You don't know what he needs," Barent said.

"I guess not. I guess I don't know him at all."

"Doc, listen to me, there's no such thing as your average murderer. I've known cold blooded killers as sweet and mild mannered as choir boys, guys who go to church every Sunday, guys who donate a tenth of their income to charity. I'm telling you, you just can't tell."

You just can't tell...Kurtz had wanted to find Sharon Lee's murderer but he had somehow assumed it would turn out to be somebody he didn't know, or at least somebody he didn't like. Not Longo. "So what now?"

"Good question," Barent said. "In the past two days there have been three more. Longo's running a regular little assembly line. We know these guys are members of Ruiz' organization. We don't know how Rivera got involved with Longo and we don't know how Longo got involved with Ruiz. And we don't know how Tony Korda fits into the picture—if he fits into the picture at all. You know anything about insurance fraud?"

"No," Kurtz said, "not at all."

"Most of it is workman's comp or phony accidents. Minor car crashes are very popular. The way it works, they take out a policy on a vehicle, maybe

190

medical policies also on the driver and passengers, then the guy runs into another car that may or may not also be insured but is full of passengers. This car is also in on the deal and they get half a dozen claims for fictitious injuries on each crack up. Another variation, the guy will stop short at a light and get himself rear-ended. The guy who hit him was set up but it doesn't matter—his insurance has to pay. You don't do it on a highway, you do it on a nice street with a lot of traffic lights where you can't go fast enough to cause serious damage. The injuries are mostly orthopedic or neurologic: lower back pain, chronic headaches, whiplash, the sort of stuff that's difficult to disprove and is likely to need repeat treatment over a long period of time.

"It's quite a racket."

"It sounds like it," Kurtz said. "And how do you figure Sharon Lee ties in to all this?"

Barent swirled his brandy and squinted into the glass. "Maybe she doesn't. We don't know that he killed her, just that they were involved." Barent took a cigar out of his pocket, looked doubtfully at Kurtz, shrugged and put away the cigar. "But now we should have enough to get a warrant."

They jimmied the lock on Longo's office suite and went in the next night. Kurtz was not with them. He had wanted to come but Barent had refused. "You're a consultant, not a cop. You wouldn't want me hanging around in the O.R. and I don't want you hanging around here. So forget about it."

Kurtz hadn't liked it but he wasn't given a choice.

Longo's suite was much larger than Kurtz'. There were three examining rooms. A fourth room was filled with weights, parallel bars, wheelchairs, walkers, canes and vinyl-covered treatment tables. The equipment in the cabinets ran to heavy-duty scissors, rolls of plaster and ace bandages, rather than syringes and vials of medication. Longo's private office was filled with a weird assortment of exotic stuff gathered from around the world: three coconuts carved into faces, one smiling, one frowning, one crying, a set of Zulu shields, a zebra skin rug on the floor, a Chinese tea table with a relief sculpture of two opposing armies set beneath a glass cover. To Barent, most of it looked like junk.

The filing cabinets were closed but not locked. Patient records, neatly typed, filled most of the drawers. There were hundreds of them. He looked under "R" but found nothing for Rivera.

"Here." A cop named Vargas whispered it to him. Sitting on the secretary's desk was a black appointment book. "Okay," Barent said, and rubbed his hands together. He flipped through it briefly. On the dates that the suspects had been seen entering Longo's office, appointments were listed for Eduardo Santana, Raymond Cisneros, Guillermo Cordova and Paul Vilas.

The filing cabinets contained records corresponding to these names and Barent quickly photographed the pages.

"Oh, boy," Moran whispered. "Look at this." He held a sheaf of paper in his hand that he had pulled out of Longo's desk. They appeared to be white typing paper. He held them out to Barent. "Be careful," Moran said. "Don't burn your fingers."

Barent read the first one and whistled. He read, *"When you put it into me I came immediately and then I must have come another four times before you finished. I've never had a cock as large as yours before and I want it all the time."* The letter—if it was a letter—was unsigned. "Are they all like this?"

"All except the last one," Moran said. "Take a look."

Barent flipped through the sheaf to the last page. He stared at it. It read: *I know what you're doing. I won't let you get away with it.*

Barent felt a ferocious grin spread across his face. The tips of his fingers almost tingled. "Put everything back neatly," he said. "Except these. These are evidence."

"He'll miss them," Moran said. "He'll know someone was in here."

"Were they on the top of the stack?"

"No. They were in the middle."

"Good. Chances are he doesn't read them every day. With a little luck, he won't notice that they're gone, at least for a while. And if he does,"— Barent shrugged—"so what? There's not a thing he can do about it."

They put a tail on Carlos Rivera and the men who had called themselves Raymond Cisneros, Guillermo Cordova and Paul Vilas. Within a few days, all four of these men were observed entering the local branch offices of various insurance companies.

One day later, Barent and Moran drove up to a State Farm Insurance office in Queens. The manager was a lanky, thin man with a brush moustache and no hair at all on the top of his head. His name was Joe Weinbaum.

State Farm, it turned out, had no record of Carlos Rivera, but they did have a policy on Eduardo Santana. "He was in an accident about three months ago," Weinbaum said. "He suffered a dislocation of the sixth cervical vertebrae. It says here he has continuing weakness and pain down both arms and is currently unemployable. The medical bills are"— he frowned— "quite extensive."

"Who's the physician?"

"Philip Longo."

Barent smiled at Moran, who sat back with his hands folded across his chest, seeming to pay the conversation no attention whatsoever.

"What's this all about?" Weinbaum asked.

"Eduardo Santana's real name is Carlos Rivera. He's employed at a nightclub in Harlem. We've seen him there. He does not appear to be disabled.

"How much have you paid out?"

"Two thousand for auto repairs," Weinbaum said. "Over five in assorted medical bills." Weinbaum looked vaguely sick.

"Any of that for physical therapy?"

"Most of it. He's still going and we're still paying."

Barent scratched the side of his nose. He said, "We came across this information in connection with another case, the details of which I'm not free to discuss. When our investigation is completed—which should be within a few weeks—we'll release all the information and then you can pursue charges."

When they got back to the office, Barent settled himself behind the desk and leaned back, his hands behind his head. Moran poured a cup of coffee. Barent felt good. Things were finally coming into focus. Sharon Lee and Longo had been having an affair. She had found out about his illegal activities and tried to get him to stop. Most likely, he had killed her for it, or had her killed.

"What's next?" Moran asked.

"Talk to Longo." Moran nodded.

A knock came on the door. A plainclothesman stuck his head inside. "Man here wants to see you, Lew. Name's Oliver Thomas."

Barent and Moran looked at each other. Moran shrugged. "Show him in," Barent said.

A few seconds later, Oliver Thomas was sitting across the desk from Barent. He seemed uncomfortable. He fidgeted in his seat. Probably worried that he'll get his suit dirty. Barent smiled. "What can I do for you, Mr. Thomas?"

Oliver Thomas looked at Moran. "Can we speak alone?" Moran put down his coffee and left without a word.

Thomas followed Moran closely with his eyes. When the door had closed, he seemed to relax. "I got a call from Gordon Stone," he said. Thomas grinned with one side of his face. "I can hardly believe it. He says his organization will be ending its business association with First Amsterdam Savings and Loan. He actually sounded sorry, like he thought I might be upset and he was breaking it to me easy."

"Congratulations," Barent said. "That's what you wanted."

"Yes..." Oliver Thomas breathed the word as if a tremendous weight had been removed from his shoulders. "It's incredible. I would never have expected it." He smiled widely. "I would like to have my notebook back."

"Really..." Barent let a doubtful look cross his face. "How is your son, by the way?"

"He's doing fine."

"And Lenore?"

Oliver Thomas shrugged. "I try to pay the relationship as little attention as possible."

Barent smiled. "Well, Oliver," he said, "that doesn't surprise me. But your little request does. By your own admission, you've been involved for a number of years in crimes that include tax evasion, money laundering and racketeering. Under the RICO statutes, the feds could confiscate your entire organization. Do you really expect me to just hand the evidence back to you and forget about it? Why should I do that?"

"Evidence?" Oliver Thomas blinked at him. "What evidence? You have a notebook with the names of people who don't exist, listing transactions that never took place. Without my testimony, you have no evidence at all. Considering that I am no longer in any danger, I'm not about to give it."

"You might not have a choice."

Oliver Thomas was looking just a trifle annoyed. He fidgeted in his seat and leaned forward. "I suppose you could launch a formal investigation. You could subpoena me. I assure you, you would find nothing, and the law does not require me to testify against myself."

"But still, I do have a notebook in your handwriting. How would you explain that?"

"I'm writing a novel." Thomas waved his hands impatiently. "Those are my notes regarding the plot."

"A novel." Barent shook his head in amazement. "I've always admired creative people." He tapped his pencil against the desk while he thought about it. Oliver Thomas was a bigoted, supercilious windbag, but he was probably right. Without Gordon Stone and Raymond Santiago, the notebook alone would not be enough to convict anybody of anything.

"You may be correct," Barent said, "but I think I'm going to hold on to it for a little while longer."

Oliver Thomas opened his mouth to say something, then snapped it shut.

"Yes?" Barent said.

"You'll regret this," Oliver Thomas said.

"Get lost, Ollie." Barent stifled a belch behind his fist. Then he smiled. "And on your way out, would you ask Officer Moran to step back in here? We were about to have a cup of tea before you interrupted us."

Intellectuals only kill their own. It wasn't quite true, Kurtz reflected. They also killed whomever they regarded as a traitor to their class. That, he suspected, was at least a part of the problem with Kathy. Kurtz was intelligent, but he was not an intellectual, not by Kathy's rigorous standards, at least. She had still not called.

194

Lenore's comment the other night, the one about staking her claim...a lot of men might have resented a comment like that. Not Kurtz.

Kathy didn't trust people who were "certain" about things. Certainty, to Kathy, was the sign of a superficial intellect. Kurtz, on the other hand, had been trained to make decisions. A necrotic gallbladder was not amenable to philosophical persuasion. Kurtz respected people who knew their own mind; he felt comfortable with them. He also respected honesty, which had been one of the things that had attracted him to Kathy in the first place and was also one of the things he liked about Lenore. He supposed he might have felt differently about Lenore's comment if he had felt differently about Lenore, but he didn't. Lenore Brinkman was a woman he enthusiastically wanted to see again, anywhere, anytime. The next time would have to wait at least a few days, however, since Lenore had taken the shuttle down to Washington to consult on the artwork for an ad campaign. In a way, though, maybe that was just as well. Kurtz needed a little time to think. The fact was, he still felt bad about Kathy. He felt bad about the way it had ended (if it had ended). A woman was supposed to stand by her man and Kathy hadn't exactly stood four square and firm by him. But then, if we're being honest, it was pretty obvious that Kathy never had seen Kurtz as "her" man.

Whatever, she had still not called, and after last night he didn't much care...which made him feel guilty. He felt like he was supposed to care.

The next day was hard. The Sharon Lee case was finally breaking and he was only a spectator. That grated on him. He knew the feeling was illogical but he wanted to be there for the kill. He wanted to look Longo in the eye while the police confronted him and see his face crumple and ask him why he did it.

He passed Longo once in the hallways. Longo looked distracted. He had lost weight. Kurtz wondered what was going through his mind. Nothing good, he hoped.

Benson had passed away two nights before. He went quietly in his sleep, his wife at his side. She seemed grateful for the little that Kurtz had been able to do for him.

Nugent had left for the nursing home. Nugent had not been grateful at all. He seemed to think that his continued existence was a disappointment to his physicians and he took a spiteful pleasure in the fact. "Good riddance," he whispered. "Good riddance." And he smiled, his stark, white face glowing with malevolent glee.

Chapter 30

"Gentlemen." Longo's eyes flicked back and forth between their faces. "Come in." Did his smile falter just a trifle? Barent couldn't be sure.

Elegant, Barent thought. Weird but elegant. A large papier-mache sculpture painted in orange and purple sat in the living room. It looked like a cartoon character, with bulbous eyes, a Pinocchio nose and a tiny hat on its head. An abstract wire mobile hung from the ceiling. The windows gave a panoramic view of Downtown, with the Empire State Building framed in the middle.

Longo shifted his feet. He cleared his throat. "What can I do for you?"

"Can we sit down somewhere?" Barent asked.

"Yes, of course," Longo said. "Come this way."

They followed him across a tiled floor into a den with thick blue carpet. An oak coffee table sat in front of a brown leather couch. Book cases lined one wall. The other three walls were covered with shelves holding an assortment of small items; knives made of ebony, obsidian and bronze, ivory figurines, feathered masks, jade incense bowls, Chinese maidens carved out of some sort of lavender stone, small boxes from Russia and China painted in black lacquer, coral encrusted candelabras retrieved from sunken wrecks, old gold and silver coins, a pewter teacup with an engraved signature of Paul Revere on its side.

"Don't touch the boxes," Longo said, "the lacquer contains urushiol, the active ingredient in poison ivy. It can give you a bad rash."

"Poison ivy?"

"They used to paint valuables with the stuff, in China. It prevented thievery."

"I'll bet." It sounded like a good idea, actually. Maybe the Department should start recommending it.

Whatever, Longo seemed a bit more confident here in his inner sanctum, among his private treasures. He smiled brightly—though the smile seemed strained—and crossed his legs. "Please sit down," he said.

Moran slumped into a corner of the couch and fixed his expressionless gaze on Longo's face. Barent also sat. Longo glanced once at Moran and frowned minutely. He shifted in his seat and looked at Barent. "Tell me about Jaime Ruiz," Barent said.

Longo blinked. After a long moment, he said, "Jaime Ruiz? I don't think I know anyone by that name."

"No? How about Tony Korda, you know anyone by that name?"

Longo shook his head immediately and said, "No."

"Then how about Eduardo Santana? Raymond Cisneros? Paul Vilas? Shall I go on?"

Longo's face grew pale and his eyes wandered around the shelves lining the room. Probably kissing it all goodbye. Barent allowed a slight note of sympathy to enter his voice. "Tell me about it. How did you get involved with these people?"

"What people?" Longo whispered.

Barent frowned. "Don't be a dope. We've had you under surveillance for two weeks. We've seen every person who entered your office. One way or another, it's over."

Longo pulled in a long, deep breath and seemed about to say something. He closed his eyes. For almost a minute, he sat there without moving. Moran gave Barent a tiny grin and Barent nodded. Then Longo blinked his eyes and looked at Barent. "I gamble," he said. "Did you know that?"

"We knew it," Barent said. "I guess you don't win much."

"I'm pretty good. I win a lot." Longo shrugged.

"But not as much as you lose." Longo shook his head. "No."

"Is that all?"

"No. If it was only the gambling, I might have been able to handle it. I've been gambling for years. Like you said, I always lost a little more than I won but I never got into a hole I couldn't get out of—until my divorce. Annette took almost everything. Do you know the laws regarding child support in this State? Plus alimony?" Longo slumped down in his seat and a pained expression crossed his face. "The more I got behind, the more I gambled, and the more I gambled, the more I got behind."

"And Sylvia..." Longo laughed softly. "Sylvia has expensive tastes."

"So then you met Ruiz."

"It was at the Showboat. We were playing blackjack."

"He beat you," Barent stated.

"Oh, yeah."

"And now he owns you."

"I know it and he knows it but you'll never prove it. Everything was done through intermediaries. Vilas is the one who set it all up. I collect nothing on the patients they send me. Ruiz gets every penny. I'm trapped, but it's better than being dead."

"I understand," Barent said. "You're in a tough spot." Then he smiled. "So what made you kill Sharon Lee?"

The blood drained from Longo's face. "What?" he whispered.

197

"You heard me, you bastard," Barent said. His voice was no longer sympathetic.

"Sharon..." Longo shook his head. He licked his lips. "You don't know what you're talking about. I never killed Sharon Lee. I never killed anyone. Sharon and I..."

"Were having an affair," Barent stated.

"Yes." Longo barely nodded.

"And she found out about your little dealings with Ruiz and threatened to expose you. So you decided to kill her."

"That's crazy," Longo said. "Absolutely crazy. I would never have harmed a hair on Sharon's head. I—" He stopped abruptly.

"Go on," Barent said mildly. "Tell us how much you loved her." Longo swallowed. He frowned at the carpet.

"I thought so," Barent said. He smiled widely, put his hands in his pockets and stretched. "Speaking of hair," he said, "you got a zebra skin rug in your office. The two of you do it very often on that rug?"

Longo's face grew red. "I don't believe you have any legitimate reason to ask that."

"Really?" Barent's grin grew wider. "We found what appeared to be horse hair on her clothing. Zebra hair and horse hair look a lot alike."

Longo shrugged.

Barent waited a moment, then said, "And how about this?" He smiled down at a piece of white paper and handed it to Longo. Written on the paper were the words: *You won't get away with it. I won't let you.*

Longo visibly winced. "Where did you get this?" he demanded.

"Where do you think? From the desk in your office. We've seen all the little messages she sent you."

"Sharon got a big kick out of these." Longo paused and grimaced in embarrassment. "The thought that she was doing it under the noses of her co-workers really turned her on. She used the computer terminal up on O.B. and sent them through the hospital mail. This one arrived just like all the others. When I first received it, I thought exactly the same thing you did, that Sharon had found out. But why send me a thing like this? We saw each other all the time. Why not confront me with it directly? Once I calmed down, I decided to take the bull by the horns. I showed it to her. She knew nothing about it."

Barent looked at him. "Then who sent it to you?"

Longo shrugged. "Somebody else."

"Somebody else," Barent said. Pretty lame story. Lame enough to be true? Barent looked over at Moran, who shrugged minutely. "Good old somebody else. Tell me, just out of curiosity, what were you doing on the night Sharon Lee was killed?"

"Sylvia and I went to a benefit dinner for Settlement House."

"And after the dinner? What did you and the lovely Mrs. Longo do then?"

"We came home and went to sleep. We were together the entire night."

"Convenient," Barent said. "Did Mrs. Longo know anything about you and Sharon Lee?"

"No." Longo shook his head emphatically. "Never."

"So even though she might have had a motive to kill your girlfriend, she didn't know it."

"No."

Longo looked pretty shaken up. Good. He deserved it. He also looked sincere, which didn't mean a thing in itself because people who made a habit of telling lies usually got pretty good at faking it. Still...

"We're going to take you into custody," Barent said. "The charge is insurance fraud, which actually I couldn't care less about; but I want to be able to find you if it turns out that you haven't been telling me the truth." He stared into space, thinking. "Then we'll call Robinson," he said to Moran. "I have an idea."

It was nearly midnight. Except for the light shining through the glass door of the Personnel Office, the Administrative Floor of the hospital was dark.

Kurtz had been thinking of going to bed when the call from Barent had come. "Meet me in the Personnel Office at Easton. You might find it enlightening."

"Personnel? What are you talking about?"

"Harry and I are doing a little research. You don't have to bother if you don't want to but I thought you might be interested."

"I'll be there," Kurtz said.

He pushed open the door and entered. A long counter contained an open section in the middle. Behind the counter, parallel rows of stacks crammed full of file folders rose almost up to the ceiling. Nobody was in sight from the front of the room but Kurtz could hear voices coming from behind the stacks. He walked through. Barent and Moran were sitting at a long table with piles of folders strewn across the top. A small man with rumpled clothes and an annoyed expression on his face stood at the head of the table.

Barent looked up at Kurtz. "Sit down," he said. He glanced at the little man. "This is Jerry Simon, the Chief of Personnel. Robinson asked him to help us out."

"This is most irregular," Jerry Simon complained. "I see no reason why it couldn't have waited until the morning."

Barent ignored him. "Take a look at these," Barent said. He handed Kurtz a small pile of folders. "Tell me what you think."

Barent looked pleased. He had a happy smile on his face. Moran, though he rarely looked anything but impassive, was smiling as well. Kurtz weighed the pile doubtfully in his hand. "What's this all about?"

"Take a look."

At this hour of the night, Kurtz was not exactly in the mood for games, but the expression on Barent's face made him pause. He shrugged.

When he opened the third folder, he blinked, then looked up sharply at Barent. Barent's smile grew wider. "Jesus," Kurtz whispered.

"Let's go," Barent said.

Five minutes later they walked through the open doors of the Obstetrics Suite. Barent and Moran were in front, Kurtz right behind them. "I figured you deserved to be here but stay out of our way," Barent had said. That was fine with Kurtz.

It seemed to be quiet for a change. The delivery room doors were all dark. Nobody was screaming. A group of five nurses sat together in the central work area, sipping coffee and talking. They all looked up as Barent approached. Barent fixed his eyes on one of them, a pretty woman with dark hair. "Hello, Mrs. Ryan," he said softly.

She frowned. "Detective Barent..."

"Yes," Barent said. He paused for a moment, smiled, then said, "I'd like you to come down to the Station House with me."

"Why?" she asked in a small voice.

Barent glanced at the other nurses, who were staring wide-eyed at his face. "I think you know why," he said.

One hand came up and lightly rested on her throat. She blinked. "I didn't do it."

"Sure you did," he said.

Chapter 31

"Could you state your full name, please?"

Peggy Ryan looked at Ted Weiss with wide, frightened eyes and said, "Margaret Donaldson Ryan."

"Mrs. Ryan, for the tape, I would like you to also state that you have been informed of your Miranda-Escobedo rights and that you have agreed to give this testimony of your own free will."

"Yes," she said.

"Yes, what?"

She said obediently, "I have been informed of my rights and I have agreed to give this testimony of my own free will."

Ted Weiss smiled. "Thank you, Mrs. Ryan."

Weiss was enjoying this, Barent thought. He was in his element, a hawk circling for the kill.

"Now, Mrs. Ryan, could you please tell us where you were on the night of December Twenty-Second?"

"Why do you want to know that?" Peggy Ryan's lawyer asked. His name was Abner Cole and he seemed out of his depth. Probably did mostly tax work, maybe divorce. Barent silently nodded, morosely satisfied with this idea. Yeah, divorce.

"Sharon Lee was murdered on the night of December Twenty-Second," Ted Weiss said.

"Murder? Who said anything about murder?"

"This is a murder investigation, Counselor," Weiss said patiently. Cole shrugged his shoulders and sniffed, expressing his contempt for the proceedings.

"I don't know where I was on that night," Peggy Ryan said. "It was a month ago."

"The work schedule on the Obstetrics Floor says that you were working the four to midnight shift."

Peggy Ryan wrinkled her brow, as if trying hard to remember. "Then I guess I must have been. I don't recall."

"As I said, December Twenty-Second was the night that Dr. Sharon Lee was murdered. Does that refresh your memory?"

"You're harassing her," Abner Cole said.

Weiss looked at him with a wooden expression. "We're not in a courtroom. She can refuse to answer any time she wants to."

Cole shrugged. Peggy Ryan looked confused. "Not really," she said. "And yet, the next morning, you were observed to be crying. That's a pretty strong reaction."

"A person that I worked with every day was dead. I don't think my reaction was unusual."

"Do you know Dr. Philip Longo?"

"What's the significance of that question?" Abner Cole asked.

"It will become clear in just a moment, Counselor."

Peggy Ryan looked at her lawyer uncertainly. "He's right," Cole said. "You don't have to answer any questions that you don't want to."

She still looked uncertain, but she said, "I used to work for him."

"Why did you leave?"

"I felt that it was time for a change."

"I understand that you got married shortly after you left Dr. Longo's employ. Is that correct?"

"I was married about two years later."

"And now you're recently divorced."

"That's correct."

"What was the basis for the divorce?

She looked away, a tense expression on her face. "He was cheating on me. I wouldn't tolerate that."

"I see." Weiss nodded. "Prior to leaving his employ, were you having an affair with Philip Longo?"

"No," she said immediately.

"Really? Dr. Longo tells us that you were."

Her lips compressed into a thin line and she sat back into her chair, her shoulders tight and hunched.

"He says that your affair with him began shortly before his divorce. He says that you were rather...demanding. You wanted him to spend all of his time with you. If he had a late case in the Operating Room or wanted to go fishing with the boys, you threw a tantrum. He didn't like that. He dropped you for Sylvia Shannon, whom he eventually married."

She stared at him, saying nothing. "So you left."

"That bitch," Peggy Ryan said in a clipped voice.

"Perhaps you'll be happy to know that she's divorcing him also." She only looked at him, breathing hard.

"What did you do on the night of December Twenty-Second, after you left work?"

"I don't remember."

"She's already answered that question," Abner Cole said.

Weiss looked at Cole and shrugged. "I understand that you share an apartment with a woman named Abby Sloane," he said.

202

"Yes, that's right."

"Do you think Miss Sloane would remember whether or not you came home that night?"

"You'll have to ask her."

"We will," Ted Weiss said. He pulled a sheet of paper out of his briefcase. The paper said, *You won't get away with this. I won't let you.* "Have you ever seen this before, Mrs. Ryan?" Weiss asked.

She barely glanced at it, then looked away. "No."

"After it's been used for a little while, the drum on a laser printer begins to develop a pattern of tiny scratches, which leave a corresponding pattern of toner on the paper. This"—Weiss shook the piece of paper, which made a rustling sound—"was printed on the laser printer on the Obstetrics Suite."

Peggy Ryan shrugged. She stifled a yawn behind her open palm. Weiss grinned. "So then there's no way your fingerprints could be on this piece of paper; isn't that so?"

She looked at him and didn't answer.

"It's laser printer paper," Weiss said gently. "It's smoother than ordinary typing paper so that it can slide into the printer more easily. Paper like this holds fingerprints quite well, much better than most paper."

Her breath came faster. Abner Cole looked as if he might say something; then he looked away and shrugged.

"No possible way your fingerprints could be on this piece of paper?" Weiss asked.

"I think I've had enough of this," Peggy Ryan said. Abner Cole looked relieved.

Ted Weiss looked at Barent. It was the signal Barent had been waiting for. He took a small, cardboard box out of his pocket. "Would you open the box, please, Mrs. Ryan?"

She did so and looked down uncertainly, then drew in her breath.

Sitting in the box was a gold ring with an inscribed 'D' and a small diamond on a black obsidian face.

"Do you recognize that ring, Mrs. Ryan?" Barent asked.

"No," she said. "I don't think so."

"No? The other nurses on Obstetrics tell me that you often wore a ring that looked just like this one, on a chain around your neck. They tell me that the ring belonged to your father."

"So?"

"As you probably know, a psychiatric patient named Bill Mose has been accused of Sharon Lee's murder. Mr. Mose is a schizophrenic. He likes to swallow things. He had swallowed that ring. Have you any idea where he might have gotten it, Mrs. Ryan?"

Peggy Ryan looked at him for a long moment. "I hated her," she said softly.

"As your attorney," Abner Cole said, "I advise you to stop."

She looked at him, uncertain. Barent nodded encouragingly. Weiss sat back, an interested, almost sympathetic expression on his face.

Finally, she shook her head, shrugged and looked down at the floor, a brooding expression on her face. "I saw what she was doing," she said in a small voice. "He met her sometimes on the O.B. floor. I saw them together. Oh, they were careful. I doubt that anybody else noticed what was going on, but I knew him. I saw the way he looked at her. I recognized the signs. And she looked so smug, so satisfied with her dirty little affair."

Weiss smiled gently. He gave an encouraging little nod. Abner Cole sighed, shook his head and looked away.

"He had other women before me, I know that, but what we had together was special. He loved me. Maybe now he's telling you a different story—men do these things. They're always trying to rationalize their stupidity. Then she came along."

"Sharon Lee?" Weiss asked.

Peggy Ryan looked at him as if he were an idiot. "Of course not. Sylvia Shannon." She shook her head sadly. "We were going through a rough time right then. His divorce was almost final but the money situation looked terrible and his wife was giving him hell. He was under a lot of tension and I"—she gave a bitter little laugh—"I was probably not as understanding as I should have been. Maybe he was coming to associate me with his problems, though I assure you, his relationship with his wife had gone sour long before I entered the picture. Still, I was with him when he was going through the bad times and maybe he wanted some- body who wouldn't remind him of them. Then he met her." She shrugged. "I couldn't take it. I quit. I saw him every once in a while after that but I don't think he saw me. I tried to keep out of his way. It would have been too painful. And then recently he began taking up with Sharon Lee." She shook her head. "Everybody hated Sharon Lee. She was an arrogant, obnoxious bitch."

Barent had heard somewhere that women doctors often had a difficult time of it with women nurses. It seemed there was a lot of resentment on both sides. Then again, from everything he had heard about her, Sharon Lee probably had been an arrogant, obnoxious bitch.

"One night, I was working the graveyard shift and she had a case, a D and C for a missed abortion. I guess he had a case too because I saw them near the elevators afterward, going up to the call rooms, giving each other little glances like love struck rabbits, and I knew then that I had to do something to stop it. I sent him that message. I don't even know why. I suppose I wasn't thinking very carefully but I knew better than to confront her. She would have just laughed at me, the woman scorned, the sore loser. I guess I thought maybe he would pay attention."

She shook her head. One slow tear began to trickle from the corner of her eye. "But they didn't stop, and I couldn't let it go on. I just couldn't. I wouldn't. But I needed help. There was no way that I could...do it by myself. I knew a man who I thought would help me. His name is Emilio Gonzaga. I was the nurse on duty the day his little boy was born with a congenital abnormality. He went crazy. He threatened to tear the place apart and then later, I heard that he tried to sue her. It wasn't hard to find him."

"How much did you pay him?"

"He didn't ask much. He wanted to do it. He really despised her. Almost as much as I did."

"Was he the only one involved?"

"No. He brought along two other men." She frowned slightly. "Carlos Rivera...I'm not certain of the other one, Delgado something."

Weiss glanced at Barent. "Herman Delgado?"

"I think so. Yes."

"Go on."

"I waited until she had a patient in labor at night. I was pretty sure she would be stuck until late and I called Gonzaga. I almost turned out to be wrong. The patient delivered faster than I expected and Sharon left. She was probably halfway home when an emergency case arrived, a teenage girl who needed a stat C-section. So we beeped her and she had to come back. I had called Gonzaga before the late shift started and he came in with his friends. The security guards are supposed to stop people who don't have legitimate business but I had given him my I.D. card to copy. He put pictures of himself and the others on the phony cards, just in case the guards were looking, but they probably weren't. It's never too hard to get past them."

Weiss glanced at Barent again. "So I've been told."

"They waited for me in the basement, in one of the old storerooms. Nobody goes down there at night. It was perfect."

Weiss nodded. "Go on."

"After the C-section was over, I went and got them." Peggy Ryan shook her head and gave a little shudder. "I was frightened, but they were waiting for me, just like they were supposed to. We went upstairs and they stayed behind for a few minutes while I went onto the attendings' wing to make certain it was empty." She shrugged. "It almost always was. We didn't have a key to Sharon's room, either. I suppose they would have broken in if they had to but the connecting room door was open." She stopped and gave a little smile.

205

"Yes?" Weiss prompted.

"They killed her."

"How?"

"They strangled her."

"Did you see it? Were you there?"

"No. I waited in the connecting call room."

"Why did you go with them? Couldn't they have done it without you?"

Peggy Ryan hesitated. "I wanted to see it. I wanted to see her face." She gave a tiny laugh. "But at the last second, I left. I couldn't bring myself to watch."

"How did you know which room she would be in?"

"The room she was in and the one it connected with were reserved for obstetrics."

Weiss nodded. "Then what?"

"Then we left. On the way out, we ran into Bill Mose, the psych patient. He was stumbling down the hall, babbling to himself. Gonzaga and Delgado wanted to kill him but I had a better idea. I recognized him. I had seen him when they took the psych patients out to the playground. I knew he was completely out of his mind. He didn't know where he was or who he was or who we were. He was hallucinating. There was no way at all that he could have remembered us or been any sort of a credible witness. We took him back to the call room and Delgado held him still while Gonzaga and Rivera lifted up Sharon's body and scratched his arm with her fingernails, enough to draw blood." She shrugged. "I found a kitchen knife in one of the call rooms. We gave it to him and put him on an elevator.

"I didn't notice until I got home that the chain had broken and my father's ring was missing. I couldn't be certain of where it had happened but it was already morning. I didn't know what else to do and so I came in to work." She shook her head and smiled awkwardly. "I was terrified that it might have fallen while we were up in the call room. That's why I was crying when you saw me; I hadn't had much sleep and I was pretty strung out. I was afraid you were coming to arrest me, but when nobody mentioned the ring, I figured it would never show up."

"So that's it," Weiss said.

She shrugged. "I hated her. I would do it all over again, even if I knew I was going to be caught. I want you to realize that."

"Thank you, Mrs. Ryan," Ted Weiss said. He glanced at Abner Cole, who was staring at the floor with a sour expression on his face. "We appreciate your candor."

"Well, I would," she said sincerely. "I really would. I wouldn't want you to think that I did it for trivial reasons. What she did was wrong, stealing another woman's husband. She deserved to die for that and I'm not sorry about it one bit."

Chapter 32

"Peggy Donaldson." Edward Ornella shook his head sadly and took a bite out of a turkey sandwich. He had brought his lunch into the office and was eating it between patients. "Little Peggy Donaldson. I remember her very well. It was an awful tragedy."

"What was?" Kurtz asked.

"You didn't know?" Ornella frowned into space. "I guess you wouldn't know. Peggy's mother played around. She left her husband for another man. Peggy must have been eight, maybe nine years old when it happened. Frank Donaldson was a real nice guy. He was pretty broken up about it. He shot himself."

Kurtz stared at him. "That's terrible. What happened to Peggy?"

"I'm not sure. I think she was raised by an aunt."

Peggy Ryan had been well liked. The people she worked with were all stunned by what had happened. Kurtz, who had never known Peggy Ryan, was willing to feel sorry for a little girl abandoned and then tragically orphaned but was not inclined to waste much sympathy on the killer she had grown into. Mostly, he was glad that it was over. Longo would probably lose his license. He might even go to jail, but in the end he was a weakling, not a murderer. Kurtz felt a little better about that. Order had been restored to the world. Here's to order, Kurtz thought, and sipped his Coke.

Barent was not as pleased. Barent and Moran had dropped in on Kurtz' apartment the evening before to tell him how it had gone. Barent sat with his shoulders slumped and barely looked at the glass of brandy that Kurtz had placed in front of him. "What's bothering you?" Kurtz asked.

"I sort of hoped that this case would go a little higher than it has," Barent said morosely.

"Ah," Kurtz said. So that was it; the big ones were swimming away. "Maybe it will yet. You still don't know who killed Herman Delgado. And you don't know what Gonzaga and Rivera will have to say."

"True," Barent said, but he sounded unconvinced.

That afternoon, Barent and Moran drove out to the warehouse where Emilio Gonzaga worked. The foreman gave them a blank look when he saw them walk up. "Gonzaga again?"

"Yes."

"He's still at the same place."

"Thanks."

Maybe Gonzaga had heard something. Maybe he saw it in Barent's face. Gonzaga was hoisting a bale in both hands when Barent approached. He froze, then without a word he dropped the bale and started to run. "Hey," Barent yelled. "Come back here!"

Gonzaga ignored him. Arms pumping, head down, he ran all out toward the entrance on the other side of the stacks. Suddenly, Moran stepped out from behind a pile of shelving. Gonzaga tried to swerve but he stumbled on the dusty floor. Moran spun once. His left foot connected with Gonzaga's abdomen and Gonzaga collapsed, gasping. "You have the right to remain silent," Moran said. He pulled a pair of hand- cuffs from his belt and snapped them around Gonzaga's wrists. "If you choose to give up that right, then anything you say may be used against you. You have the right to an attorney..."

"I thought you said Shotakan didn't use kicks," Barent said as he sauntered up to them.

Moran smiled. Gonzaga looked back and forth between the two policemen. A drop of blood trickled from the corner of his lip. "Shotokan encourages the practitioner to express his latent creativity."

Gonzaga glared at them. "I tell you nothing," he said. "Nothing!"

"Who asked?" Barent said.

"Hey, man, you can't come in here," Carlos Rivera said.

The little man wore dirty denim jeans and a worn out olive colored parka that leaked stuffing from a small hole below the front pocket. He looked up blearily. "Why the fuck not?" he slurred.

"Cause we got a dress code. Nobody comes in here dressed like that. You want to come in here, you got to wear clean clothes, get a shave, look nice."

"Shit..." He peered up at Rivera uncertainly. "It's cold out there," he whined.

Rivera shrugged. "Tough."

"Say," the little man said. "Don't I know you?"

"Not a chance," Rivera said.

"Sure. I know you." The little man squinted, then nodded his head firmly. "You're Carlos Rivera."

Rivera's nostrils flared. A tense expression crossed his face. "Get out of here," he said.

"Sure." The little man bobbed his head. "Carlos Rivera."

"Out." Rivera reached out and attempted to grab the little man by the collar but he backed away.

209

"Hey, Carlos, you need any help." Two enormous bouncers wearing suits and ties approached from the rear of the club.

"No," Rivera said.

"Jeez," the little man said, and smiled. "How long you been working here, Carlos?"

"Get out!"

The little man shook his head, reached into his jacket, pulled out a badge with one hand and a gun with the other and said, "You're under arrest."

Rivera stopped abruptly. He stared at the little man. The little man smiled widely and said, "You have the right to remain silent..."

Gonzaga, as he had promised, stayed in his cell, glared at them sullenly from under hooded eyes, set his lips and refused to talk. Carlos Rivera also shook his head and said absolutely nothing. Barent was not surprised. "These guys talk, somebody will break their skulls with a baseball bat as soon as they hit prison. Forget it."

"Peggy Ryan's testimony ought to do it," Moran said. Barent hardly heard him. "Yeah," he said. "Sure."

"What's on your mind?"

Barent's eyes flicked to Moran, then away. He shrugged. "Ruiz," Moran said, "and Korda."

"That's right: Ruiz and Korda." Moran looked at him questioningly and Barent shrugged. "When all is said and done, the case is solved but we've hit a dead end. We'll never find out what happened to Herman Delgado and we've got no way to connect Ruiz or Korda to any of it. At least, no way that will hold up in court." Barent shook his head sadly.

For the next two days, Barent moped around the house. He seemed distracted. Betty tried more than once to talk to him but he barely heard her and finally she gave up and let him stew. The Priest, Father Michael, visited once to discuss the wedding plans. He pointedly avoided Barent. Barent barely noticed. Barent was thinking. For two days he sat in his chair in front of the television, staring at the list of deposits that Oliver Thomas had given him. By the end of the second day, he came to a conclusion. He copied the list on the Xerox machine at the office, put the copy in an envelope and dropped it in the mail. Then he waited.

Three days later, at two o'clock in the morning, Jaime Ruiz and his bodyguards left the Vanity Social Club. Jaime felt good; all of his plans were going well. He was rich. His head spun with fine cognac and the best cocaine. The night was cold, clear and still, and he breathed in the crisp air like it was another line of coke. He shook his head slowly as he considered where he had come from and where the future was taking him and he thought, *No, I don't feel good. I feel wonderful!* It was a thought that Jaime cherished and had grown used to. He laughed a little and rubbed at his nose. The tip was numb.

One of his men went to get the car. A minute later, the limousine came around the corner and pulled up to a stop. The doors opened. Jaime Ruiz barely had time to register the single man in the front seat and the two others in the back before their weapons opened fire. Gouts of orange flame pierced the air. Jaime felt something thud against his chest and then, his legs suddenly weak, he slumped to the ground. He tried to gather his feet underneath himself and rose fitfully to his knees but another bullet hit him in the back and he fell. The car doors closed and the limousine pulled away from the curb. Jaime Ruiz blinked his eyes once at the stars twinkling so high overhead, shuddered once and then lay still.

The shooting took place in another precinct and so Barent did not get the call. He first received the news from a third page story in The Times. He noticed the heading, read it carefully through twice, nodded silently to himself and closed the paper.

That afternoon, Moran said to him, "You hear about Ruiz?"

Barent smiled into his cup of coffee. "Uh-huh."

"What do you think?"

"You know that list of deposits that Oliver Thomas gave us?" Barent allowed a small, grim smile to creep across his face. "I wonder about that list, the amounts that Ruiz put in. You think those are the amounts that Ruiz told Korda?"

Moran looked at him.

"The insurance scam, the nightclub...who knows what else Ruiz was into? A guy like Korda, he expects his take. He doesn't get it, he won't be pleased."

"How would he know?"

Barent nodded his head. He stared at the smoke rising from his cigarette, then he shrugged. "These things have a way of getting out," he said.

Moran stared at him for a long time, while Barent sipped his coffee and blew smoke rings at the ceiling, then he slowly smiled. "What about Gordon Stone?" Moran asked. "What about Korda?"

Barent shrugged again. "Patience, Harry," he said. "We're only human."

Peggy Donaldson had been seven years old. She had awakened at night, hearing noises coming from somewhere in the apartment. "Daddy?"

she whispered. There was no answer. Sleepily, she got out of bed and toddled down the hall. The sounds were coming from her parent's bedroom, rhythmic gasps, whistling moans. She pushed open the door. Her mother was on her hands and knees in the dark. The sounds were coming from her. She was naked. A man Peggy didn't recognize kneeled on the bed behind her, moving back and forth. He was naked too. "Mommy?" she asked uncertainly.

Her mother's eyes snapped open. She saw Peggy and began to laugh. "Come here," she said.

The man behind her stopped moving and slowly smiled...

Abner Cole had posted her bond and now Peggy Ryan was back home after a long two days in jail. Peggy's roommate had moved out in her absence, evidently unwilling to share an apartment with a murderess. It was almost midnight. Peggy Ryan sat at the kitchen table and filled a glass full of vodka and drank all of it in a single gulp. Then she took a Valium out of a pillbox, put it in her mouth, chewed it and swallowed. There had been twenty Valiums in the pillbox; this was the last. She emptied the final shot of vodka into the glass and slowly sipped until it was finished, then she rose to her feet, slid open the door leading to the balcony and walked slowly over to the edge. Her entire body was numb. She barely felt the cold. She closed her eyes, deliberately relaxed her legs and slumped forward, over the railing. She felt as if she were drifting as the ground rushed toward her and she almost giggled. What she did was wrong, Peggy Ryan thought fuzzily. She wondered, in the instant before she hit, exactly who it was that she meant.

He sat on the couch in his living room, sipping brandy, and watched the river flow by. It rippled in the moonlight. "In a Sentimental Mood," Ellington and Coltrane, was playing on the stereo—a very sad piece. Sharon Lee, Peggy Ryan, Jaime Ruiz...they were all dead. Kurtz was alive, reason enough to feel good about things, considering the alternative.

He stared at the phone, brooding, and at that instant, it began to ring. Kurtz smiled wryly and picked it up.

"Richard?" It was Kathy. She sounded hesitant.

For a moment, he could barely speak. "Yes," he said. "How are you?"

"I'm fine." He could hear her swallow. Her voice wavered for an instant, then she said in a rush, "I know it's been a long time but I've been thinking. I've been thinking that perhaps I was too hasty. I miss you.

"Could we get together, please, maybe on the weekend?"

"I see." There was silence for a long moment. "I've been thinking about you, too." He paused, the words suddenly sticking in his throat. He opened his mouth and then closed it. He stared at the phone. He shook his head slowly and said, "I'm sorry, Kathy, but I've come to think that your misgivings were justified. Remember when you said we were different sorts of people? Well, I think you were right."

"Oh..." She sounded surprised. He waited a long ten seconds, then he sighed and gave a little shrug. "Goodbye, Kathy," he said. He hung up the phone so softly that it barely clicked.

Just like that.

Lenore had been home for at least two days. He picked up the phone again and dialed it. Her deep, husky voice answered. "Yes?"

"Lenore? Hi. It's Richard Kurtz."

"Well, hello." The slightest tinge of amusement colored her tone. "I was beginning to wonder if you were going to call."

"I'm sorry," Kurtz said. "I really am. I had some things I had to work out first. Would you like to have dinner with me, maybe tomorrow night?"

"Tomorrow? Let me see...tomorrow is Thursday. Yes, I think tomorrow would be just fine."

"Pick you up at seven?"

"Seven is perfect."

"Is there anyplace special you'd like to go?"

"Not really. Why don't you meet me at my apartment and we'll play it by ear?"

"Okay, I'll be there at seven."

"Great," she said. "I'll see you then."

He leaned back into his couch, sipped his brandy and watched the river drift by. The stars twinkled overhead; the city lights reflected on the water; the moon was full. Nice view, Kurtz thought. The stereo faded into silence.

He glanced at his watch, finished the brandy and rose to his feet. He had a tough case scheduled for the morning, a gallstone stuck in the ampulla of Vater, where the common bile duct and the pancreatic duct join together before entering the duodenum. The stone had caused obstruction and scarring of both ducts. The indicated procedure was to take everything apart and sew the pancreas and the remains of the bile duct directly to the duodenum. It was a tough case, Kurtz thought, an interesting case.

He could hardly wait.

—The End—

Information about the Kurtz and Barent Mystery Series

I hope you enjoyed *Surgical Risk*.

The series continues with *The Anatomy Lesson*, in which surgeon Richard Kurtz and police detective Lew Barent are determined to solve the brutal murder of Rod Mahoney, a respected Professor of Anatomy at Staunton College of Medicine. Please read on for a preview of *The Anatomy Lesson*.

For updates regarding new releases, author appearances and general information about my books and stories, please sign up for my newsletter/email list at www.robertikatz.com/join and you will also two **free short stories**. The first is science fiction, entitled, "Adam," about a scientist named Fischer who uses a tailored retrovirus to implant the Fox P2 gene (sometimes called the language gene) into a cage full of rats and a mouse named Adam, and the unexpected consequences that result. The second is a prequel to the Kurtz and Barent mysteries, entitled "Something in the Blood" featuring Richard Kurtz as a young surgical resident on an elective rotation in the Arkansas mountains, solving a medical mystery that spans two tragic generations.

Preview: The Anatomy Lesson

Chapter 1

Two white, protruding fangs peeked out over Nolan's lower lip while a tiny red dribble of dried blood trailed down his chin. His skin was the color of flesh that has lain for many years at the bottom of a grave. His clothes were jet-black and rippling. "It's not bad," he said, and frowned down into a styrofoam cup. "Still a little weak, though."

The ghoul grunted and poured a thick, brown liquid into the bowl. "Try it now."

Nolan dipped his cup into the bowl and sipped delicately, then nodded. "Perfect," he said, and smacked his lips.

"Good." The ghoul took a greenish-looking hand out of a bag and placed it into the bowl, where it floated. "You like?" he asked.

The vampire smiled. "Definitely."

The ghoul smiled back. The ghoul's name was Redding. Redding was almost six and a half feet tall and cadaverously thin, which went along perfectly with his gray skin and decaying features. The vampire looked at him and despite himself, almost shuddered.

"Help me with these, will you?" Redding asked.

Gingerly, Nolan reached into the bag, retrieved more body parts and scattered them strategically around the room. "How about the head?" Redding asked. "Hang it from the chandelier?"

The vampire considered the suggestion, then nodded. "I'll do it," he said. He stood on a chair and attached the head with a piece of twine so that it hung suspended in mid-air a foot below the ceiling. The head's eyes drooped slightly open. They seemed to stare at him accusingly.

"Beautiful," Redding said, "just beautiful."

The vampire examined the head, reached out a clawed hand and fluffed up the red, matted hair. His fangs protruded as a slow smile spread across his face.

Both of them took a moment to admire their work: neatly laid-out platters of hors d'oeuvres, cold cuts and smoked salmon, loaves of bread and soft rolls already sliced, green salad, macaroni salad and potato salad and a pot of baked beans bubbling over a portable heating coil, pretzels, bottles of wine and soda and beer, assorted cakes and pies and sweet pastries and a small cooler set up in the corner of the room with gallons of ice cream inside, and of course the *piece de resistance*, the enormous bowl of rum-laden punch in the center of the table, with a green plastic hand floating on top.

"Beautiful," Redding said again.

The vampire nodded and looked at his watch. "They'll be arriving in less than an hour. Help me set up the VCR."

"You got Nightmare on Elm Street?"

"Yup. And Fright Night and the original Dracula with Bela Lugosi."

"You dog," Redding said.

The vampire shrugged modestly and switched off the light as they left the room.

"I love Halloween," Redding said.

"Trick or treat," the vampire said, and giggled.

Within an hour, the guests began to arrive. Nolan met them at the door, shook the men's hands and pretended to bite the women on the neck. Most of the women responded with mock shrieks. One, a tiny witch with

215

straggly orange hair and a crooked plastic nose, merely yawned. Her name was Carrie Owens.

"So young and so blasé," Nolan said.

Carrie Owens yawned again. "I was on call last night."

The vampire smiled sympathetically. "Go on in and sit down," he said. He waved a hand at the door to the outer office, where Redding had set up bowls of pretzels, potato chips and dip on a corner table between two couches. Fright Night was playing on the T.V.

Carrie went in and flopped herself on the couch. She felt numb. The night before, a fifteen-year old had blown off three fingers with a cherry bomb ... not exactly appropriate to the season but there you were, and after the kid was worked up and sent to surgery, a five year old who had swallowed her mother's asthma medication had arrived in the ER, seizing. After that had come a routine stab wound followed by an old geezer brought in by ambulance complaining of chest pain, who promptly arrested. They had worked on the old guy for over two hours. Every time they got a rhythm going, he would wake up for a few seconds and start screaming. Then his heart would fibrillate again, his eyes would roll back and he would go limp as the blood flow to his brain began to fall. In between shocks they pumped on his chest. He was finally stabilized on amiodarone, lidocaine, pronestyl and bretylium drips and sent off to C.C.U. but it had not been a pleasant night for the patient or for Carrie.

On the T.V., somebody was being stabbed in the chest with a wooden stake. Carrie winced.

A man in a pirate's hat flopped down on the couch beside her, a Heineken bottle in one hand and a half-empty glass in the other. His name was David Chao, one of the private surgeons. "Hey, there," he said. "How you doing?"

She yawned again. "I'm tired."

"Rough night?"

"It sucked."

Chao nodded sympathetically. "You here with anybody?"

"I was supposed to meet Angie West but she got stuck in the ER."

Chao cocked his head to the side and gave her a speculative look. "Where's Frank Merola these days?" he asked.

"I don't really know," Carrie said. "And I don't really care."

"Ah..."

Carrie shrugged. On the T.V. screen, an enormous bat was blasted into gouts of ugly-looking smoke by a beam of sunlight. On the other side of Chao, a mummy and a pint-sized Darth Vader flopped down onto the couch, munching pretzels. A devil with a long red tail and an alien in a silver spacesuit came in and leaned against the wall. The little room was

216

getting crowded. A woman dressed in a Tinkerbell costume opened up a window.

"Attention, everybody ..."

Nolan stood in the doorway, his cape spread wide, his fangs bared. "Dinner is served."

Carrie rose with an audible groan as the party trooped out and into the next room.

"Very nice," Chao said.

"Yuck," Carrie replied. She was staring at the head hanging from the ceiling. "A little too realistic, if you ask me."

Redding went over to the punchbowl and started to fill the glasses with a metal ladle. People grabbed plates and Redding handed out the punch as the line went by.

Carrie sipped. The punch tasted...strange. She peered into her glass. Floating on the surface was a gray and pink glob, with tiny white strands floating all around it. "God ..." she whispered. She looked at all the animated, happy people, talking, eating their food, sipping their wine or beer or punch. One or two, however, were staring uncertainly into their glasses. She walked over to the bowl. Submerged beneath the surface was a human hand.

Redding looked at her with concern. "Something the matter?" he asked.

Carrie plucked a serving spoon from the table, dipped it into the bowl and brought out the hand. It fell off the spoon and dropped to the table, pink and gray and silent, the fingers curled into a shrunken claw. Carrie's stomach did a flip-flop. Redding grinned, looked at the hand and started to say something. He stopped. An uncertain frown crossed his face. Gingerly, he reached out a finger and touched the soft, yielding flesh. It made a squishing sound.

"That looks real," Carrie said in a clipped voice.

"Yes, it does," Redding answered. "It really does. Jesus ..."

Carrie leaned over the table and threw up.

Chapter 2

"Cause of death?" Barent asked.

The Medical Examiner squinted down at the head, which was perched on top of the table like an exotic mushroom. The cops were still scouring the room, coming up with more stray body parts

"Hard to tell, actually," the M.E. said.

"Why is that?"

The M.E. looked at Barent as if he could barely restrain his glee, slapped his thigh with an open palm and cackled. "Because they've been embalmed. They're soaked in formalin." The M.E. cackled again, his beady eyes bright. He sounded, Barent thought, like a demented chicken. "This isn't murder, Barent. It's some bright young idiot's idea of a joke."

He picked up a hand and held it under Barent's nose. Barent reared his head back and blinked rapidly. "You smell it?" the M.E. asked.

"Yes," Barent said. His eyes were tearing.

"Formalin." The M.E. smiled in genuine delight at the assortment of body parts. "So far, we've got three hands, one whole torso, one foot, two heads, a liver, a heart and two mismatched lungs. They're from at least three different bodies. I suggest you take a look up in the anatomy lab. You'll find that somebody has pilfered a few cadavers. Like I said, a joke."

"Some joke."

The M.E. shrugged, still smiling. "Reminds me of my medical school days."

Barent shuddered.

The M.E. waved a hand toward the door where the partygoers were clustered outside the room, peering in over the yellow crime-scene tape and grinning. "Look at them," the M.E. said. "They've figured it out for themselves."

The ones who had drunk the punch with the hand in it were generally not so happy.

"Think any of them had something to do with it?"

"Who knows?" The M.E. shrugged. "I critique the performance. You seek out the artist. Happy Halloween."

"Right," Barent said. "Sure."

Barent walked over to the doorway with the Medical Examiner, and after the M.E. had pushed his way out, Barent spoke to a tall young man dressed as a vampire. "I understand this is your party?"

The vampire looked around, first left, then right, then grinned sheepishly. "Not exactly. Bob Redding and I organized it."

Barent lifted one edge of the tape. "Come in," he said. Nolan did so and Barent squinted at him. "Don't I know you?"

"Steve Nolan. You met me last year at Easton."

"That's right." Barent nodded. "What are you doing here?"

"I finished my residency in June. I'm on staff."

Barent grunted. Harry Moran, a burly cop in a blue suit and swept back brown hair came up to them. He didn't look at Nolan. "That seems to be it."

The assortment of body parts lay clustered together on the table next to the punch bowl.

Nolan glanced at them with casual interest. He seemed to be trying not to smile. Barent, whose work as a homicide detective had exposed him over the years to more corpses than he cared to remember, had difficulty seeing dead bodies–particularly dismembered dead bodies–as funny. He found himself frowning. "I've been told this was a joke."

"Yeah," Nolan said. "It does seem likely.

"Nevertheless, I imagine that whoever is in charge of the bodies, and also the administration of the medical school, will not be pleased."

Nolan shrugged.

"You have any idea who might have done it?" Barent asked.

"Not a clue."

"I understand that you and your friend Redding put a bunch of plastic body parts around the room."

"That's correct."

The dismembered plastic corpse had been found stuffed in a closet. "Who had access to this room?" Barent asked.

"Damned if I know. I locked the door after we finished setting up but plenty of people must have keys."

"I understand this room is part of the faculty club?"

Nolan nodded. "It's usually used for meetings. We generally have a Halloween party here and a Christmas party for the staff, and also a graduation party for the medical students."

"So what you were doing was nothing unusual."

Nolan shook his head. "No."

"When did you finish getting ready for the party?"

"About an hour before."

"What did you and Redding do then?"

"I went back to my apartment for a little while."

"Where is that?"

"Right down the street. The Medical School owns the building. It's faculty housing."

"How about Redding?"

"You'll have to ask him."

Barent grunted again. He was not pleased. Despite his relief that nobody had been killed, he resented being here. Halloween was a lousy time of the year for a cop. This was only the beginning of what would most likely be a long, miserable night, and he resented wasting his time. "You know, it might be just a joke but vandalism, thievery and desecration of the dead are all against the law."

Nolan held up one hand and moved it back and forth, as if weighing the options. "Medical school is a gruesome business. After awhile, you stop thinking of the cadavers as people, or even as dead bodies. After a

219

little while, they're just an unpleasant source of information. I know that sounds insensitive but none of us could survive emotionally if we didn't learn to look at it that way."

"Regardless of your sensitivity or lack thereof, it's still a crime."

Nolan shrugged. "I suppose so."

"This sort of thing happen often? Little jokes with the cadavers?"

"No." Nolan shook his head. "Not at all. The administration is quite aware of the effect such incidents would have upon the school's reputation. Any student who screws around with their cadaver would be instantly expelled. They let you know that."

"Who's in charge of them?"

"The cadavers?"

"Yes."

"Rod Mahoney is the professor in charge of the Anatomy course."

"Where would I find him?"

"Probably at home, watching T.V."

Barent nodded his head and made a notation in his notebook. "I'm going to want to look over the place where they keep the cadavers. Who can take me there?"

Nolan looked at the table spread with Halloween goodies. The crime lab techs were dusting for fingerprints, peering through magnifying glasses and collecting samples of dust from every corner of the room. "What about our party?"

Barent raised an eyebrow. "You can party somewhere else."

"What about the food?"

"You really want to eat it? There's a mummified hand in the punch bowl. Who knows what you'd find in the dip?"

Nolan sighed. "True. I guess the party's over." He shook his head sadly. "Give me a minute. I'll take you up there."

Barent, Harry Moran and Nolan took an elevator up to the Eleventh Floor, where the Gross Anatomy and Histology courses were taught. A faint, decaying odor permeated the entire floor. There were ten classrooms, five on each side of the hall. Each classroom contained four workspaces, and each workspace contained three low tables set against each other in a U with a book shelf running above them, three small lockers, recessed lights set beneath the book shelves and three chairs. Between adjoining workspaces, beneath the tables, were what appeared to be two long metal safes with combination locks on the doors.

"The lockers are for microscopes. The cadavers are kept in there," Nolan said, and pointed to a safe. "Four cadavers in each classroom. Three students to a cadaver."

"Show me one," Barent said.

220

"I can't. I don't know the combinations."

"Who does?"

"Each student gets the combination to his own cadaver."

"Anybody else?"

Nolan shrugged. "I wouldn't know."

"Mahoney have the combinations?"

"I would think so. He probably assigns them, or one of his assistants."

Barent grunted and turned to Moran. "Give Mahoney a call. Get him here."

"Suppose he doesn't want to come?" Moran asked.

"A crime has been committed. We're not giving him a choice," Barent said.

Rod Mahoney was a tall, thin man, with light, blue eyes behind wire-rimmed glasses. The remnants of his thinning, brown hair were combed carefully over the top of his head and then plastered down. He wore a plaid bowtie in pastel pink and green, a light blue oxford shirt, brown corduroy pants, brown leather loafers and a white lab coat. He wrung his hands as he talked. "This is terrible. Simply terrible. You won't tell the newspapers, will you?"

Fat chance. The media were not exactly the cops' best friends. Barent scratched his head. "It's not our job to keep the press informed."

Mahoney sighed, obviously relieved. "Thank you," he said.

"Dr. Nolan tells me you have the combinations to the safes where the cadavers are kept."

"That's true." Mahoney blinked at Moran, looking like a bewildered rabbit. "I was asked to bring them along."

"Alright, we'll start here. I want you to open every one of them." Mahoney looked even more bewildered. "Is that really necessary?"

Barent wondered. Most likely, the M.E. was correct. It was all just a "joke." Certainly, Nolan seemed willing enough to accept it as such. But something about the whole thing stuck in Barent's craw. Barent wasn't a physician. Maybe he just lacked a sense of humor but a crime was still a crime and fuck Nolan and his amused, long-suffering attitude.

"I think so," Barent said.

Mahoney shrugged, pulled a sheet of paper from his pocket, leaned over and spun the combination. The door swung open. A sharp, pungent odor came from the locker and filled the room. Mahoney reached in and pulled out a low metal table on wheels. As the table rolled out it rose on a spring mechanism and then locked into place, so that the body lying on it was about waist high. The body was male, emaciated and gray, the skin leathery. The features of the face were blank and shrunken together, so that it was impossible to tell what it had looked like when alive. The muscles of the left arm had been dissected neatly out.

Barent swallowed. "Now the next one," he said. "I want to look at them all."

Mahoney frowned. A sheen of sweat covered his face and he blotted his forehead with a handkerchief. "Why?"

"Isn't it obvious? I'm looking for bodies with pieces missing."

"Ah …"

Barent smiled thinly. Mahoney stepped on a button on the bottom framework of the table and pushed down. The table collapsed slowly and Mahoney shoved it back into its safe, closed the door and spun the combination.

They found what Barent was looking for in the fifth classroom. All four bodies had been mutilated. Two were without heads. Another was missing both hands and a foot. A third body's chest and abdomen had been hacked open, the heart, liver and one lung removed. The fourth table contained only the head and limbs lying together; the torso was gone.

Mahoney looked wilted. He stood with rounded shoulders and a distraught expression on his face. Even Nolan seemed subdued. Moran was pale. Barent broke the silence. "Four different cadavers. Four different combinations. That would imply that at least four different people were in on it."

Mahoney cleared his throat. "Not necessarily," he said. His voice was barely a whisper. "The faculty, the teaching assistants and the dieners all have access to the combinations."

"What's a diener?" Barent asked.

"They're like morticians. The dieners prepare the bodies when they arrive at the school: clean them and preserve them in formaldehyde."

Barent looked at the four tables, the four mutilated cadavers, and grimaced. Already his nose had grown so accustomed to the stench that he could barely smell it, but his mouth tasted foul. "I'll want a list," he said. "Two lists. Everybody who might have had access to the combinations and the names and backgrounds of all four cadavers in this room."

Made in the USA
Lexington, KY
20 May 2019